THE SLEEPWALKER

www.penguin.co.uk

Also by Joseph Knox

Sirens
The Smiling Man

For more information on Joseph Knox and his books,
see his website at www.josephknox.co.uk

THE SLEEPWALKER

Joseph Knox

doubleday

TRANSWORLD PUBLISHERS
61–63 Uxbridge Road, London W5 5SA
www.penguin.co.uk

Transworld is part of the Penguin Random House group of companies
whose addresses can be found at global.penguinrandomhouse.com

Penguin
Random House
UK

First published in Great Britain in 2019 by Doubleday
an imprint of Transworld Publishers

A CIP catalogue record for this book
is available from the British Library.

ISBNs 9780857524386 (cased)
9780857524393 (tpb)

Typeset in 12/15 pt Adobe Garamond Pro by Jouve (UK), Milton Keynes
Printed and bound in Great Britain by Clays Ltd, Elcograf S.p.A.

Penguin Random House is committed to a sustainable
future for our business, our readers and our planet. This book
is made from Forest Stewardship Council® certified paper.

MIX
Paper from
responsible sources
FSC® C018179

1 3 5 7 9 10 8 6 4 2

For Elizabeth K.

'The craving to risk death is our last great perversion. We come from night, we go into night. Why live in night?'

John Fowles, *The Magus*

Tessa was ready and packed with a few minutes to spare, standing in the open doorway enjoying a gentle evening breeze. It wasn't quite dark, and the vivid powder-blue twilight felt like something she hadn't had time to stop and contemplate in years. It struck her as a premonition, a promise of all the good things still out there on the horizon, and her hand went unconsciously to her stomach.

The street was quiet and Tessa could hear the little girl next door rehearsing at her piano, playing Beethoven's Moonlight Sonata. She'd improved so much in the last few months, her rendition transforming from the halting scales of an amateur into something elemental, flowing out of her like water. A set of headlights turned the corner, strafing the houses on the other side of the road, and a matt-black Mercedes pulled up at the end of Tessa's drive, precisely on time. The driver was dressed in a smart, dark suit and when he came up the path she saw he was wearing tinted glasses.

'Miss Klein?' he said.

'Call me Tess.'

He asked if he could take her suitcase and she caught her reflection in his lenses. The amused smile in her eyes that said she didn't do this often. She followed him to the car, where he held open a door for her and loaded her case into the back, before taking up his position in the driver's seat.

'Where to?' he said, clearly in on the joke.

'Oh, surprise me,' she answered, feeling the smile split her face in half.

The driver gave her a nod in the rear-view and pulled out into the road. Tessa looked through the window, at the houses, the lit windows and lives she was leaving behind. She felt her eyes growing heavy, sinking shut, and when she opened them again it was full dark outside. The driver turned into a narrow country lane, crunching gravel beneath the tyres, approaching a small cottage with no lights on. He pulled up and touched the ignition.

'Surprise,' he said.

It was so quiet that Tessa could hear herself breathing. The driver climbed out and went to the car boot, taking her suitcase, and returning to open the door.

He clicked on a Maglite and led them towards the cottage.

'We're looking for a cactus,' he said, examining the pots lined up against the wall. Tessa bent to the plant and found the spare key hidden beneath it. The door opened with a sigh, as though the building had been holding its breath, and she felt along the wall for light switches, pressing all of them at once. The bulbs were energy efficient, her preference, and she smiled to think that he'd probably had them changed especially for her. They gave off a soft glow that didn't quite reach the corners of the room, making it seem even more cavernous than it was. The space was large, open-plan, including both kitchen and lounge, with enormous wooden beams lining the ceiling. Tessa forgot the driver for a second, and when he discreetly cleared his throat she twisted round to him.

'I'm sorry, please put that down anywhere.'

He stepped inside and placed the suitcase beside a sofa.

'Can I get you a drink?' she said, moving to the kitchen. 'Not that I know where anything is. We should probably wait for his lordship.' When the driver didn't respond, she turned to him. He was much closer now, and she wondered how he'd moved so quietly.

'I'm afraid he's not coming.'

She took half a step backwards. 'Some kind of problem?'

'You could say that.' His tinted glasses made the expression unreadable. 'I'm afraid it's over, Miss Klein.'

'OK,' she said, catching her reflection in the lenses again. She looked afraid now, and tried to go on in a calm tone of voice. 'That's OK, but in that case I'll be going home.'

'It's all over,' he clarified.

'You've got it wrong.' She smiled, relieved that the answer had come to her. 'We were together yesterday . . .' She thought of their bodies intertwined on his office floor, her ear pressed against his chest like she was guessing the combination to a safe. '. . . I'm pregnant.'

'Exactly,' said the driver, sounding grateful that she'd broached a difficult subject. 'Exactly, so you just take a seat for me,' he said, motioning to the table. 'There's one thing I need and then we'll be square. I'll sit over here.'

He touched the furthest chair from her.

'I'd rather stay standing, thanks.'

'That's fine,' he said. 'Me too.' He reached inside his pocket, found a pen and paper and placed them on the table. When he slid them towards her she recognized the items from her own home. 'These are for you. I need you to write something down for me.'

'If this is about the baby—'

'No, no,' he said. 'Just pick up the pen, it's all very simple.' Not taking her eyes off the man, she bent to pick up the pen, holding it up to him. 'Good. Then all we need you to do is copy this down.' He searched another pocket and found a printed piece of paper, placing it on the table, sliding it towards her. She started to read and then took a step back, covering her mouth.

'Let me talk to him,' she said through her hand. The man didn't move. 'I'm not writing that, not ever.'

The man took off his glasses, looking at her with such sympathy that she thought she'd got through to him.

Then he took another item from his jacket pocket, a pair of pliers.

3

'Sorry,' he said, searching for something else. 'Oh, here we go.'

He dropped a heavy envelope on to the table.

'Money?' she said, incredulous but feeling the relief work through her. 'He thinks he can pay me off?' The driver waited in silence, not looking at her now. She bent to open the envelope and poured out the contents.

They were glossy photographs.

The first showed her mother, working at the co-op, and the second was her dad behind the wheel of his car. The bulk of them were pictures of her sister, her brother-in-law, their two toddlers, Sarah and Max. The final three were taken from inside their bedroom, while the children were sleeping. Tessa looked up but she couldn't speak, suddenly she couldn't breathe.

'Something really good can come of all this,' said the man. 'You can save their lives tonight, Tess. And all you've got to do is write that note for me.'

'I don't believe you,' she said, running out of air. 'I don't . . .'

He took his phone from his pocket, scrolled to an entry and slid it towards her. She recognized it as the landline for her sister's home, a number she didn't think she'd dialled in years. The adrenaline was making her fingers shake but she pressed 'call', looking defiantly into the driver's face. It was picked up on the first ring.

An unfamiliar male voice: 'Made up your mind?'

'Who are you?'

'You just worry about where I am. Where I'll be when your sister gets home with the kids in ten minutes. Sign the note, Tess. I don't know how to make it easy on them.'

The man hung up and Tessa felt the phone growing slippery in her hand. She dropped it and looked about her, then sank to the table, drying her right palm against her blouse so she could hold the pen. She'd copied down two halting lines before coming to a stop, hovering over the third for a long moment.

Don't look for me, it said. *I've made it so my body won't ever be found.*

4

Slowly, deliberately, she copied down the line, ending with a single initial. When she looked up the man had moved even closer, was standing almost directly behind her.

'They will look for me,' she said.

'But they won't find anything.' He smoothed her shoulders. 'Not anything at all. It's the baby, see. It could lead back to him and, well. He's a family man now.' As Tess stared ahead at the empty room she thought she could hear the sound of a piano playing somewhere in the distance.

'Do you hear that?' she asked, holding up a hand, straining to listen.

'People often hear things,' said the man. 'Can I ask what it is?'

'Beethoven,' she said, eyes falling to the pliers on the table. 'Moonlight Sonata.' The driver gripped her shoulders and she looked up at him, trying to smile. He gave her an affectionate squeeze and smiled back.

'That's magic, that is.'

———

I
Night People

1

Later, they'd call it the lost weekend. A series of rolling blackouts disconnected entire city blocks for hours at a time, from Friday afternoon right through to Sunday evening, and the centre became temporarily exciting and unknowable again. Without the ambient glare of the high-rises and street lamps, the garish storefronts and facades, people returned to a kind of innocence that had seemed lost to them just a few hours before. The elderly were coaxed out to the ends of their paths, remarking on constellations that hadn't been visible in decades, and packs of teenagers roamed the streets without destination, ignoring the police-imposed curfew and making each other jump, lighting up the faces of new friends with precious electricity from their phones. When the power came back it ignited the town, dazzling onlookers like some lavish Broadway set, and there was a kind of thrill as people really saw each other, tried to best use what now felt like essential, borrowed time.

With the lights out there was a sense that you could easily disappear or reinvent yourself, walk out of one life and into another. Crossing town on the way to my shift, I'd have said that this feeling was communal, in the air somehow, but on reflection I think it was just a feeling in me. I'd spent thirty-something nights in a row sitting in St Mary's Hospital, off Oxford Road, watching a mass murderer slowly die.

When the lights went again, that's where I was.

We were in a small room on an otherwise empty corridor, just me and Martin Wick. He was bound to his bed, too sick to stand now, and the restraints meant that he couldn't raise a hand to wave at me if he wanted to. His arms were thin, allowed very little movement, and wasting away so quickly that the straps had to be adjusted each morning. So when the power cut out I had no reason to look away and no reason to be nervous. Except that, in those seconds before the back-up generator kicked in, it felt like I could really see him.

He always seemed more visible to me in the dark.

His eyes gleamed like they were backlit, as though there was something incendiary behind them. A cold flame that threatened to burn on long after his body died. I let out a breath as the power came back, and a muted light swelled through the room.

When I raised my eyes to Martin Wick he was smiling.

He said he didn't remember killing them, so that was where the nickname came from. Nobody believed his version of events, that he'd woken up covered in blood, and the headlines, think pieces and profiles referring to him as *The Sleepwalker* were all dripping with sarcasm. Even people who didn't know what he'd done felt uncomfortable around him. I'd heard one of the new nurses say he gave off a sense of impending doom, but she clearly didn't know her history.

The doom had happened already.

Sent him slightly off course years before and taken him deep into this uncharted territory. There was no roadmap for the Martin Wicks of the world, no possible way back to civilization. So now, if you believed him, he'd found himself hopelessly lost and strapped to a hospital bed. If you believed him, he had no idea how he got here.

If you believed him.

In spite of the twinkle in his eyes, they were lifeless, full black, and slow-moving. Sometimes he slept with them wide open. You couldn't distinguish the pupil from the iris, so you couldn't tell whether he was staring into thin air or looking directly at you. Some nights it felt like neither, some nights it felt like both. Some nights, when his eyes moved on to mine, it felt like being under surveillance, and I could never quite shake the feeling that some third party was reviewing the footage from inside his head, going frame by frame looking for weakness.

My job was to sit there for ten hours at a time, waiting for him to say or do something, documenting his every move. When he remained silent throughout my shifts, I thought it was in the same way you'd keep a secret. The same way you'd grip the change in your pocket on a bad estate. I thought he was just making sure he didn't jingle too much or give anything special away before he died.

Of course, it turned out he was just waiting.

I'd been there an hour or so when I sensed some movement. Looked up from my paperback and saw him reaching for the note-pad. He lifted his pen, wincing at the limitations of the restraints, and wrote something down. His handwriting was the smallest I'd ever seen, and if I hadn't read the transcripts of his plea agreement, squinted to find that half-empty signature hiding at the bottom of each page, I'd have thought the notes were some kind of mind game to get me out of my seat.

'Don't get up,' I said, folding the page on my book and crossing the room.

Lying there beneath the hospital lights, Martin Wick was beyond pale. Whiter than one of Hitler's cum stains, as Sutty said. The result of twelve years chain-smoking on the segregation wing, followed by a diagnosis of terminal lung cancer. He had a crumpled old rag for a face and his skin was as thin as tracing paper. You didn't want to see what was underneath it, though. He'd had one lung removed and the other was knitted together with tumours, the effects, apparently, of running a cavalier asbestos clean-up crew, back before they put him in Strangeways.

I watched the heart monitor while he finished writing. The jagged peaks and troughs looked like a lie detector test that he was failing. When he dropped his pen on the bed I took the notepad and felt a jolt of electricity. Wick reacted strangely with the bedsheets, his every movement creating static, and any time I touched him I seemed to get a shock, like there was some dangerous current coursing through his body, something beyond a bad vibe. I could never quite shake the feeling that he intended something to pass between us with each spark, that he was contagious, and he knew it.

Sutte, said the tiny, joined-up handwriting. I dropped the pad on the bed so I wouldn't have to pass it back to him, then crossed the room. I'd only relieved Sutty, my superior officer, one hour before, but our orders were clear. Until the day he checked out, what Wick wanted, Wick got.

'I hope you'll have something to tell him tonight, Martin,' I said, opening the door.

'What's the difference?'

I turned. In more than a month on the ward I'd never once heard Martin Wick speak. He'd removed the respirator from his mouth and when I looked into his gleaming, black eyes I couldn't tell if he was staring up at the ceiling or directly at me. It felt like neither, it felt like both.

He coughed, hacking the gravel out of his one remaining lung. 'Waste your life, son . . .' It came out as a painful whisper. '. . . It's all mean time, anyway.'

I stood there for a moment, saw he was sweating from the effort of speaking, then nodded and backed out of the room. Walking down the corridor towards the armed guard, I found myself rubbing my hands into my trousers, thinking of those sparks, wondering if I'd imagined him speaking.

For weeks it seemed like I hadn't really slept and I hadn't really woken up, either.

Each shift had felt like entering into some kind of stasis, like an episode of temporary insanity. So when the lights went out again I kept on going, feeling my way along the wall. The armed guard turned, blinding me with the torch attached to his Heckler and Koch, but I wasn't afraid yet. I felt no more powerless or in the dark than usual.

2

I'd only seen the footage of Martin Wick's arrest once, some years before, but it had made a strong impression. It had been early, about an hour before dawn, and he was invisible against the dark until the door closed behind him, silhouetting his frame against the dull grey of the train station facade.

Wick's head, neck and shoulders remained downcast, like a limp marionette, and when he lumbered forward into the light, he was dragging one leg. His clothes looked black all over and, even though the detail on the video wasn't great, you could see that the buttons on his jacket were fastened all wrong, causing it to bunch up, giving him a hunch across one shoulder. He moved in spasms and jerks across the empty concourse, towards the unmanned ticket desk.

The grained image from the video feed behind the counter felt appropriate. As if a cloud of static surrounded him, an electric mist that made his body seem blurred and hazy at the edges. Then he shunted forward into the clarity of the dirty yellow lights, bringing himself finally into focus. The collar on his shirt was pulled inside out, the sleeves on his jacket were one up and one down, and his trousers were on sideways, the seams running diagonally across his legs.

If I remember rightly, he was only wearing one shoe.

The right foot was covered by a loose, wet sock, and it left red prints across the floor as he walked. When he reached the counter, it became clear that his clothes were a glistening wet-black, that they were stuck to his body in strange places. Over his shoulder, the blue lights that had appeared ghostly and distant began drawing nearer, pulsing through the windows.

Martin Wick raised his head and looked, blankly, into the ticket desk. At length, his gaze shifted from its interior to his own reflection in the Perspex window and he took a step back. A look of appalled recognition crossed his face, like a man waking up out of one nightmare and into another. As he staggered back, away from himself, his eyes flicked up at the camera that had caught his march across the concourse.

The image would be endlessly debated.

Was it the innocent flinch of a man who didn't know where he was, what he was doing, or was it the calculated appraisal of a psychopath, making sure that his performance had been properly documented? After that he'd crumpled to the floor, where he lay flinching and foaming at the mouth.

They found the family home a few hours later, front door wide open.

Martin Wick had walked through town with the blood of five different people drenched into his clothes, and he spent the following twelve years in Strangeways.

It wasn't quite enough.

3

Detective Inspector Sutcliffe wasn't answering his phone, but I found him in the first place I looked. The Temple was a small subterranean bar beneath Great Bridgewater Street, a brisk twenty-minute walk from the hospital. The room had been an underground public toilet in Victorian times, before being repurposed into a rock-and-roll boozer in the eighties. The tables were small and close together, and the surfaces were absolutely covered in band flyers, tour posters and graffiti. Sutty was standing in the corner, explaining something to one of the other customers. To make sure the man was really listening, he'd lifted him off the ground by his ears and begun banging his head into the wall with the beat of the drum.

He let the smile slide, dramatically, off his face when he saw me.

'Oh,' he said, over the music. 'It's the Great Depression. Shouldn't you be queuing up for a loaf of bread instead of buying beer?'

'Wick wants to talk to you.'

Sutty nodded, lowered the man to his feet and told him to get lost. 'Strange, innit?'

'What is?' I said, watching the man walk away, rubbing his ears.

Sutty wiped his brow and gave me a slice of his dull-yellow grin. 'That Wick prefers me so much to you.'

'Yeah, funny that. He's talkative tonight . . .'

'Is he now?' It took a lot to surprise Sutty but that got his attention. 'Maybe this is it, then. What did he say?'

'Told me I should waste my life.'

He snorted and turned to drain his glass. 'You're one step ahead of him.'

Standing there watching Sutty drink, it was difficult to argue.

My partner was built like a hip flask. A stout, neckless head on top of broad shoulders, with the whisky breath to match. There was something off, curdled even, about his face, which was bleach-white all over and studded with strange lumps beneath the skin. Somehow it suited his personality, like the warning sign printed on rat poison. He never ironed either of his suits, but filled them to absolute breaking point so they appeared perfectly pressed. He slammed down his glass and looked at me as if I was a stranger.

'How do I know you don't just want the night off? Didn't your old bit used to work in here?'

'She left,' I said, searching my pockets for the note that Wick had given me.

'The one of many that got away. You must've been coming in too often.'

'One of us must.'

I found the folded slip of paper.

'Yeurgh,' said Sutty, scrutinizing it. 'Pity we can't tie his hands behind his back.' He picked his blazer up off the bar stool and forced himself into it like a straitjacket. 'Come on then, Bi-Wonder, to the twat mobile.'

'I'm afraid I walked,' I said.

'Well then, I'm getting a cab and you're coming with me. Soon as he nods off again, you're back on duty.'

I nodded and followed him to the door.

We climbed the steps out on to the street and hailed a taxi, both staring out the windows as we rode, watching the city stream by. Charity workers going between wild-eyed homeless men. Boys peacocking, loaded with drink, on their way to or from pubs or clubs. And the girls gliding along in formation, doubling up and laughing at life. Usually, this would be our beat, but things had changed. Sutty sat beside me grumbling, rubbing antibacterial gel into his hands. He went through a bottle a day but somehow never got clean enough. Sometimes I wondered if he was absorbing the alcohol through his pores and into his bloodstream.

When we arrived at St Mary's we saw two men carrying an unconscious teenage girl inside, holding her between them like a rolled-up carpet. We entered the building and the lights in reception cut out for a second then came back. I looked about me. Bloodshed, fist-fights and stab-wounds. Confused, stunned people, drunk, on drugs, with life-altering injuries. Stick-thin single mothers on food bank diets, with morbidly obese babies. Sutty and I turned as the girl came to, fought free of her helpers, and made a break for it, back into the street. It seemed like the only rational response.

4

Since the May 22nd suicide bombing, firearms officers were an increasingly common sight in the city.

It still felt unusual to see one stationed inside a hospital.

There had been some resistance from the health trust at first, until we presented the Osman Warnings on Wick's file. These were risk-to-life alerts, letters which the force were legally obliged to deliver when we received credible death threats. Wick had amassed a long list of credible death threats in his years at Strangeways, and in the hour we'd had with the board, we hadn't managed to get through them all. They declined to hear any more, and approved an armed guard for his hospital room immediately.

It had been an intentional strategy.

To use up the time discussing death threats against our prisoner, so we wouldn't have to tell them about the actual attempts on his life. One cellmate had stabbed him through the ear with a sharpened ballpoint pen, another had tried to hang him with his own bedsheets. In the most inventive example, an unknown number of inmates had banded together to drown Wick in his cell toilet. Prison latrines are built in anticipation of this group activity and feature large trapways with low-volume flushes, so there's not enough liquid for it. According to the report it would have taken at least five men with full bladders to fill the bowl, to keep it at the right level for the minute or more that Wick's face was submerged. The screws got to him just in time, but on balance I thought it had probably been a relief when he was diagnosed as terminally ill and transferred to a hospital ward.

Sutty and I had been told that, where possible, one of us should stay with him at all times. Not because he posed any kind of threat to anyone, but because it was hoped that his proximity to death might make him talkative. Even now, twelve years after his original arrest, question marks hung over Martin Wick's head.

When we'd first accepted the assignment, they'd said he only had five or six days left to live, and I'd felt relieved that we wouldn't be here too long.

That had been five weeks ago.

Sutty's presence had proved restorative, like he was draining the life out of me and donating it directly to our prisoner. By the end of the first week, I'd been certain that Wick would die in the second. By the third I'd thought he was rallying, and recovering by the fourth. Now, at the close of our fifth week on protective custody, I was afraid that Martin Wick might live forever.

Housing a national hate figure can be a delicate business, and it was agreed that Wick would be roomed in secret, on a dilapidated first-floor hospital wing undergoing renovation. It was one quarter of a corridor, rendered inaccessible by all but one entrance. The lift doors had been deactivated and a makeshift partition had been built between this and the rest of the ward. The only way in or out was through a fire escape which led on to a barren cement staircase. To access the rest of the hospital you had to descend these steps, cross reception and climb the central staircase on the other side of the partition. In theory, this meant there was only one way to or from Martin Wick's room.

In practice, it made me feel like a rat in a trap.

Rennick, the armed guard, was in position as I emerged from the stairwell, Sutty still some way behind me. He was sitting behind what would have been the nurses station when the wing was fully functional, and he wore full tactical-style uniform. Body armour and fingerless gloves, as well as the newly issued black baseball cap. With the amount of equipment strapped to his vest, including speedcuffs, radio and taser, as well as the sidearm, medical kit and back-up rounds, he looked like a little boy's action figure. He was reading the newspaper and smiling to himself. Scratching his ear with a G36 assault rifle.

I tried not to startle him.

'Rennick,' I said gently.

'Waits,' he answered, without turning his head. He placed the newspaper on the counter before him and stood, sweeping the gun barrel past me in one fluid movement.

'You were about to give yourself a centre parting, there.'

'Safety's on,' he said, voice level.

'Well, Sutty's right behind me, so you'd better look alive.'

He shot me a glance and then moved, slowly, round the counter, like it had been his idea. It didn't seem worth making an issue of. Rennick was in his mid-twenties, four or five years younger than me, but we were still the same rank. I'd recently passed my sergeant's exam but I wasn't expecting a promotion. There were so many black marks on my file you'd think it had been dipped in shit.

Sutty burst through the door, strode past me and approached the nurses station. He turned out his pockets, handed over his phone and then leaned into the counter, spreading his legs.

'Aren't you gonna frisk me?'

Rennick slid the sign-in sheet towards him without comment. Sutty pushed himself upright, scrawled his name and carried on down the corridor. He had an uncanny knack for upsetting people, and the pleasure he took from it was nearly life-affirming. He turned to Wick's room and went in.

'How's my big brave boy?' he bellowed, before the door closed behind him.

Rennick looked at the sign-in sheet with distaste. 'He always been like that?' he said.

'As long as I've known him.'

He looked towards Wick's room, trying to maintain the cold

front, but his curiosity about Sutty won out. He gripped his gun and nodded at me.

'You're both from the night shift . . .'

'For our sins,' I said. Between Sutty and me we had enough of them to send a priest screaming from confession. The night shift was the lowest possible rung of the force, and held some grim fascination for those who weren't on it.

There were just two long-term members.

Myself and Detective Inspector Sutcliffe. Other officers worked it rotationally, and they were wary of us, afraid of contamination or the threat of permanent reassignment. As a consequence, we dealt autonomously with low-level, unglamorous crime, with little oversight or overlap from the force at large. Our official street-time went from the evening right through to the early hours of the morning, in a city with an expansive, thrilling nightlife. Problem officers occasionally got rotated through, until they changed their ways or put in their papers, but Sutty and I had been deemed beyond rehabilitation.

'Detective Inspector *Peter* Sutcliffe . . .' said Rennick, reading the sign-in sheet. 'That's a bit unfortunate, innit?'

We heard soft murmurs coming down the corridor.

'I don't know, I think it suits him.'

Rennick smirked. 'Our DS said I must have heard wrong when I told him you two were assigned to Wick. Said the night shift couldn't be trusted to count the cocks on a toilet door.'

'Just the ones on a hospital ward, Rennie.'

'Didn't know they even sent people our age on nights,' he said, ignoring the insult. 'Permanently, I mean . . .' He lowered his voice. 'What did you do to earn that?'

'Nothing exciting.' He waited and I went on. 'The right thing in the wrong way.'

'That's not what I heard,' he said with a smile. 'I take it you're clean now?' When I didn't respond he moved on. 'So, why the change, then? This feels a bit like the big leagues after all that.'

21

Of course he thought it was the big leagues. He was here, after all.

'Sutty was one of Wick's original arresting officers, back in the day.'

'Him?' Rennick looked impressed. 'Thought it was that guy Blake . . .'

'Blake got the conviction, but Sutty was first on scene. Someone called in about a man walking through town covered in blood and he dropped everything to get there first.'

Rennick frowned. 'So they took him off the night shift twelve years later to come and hold Wick's hand while he died? I don't get it.'

'You know one of the kids was never found . . .'

'Course,' he said. 'Lizzie Moore.'

'Right.' I nodded up the corridor. 'With Wick dying, it's the last chance for the family to find out what he did with her.'

'Yeah, but why you two?'

'What's the one word you'd use to describe the prisoner?'

'Cunt,' said Rennick, without hesitation.

I nodded. 'Well, Sutty speaks the language. He's fluent in it. They got along when he brought Wick in the first time. The higher-ups thought he might be their best bet to get him talking now.'

'They got along?' Rennick screw-faced and I thought I could see him bristling, hairs standing on end. 'Wick murdered a woman, three kids . . .'

I nodded but it was hard to explain.

On the surface, Sutty had more in common with a career criminal than a cop. Except, where criminals act emotionally, out of anger or economic need, Sutty loved crime, and the lower down it went the better. His law-enforcement career was simply a way to be around it at all times without ever risking his liberty. Some days, when we'd gone too long without encountering trouble, he had a way of making things happen.

Privately, I agreed with Rennick.

Our being reassigned was unusual, unlikely even, but I didn't want to know what had really motivated it. When the answers get worse and worse, you stop asking questions.

I wasn't exactly sure how this change had come about, but I sensed Sutty's antibacterial hand behind it.

'What's he like?' said Rennick, breaking into my thoughts.

'Sutty?'

He rolled his eyes. 'Martin Wick.'

'I don't know,' I said, and he made a dubious face. 'I mean it, he doesn't talk to me.'

'So, when you're in with him for ten hours at a time . . .'

'I write down whatever he does and call Sutty if he asks for him.'

'Sounds like you've landed on your feet.'

'Yeah,' I said. It felt more like they were nailed into the floor.

I moved around him, turning the newspaper over on the counter. The front page showed a picture of Martin Wick, our prisoner, sitting in his hospital bed eating cornflakes. It had been taken on a mobile phone, from the doorway of his room.

Cereal Killer!

'Fuck sake,' I said, looking at Rennick.

'Not on my watch, I'm always relieved by breakfast.'

'If Sutty sees it he'll relieve himself in your eye.' I checked the date. It was the early edition of Sunday morning's paper. The world would wake up to it in a few hours. 'Where did you get this?'

'Picked it up in reception on break.'

'And you didn't think it was worth mentioning?'

'It wasn't taken on my watch,' he repeated.

'You're turning out everyone's pockets, though?' Only vetted personnel were allowed past this point. The presence of orderlies, cleaners, even doctors and nurses, was strictly scheduled. It was the FO's job to search them all.

No one was allowed to take a phone any further.

He frowned. 'Course I fucking am.'

We both turned to see Sutty emerging from Wick's room. He

23

looked troubled, and I tried to stand between him and the newspaper.

'Got a sec, Aid?' he said.

'Sure . . .'

I turned out my pockets, handed over my phone and signed in so I could cross the checkpoint. I went past Rennick and walked up the corridor, wanting some distance before I gave Sutty the bad news.

There were large plastic sheets covering the walls.

Buckets filled with rubble and dust. Remains of the refurbishment work that had been postponed until after Wick died.

Sutty held open the toilet door like he was inviting me into his office. I went inside and found the light switch. No one had been here in weeks, and it was probably the cleanest room in the building. I sat on the sink. Sutty drew the door closed behind him, then leaned on it so no one could get in or out.

'Wick says he never asked you to come and get me . . .'

'He did. I mean, he wrote that note. If I read it wrong, I'm sorry for dragging you in.' Sutty was quiet, taking this in, and I watched his face changing.

'Yeurgh,' he said, finally. 'I believe you. He wrote that note and he meant you to come and get me. Something's up.'

'Do you think he's dying?'

'He's been dying for months. Should be used to it by now. Nah, this is different. He seems, I dunno. Scared.'

'You think someone's got to him?' I said, thinking of the newspaper. He didn't say anything and I lowered my voice. 'Why? How?'

Sutty scowled down at the ground for a moment, then leaned off the door and opened it. When he looked down the corridor, he shook his head. I stuck my neck out to see Rennick reading the paper again. He was using the assault rifle to hold up his chin.

'Koch in hand,' said Sutty. We stepped through and he slammed the door with all his might. Rennick jumped out of his skin, got up and fumbled for his weapon. He was lucky he hadn't blown his head off. Sutty marched to the counter, looked at the sign-in sheet and went face-to-face with him.

'Constable, in our absence has the prisoner had any visitors?'

'What?'

'What, *sir*,' said Sutty. 'I think someone's spoken to Wick while we've been gone. Might've been an unscheduled doctor or nurse, might've been someone you didn't sign in. Maybe curiosity got the best of you, I don't know. But I think a man who was about to tell us what he did with the body of a twelve-year-old girl's suddenly clammed up.'

'No one's been past me.'

Sutty's eyes went to the newspaper on the counter. He saw the picture of Wick in his hospital bed and picked it up. I knew that look, and was grateful not to be on the receiving end of it. Like a watched pot of piss, coming slowly to boil. He collected his wallet from the counter, opened it and began counting his cash.

Rennick snorted. 'I wouldn't touch your money, sir.'

'I know you wouldn't,' said Sutty. 'Aid, what was that Mick called who was advertising his services in the Rising Sun?'

I thought back. 'Pipebomb Willy.'

'That's the guy. Said he'd break any limb on anyone for fifteen quid.' Sutty slammed down his wallet and leaned into Rennick. 'Well, I've got his phone number and two twenties, so you'd better make this good.'

'I'm never on duty for breakfast. I wasn't here when that photo was taken.'

At length, Sutty turned. 'Confirm that for me, Aidan.' He ripped the newspaper off the counter and thundered back to Wick's room. 'And get me a coffee. Blacker than the hundred-metre sprint.'

I waited until I heard the door slam, then I nodded to no one in particular and walked to the stairwell without meeting Rennick's eye.

5

As I made my way down, the lights waned, dimmed and died out again. Sutty lost his temper like another man lost his keys. Carelessly and completely without thought, and sometimes it seemed like he'd never get it back again. Rarer were these occasions when he trained it on people like a spotlight, stopping them in their tracks and illuminating things they really didn't want to be seen. If he was unnerved by Wick's apparent change of heart, then there was probably something in it. That his nose had led him immediately to Constable Rennick was concerning.

We had a long shift ahead, and firearms accidents happened all the time.

The back-up generator kicked in and the lights returned at about half their previous strength. I rubbed my face to try and activate myself, then stepped through the door, into the organized chaos of a city centre hospital reception on a weekend.

I went across the scarred linoleum as fast as I could, weaving through a riot of in- and out-patients.

I climbed the central staircase, away from it all, just in time to see a crash team of doctors and nurses pass by, wheeling someone towards surgery. There were no windows in this part of the building but I could usually guess the time by what state the patients were in. Tonight the beds were lined along the walls containing people in varying levels of distress, all queuing until more space became available. I wedged myself between them as another triage team passed, followed almost immediately by a third.

Saturday night fever.

As a final crash team blasted by, I looked into the blank, open eyes of the man on the gurney, taking in the cavernous head wound that he'd sustained. The team turned into a side room and the doors wafted shut behind them.

'Excuse me . . .' I looked down at a small woman who'd been following the team through the corridor. I tried to move past her but she put a hand to my chest. She looked bewildered, lost, and I saw that there was blood smudged about her forehead. I thought she was in shock. 'Do you work here? Do you know if he'll be all right?'

'No,' I said, stepping back from her hand. 'I mean, I don't work here.'

I walked around her, to the end of the hall, and turned the corner without looking back. I kept on going, following my feet, intentionally trying to lose myself in the maze of units and wards. I came to a completely empty stretch, leaning into the wall, closing my eyes.

Half the man's head had been missing.

At length, I went to the coffee machine and searched my pockets for change. I was only a few feet further along the corridor that Martin Wick was on, but because of the partition it took ten minutes to get here.

Sliding the first coin home I caught my reflection in the black plastic. Looked down and saw the blood-red smear that the concerned woman had left on my shirt. I could have probably lifted her prints from it. I put the coins back in my pocket and pushed open a toilet door to clean up.

6

The mirror above the sink was a slab of polished metal, so the junkies couldn't smash it and use the shards for knives. Its surface was dulled, though, dented from some of their best efforts, and my image felt surreal, like the straining, de-tuned broadcast from another dimension. I looked at myself. The dark rings around my eyes that were slowly turning red.

Confirmation that I was the man in the mirror.

There was no soap inside the first two hand dispensers, but I tried the third out of a sense of completism. When I found that empty as well, I gave up on the bloodstain, fastened the button on my blazer to cover it, and went for the door.

I had it open when I heard a strange sound coming from one of the cubicles.

Something like a gurgle. Looking back, I saw two plastic gel bags which had been ripped from the soap dispensers, shredded and drained. They lay glistening and flattened on the tiles like enormous squashed slugs. Then I heard another sound from the cubicle. A long, wet kiss.

'Hello?' I said.

No answer.

The lights dimmed as I went towards it and I stopped halfway, knowing full well what I'd find. The door was ajar and when I pushed it open I saw an emaciated woman wearing a green tracksuit with the hood up, sitting on the closed toilet lid, sucking the life out of a bag of liquid soap. They said each pack was equivalent to six shots of vodka, and it hit you hard. It didn't exactly clean out your insides, though, and the after-effects were as drastic.

Amnesia, blindness and loss of bowel control.

At least she was in the right place for it.

She had green fingernails and tattoos on her face, pentangles of varying sizes around her eyes, but I couldn't guess her age. That kind of life puts a lot of miles on the clock, or takes a lot of them off, depending on how you look at it.

'Fuck off,' she said, sucking another mouthful from the gel pack. I felt sorry for her, so I didn't pay attention like I should have. I nodded and left her to it, hearing the door slam and lock behind me. I'd have told her to wash her mouth out but it was too depressing.

7

I returned to the wing with two coffees, finding Rennick standing to attention. When I left a cup on the counter for him he didn't look at me, and I wondered if it was wounded pride or something more serious.

'Cheers,' I said, but he didn't answer.

I went towards Wick's room feeling hyper-aware, like I had a target taped to my back.

There were soft murmurs coming through the door, and I listened for a moment before I knocked and stepped inside. Sutty was sitting next to Wick, concluding a dirty story.

'I said, I've heard of ministers kissing babies before, but he's the first one to use tongue.'

Sutty usually came alive as a filthy raconteur but his delivery seemed flat tonight, and I thought he was covering an abrupt change of subject.

'Black,' I said, handing him his coffee.

He took the cup and left it steaming on the table, then cracked open a new bottle of antibacterial gel, rubbing it into his hands.

'Still busy down there?' he said.

I nodded and looked at Martin Wick. It felt like I was interrupting something, but his gleaming, CCTV eyes hadn't moved since I'd entered the room. 'Is he awake?'

'Can't you tell?' said Sutty.

'How are you feeling, Martin?' There was a flicker in his face, and I felt a familiar chill as those black eyes moved on mine. Sutty leaned in, put his ear beside Wick's mouth and listened to the whispered answer.

'Says if there's any justice in the world he'll make a full recovery.'

'If there was justice in the world, we'd be out of a job. How is he really?'

'We were about to read his prognosis.' Sutty held the paper up for Wick to see. Looking closer I saw that the picture they'd printed showed him in obvious discomfort and distress. '*The cost of living*,' said Sutty, reading the caption. '*Hospital insiders say that Mr Wick is clinging to life but has only a matter of days left.*' He put the newspaper down and looked at our prisoner. 'Don't believe everything you read, Mart.'

Wick's lips started to move and Sutty leaned in to listen.

'Hm,' he said, as if answering a question. 'Hospital insider could be anyone who's been on the ward. Doctor, nurse, cleaner. You wouldn't sell your story, would you, Aid?'

'Who'd believe it?' I said. 'Are you sure he wants to be reading that?'

Sutty turned to a page with a picture of a smiling family. There were five of them. Mother, father, two girls and a boy. The Moores.

'Nothing wrong with a trip down memory lane, is there, Mart?' Wick's lips started to move and Sutty leaned in to listen. When he sat up again his face had darkened, and his eyes came slowly to me. 'Maybe you should go and wash that shit off your shirt?'

I looked down at the dried blood, still on my chest.

'Course,' I said, backing out of the room. 'Don't let your coffee go cold.' Sutty didn't look at me or the coffee but turned to Wick. Once I was out in the corridor I could hear the low murmur of his voice from inside. Glancing towards the nurses station I saw that Constable Rennick was watching me closely. From the way he just happened to be standing, I found myself staring down the barrel of a gun. I crossed the corridor to the toilets, wondering what was going on.

8

When I switched the light on I saw another drained, flattened pack
of liquid soap, like the ones in the toilet beyond the partition. It
hadn't been here when Sutty and I spoke earlier, and I looked at the
hand pumps above the sinks. They were all empty. The cubicle
door was half-closed, and when I pushed it open I saw the remaining two gel packs floating in toilet water. I stepped back, looked up
and saw a loose ceiling panel directly above the stall.

My heart rate registered the anomaly and I left the toilet.

Rennick was watching me closely.

'Everything OK?' I said.

He didn't answer.

'Is everything OK, Constable?'

He nodded and I walked past him, into the stairwell.

'There's blood on you,' he called after me.

I'd gone up and down these steps so many times in the last few
weeks that I'd felt my leg muscles hardening, and I moved fast
now, banging through the doors on to the floor below. I fought my
way through the reception crowd, hoping I was being paranoid,
then climbed the central staircase on to the ward again. It was still
busy and I pushed through the corridor towards the toilet where
I'd seen the junkie, twenty minutes or so before. There was a man
at the urinal, and I felt the look he gave me as I began thumping
on the cubicle wall.

There was no sound from inside.

I took a step back, looked up and saw that the ceiling panel above this toilet was missing, too. I shoulder-barged it open to find the stall empty, a drained gel-pack floating in the basin. There was only a small gap above the door. Either the woman had flushed herself down the toilet or she'd climbed up into the ceiling.

'Fuck,' I said.

The man at the urinal left without washing his hands. I followed him out, pushing past patients and hospital staff, projecting people out of my way and descending the central staircase. By the time I'd navigated the gridlock of reception and re-entered the stairwell, the lights were flickering, dimming, dying out again.

I felt for the handrail and started up.

There was a strong chemical smell and I thought I could hear footsteps descending. My heart was beating so hard I thought it might bruise a rib, and something cold brushed past me as the lights flickered back to life. I turned to see the emaciated woman in the green hoody, first walking, then running down the stairs.

'Hey,' I called after her, jumping as the fire alarm went off.

Between such narrow walls it was like a pneumatic drill at each temple, and I covered my ears, continuing up the stairs. Pushing open the door I could see immediately that something was wrong, because Rennick was no longer in position. There was no sense in calling out for him over the din of the alarm, and I edged forward into the corridor. When I reached the nurses station and looked across the counter I took a step back. The constable was lying on the floor behind it, both hands around his neck. There was blood seeping out through his fingers and it looked like he was drowning.

At that moment, Sutty exploded out of Wick's room, rolling in flame, banging from wall to wall and sending a roar of heat down the corridor. Coming back to life, I pulled a fire extinguisher off the wall and opened it up on him. He fell down and started to roll out the flames as the sprinkler system came on, soaking us both and finally extinguishing him.

Edging past my partner into Wick's room, I was struck by the stink.

He was blackened and writhing, handcuffed to the still-burning bed. I turned the fire extinguisher on to his body, covering his torso. The flames went out but I could smell burned skin and hair, and I covered my face with my forearm to keep the taste out of my mouth. I wanted to back out of the room but could see that he was still alive, struggling for attention over the alarm.

I went to him, closed my eyes and put my ear beside his mouth. '*Not me*,' I thought he said.

I could feel the heat pouring out of him. 'I know that, Martin . . .'

'*Not this*,' he said urgently. I looked at him. Those black eyes staring out from charred, blistered skin. They were lit with anger. '*The Moores*,' he said. The skin about his mouth broke and he began beating his free fist against my chest. Perhaps there was something else, but the fire alarm was exploding out from every surface. By the time his body slumped down into the smouldering bed, I didn't need to check his pulse.

I staggered out into the corridor, stunned and soaked by the sprinklers. Sutty had crawled towards Rennick, and was using his hands to try and stem the blood flowing from the constable's neck.

The water around his body was turning red.

I went towards them, past them, and on to the staircase. Three floors below, I thought I could see a figure running down. I went after it, throwing myself down tens of steps at a time, sliding on wet shoes, and tearing round each landing.

Looking over the railing I could see more shapes on the staircase, and when I reached the next floor down the door beside me slammed open.

People were flooding through the fire escapes.

Pushing through them, I thought I could still see the woman, but after a few seconds more I knew I'd lost her. Even shoving, shouting at the top of my voice, it took minutes to get to the ground floor. When I reached the people congregating by the exit everyone had the same sick, stunned look on their faces. They saw the blood on my hands, face and shirt, fresh and wet because of the sprinklers. I lifted myself on to the bonnet of an ambulance, then climbed on to the roof, but squinting into the sodium lights of the car park I could just see the same thing in all directions.

People, madness, everywhere.

9

It was gone four in the morning. Statistically, the time that most deaths occur. For once we were ahead of schedule. I'd made a distress call from the ambulance and a firearms unit had arrived within minutes, securing the scene. After that, I'd given a full description of the junkie I'd seen juicing up in the toilet and the circumstances, as I understood them, that had led to the attack on Rennick. To Sutty's life-threatening injuries and Martin Wick's assassination. As I spoke I found that I didn't understand much, and the Chief Inspector on point dismissed me with a curt nod. I'd stood up, hoping to find a bar that I could go and fall down in, when a hand touched my shoulder. It was the padded glove of an armed response officer, so I listened when he spoke into my ear.

'Superintendent Parrs,' he said simply.

I closed my eyes, half-expecting my life to flash before them.

'Lead the way.'

He took me back into the stairwell and we climbed. I felt so dirty that my skin was itching, and my body reeked with blood, burned flesh and hair. There were firearms officers stationed at each floor and they gripped their rifles as we approached. When we reached the final door it didn't budge and the officer shoulder-barged it open. I saw weak light and felt the wind rearranging my hair.

We were standing on the roof of the hospital.

This area hadn't been built or maintained with the public in mind, and the walkway consisted of thinning gravel with weeds

36

fighting their way up through the cracks. There were rusted Coke cans filled to the brim with cigarette butts, and I even spotted some empty gin bottles, half-hidden behind stacks of bricks. The FO held out his arm like a gameshow host showing me what I'd won.

It didn't look like first prize.

Superintendent Parrs was standing with his back to us, alone, looking down on the floodlit chaos below. His grey hair, grey coat and grey trousers blended in with the bruised skyline, making him look at one with the city, inseparable from it. The dawn hadn't quite broken but there was a thin strip of hazy light on the horizon. When the door slammed behind me the Superintendent's head moved, acknowledging my presence, and I realized that the FO had left us to it.

'Aidan Waits,' said Parrs. His Scottish accent sounded even harder than usual. Like a blade being sharpened on a cinder block. 'When I heard I had an officer down, somehow it was your name that went through my mind . . .' When he turned to look at me his eyes were so bloodshot I thought he must be seeing red. 'But here you are, alive and kicking.'

'Every cloud, sir.' He didn't say anything and I looked at the floor. 'Good morning, Superintendent.'

'Shouldn't that be *in mourning*, Detective Constable? We appear to have another fine Aidan Waits fuck-up on our hands.'

I squinted into the pre-dawn light and kept my mouth shut.

'I've received Chief Inspector James's report,' he said. I frowned. I'd only finished speaking to James ten minutes before. 'He tells me that you don't know anything. Somehow, that has the ring of truth to it. So, I'm assuming there's nothing you left out of your little debrief with him that you'd like to share with me.'

I'd described the facts to DCI James, leaving out what felt like some personal interpretations. I hadn't known whether to describe my brief conversation with Martin Wick, and had finally opted against it.

Parrs suspected something already, though. He could always

spot the outline of an omission on my person, then lift it from me like a pickpocket.

'There was one thing, sir.'

'You do surprise me.'

'Wick tried to tell me something before he died.'

'Unless it was the location of Lizzie Moore's corpse, I'm not sure I need to know.'

'He said he didn't do it.'

'He was bound to his bed at the time of the attack, Aidan. Of course he didn't do it.'

'I mean the crime that he was bound to the bed for, sir.' Parrs still didn't move and I went on. 'I think he was trying to tell me he didn't kill the Moores.'

'The old deathbed conversion, eh?' The Superintendent seemed relieved. 'What were his exact words?'

'Pretty much those.'

'Pretty much?' he said, taking a step towards me.

'He tried to say more but the alarm was going off. I didn't catch it.'

Parrs thought for a moment. 'And you didn't direct this information to DCI James because?'

'I thought you'd want to hear it first, decide what we should do.'

'The man was a convicted killer who died in police custody. I'd say we've done all we can.'

'There was something in the way he said it, sir.'

'A great deal of pain, one would hope. Anyway, I've got a signed confession that begs to fucking differ, and we've got enough on our hands without that kind of carry-on.'

'Sir.'

'James says you didn't get a good look at our flamethrower . . .'

'No, sir.'

'Convenient.'

'For who?'

'For the thrower. Forensics are still picking their way through the debris but it looks like a classic. Makeshift incendiary devices. Glass bottles and pints of kerosene.'

'Petrol bombs,' I said.

'Molotov cocktails for two. Someone kicked open the door and bought them a round. At least one apiece, thrown into Wick's room. They think the assailant held the door shut on them . . .'

The petrol bombs I'd seen in my time were usually exploding against the hulls of riot vans, and I winced at the thought of being in an enclosed space with one.

'So, come on,' said Parrs. 'What do you think happened here?'

'The obvious answer would be a friend or relative of one of Wick's victims, someone connected to the Moore family. Someone who saw their last chance for revenge. As far as I know, Wick hadn't been out in the open like this since his conviction. Maybe they found out where he was and took a chance.'

'Sounds plausible . . .'

'We saw Sunday's *Mail* shortly before the incident took place. The leaked photo. It could have brought the killer here . . .'

'Breakfast in bed?' said Parrs. 'Any idea where that picture came from?'

'I questioned Constable Rennick about it before the attack. He said he was never on duty for breakfast. DCI James and I consulted the rota and that checks out.'

'Do you have the name of the officer who was on duty?'

'A Constable Louisa Jankowski,' I said. 'He only had cornflakes when she was on duty. New to firearms, apparently, but—'

'But already making a name for herself . . .'

Although Jankowski's name hadn't appeared in the press, her work had. In December of the previous year she'd been on patrol when a large goods vehicle careened into the Albert Square Christmas market, intentionally mowing shoppers down. She'd reacted fast, delivering a mid-range headshot to the driver, possibly saving dozens of lives.

'She doesn't seem a likely culprit,' said Parrs. 'Where do you stand on Constable Rennick?'

It didn't seem worth reporting his lax behaviour in light of what had happened. 'He's a valuable eyewitness,' I said, understating it somewhat. The stab-wound to his neck had come from the front. As long as his eyes had been open, he could tell us a lot. 'He's probably the key to closing this thing quickly.'

'Are you volunteering for the job?'

'No, sir,' I said firmly. I could feel his red eyes, burning into me. 'I assumed I'd be re-posted to the night shift.'

'Someone just flame-grilled your partner, Detective Constable. I know you probably wouldn't piss on him if he was on fire, but—'

'I was the one who put him out.'

'And he'll spend the next seven days in a medically induced coma. Christ knows how we'll tell the difference, though. I'll ask again, are you volunteering for the job?' I didn't say anything and he snorted. 'Anything for a quiet life, eh?'

A quiet life.

I'd been given a few special jobs by Superintendent Parrs, and my ears were still ringing from the last one. He knew this all too well, but sometimes he liked to go over old ground. In the last couple of years he'd rubbed so much salt in my wounds I could have gritted the garden path with it.

He smiled. 'I'm not too sure about sending you back on nights without Detective Inspector Sutcliffe acting as chaperone. See, with him, I could always see what was slowly walking down the hall. He lit up the room, even before someone set fire to him. You're more like a dimmer switch. I'm not sure I want you skulking around in the shadows at the moment, especially without him to curb your worst instincts.'

'They're under control, sir.'

'Oh? Why don't you wow me with some insight, then? Tell me which of those instincts I'm most worried about right now.'

I paused. There were so many to choose from.

'Self-destruction,' I said finally, covering them all.

'I'd go further than that, I'd say your great talent's for

40

self-immolation. I'm surprised Sutty set off the sprinklers before you did. You've managed to stop, drop and roll your way out of it once or twice now, but you know what they say. Where there's smoke . . .'

'There's no smoke, sir.'

'Oh, but there is.'

I waited.

It looked like he was about to expand on the thought when he shook his head and went in another direction. 'Never let it be said that I don't take your mental health seriously, Aidan. I thought we could meet up here as a kind of psych evaluation. If your heart's really in this suicidal streak then feel free to throw yourself off the fucking building.'

I didn't move.

'Good, then we won't hear any more about you returning to the night shift.'

'There are better people for this job, sir.'

'Oh, decidedly, and DCI James will be leading the official investigation, don't worry about that. His team can spend the next few days tracing everyone who was here tonight, talking to Wick's former cellmates and reworking the original case file – all that good stuff that won't get them anywhere. But you? You just have this knack for putting people on edge and then pushing them over it. I have a feeling this case could put it to good use. You said a revenge hit against Wick for his crimes was the obvious answer to all this, so I'm intrigued. What's the less obvious one?'

'If Wick was telling the truth about not murdering the Moores, then their real killer might have been attempting to silence him.'

'It wasn't an attempt, Aidan. It was a roaring success.'

'I just don't buy the relatives having him killed when he was already at death's door. Did they know we were trying to extract Lizzie Moore's location?'

'I believe that they had been informed . . .'

'So why would they eliminate all hope?'

41

'You could argue that Wick did that twelve years ago. Y'know, there is a third option for all of this. It was good thinking, there, checking Rennick's word against the rota. I had a similar brainwave myself. Turns out *you* were supposed to be the one on duty at the time of the attack.'

I rubbed my face. 'My job was to wait with Wick, to find Sutty if he felt like talking. He'd lived a lot longer than expected but clearly he didn't have much time left.' I looked at Parrs. Felt those red eyes burning into me. 'He woke up and wanted Sutty, so I went and got him.'

'I don't dispute that. My point is that anyone who'd been watching your movements, or those of the team, would have expected Detective Constable Aidan Waits to be on duty in that room in the early hours of the morning.'

'So what?' I said.

'So, it may have been a hit after all. But what if it was your name on their list? They're told to get inside that room and rub out the gormless prick standing beside the bed . . .'

'I'd like to think that no one would mistake me for Sutty, sir.'

'Sometimes I see a certain resemblance. Do you know why you were given this detail, Detective Constable?'

'To get Lizzie Moore's gravesite out of Wick,' I said. When his face didn't change, I started to get a bad feeling. 'To assist Sutty, to offer round-the-clock protective custody—'

He was shaking his head. 'You don't think I could have assigned anyone to sit downstairs listening to a fantasist saying fuck-all? No, I'm afraid you were here for your own safety.'

'Me specifically?'

'You specifically. We have reason to believe that your life is in danger,' he said. 'When I discussed the matter with Detective Inspector Sutcliffe a few weeks ago, we agreed it might be best to get you off the streets for a while until we knew more.'

'And?'

'And you said it yourself. Why would what's left of Lizzie Moore's family kill the one man who might be able to tell them where their daughter's buried?'

I shook my head, trying to clear it. 'Where does the threat against me come from?'

'Old friend of yours, but I'm afraid I can't say any more than that.' His smile was pure malice. 'You're standing here refusing the investigation, after all.'

'I thought you were giving me the choice.'

'I am. Either you can do as you're told or you can get dug out of the ground in bin bags. Given that this old friend of yours is the reason you're so keen to get back on to the night shift, back into hiding, you have to accept that it's within the realms of possibility that he'd pull a stunt like this.'

'Anything's possible.'

'So I'll ask again. Are you interested in this case?'

I tried to think of another answer and my eyes went briefly to the ledge.

'Look,' he said. 'It's very simple. Chief Inspector James and his team will be on the surface, pushing the boulder up the hill. I want you examining the insects underneath it. I anticipate a difficult, thankless and likely violent task, which may conclude with a head rolling, one way or another. We need someone we can live without – and believe me, I'm looking at him. So, here we are. Your latest last chance . . .'

'Thank you for the opportunity, sir. Will this be a permanent or temporary assignment?'

He smiled. 'Look at where you're standing, son. *Life* is a temporary assignment. Let's just see how long you last, eh? You should try to look on this as an opportunity to rehabilitate yourself, try to live a little, because people in your position die a lot. Do right by me and this case could be your lifeline.'

I didn't believe him for a second.

The Superintendent's lifelines had a strange habit of choking you, and the ones he'd thrown me had all come with strings attached. You might not know until the end of an assignment if he was setting you up to succeed or setting you up to fail, and you might never grasp the larger picture or see what he was really going for. He'd sent me into situations where I had to break the law to live, then threatened to have me arrested for it. Afterwards, he'd made sure that the world knew how dirty I was, discredited me with the things he'd forced me to do in the first place. He was a master when it came to isolating people, and it had taken a couple of bad cases for me to realize that he always appeared at my lowest moment, right as I was going under. He'd make sure I understood that he was my only friend, then throw out one of his famous life-lines and drag me even further from the shore.

This time I wasn't going to take it.

As soon as he'd mentioned the threat against me, my mind had begun racing. Storming through possible solutions. Exit strategies and means of escape. I nodded along and accepted the case with no intention of actually working it.

The only other way off that roof was head first.

'Speak to whoever let that photograph of Wick get off the ward, and find this junkie. I'm sure you're familiar with some of the holes she might have crawled into. Do you think she's our flamethrower?'

'I don't know,' I said, coming slowly back to him. 'It looks like she was able to cross the partition by climbing up into the ceiling panels. Too unusual to be innocent.'

'Whether she did it or not, I don't need to tell you what'll happen if firearms find her first.'

'No, sir.'

'Speaking of which, you'll want to keep a close eye on Rennick.'

'Do we know his prognosis?'

'Same as yours, son. Stable, for the moment.'

'I'll talk to him as soon as he's awake.'

'So we're agreed, then. We'll be pursuing the murder as revenge motive . . .'

'I think you should at least consider the possibility that Wick was telling the truth when he died.' I said it mainly to rile him, so the detail would definitely end up in the case file, and he blinked suddenly, like I'd spat in his eye.

'Fine. You'll be wanting to speak to former Detective Inspector Kevin Blake. He wrote the book on it, after all.' Literally. Blake had been the man responsible for Wick's eventual confession. A twenty-five-page document that the killer had signed and then attempted to withdraw the week after sentencing. That wasn't uncommon, and Blake had gone on to write a bestseller about the arrest, trial and conviction. 'Get to him before the press do. He's not much of a writer but he could talk the arse off an elephant.'

'Sir.'

'And in the interests of being truly thorough,' he said, hitting me back twice as hard, 'you'll also look into the possibility that *you* were the hit's intended target.'

'How do you suggest I do that?'

'Well, think it through. If you walk around long enough, they might try again and then we'll know for certain. Besides, I'm sure we can both think of someone who might hold a grudge against you.' I was actively trying not to, but he saw through that and smiled. 'You should go and talk to him, have a little catch-up . . .'

'I wouldn't know how,' I said.

'I hear he owns a club in town . . .'

I didn't say anything and he nodded the subject closed.

'Now, with Sutty even more off his feet than usual, you'll probably be needing some help. Someone to keep an eye on you. I'm assigning you a new partner.'

I thought I'd misheard him.

'In light of your recent test results, and the situation we now find ourselves in, I'm seconding you to the position of detective sergeant. More responsibility. More pressure. Not much more money. When I shared this decision with Chief Superintendent Chase, her opinion was that you couldn't lead shit out of your own arsehole. So, let's prove her wrong, eh?'

'Lead?' I said.

'You know Constable Black.'

'Constable Naomi Black?' He flinched at my using her first name, but nodded. I was surprised. She'd done some surveillance work for me, and she'd seemed intelligent. Professional, hardworking and with both eyes on her career.

She must have had them closed for a second.

Parrs answered the question on my face. 'She's just transferred to CID, and when I asked for volunteers to assist Aidan Waits, hers was the only hand in the air. Too young to know better.'

'She's good,' I said. 'She helped me with a case last year.'

'That's right, the smiling man,' he said. 'I remember. You very nearly solved it. Maybe this is the big one, eh?'

He looked over my shoulder in a way that gave me a very bad feeling. Sure enough, I turned to see that Naomi Black was there with us. Had been standing on the roof the entire time. She was concentrating on the ground but gave me a quick look.

'I thought it might be useful for Constable Black to see what she was up against,' he said. 'I think our boy might need some sleep now, Naomi. Perhaps you could run him home? I'll expect to see you both fresh-faced and raring to go on Monday morning.'

I didn't know Black well, but I could see that this introduction hadn't been her idea, that she felt uncomfortable with what she'd witnessed. She moved from beside the door and went down the staircase. I made to follow her and heard Parrs coming up behind me.

'And Aidan . . .'

I turned.

'. . . If you think this is the moment for a bit of soul-searching, then let me save you the bother. You haven't got one.' I looked into his red eyes. 'You sold that to me a long time ago. I want you on deck here, son.' He gave me his shark's smile again. 'So no going overboard, eh?' He nodded after Constable Black. 'And double-knot your dick. That's an order.'

10

I followed Detective Constable Naomi Black, wordlessly, down the staircase. In the time I'd known her we'd only spent a few hours in each other's company. When I'd asked her to join me for a drink afterwards she'd declined, forcing me to question what my motives had been in the first place.

I didn't think I'd seen her out of uniform before, and was trying to get a read on her style. Black jeans, Doc Martens and a thick, dark green parka jacket. She had short, Afro hair with the tips dyed blonde and, taken altogether, looked a little like Liam Gallagher's half-sister.

She was mixed race in a way that would both help and hinder her career. The force was desperate to find faces with some colour in them, and if they were attached to intelligent people then so much the better. On the other hand, the promotion of a minority – which in our line of work was anyone other than a straight white male – was met with cynicism and innuendo in the ward rooms, and you could make that a double in police bars. The promoted subjects of this scorn were faced with a stark choice. Laugh along and be good sports, or risk isolation. It was my impression that Constable Black's choice had been the latter.

Partnering with me was something else, though.

Maybe we were both suicidal.

Sutty, usually a good barometer for the heavy weather of station discourse, had encountered her name in my final report on the smiling man. He'd made a satirical note in the margins: *Shouldn't that be Naomi Half-Black?*

The racial profiling went further than that, though.

I hadn't been welcome in a cop bar, or drank with any officer other than Sutty, in a couple of years. The last time I went to the Crown, the closest pub to police headquarters, it was to break up a fight that had long dispersed by the time I arrived. I needed to use the toilet before I left, and was amused to find a painstakingly compiled legend of local police officers on the cubicle door. There was a nickname beside each entry, alongside a precis of whatever the received wisdom was about them. I found my own, 'Toxic Waits', with ease. There was a snake drawn beside it, denoting that I'd been responsible for the arrest of a fellow officer.

The snake was swallowing its own tail to indicate said officer's subsequent death.

I'd seen worse things beside my name and, for a moment, I was transported to another time and place, where I'd felt like a part of this culture, working alongside people I liked. I began tracing the names of old colleagues I hadn't heard from in years, likely would never hear from again, and then I stopped. I saw that there were marks out of ten next to every female officer's name. Some had crude descriptions, some had sexual acts listed beside them, often in differing styles of handwriting, things they did in bed, or things their male counterparts wanted to do to them. I'd seen Naomi's entry by chance and then left the cubicle altogether.

8/10, it said. Nickname: *The N Word*.

11

When we reached the bottom of the stairwell, even the weak morning light hurt my eyes. Naomi turned, looking over my shoulder to confirm that Parrs was no longer with us. She stuffed both hands into the pockets of her parka.

'Sunday, bloody Sunday,' she said. 'He didn't tell me he was gonna do that.'

I nodded, looking out at the carnival of police and firearms officers surrounding us. The car park was alive with activity, as one shift ended and another began. Ambulances were still queuing to get in and Tactical Aid Units stood out, ominously, from everything else. I wanted to say something in return, to put her mind at rest, but instead I heard myself changing the subject.

'Is there anything I should know? Aside from the obvious.'

She nodded towards the fire escape we'd just come from. 'Did you notice the door?'

'Forced entry from the outside,' I said, turning to look. I'd missed it on the way up and on the way down.

'Why would your junkie have done that when she could get on to the ward undetected through the air vents?' I didn't want to give her the obvious answer. That someone else, someone worse, had broken in to do the job.

'CCTV?' I said.

'There's no surveillance on the wing itself but they're working on

49

footage from reception, and I've also requested the car park tapes. We might have to get in line behind DCI James and company, though.'

'I'm sure we'll all be working hand in hand.'

'Something in hand, if I know him . . .'

'You've worked under him before?'

She watched me from the depths of her parka and rocked back on her Docs. I could see that she didn't know how far she was allowed to go.

'I take it you weren't under him in quite the way he would have liked?' I said.

She laughed. 'To put it bluntly . . .'

'He took my statement earlier.'

'How was that?'

'He wrote everything down, at least. I got the impression he wouldn't fuck up a coffee order.' We shared a smile. 'What else have we got?'

'A car stolen, Fiat, pretty much immediately after the fire alarm went off.'

'So pretty much immediately after the attack?'

Naomi nodded. 'It gets better. The owner saw the girl . . .' She consulted her notes. 'IC1 female. Skinny with facial tattoos. Green tracksuit.'

'Sounds familiar. We've got the description out there?'

'So far nothing, but we'll find her. Who do you think she is?'

'Maybe she's the attacker. Maybe she's just involved somehow – a lookout, possibly? Maybe she was just in the wrong place at the wrong time.' I happened to look down at my charred and bloodied suit. 'It happens . . .'

'Sorry,' said Naomi, suddenly remembering something. 'Would you like to visit Detective Inspector Sutcliffe before we leave?'

'No,' I said. When she frowned, I explained. 'We don't have that kind of relationship.' I could see that she didn't know what to say, and was grateful for the distraction coming from the hospital.

Officers started speaking animatedly or listening intently to their radios, and we approached the nearest two for the news.

'What's going on?' asked Naomi.

'Rennick,' answered one of them, darkly. 'Internal haemorrhage. Poor bastard's dead.'

12

I was out on my feet but declined Constable Black's offer of a lift, mainly because the Superintendent had suggested it. My being assigned to Sutty for the last few years made perfect sense. Parrs liked to keep compromised officers in his pocket, feeding them to the higher-ups or the press as necessary, and I was the gift that kept on giving. Drug addiction, evidence-tampering, falsified reports and suspicious deaths. When the time came, there would be nothing they couldn't attach my name to, and it gave Parrs leverage, allowing him to press me into these off-the-books investigations.

It all made Naomi Black too good to be true.

She was clean, clearly being fast-tracked for promotion, and so over-qualified for the position that it was laughable. It suggested a deeper reason for her new assignment. An open pair of eyes and ears to follow me wherever I went. A trustworthy source who could convincingly report back on my conduct, filling in some of the blanks I always left in my reports to the Superintendent. With him, anything I said might be used against me.

If he was building a case, then I was sure Naomi would do a good job.

She was quick-witted and had a keen eye for bullshit. It was all the more reason to keep her at arm's length, and I hadn't felt like giving her my home address.

It was 6 a.m. on Sunday morning. The bloodshot autumnal sky tinted the air red, and the whole city looked like a bar with the lights up at last orders. I watched the men still ending their Saturday nights, draining crinkled beer cans, queuing for takeaways. Brand-new couples flagging down taxis, the boys attaching themselves to girls like barnacles. I turned on to Portland Street, skirting Chinatown, passing the twenty-four-hour casinos and strip clubs, the raw-eyed patrons squinting into the dawn.

When I looked up I saw that my feet had taken me to the door of one of the newer clubs in town. The Light Fantastic. Parrs hadn't said the name, but we both knew that if there was a death threat against me, it came from the man at this club's centre. And we both knew that we'd never prove it. He was young, handsome and wore his immovable gleaming grin like a mask.

I'd simply made the mistake of seeing behind it.

Standing there, looking up at the solitary lit window on the first floor, I finally came to a decision I'd been putting off for years. Two deaths while working protective custody was a new record, a new low, even for me, and whether Sutty pulled through or not, I knew that there'd be more, each one closer than the last, until . . .

I decided I wasn't going to wait around for them.

There was nothing left for me here but a blunt object to the back of the head and an unmarked grave. Agreeing to the case had been a way off that roof and out from under the Superintendent's red glare, but I wanted to go further than that, as far as humanly possible, with no forwarding address. There was only one person I had to say goodbye to, and it wasn't the psychopath behind the Light Fantastic.

Rubbing my eyes, I turned for home. In recent years I'd lived a few different lives in this town, but it felt like I'd died as many deaths. Looking over my shoulder at that solitary lit window, I got the feeling I was down to my very last one.

II
Shadowplay

1

I rolled up one sleeve and took the lid from the cistern. The water was freezing but I reached all the way inside, peeled away the gaffer tape and withdrew the sealed plastic envelope I'd fixed to the porcelain. I replaced the lid, dried up and went into the front room. It was Monday morning but I was wide awake, still a little night-headed when I looked out of the window. My eyes drifted from the grainy, low-resolution skyline to the building opposite, where a man was watering his window plants.

I told myself I was just drawing the curtain against the glare.

I lived alone, on the first floor of a small apartment block in the Northern Quarter, the beating heart of the city centre. Somehow I'd never been able to settle in the suburbs. The Quarter was a popular nightspot, rammed with cafés, bars, pubs and clubs, as well as clothing bazaars and scuzzy, rough-and-ready art galleries. Independent bookshops rubbed shoulders with record stores and fashion outlets, and the streets were vibrant, populated with colourful, non-binary young people who it was difficult to stay cynical about. It could get loud in the evenings as they flooded the streets, drinking in the nightlife, but I was usually at work by then anyway. When I got home, and when I was in the mood, sleep came easily enough. The entire quarter was hung-over or coming down during the day.

I knew that the decision I'd made to leave was emotional, fresh from the fire and Martin Wick's murder, from the suggestion by Parrs of some larger threat against me. Looking at it in the cold light of day, though, it seemed like the only option, and I'd spent several hours the night before composing a letter to my younger sister, the only person I could think of to say goodbye to. Separating myself from people, permanently cutting all ties, was one of my few natural talents, but this had tested it to the limit.

To say anything to her at all was a difficult impulse to explain.

An almost impossible one to go through with.

We'd been separated as children, shortly after being taken into care, and hadn't spoken in more than twenty years. Our relationship had never ended, though, and each of us seemed to haunt the other, resulting in several near misses. Moments where I'd swear blind that we'd passed in the street. I'd even made one aborted visit to the shared house she lived in, south of the city. It had left me short of breath, seeing sunspots, paralysed on her doorstep, and I'd never got any further.

Anne had tried, once or twice. She knew I was a police officer, and had asked after me when her home had been broken into. She'd even sent a letter after seeing my name and face in the news, when I'd been arrested for stealing drugs from evidence. I unfolded her letter now, having opened and closed it so many times in the last two years that the paper was thinning at the seams. Given time, it might have disintegrated completely, absolving me of any need to respond. Tracing my fingers across the lines, I saw again why I'd never felt able to.

There was no judgement in what my sister had written to me, just compassion, goodness, an effort to close a widening gap.

How could I insert myself into the life of someone like that?

In a sense, the mess I'd found myself in had provided the perfect solution. I had to act quickly, make an immediate connection, and then I had to walk out on her forever.

Hello and goodbye.

I gathered up my own notes, the reply I'd finally arrived at, feeling myself blush, feeling faintly ashamed by it. All I could see was a long list of reasons. Why the things that she'd read about me weren't true, why it had taken me a lifetime to get in touch, and why I was only doing so now to tell her that there would be no reunion between us, to definitively end even the shadow relationship we'd had up until now.

My letter made me look a man with an excuse for everything, a pathological liar, and in that sense at least, I suppose it was honest. I began to re-read it but folded it shut before I was even a few sentences in, then I halved it again, and again, pressing it smaller and smaller, until I could crush the paper inside my fist.

The walls in the front room were closing in on me with bookcases, about the only personality I'd imposed on the place. I ran a finger across the spines, looking for certain titles, taking down ten different paperbacks and removing various amounts of cash I'd hidden between the pages. I piled the notes on top of the plastic envelope and went out into the hallway for the stepladder. I stood it in the centre of the room, collected my valuables, and climbed up. Common sense had suggested that I keep each of these items separate, but it was time to put them all in one place.

Time to get paranoid.

Carefully, I removed the light fitting, then climbed up another step and reached into the void, twisting my arm around until I touched the handle of a bag. After the events of Saturday night and Sunday morning, I'd decided to keep it packed and ready to go.

As I drew it towards me, there was a knock at the door.

It was 6.30 a.m., and the building's imposing street entrance meant that visitors had to be buzzed inside. I remained still for a moment, holding my breath. There was another knock, more insistent this time. I placed the plastic envelope and the cash inside the ceiling cavity, then as an afterthought stuffed my sister's letter and my reply in after them.

The light fitting slid easily back into place. I climbed quietly down from the ladder, drew it closed and placed it against a bookcase, wincing as the frame rattled. Then I went to the door and opened it to Detective Constable Naomi Black.

She held out a coffee and smiled. 'You heard the man. Monday morning, raring to go.'

'How did you get in?' I said, blocking the doorway.

'Your neighbour.' I frowned at her. 'The older guy?' The flat opposite mine was empty. There were two students below and an elderly woman on the top floor. No older guy.

'Just a second,' I said, moving around her and drawing the door shut so she couldn't see inside. I went out to the landing and looked down. There was nobody in the hallway but the front door was ajar.

'He let me in as he was going out,' said Naomi. 'You're being weird.'

'Humour me.'

She muttered something about my sense of humour as I went down the stairs. I could hear a hairdryer from one of the ground-floor flats and street sounds from outside. There was the outline of someone through the glazed window and I threw open the front door, startling a man in his sixties, who dropped a large cardboard box, filled with blankets.

He was meaty, bearded and bald.

'Christ almighty,' he said, holding his chest and laughing at himself. Then he looked at me. 'Waits?' he said. 'I'm not psychic, I've just met the others. I'm moving in on the first floor.' He left the box at his feet and stuck out a fleshy hand. 'Robbie Grant.' I accepted it and stammered an apology for surprising him. 'Well, I'll tell you what,' he said. 'All my stuff's in boxes but I'd kill for a coffee . . .'

As a rule, I didn't enjoy my neighbours knowing my name, but it felt like I'd asked for this one. I picked up the cardboard box and we climbed the stairs. When we reached my flat, Naomi was inside. She'd opened the curtains and was looking quizzically at the step-ladder leaning up against the bookcase. I handed Robbie the box, found some instant coffee and balanced it on top for him.

'Give us a sec,' he said, leaving to cross the corridor. He had the look and authority of an ex-police officer, voice one decibel too loud, and it unnerved me slightly.

Naomi smiled. 'Like I said, the older guy. You wanna be careful, jumping out on pensioners. You'll end up giving him mouth-to-mouth . . .'

I tried to think of a comeback but it sounded like the kind of thing that might actually happen to me, so I got on with taking down the stepladder, carrying it back out on to the landing.

'Am I interrupting some Monday morning DIY?' she said, when I came back.

'Nothing like that . . .' She tilted her head to one side. '. . . I'm just so broken up about Sutty I was going to hang myself.' She didn't laugh. 'It's six thirty in the morning, Constable, and I've never told you where I live. I wasn't expecting you.'

'It's Naomi,' she said coolly. 'And you've got no secrets any more.'

If that was true then I'd probably be in prison.

We were still looking at each other when Robbie returned with the coffee. He began making small talk but Naomi interrupted.

'Press conference in an hour,' she said. 'We should probably get going.'

'Which one of you's in charge, then?' Robbie asked.

I looked at Naomi as she walked past us, Doc Martens thumping on the floorboards.

'It's complicated.'

2

'The entire service is in mourning today, and we are determined to carry out the fullest possible investigation into this attack. There will be no place to hide for the killer, nor for anyone who may be harbouring, aiding or abetting them . . .' Chief Superintendent Chase paused, sweeping her eyes across the captive audience for a beat before releasing them. 'Thank you.'

An explosion of flash photography greeted the close of her prepared statement, and she faced it seriously. She was flanked by Superintendent Parrs on one side and Chief Constable Cranston on the other. Usually, a conference of this magnitude would have fallen to Cranston, but his retirement was due at the end of the year and it was likely deemed a good opportunity to show the press a senior female face.

Who knew when the next one might come along?

Chase was younger than both men, in her early forties, and hadn't allowed the youth or colour to be bled out of her in the same way they had. Parrs conducting the conference would have been out of the question. Sitting there in his grey hair, suit and skin, his red eyes looked like twin laser sights mounted on some new and terrible weapon. With Chase there was just a glint in her eye, and she was able to tune it in for different occasions. Professionally, it could imply a sharp intelligence. Socially, it augmented a probing sense of humour, likely informed by years of interviewing men who'd underestimated her.

Now, the glint in her eye was determined.

The press conference had begun at 8 a.m., at police headquarters, and there was standing room only. Naomi and I had both watched from the back as Chase briefed the official version of events from St Mary's Hospital, with particular emphasis on the death of Constable Rennick. I wasn't mentioned by name but heard something faintly hostile in her voice when describing the one unharmed officer who'd been at the scene.

I'd spent the drive over dwelling on Naomi's unexpected visit that morning, thinking about the bag in my ceiling cavity. She was wrong when she said I had no secrets, but I had a feeling they were about to get scarce. When I glanced over, I caught her watching me, trying to read the look on my face.

I put it all out of my mind in case she could read that as well.

Chase began taking questions as the flash photography died down.

'Thank you, Chief Superintendent,' said one woman, standing up. 'Can you tell us any more about the person of interest?'

'As I said, we are pursuing *this* individual.'

Chase pressed a button on the desk and the image in the background changed from Rennick's face to a CCTV still of the young woman I'd seen in the toilets.

The picture wasn't great but she was distinctive.

'We believe that these marks on her face,' said Chase, turning to illustrate, 'are tattoos. Furthermore, this individual may have serious issues with substance abuse. Somebody out there knows who this is, and we ask them to come forward.'

'Is she considered a risk to the public?' asked the journalist.

Chase looked as though she were about to give a forthright answer before locating the soundbite. 'I would certainly urge members of the public not to approach this individual, as we do consider her to be extremely dangerous.'

I hadn't quite known that we considered that, and I sank a little as I saw fifty reporters adding the detail to their notes. The journalist nodded and took her seat. Chase pointed to a man in the front row. He was squat with a red face and a drawling, accusatory tone.

'Chief Superintendent, as I'm sure you appreciate, our readers are terrified today. Can you give them assurances that security will be tightened in the wake of this attack?'

Chase nodded. 'Armed police will remain on duty at St Mary's and in the city centre itself twenty-four hours a day, seven days a week, until further notice. These officers are highly trained to deal with a range of events, and they have my full support.'

'Thank you, Chief Superintendent,' said the man, setting up his real question. 'Are you happy that the security measures surrounding Martin Wick were sufficient for a man who'd survived seven attempts on his life while incarcerated?' There was a rumble of voices from the room. Not all of those attacks had been made public. The man turned to his colleagues with a smile. 'I mean, it seems like our prisons are safer than our hospitals these days . . .'

Chase blinked, internalized the question, and then turned. 'Perhaps Superintendent Parrs could elaborate on that.'

'Good morning, Charlie,' said Parrs, red eyes locking on to the man. 'In light of Saturday night's events, we are, of course, reviewing the security measures which were in place for Martin Wick.' His voice was a controlled growl. 'It does, however, seem worth re-stating that we'd received no intelligence of an attack before it took place.'

'Don't seven attempts on a man's life constitute something of an ongoing threat?' the man interjected.

'Furthermore,' said Parrs, ignoring him. 'We *had* managed to keep Martin Wick's location confidential until your publication put him on the front page yesterday.'

'Superintendent, you're suggesting that a photo printed a few hours before the attack was its cause? This was public interest. Patients at St Mary's had a right to know they were sharing air with a child killer.'

The room came alive with conversation and Parrs let it die down again before continuing.

'I'm suggesting it's a serious line of enquiry, and if it is connected I'll consider the reporter responsible as complicit in the murder of Constable Rennick.' There were raised voices and overlapping questions in the wake of this. 'Perhaps then you'll find out first-hand how safe our prisons are,' Parrs concluded.

Chase gave him a measured stare before waving the room quiet again.

'Please,' she said. 'Mr Sloane, as you know, following the tragic events of May twenty-second, I have campaigned tirelessly, and successfully, for deeper integration of armed patrols and personnel into everyday police life. This shocking and premeditated attack will only strengthen my resolve to go further.'

It was the all-inclusive tough talk that they wanted to hear, and you could almost feel the room mentally filing their copy. The man smiled between her and Parrs and resumed his seat. With the press under control again, Chase began bringing the conference to a close.

'I can only take one or two more questions. Yes,' she said, pointing at a younger man.

'Chief Superintendent, picking up on the thread of the prison attacks on Martin Wick, have those responsible been interviewed by the police?'

Chase nodded. 'Although at this time we do not believe that the attack is related to the prison assaults, we are pursuing all lines of enquiry. I can confirm that those inmates are being interviewed and eliminated as we speak. This is a relatively straightforward exercise, if only because most of Wick's former attackers are still serving their own life sentences. I am also in a position to confirm that one former inmate of Her Majesty's Prison is assisting us with our enquiries.' Naomi and I exchanged a look. DCI James and his team were one day ahead of us, and we hadn't been told that any of Wick's prison attackers had been released. 'Last question,' said Chase. 'Yes.'

A young woman stood up. 'Prior to his death, there were rumours that Martin Wick was willing to assist police looking into the location of Lizzie Moore's final resting place. Can the Chief Superintendent confirm whether there were any developments in this regard before the attack, and if not, does that spell the end for the hopes of the Moore family?'

Chase softened here, recalibrating for the more personal question. She opened her hands and laid them flat on the table. 'Unfortunately, despite the best efforts of our team, Martin Wick revealed no further details about the death of Lizzie Moore.' I looked at Parrs but he didn't move. 'Ladies and gentlemen, this is a dark day for Greater Manchester Police, and for the force at large. We have lost not only a protected prisoner but a deeply loved and valued colleague. We are shattered by the weekend's events, and ask for your understanding as we bring this killer to book.'

Chase clearly intended this to be the final note of the conference but the journalist pushed on. 'Chief Superintendent, as you know, Tessa Klein was officially declared dead by the coroner's office last week. Given that her body has never been recovered, and that this crime feels like an attack on the force itself, will you be exploring the possibility of a connection?'

Tessa Klein had been a young detective constable who'd resigned her position citing stress and depression, then taken her own life six months ago. Her car had been found at the banks of the River Irwell, doors wide open, with a suicide note on the dashboard. Chase seemed momentarily perturbed that the subject had intruded into an otherwise successful press conference, but she turned the look into a kind of universal concern.

'Tessa Klein is a tragic case of an officer suffering from depression, resigning her position and taking her own life outside the support systems of the police force. While I know that she's a favourite subject of the press, I would ask that her family be allowed to grieve. Today, we're talking about an entirely separate, vicious and premeditated attack.'

The journalist still hadn't sat down. 'And given that violence, would you hesitate to sanction lethal force in the pursuit of your person of interest?'

Chase looked grateful for the opportunity to end the conference on the correct note. She looked down the centre of the room, tuning the glint in her eye to one setting beyond determination.

'We will do whatever it takes to bring Constable Rennick's killer to justice.'

3

When the conference ended, the collected members of the press stood and began leaving the room as one mass, comparing notes, jokes and hangovers. I saw Parrs set his red eyes on to me and then look to the reporter he'd quarrelled with. I nodded and pushed my way through the crowd, getting a hand on Charlie Sloane's arm.

It felt like warm sausage meat.

He turned slowly, showing me his red, speckled spam face. The flared nostrils that implied he'd literally sniffed this story out.

'Excuse me, Mr Sloane, could I have a word?'

He followed me into a side room and I closed the door.

A moment later Naomi entered, taking a seat beside me. I hadn't asked her to join us, but was getting used to having a shadow. I had no real interest in speaking to Sloane, but if Parrs had seen him leaving unimpeded I'd probably end up on a hospital ward myself. The conference space and interview rooms had a bland, mass-produced, modern aesthetic. If Hitler's bunker had been designed by Travelodge, it couldn't have communicated quiet despair any more effectively. Sloane slouched into his seat and twisted a little finger in his ear, like he was winding himself up. He had the build of a tree stump and a dissatisfied crease for a mouth.

'So,' he said, drumming the desk with knuckle-less hands. 'What can I do you for?'

'We'd like to talk about the picture of Martin Wick you printed in your Sunday edition.'

'The *Mail* printed in their Sunday edition,' he said, correcting me.

'With your byline beneath it . . .'

'Nothing escapes you lot, does it?' he said with a smile. 'Except protected prisoners.'

'I'm not sure Martin Wick would describe his agonizing death as a jailbreak, Charlie.'

'And I'm not sure who I'm speaking to,' he said folding his arms. They were so short that he had to grip on with both hands to keep them together.

'I'm Detective Sergeant Waits, and this is—'

'Waits,' he said. 'The avant guard himself. You were there, or s'posed to be . . .'

'That wasn't a part of the public record, so I won't ask who told you. You can appreciate why I'd like to know who took that picture, though.'

'Well, from what I understand, aside from Wick, there were only three people present, two of whom have had the air let out of them.' He looked at Naomi. 'Whoever smelt it, dealt it, I say. You should arrest this man.'

She smiled. 'You won't tell us who sold you the picture, Charlie?'

'I protect my sources.'

'Your headline doesn't even work,' she said. 'Wick wasn't a serial killer . . .'

'That you know of. Kevin Blake's book acknowledged it as a possibility and, as I told the dark lord out there, people had a right to know their babies were being born in the same building where he was filling a bedpan.'

'Would you rather he went on the floor?' she asked.

'I'd rather he died in jail, as planned.'

'He was sentenced to life,' she said. 'Not death.'

'Well, more's the pity.' Naomi started to respond but he interrupted her. 'Nah, I'm not finished, young lady. If I talk to someone about this, it'll be one of the grown-ups. Someone who can give me something back for my trouble. Chief Inspector James has got this case, from what I understand.'

'We're following supplementary lines of enquiry,' said Naomi.

'Your Chief Super wasn't interested in the most promising one.'

'Which is?'

He reached into his pocket and showed us his phone, a picture of the missing former detective constable, Tessa Klein. She was dressed up for a night out, wearing a black dress and an eye-popping pink handbag. It seemed likely that she and I had passed each other in a corridor or two, but I couldn't recall ever meeting her.

'What do you think she's got to do with this?'

'According to my information, she graduated in the same year as Rennick . . .'

'So did I,' said Naomi. 'I never met him. Why would a six-month-old suicide be linked to what happened on Saturday?'

Sloane shrugged. 'Why did she book a weekend break for two and then top herself? Why did you never find the body?'

'Because she wasn't thinking rationally,' said Naomi. 'The body? It'll turn up, Charlie, they always do.'

'I'm sorry,' he said. 'What was your name again, darling?'

'Constable Black.'

'Well, give us a minute, eh, Constable Black?'

She looked at me then got up and left, doing a good job of seeming unfazed. I didn't have the same grace, and as soon as the door closed I leaned forward:

'Well?'

'Well, what?'

'Well, what do you have to tell me?'

'Tell you?' He laughed again. 'Nah, boy.' He nodded after Naomi. 'I was just enjoying the front of Black Beauty so much I couldn't wait to see the back of her. You're still young. If I were you, I'd try and find a way to give her a bit of the old nightstick.'

I got up and went to the door. I'd been hoping for an ambling conversation that went nowhere so I could creep out of the building without Naomi following, but nothing was worth this.

'Hang on a sec,' he said. I turned. 'You do know. Don't you?'

'Know what?'

'This play-acting, this fancy-dress ponce police work you think you're doing, this shadow investigation you've got going on . . .' I waited. '. . . You're just a fresh pair of pants, boy. When the time comes, they'll hang you out to dry. Here's hoping there's no shit stains in your kecks, eh?'

I could think of a few things to say in return but instead I crossed the room, pulled him on to his feet and projected him through the door.

'Thanks for your help.'

Naomi was standing outside, wide-eyed at my rough handling of an interviewee. If she put it in her report to Parrs it was one of the few things he might pat me on the back for. Sloane was used to it, anyway, and it seemed to shake something loose. He checked his watch and sucked on his teeth.

'Getting on for half nine . . .'

'That's right,' I said. 'Shouldn't you be hiding outside some school gates or something?'

He laughed. 'Y'know, the real detective, the man who actually caught Martin Wick, is about to go on the radio and talk all about it.' He saw the look on my face. 'And I'm betting you haven't got around to him yet. You should have a word, one of these days. Might learn a thing or two.'

71

4

'Excuse me,' said the security guard. 'You can't go in there.' We were in the lobby of Quay House, BBC headquarters in Media City. We badged the guard and asked to be escorted into the studios. Media City's a 200-acre property development on the banks of the Manchester Ship Canal. What had been a barren wilderness of industrial decline just a decade before was now a sprawling new media complex worth more than a billion. Across seven monolithic facilities it housed television networks, content creators, radio stations and more.

The largest of these buildings, Quay House, was home to the BBC.

It was a seven-storey glass structure, and towered over the canal like some prehistoric glacier that had drifted in on the tide. Stepping into the atrium at its centre was overwhelming and, craning your neck, you could see each of the five floors above. It felt like standing at the centre of an improbably empty Olympic stadium. The security guard led us up, past open-plan offices, meeting areas and breakout spaces.

We reached the broadcast facilities too late.

A large pane of glass walled off the studio where Kevin Blake was already being interviewed about Martin Wick's death. The audio was being broadcast out to the floor, and to the nation.

The presenter glanced at us through the glass. 'For those just joining us this morning, we've been speaking to Kevin Blake, the former detective inspector who secured a conviction against Martin Wick. He's also the author of the bestselling book, *The Sleepwalker*, which examines the case. Kevin,' she said, 'it's your belief that Saturday night's attack was premeditated . . .'

Blake nodded. 'This killer neutralized two police officers, carried out the execution of a protected prisoner and managed to get away with it. Now, that doesn't happen by accident.'

Blake was somewhere in his early sixties, and better groomed than any former DI I'd ever seen. No spider legs of nasal hair or burst capillaries for him. It was smart, dark suits all the way, and they had the effect of making his skin seem even paler than it already was. The thin, brass-rimmed glasses felt like an affectation, making him look like a pre-war intellectual. I didn't think he was vain, necessarily, just a man who expected to be noticed. He had a broad Yorkshire accent and it sounded honest against the received pronunciation of a BBC presenter.

'Final question,' said the host. 'We know that a woman in or around her thirties with facial tattoos is being sought in connection with this attack. Are there any further details on her?'

'Not according to what I'm hearing although, once more, I must stress that I am not a part of this investigation. Anyone with information relating to this attack should get in touch with the proper authorities. My sources do indicate that this woman is a significant person of interest, but I think Chief Superintendent Chase's press briefing this morning told us far more than that . . .'

'For those who didn't hear this morning's briefing, the Chief Superintendent advised members of the public *not* to approach this woman, as she is considered extremely dangerous.'

'In fact, she went further,' said Blake, holding the presenter's gaze. 'When questioned on public safety surrounding this attack, and on the person of interest still at large, the Chief Superintendent all but said that she wouldn't hesitate to approve lethal force in her apprehension . . .'

He let that sink in for a second.

'. . . As you know, that's extraordinary language, Miranda, usually reserved for acts of domestic terrorism.'

'Extraordinary, indeed. You mentioned domestic terrorism. Do you believe that the public are safe in the wake of this attack?'

Blake considered this. 'Martin Wick was a one-of-a-kind target, believe you me. Whoever killed him likely felt they had a strong motive for doing so. I'd be surprised to see any similar attacks. That said, this is one dangerous individual, and I'd echo the Chief Superintendent's warning to give them a very wide berth.'

'Kevin Blake, thank you.'

The presenter wrapped up the broadcast and they both removed their headsets. Behind the glass window, we couldn't hear what was being said off-mic but they had a brief conversation before Blake gave her a meaningful two-handed handshake. He got up, opened the door and stepped out of the booth. To avoid any possible confusion about his identity, he carried a copy of his own book.

'Kevin Blake,' said Naomi, stepping forward. 'I'm DC Black and this is my colleague, DS Waits, we've been trying to get hold of you.'

'You and the rest of the world,' he said.

The way his lenses caught the light meant that I couldn't see his eyes, and I couldn't tell if he sounded arrogant of the attention or weary of it.

5

Blake led us into the coffee shop over the road, motioned us each to a seat and then sat opposite, sliding a menu out of our sightline. Ordering coffee and water to the table, I could have almost believed he was there to interview us. He placed the copy of his book face down, so that the author photo was staring up. In the picture, Blake's jawline looked a little firmer, but it was the same honest, open face. The book had been successful enough for him to launch a career making press appearances pontificating on notorious killers, as well as fulfilling more general rent-a-quote duties. Though he'd retired soon after the case that made his name, he was still well regarded in police circles, maintaining the public image of a man on the inside, despite having been a civilian for the past decade. The waitress brought three coffees, some water and his change to the table.

When she left, he drew a cup towards him and smelt it. 'I'm not allowed coffee any more but I still get a kind of contact high from the fumes.'

'Does it keep you up?' I said.

He laughed. 'Might put me down for good. Heart problems, unfortunately. Don't ever get old. I'm sorry,' he said. 'Your name was . . .'

'Waits.'

'You were on the scene, if I hear correctly . . .'

'You're well informed,' I said. If he still had sources on the police force, then he'd heard a lot more about me than that.

'Sorry,' he said. 'After twenty years on the beat, I think it's just boiled into me. I try and keep my finger on the pulse, especially when it comes to Martin. I was bloody sorry to hear about Detective Inspector Sutcliffe.'

'Of course, you must have worked together . . .'

'You were his partner?' said Blake. I nodded. 'Then you probably know Sutty could be a bit . . .' I nodded again. 'You might know, or you might not, but I had Sutty taken off the original case.'

'All I know is he was the first on the scene.'

'And he wasn't without his talents. I just thought they'd be better used elsewhere.'

'How did he take it?'

'You don't know this? He handed in his notice.' I was surprised. I couldn't imagine Sutty being invested enough in anything to react so strongly. 'Someone must've talked him down from the ledge, though, because next thing I knew he was on the night shift.'

'It's all news to me,' I said, realizing that a man who'd been retired for more than a decade knew my partner better than I did. I wondered if that was Sutty's fault or mine.

'Who's got you running round after this?' said Blake.

'Superintendent Parrs.'

'The greyhound himself, eh? Good man, you must give him my best. I'm sure he'll be expecting yours. I've never worked with Alistair directly but my impression is he's always willing to lend a hand . . .'

'It's just that his grip can be a bit firm.'

'Well put,' said Blake, recognizing that he'd focused on me for too long. 'Black,' he said, turning to Naomi. 'Now, you wouldn't be related to a Constable Terry Black, would you?'

'He's my dad.'

'You're kidding?' he said, slapping a hand on the table. 'Then we've met before. I was at your christening.' I hadn't known that Naomi's father had been a police officer and when I risked a look I saw she was blushing, making the freckles visible against her dark skin. Blake noticed this as well. 'Nothing ages a man like a long memory, eh?'

'We're counting on that memory,' I said. 'Both Naomi and I are relatively new to the world of Martin Wick. In light of the events at St Mary's, we were hoping for some background on the case.'

'I don't envy you,' he said, 'working out who killed him.' He swept his change off the table, sifting it in his hand. 'First thing you should know is, if I threw this over my shoulder I'd probably hit someone who wanted Wick dead.'

'If you could hit the killer, we'd be grateful,' I said.

No one laughed, and Naomi leaned in. 'We know he was a hate figure for the tabloids, but we're more interested in people with real-world connections, real-world grudges. People who might actually go through with something like this. The statistical likelihood is that Martin Wick knew his killer, so it makes sense to start with those closest to him.'

'Of course,' said Blake. 'Although it's worth remembering that those closest to him for the last twelve years have been his cellmates. From what I hear, there was no shortage of blokes in there who felt like pulling the flush.'

'Handily for us, most of them are still serving their own sentences in Strangeways.'

'Most?' said Blake.

'One of his attackers is out on licence,' said Naomi, repeating what we'd heard in the briefing.

'Course,' he said. 'That spice dealer . . .' Blake squinted, trying to remember the details. 'Short Back and Sides, I think they call him.'

'Why's that?' asked Naomi.

'Not sure I want to ruin the surprise, but it won't shock you to hear he's the scum of the earth.'

'You've had dealings with him?'

'Happily not, he's a kid, long after my time. Only went into Strangeways last year and came out a few months back. I've just tried to stay up to date with Martin's play pals over the years. If I remember rightly, this Short Back and Sides bloke tried to hang him in his cell with the bedsheets.'

Naomi shook her head. 'Sounds like Short Back and Sides should be in prison . . .'

'Or six feet under one. His conviction was overturned, if you can believe that.'

'All these death threats and acts of violence against Wick,' I said. 'I've always wondered why he got it so bad inside?'

Naomi looked at me. 'He killed three children . . .'

'He's right, though,' said Blake. 'In Strangeways, who hasn't? They could fire a child killer out of a cannon every day of the year and still have some left for Christmas.'

'Is it the sleepwalking thing?' I said. 'His denial? Not facing up to what he did?'

Blake shrugged. 'There might be something in that. Going inside with these guys who are all pretty upfront about what they've done, and then playing innocent, or saying you don't remember, it's always gonna rub them the wrong way. I think there's more, though.' He thought for a second. 'Well, he was weird.'

'Weird?' said Naomi.

'I don't like it, but there it is. Look around the schoolyard and you can see at a glance who'll be getting their head flushed down the shitter from day one. I'd have put my mortgage on Wick having a hard time inside, unfortunately.'

'Unfortunately?' I said. I didn't disagree, but my experience of older officers was that they usually took a hard line and then doubled it.

'A campaign like that, unchecked, in what's supposed to be a high-security institution?' Blake affected a pained expression. 'That's the opposite of what we should be striving for. And as for some of the other blokes who've attacked him inside . . .'

I nodded. 'But as we say, these men are easily eliminated.'

'That's right,' said Blake. 'You want the background.'

'You were the senior detective inspector on N Division when the original call came in . . .'

He nodded. 'I can't tell if it's because I spend so much time stewing on it now or if I had a premonition back in the day, but I always say that was the year the worm turned.'

'Turned?'

'Or the bubble burst, went sour, whatever. You had the mortgage crisis, recession, foreclosure, all that, then Iraq going south and the launch of the iPhone. The start of all this social media shit. Loss of nuance and attention spans.' He shook his head. 'For me, that's the year the pilot light went out in us. We lost our spark.' He rubbed the bridge of his nose and smiled, self-effacingly. 'I lost mine, at any rate. Yes, I was the senior officer on N, but my first interaction with the case came when Wick was brought into Chester House, covered in blood. Clearly, it was serious but at first we struggled to get any sense out of him.'

'What sort of state was he in?'

'Agitated, confused. When we questioned him about the bloodstains on his person, he said he couldn't remember how they got there, as you probably know. He was such a mess that we had to move carefully. He was shivering, talking gibberish. In shock.'

'That must have been frustrating.'

'Ordinarily, it would have been, but a girl in dispatch connected his description with a suspicious persons report from 11 Briars Green. The Moores' property. There was plenty for us to do there, believe me.'

'Could you describe the scene?'

'I wish I could forget it. Semi-detached house at the end of a cul-de-sac. Neighbours slept through the lot, somehow. Front door was wide open when we arrived and Maggie . . .' He stopped. Took a drink of water and continued. 'Margaret, the mother, was lying at the bottom of the stairs. There was a lot of blood, stab-wounds to the abdomen and chest, defensive wounds on her hands and arms. We concluded that she'd fought her attacker, tried to prevent him from getting to the kids. We found them upstairs, the twins. They were both in the bath. They'd got in and hid behind the shower curtain, but . . .'

'Say no more,' I said. 'When did it become clear that the eldest was missing?'

'We were looking at the pictures on the walls,' he said. 'It was always all five of them in every frame. Maggie, the mother. Arthur and Mary, the twins. Frank, their dad. And then Lizzie, the eldest. Of course, our immediate focus became locating Frank and Lizzie, the only two not at the house.'

He nodded at the memory.

'There was an hour, a good hour there, where I convinced myself they'd be safe, together somewhere. My daughter was her age, twelve, at the time, and I don't mind telling you I called the wife and told her to give our Lucy a hug.'

It was a moving addendum.

One I remembered, word for word, from several different interviews he'd given over the years. I didn't doubt its sincerity, though. It was the kind of detail you only put into words once and never tinker with again afterwards.

'When did you realize Lizzie was among the victims?' asked Naomi.

'Unofficially? When we found Frank Moore, the father, and he hadn't seen her. The neighbours had already told us Frank and Maggie were . . .' He searched for the right phrase.

'Semi-detached?' Naomi suggested.

'Something like that.' He nodded. 'A trial separation, I suppose you'd call it. He'd moved out, and it was her weekend to take the kids, so he'd been working.'

'What was his reaction?'

'What do you think? There are some parts of the job I'll never miss and that's one of them. I mean, he just fell apart. He's a big man, physically and mentally, was in the marines at one time. It was like seeing a building come down, or a landslide. Hard to watch. He kept saying, "I should have been there, I should have been there."'

'And when did you officially know that Lizzie was among the dead?'

'Well, we never recovered the body, but DNA at the scene clarified things.'

'From what we understand, there was plenty of it . . .'

'A bloodbath,' he said, looking into his coffee. 'Quite literally.'

I was starting to get some idea of why he'd taken early retirement and why, perhaps, he still felt some responsibility to the victims all these years later. A mute killer, a missing girl, a mother torn apart trying to save her children. The kind of case you could get lost in.

'What took Wick there, do you think? Why them?'

'Madness,' said Blake, shaking his head. 'He was travelling a lot at the time, staying in cheap hotels, B&Bs. Some asbestos job had brought him into the area and he was at an inn nearby, the White Swan. It was our theory that he fixated on Lizzie, the eldest. Parents said later they'd seen a man matching Wick's description hanging round at her school. We also found some of her clothes in his hotel room and, of course, finally, the murder weapon.'

'It was the kitchen knife from the Moores' house?' I said, dredging up the memory.

'Found behind the radiator in Wick's room, on our third or fourth time round.'

'So, the full sequence of events was . . .'

'Wick arrives in the area for work, a week before the murders. He sees Lizzie, the eldest, on the street somewhere and follows her, either to school or home that first time, just so he had some means of finding her again. We had witnesses who could place him at both, later on. He stalked her, became infatuated, maybe even made contact or imagined they were in love. One night he snaps, has to have her. Breaks in the back window, murders Maggie at the bottom of the stairs, butchers the twins in the bath and snatches Lizzie. We were able to track his movements through the house because he cut himself breaking in through the back window. Trailed blood from the kitchen, to the staircase, to the bathroom, then back down and out the front door. Then he drove into town and walked into Piccadilly station, where he was apprehended. Five different blood types on his clothes. His own, Maggie's, Arthur and Mary's, and, of course, Lizzie's. Unfortunately, we're certain she was bleeding when she left the house.'

'What happened to her body?'

'That's the great mystery. I know they hoped he'd spill the beans to Inspector Sutcliffe but I never saw it happening, myself. I s'pose now we'll never know. Poor Frank, eh?'

I nodded. I wasn't sure what had become of Frank Moore but we'd have to speak to him.

'Was there anything like this in Wick's past?' I asked.

'No criminal record but with regards to his behaviour, it was difficult to get any kind of clear picture.'

'Because he was a loner,' said Naomi.

Blake nodded. 'And afterwards, people weren't exactly crawling out of the woodwork to admit knowing him. His work had him moving around a lot. He cleared off asbestos but as a freelance contractor. Job like that was perfect for a nomadic, lonely life, and that's what he seemed to be after, until he saw Lizzie Moore, that is. I interviewed some of the guys he worked with more regularly but it was all pretty weak beer. Quiet, kept to himself.'

'So there was never any suggestion he'd killed before?'

'Personally? I never discounted it. There were unresolved missing persons cases in the area, similar-looking girls, but we could never definitively say whether he was involved or not. All that moving around and so few people in his life.'

'What about his family?'

'Only child, parents dead. There's the ex-wife, of course . . .'

I looked up and Naomi stopped writing. 'Ex-wife?' we said at the same time.

'Married less than a year, divorced before the murders. Not much to say but I might have her number somewhere.'

'That could be a big help.'

'You said Frank Moore came apart,' said Naomi.

'But he put himself back together again. We actually spoke this morning, we're involved with some of the same charities.'

'May I ask what the substance of your conversation was?' she said.

'You're asking if he was happy to see Martin Wick get cremated? He wouldn't be part of the human race otherwise . . .'

'We'll need his details, too.'

'By all means. You should try and catch his talk today. I think it's still going ahead.'

'His talk?' I said.

'He gives these motivational speeches, I s'pose you'd call 'em. Survival seminars. To take all that trauma and turn it into anything remotely positive, it's impressive work. Sheer force of fucking will. Pardon the French.'

Naómi made a note. 'Did you ever have any contact or correspondence with Wick after his conviction?'

Blake shook his head. 'The publisher suggested we do an interview with him for the book, give his side of the story, but I objected. Anyway, like I said, he wasn't exactly talkative. And there was that whole business of him disavowing the confession he finally did sign.'

'Did you ever believe him?' she asked.

'Believe him about what?'

'That he couldn't recall the crime . . .'

He considered this for a moment and turned to me. 'You must have met him, Waits. What did you think?'

'Something certainly slipped his mind.'

'My conclusion, too,' said Blake. 'It took a long time for him to come around to signing his confession in the first place, dropping all that sleepwalking business, but he got there in the end.'

I didn't want to tell him that Wick's final words had been to forcefully withdraw that confession, but I did want to push him on the subject.

'So you never had any doubts?'

'I wouldn't say that, exactly. I had some reluctance committing to him as the perpetrator. The way he held himself back, you sometimes had to be mindful of projecting things. He had those big, black eyes and didn't show much emotion, so it was easy to attribute things to him. I had to keep in mind that we might be filling him up like a pint glass. A lot of the lads hated him from the off.'

'Sounds tricky.'

He nodded. 'And especially because, on the other hand, I had to follow my instincts – and all of them were screaming that Wick was my man. All the evidence, too. You're always gathering evidence, even when you don't know it. Sometimes what's called intuition is actually your subconscious coming to a logical conclusion sooner than the part of you that second-guesses everything. For what it's worth, my advice is follow your instincts.'

'Where would you be looking?' I said.

'For Wick's killer? Revenge seems like the most obvious reason for his death, but what slows you down are the rules of the road. Second-guessing yourself because your brain's looking for logic. You think that, surely anyone who'd kill a murderer wouldn't take down an innocent policeman with him? Wouldn't set fire to another one while he was at it.' He looked between us. 'My real advice is not to go chasing a case like this looking for logic. You'll never sleep again. Murder's not rational, except for the killer. For someone, what happened on that ward felt like the only possible course of action. That's who I'd be looking for.'

6

'And that was me,' said Frank Moore. We were standing at the back of the event space in the Radisson Hotel, inside the Free Trade Hall. Moore was concluding an hour-long speech on the subject of surviving grief. He was the father of three murdered children and the husband of a murdered wife.

I thought if anyone had the answer it was probably him.

We'd arrived late and found there were a couple of hundred people in attendance, in a space that would usually host weddings or charity functions. Most were smartly dressed. Well-to-do people prepared to pay the admission fee, comfortable with an afternoon out of the office. Looking more closely, though, the links were apparent.

Exhausted faces and red eyes.

Scanning the crowd, you could see the burnouts. Restless people, itching inside their skin. Some carried the recognizable scars of grief. Gaunt, haunted faces. Drinkers' noses or delirium tremens. Eating disorders and self-harming scars. Others hid them behind designer clothes and well-exercised gym memberships. All of them watched Frank Moore closely, like he was their last hope.

It was easy to see why.

He was strong, handsome, a full six feet four of self-assurance, wearing a crisp, fitted shirt over a well-developed chest. The look was completed with blue slacks and cream loafers but he made the clothes look somehow more like a uniform than a personal choice, perhaps an echo of his military days. His hair was black, buzzed short in a high and tight style with a lightning bolt shock of white straight through the centre.

He was unnervingly symmetrical, like a photoshopped picture of himself, and in his comfortable persona and easy speaking manner, in his certainty, he reminded me of a good barrister making his closing argument in court.

'I was living through these photo albums,' he said to the crowd. 'I was dwelling on the past, because I didn't have a future. And that was when I did the most difficult thing of all. I turned the page. And where I'd been looking at this family that I'd been in charge of, my girls, my little lad, a wife I was supposed to protect, on that next page I saw something else.'

He looked up at the crowd significantly.

'I saw myself. See, I'd forgotten that I was in there, too. I'd forgotten I was in that photo album, and I'd forgotten I was in that family. I'd forgotten that I loved that man, once, as well.' He flipped the picture of the Moore family on an A-frame behind him, revealing a close-up of his own face. 'It was one of those bankers we've been talking about. One of those moments of good feeling that you want to bottle up, to try and future-proof yourself against grief.'

Understanding nods throughout the room.

'But grief's a bit like a debt collector, isn't he? Always turns up at the worst possible moment, always takes a bit more than you can afford to give. If bereavement of some kind's found you already, then you'll understand what we've been talking about this afternoon. If it hasn't touched you yet, then I'm afraid that one day it will. Because the books tell us there are five stages. Denial. Anger. Bargaining. Depression. Acceptance.' He looked around the room and then shook his head. 'The books are wrong, though, because there's actually just the one. William Shakespeare said "all the world's a stage". I say all the world's a stage of grief. So, how do we re-learn our lines? How do we go out there and perform again?'

He looked at the crowd and, for a moment, I thought he might actually have the answer. 'I hope you'll join me next time to find out.'

He stepped down from the stage to a standing ovation, ran a hand through the shock of white in his hair and walked through the centre of the room to the exit.

I couldn't believe this was the conclusion of his speech.

It felt too much like the night shift to be funny. A dealer giving his customers their first taste cheap, then jacking up the price once they were hooked.

When Naomi and I followed him outside, Frank had taken up position at a large signing table covered in leaflets, flyers and promotional materials. We were first in line but people were already flooding out of the ballroom behind us.

I approached the table. 'That was a powerful speech.'

He seemed to consider this, as though I'd said something that hadn't occurred to him before. 'Thank you,' he said, after a pause. 'You've lost someone recently?'

'Quite recently.'

'You arrived late,' he said. 'It's OK, but I don't think you got the full breakdown of what we can offer. You'd probably both benefit from one of our four-week survival courses.' He looked past us at the growing line. 'We'll discuss my story and you'll have the opportunity to share your own. There'll also be input from some of our other long-term survivors.'

'And what is your story?' I said.

'I think you know my story, Officer.' He threw in a smile. 'As you can see, I'll probably have my hands full for the next couple of hours, but we could arrange a meeting for later today? I'd be more than happy to discuss it then.'

'I'm sorry, we didn't mean to—'

He shook his head. 'I'm flattered that you're interested in the programme. And I meant what I said, I think you'd both get a lot out of it – a lot of cops do.'

'How much is the programme, out of interest?' asked Naomi.

'We've got a variety of plans, something to suit all income levels. If you need help, then by hook or by crook, we'll make it work.'

'Did Kevin Blake call ahead to say we were coming?'

'Kevin? No. You just look like a police officer, Mrs . . . ?'

'Detective Constable Black,' she said, with a smile.

I glanced at the growing line. 'We could visit you later today, at home, or wherever's convenient.'

'I'd like that,' he said, standing to shake my hand but not Naomi's. He passed me his card and we stepped out of the line.

7

'Do you think he'll speak to us?' said Naomi as we returned to the car.

'I don't think he was ducking it. If you've got something else on later I can easily talk to him alone.' I knew I was chancing my arm, but if I was ever going to abandon this case and blow town, then at some point I needed to shake Naomi off it.

'Is that what you'd prefer?' she said, after a beat.

I'd almost have preferred to be working the case with Sutty. Superintendent Parrs had always made our dynamic clear. One of us to carry the casket and one of us to carry the can. He didn't care which of us did what. With Naomi, I didn't know what her role was, what she was carrying. It might have been an olive branch, it might have been a wire.

It had been interesting to see Frank Moore bristle at her, though.

'As long as we're looking into this, it might make sense to attack it from different angles,' I said. 'I don't know what both of us being here adds to anything . . .'

She was quiet for a moment. 'What did you make of the Super's theory that you might have been the intended target of the attack?'

'I'm sorry?'

She looked guilty, like she wasn't supposed to know. 'When we were on the roof with Superintendent Parrs after Wick's murder, he said we should look into that possibility. It seems like the only angle that we're not—'

'I don't think it was a serious concern,' I said. She didn't respond. 'Is there anything else on your mind?' I knew that Naomi had questions about me, that she must have seen her share of scandalous graffiti with my name attached to it. I hoped that if I asked her straight she'd back down.

It didn't work.

'Parrs said this man who wanted you dead was an old friend of yours. Who was it?'

'It was a figure of speech,' I said, grateful that we were nearing the car. 'A figment of his imagination.'

'You don't trust me, do you?'

I could feel her eyes on me but didn't look up as I opened the door. 'Should I?'

She didn't answer, and when we climbed into the car I thought I could see her mind working, approaching the problem differently. Her eyes went to the copy of Kevin Blake's book, which he'd given to her after our meeting.

She handed it to me. 'This is yours, by the way. I got the paperback on Sunday.'

'Any good?'

'Like the Super said, he's not much of a writer. Felt like a police report crossed with a thesaurus. I couldn't get through it . . .'

'*The Sleepwalker*,' I said, reading the dust jacket. '*Awakening the Beast*.' I put it down on the dashboard. 'I can barely get through the title.'

'I thought you were a big reader . . .' I looked at her and she shrugged. '. . . Your flat, the bookcases.'

'Cheaper than insulation,' I said, shutting the conversation down. 'Look, once we get back to the station I'd like you to liaise with DCI James and his team on the CCTV footage from St Mary's. That's our best bet for solving this thing quickly.'

She looked at me but didn't reply.

'Might take a few days sitting in with them, if you're up to it . . .'

'Sure,' she said.

'And you should probably write up a report of what we got from Blake and Moore, although I'm sure James is hot on our heels.'

She nodded.

Parrs couldn't complain if I entrusted a job like that to her, and it might give me some breathing room. I wanted to discourage Naomi from following up on the possibility that I'd been the intended target of the hit. Whether it was true or not, there was nothing good at the end of that thread for either of us. The scanner glitched into life but she got to it before I did.

'Constable Black, receiving.'

Her eyes lit up as dispatch relayed a possible sighting of the woman in the green tracksuit. She started up, switched on the sirens and made a U-turn. We were forging ahead, despite my best efforts.

8

We found the Fiat that had been stolen from St Mary's car park on Lower Ormond Street, a well-heeled part of town that was home to an arts centre and walled in on both sides by redbrick apartment blocks. It had been torched, implying that the woman I'd seen at the hospital had been in possession of it for a full twenty-four hours without being caught.

Maybe she hadn't been quite as fried as she'd seemed.

We arrived in time to see the fire brigade extinguishing the flames. An efficient means of wiping your fingerprints.

'Yeah,' said the woman who'd called it in. 'Green tracksuit. Looked all wrong round that car. Next thing I know, it's smoking.'

'Did you notice if she was carrying anything?' asked Naomi.

She closed her eyes. 'I think there was a backpack – light-coloured but minging. She the one off the news?'

'Sounds possible,' said Naomi, making a note. 'Do you have any idea which direction she went in?'

'I was getting the kids together, sorry.'

We crossed the road and watched the fire brigade packing it up.

'Clever girl,' said Naomi, balefully. She left a pause for me to contribute something but I just watched the fire crew disassembling. 'So, what do we do now? Look around?'

She was trying to avoid me dumping her back at Central Park.

'Where would we even start?' I said. 'We're a two-minute walk from the busiest road in the city, at the busiest time. North and you're at the station, then anywhere. South and you're at either of the universities. We can send some uniforms door-to-door, but the best we can hope for's which direction she went in.'

'It feels like we're five minutes behind her . . .'

'I suggest you make peace with that.'

'Ha,' she said flatly. 'You're not interested in this . . .' I started walking towards the car. '. . . at all, are you?'

'No one's interested in this,' I said, without turning round.

'Every newspaper on the stand this morning says you're wrong. That press conference says you're wrong.'

'They're interested in some ghoul who went up in flames, not the truth behind it.'

'Good job we are, then,' she said, coming alongside me. 'Superintendent Parrs said we should find this girl before the firearms unit, why was that?'

'If you were listening to Chase this morning then I'm sure you can work it out.'

'But I'm wondering if you know.'

'Because they think she killed Rennick,' I said, looking at Naomi. 'If they find her they'll gun her down in the street.'

'And you're OK with that?'

'I've just been here before.'

'And where exactly is *here*?'

'On the losing side, Constable Black. Welcome aboard. Find her first and lock her up, they'll kill her there instead. That's what they do.'

'Who's they?' I ignored her and turned for the car. 'You went undercover,' she said. I stopped and she spoke to my back. 'Looking for police corruption, I heard.' I didn't say anything. 'I take it you found it, then . . .'

I caught my reflection in the glass. 'Everywhere I looked.'

She was silent for a moment.

'Fine,' she said finally. 'That's them. We're talking about you. You're happy with them finding her first and shooting her down? A woman's death on your conscience?'

'What's one more of them?' I said, opening the door and climbing inside the car.

When I looked back at Naomi she was staring straight ahead with a slight frown on her face, like the street was unfamiliar to her, and she was lost. I didn't meet her eye when she got into the car. She started up without saying anything and I caught my reflection again in the wing mirror. Then I leaned back so I wouldn't have to see myself.

9

We didn't speak to each other on the drive back to police head-quarters, and I was looking forward to breaking off from Constable Black, allowing her to be absorbed into the tedious due diligence of DCI James and his team. The first few hours of our partner-ship hadn't been promising. I knew most of that was down to my cynicism and lack of investment, but given the circumstances those weren't personality traits I expected to change. For Naomi's part, her frustration with me presented itself in an abrupt, impa-tient driving style, punctuated with obscenities projected at other drivers.

'Get a life, dickhead,' she shouted at a man who cut her up.

When he stopped and tried to give her a menacing look, she held two fingers up to the windscreen, daring him to do something about it. He drove on.

When we passed the station without stopping I gave her a look.

'Where are we going, Constable?'

'I thought—'

My phone started to vibrate against my chest. 'One second,' I said, pulling it from my jacket pocket and picking up the call.

'Aidan Waits?'

The woman said my name strangely, like it was an instruction for me to stay put.

'I'm looking for Aidan Waits.'

'Speaking,' I said.

She started to say something else but the line cut out and I looked at the screen. It had come from a withheld number. I thought she'd sounded familiar somehow but I couldn't place her. At length, my mind came back to where we were.

This unexpected deviation.

'Well?' I said, looking at Naomi.

She nodded at the windscreen. 'We're here.'

We pulled into a side road in Newton Heath, not far from police headquarters. Naomi leaned out of the window and badged a constable in a filthy high-vis jacket. He waved us through and she coasted on to an enormous, abandoned-looking warehouse with a sign that read Coleridge and Whites. For a moment I thought this was the kind of place a killer might dump a body, another crime scene, but when she switched off the engine I could hear gunfire.

'Tell me you haven't arranged an interview with firearms on the shooting range . . .'

'I haven't, I promise.'

'I can hear them, Naomi.'

'Yeah, but they don't know we're here,' she said, opening the door. 'Come on.'

I thought about my new neighbour's question, earlier in the day: *Which one of you's in charge, then?*

Firearms units train at several remote sites in and around the city. This, I assumed, was one of them.

'Louisa Jankowski,' said Naomi as we approached the building. The officer we believed to have been on duty when the photograph of Martin Wick was taken in St Mary's. 'I thought we could probably catch her off guard.'

'I'm not sure you want to surprise someone who's carrying an assault rifle.'

She winked at me. 'That's why I brought my human shield.'

Before I had a chance to laugh, a firearms officer stationed at the factory's entrance took a step towards us. He had a hipster beard that curled upwards, like it was climbing off his face, and I hated him on sight.

'DC Black,' said Naomi, holding up her card. 'This is DS Waits. We'd like to speak with one of your officers.'

'Sorry, sweetheart,' he said, like he was talking to a ten-year-old child. 'We only interrupt them if it's life or death.'

'We're in luck, then,' she said. 'Because it's the latter.'

'Which death?' He looked between us and smiled. 'Only we get so many.'

'We'd rather discuss that inside,' said Naomi. 'But if we need a fresh corpse . . .'

He made a face and I broke in. 'I know guard duty gets boring, Constable, but we're not here to chat. Someone put air vents in one of your colleagues in the early hours of Sunday morning and we're looking into it.'

'Rennick?' he said darkly. I nodded. 'You could probably phrase that a little more tactfully, couldn't you?'

'Anything you say, sweetheart.'

He glared at me. Somehow I can never tell men with guns what they want to hear.

'Follow me,' he said, hitting the F sound. 'I only hope we find the fucker first.'

Naomi raised an eyebrow. I thought I'd travelled in her estimation but I couldn't tell whether I'd gone up or down.

10

We were led through, into an enormous wide open space. The walls were made of cinder block up to about six feet and sheet metal thereafter. One benefit of catastrophic industrial decline was that it opened up plenty of ad-hoc shooting ranges.

The sound of gunfire was absolutely deafening.

There were six firearms officers standing in formation with their backs to us, discharging their weapons into targets about fifty feet away. Standing at the rear was their sergeant, who frowned and removed his ear mufflers as we entered. He spoke to the man from the door, looked at us and then nodded. One by one the others ceased fire and turned. All except the lone female firearms officer.

Louisa Jankowski.

She continued firing into targets, reloading and repeating, as if she were pushing back some unstoppable force. Finally, she sensed her colleagues looking at her, lowered her weapon and turned. I thought I saw a moment's flight in her eyes, an almost imperceptible step backwards, until she calculated the odds, removed her ear mufflers, and came towards us.

I recognized her from the ward.

She'd signed me in and out several times while inside the hospital, but we'd never had much cause to talk. She was second or third generation Polish immigrant, I thought. The kind of bone structure, luminescent skin and white teeth that rarely floated to the top of the city's gene pool. She was athletic and tall, at least my height, and as she drew closer I saw that she was out of breath, sweating slightly.

Alongside the firearm, it made her look strong and fearless.

'Louisa,' said her sergeant. 'These two officers would like a word with you.'

'Waits,' she said, recognizing me from the ward. 'What's this about?'

'Perhaps we'd better talk outside,' said Naomi.

'You won't need the gun,' I added.

As we left the building I saw the other officers exchanging looks. Louisa strode ahead of us, as if eager for confrontation. There, she went comfortably to the far side of the car we'd arrived in, leaning into the roof like she was wearing it as body armour. She'd been highly trained to find the best vantage points, and I wondered if that would be reflected in her conversation.

'This about Rennick?' she said.

'We're sorry about your loss, Louisa.'

'Well, I think you're wasting your time here.'

'I was there when the attack took place,' I said, hoping to find some common ground. 'Rennick was a good man.' I hadn't known him personally but maybe it was true. People seemed to get a certain grace period immediately after death.

'Tell me what happened.'

'I don't know,' I said honestly.

'But it's what we'd like to find out,' Naomi resumed. 'Were the two of you close?'

'Close?' said Jankowski. 'I think you know that's a loaded word between male and female officers. What about you two? Are you two close?'

'No,' said Naomi, more forcefully than I would have expected.

Jankowski half-laughed and nodded, looking down at her reflection in the car roof. 'Well, me and Rennie were mates. I kept expecting him to walk through that door today . . .'

'You were going pretty hard out there,' said Naomi.

'Visualization. Thinking about the bitch who did him. What's going on with that, by the way? We heard there'd been a sighting of her but then nothing.'

'We're not entirely sure she was even the attacker,' said Naomi, her eyes drifting to me for support.

'You what?'

'The situation's complicated by Martin Wick,' I said. 'We're investigating his murder, alongside Rennick's.'

Jankowski snorted.

'Is that a problem?' said Naomi.

'Rennie deserves better. They're tied together now, and they always will be. It's disgusting.' She unballed her fists. 'How does Wick's murder make things more difficult?'

Naomi looked at me to answer and I did it grudgingly. 'He muddies the waters of whatever the motive might be.'

'The motive? What else would it be but vigilantism? People hated him, that's why we were there in the first place . . .'

'There could be an unrelated issue, or there could be unanswered questions from his original conviction,' I said, throwing out two options. 'For all we know, one of the police officers on duty might have been the intended target.'

I felt Naomi's eyes move on and then off me.

Jankowski thought about it and frowned. 'So tell me how I can help.'

Naomi took her notebook from her pocket. 'You were working on Wick's protective detail in the weeks leading up to the attack. Did you see or hear anything unusual?'

'No,' said Jankowski. 'I'd have reported it. You think she'd been hanging round St Mary's a while, then? This tracksuit girl?'

'And the searches?' said Naomi, ignoring her question. 'Were you satisfied with the rigour you applied to the sign-in procedure?'

'What are you saying?'

Naomi's voice remained steady. 'I'm asking if you were happy with the rigour you applied to the sign-in procedure?'

'Always,' Jankowski said. 'Procedure's there for a reason. I can stop and search in my sleep, Constable Black. Can you? What's this got to do with someone stabbing Rennie? I wasn't even there.'

'Where were you, out of interest?'

Her jawline tightened. 'On duty.'

'Did you see yesterday's *Mail*?'

Jankowski shook her head but I found it hard to believe. It was the biggest story of the day and affected her personally. I found myself looking at her a little more closely.

Naomi opened the driver's-side door and found a copy of Sunday's paper. She laid it on the roof with the picture of Wick facing up.

'We have reason to believe that this photograph was taken while you were on duty, Louisa.'

Jankowski leaned off the car roof and stood up to full height. 'Bullshit,' she said. 'I'm not the only guard he had for breakfast.'

'You're the only one who was on duty when he had cornflakes, as pictured . . .'

I picked up the thread. 'When Rennick was assaulted I couldn't call for help immediately, because I'd signed in my phone before entering the wing.'

'Rennick had done his job,' said Naomi. 'It looks like whoever was on duty when this picture was taken didn't do theirs.'

'I object to this version of events,' said Jankowski.

'This version of events is the one we've got,' Naomi answered.

Jankowski shook her head and looked at me. 'You're here, talking about conduct? You? What's your superior called, again?'

'Sutcliffe,' I said.

'Yeah, him. Screaming with laughter all day long with a child killer. He should be ashamed of himself.'

'His face is pretty red now, if that's any consolation.' She looked appalled that I was prepared to joke about Sutty's injuries but I thought it was worth making the point. 'There's no love lost between the two of us, and if the evidence leads his way then I'll cuff him to the gurney myself. There is one detail that hasn't been made public, though. His job entailed winning Martin Wick's trust. He was there to extract the burial site of one of the victims, Lizzie Moore.' I thought Jankowski's face changed subtly. 'Perhaps the things you saw weren't quite what they seemed,' I suggested.

She looked at the paper. 'I had nothing to do with this.'

'The sign-in sheet says Sutcliffe and Waits were swapping over,' said Naomi. 'Neither one of them was on the wing. It shows there were no doctors or nurses present. And, correct me if I'm wrong, but procedure dictated that you escort orderlies to Wick's room with his meals?' Jankowski nodded. 'Did you follow that procedure?'

'To the letter.'

'Then you were the only person on that stretch of corridor,' said Naomi. 'And you saw nothing unusual?'

'You keep asking that. He was there when the execution took place,' she said, nodding at me. 'Did he see anything unusual?'

I nodded. 'A firearms officer with his throat cut and a protected prisoner burning to death.'

'It's starting to feel like I should have my rep present.'

'We're here with an open mind,' I said. 'But we are certain that someone told Wick's killer where he was, what the security measures were, and how to get to him. That suggests some inside knowledge. I'm sure DCI James will be looking at everyone.'

'Not at your gaffer.'

'He's not so pretty at the moment,' I said. 'In fact, he's in a medically induced coma. Believe me, my face will be the first thing he sees when he wakes up. If he wakes up.' With that she nodded, seeming finally to accept that we weren't there to exonerate Sutty.

'Are we done here?'

'For now,' said Naomi.

'If you do think of anything, give me a call.' I handed her my card and she rolled it across her fingers like a blackjack dealer. 'We don't have any agenda other than finding the truth.' The conversation hadn't gone well, and I wanted to end on some kind of positive.

I didn't need any more trained killers cursing my name.

Jankowski walked round the car and returned to the factory. When we turned to watch her go we saw several armed officers standing in the doorway. They parted so she could pass through them, then closed ranks again, eyes on us.

She was distrusted but we were despised.

I counted five assault rifles pointing vaguely in our direction.

Naomi turned to me. 'Thanks for waking up at the end, there . . .'

'This was all yours. Anyway, it looked like you knew what you were doing.'

'I didn't know I was doing it with a silent partner. Do you think she was lying?'

'Why not? Everyone's at it.'

We climbed inside the car and Naomi changed the subject. 'See the way they all looked at each other when we took her outside?' It was another thing I was hoping she hadn't noticed. 'It was like they didn't trust her.'

'Could mean anything. It's not easy, working under a cloud.' Naomi looked at me and I assumed she thought I was talking about myself. I could only imagine the kind of cloud she envisioned.

'Think they could make life hard for her?'

'It's not her life I'm worried about. I wouldn't expect to make any new friends this go around.'

Naomi started up. I turned down the scanner and switched on the radio, trying to fill the growing silence between us. I didn't like the rate that the case was progressing at, the way that people seemed to be shape-shifting before our eyes, and I couldn't drag my feet much more without arousing Naomi's suspicions.

She was too intelligent to lie to, and her relationship, whatever it was, with Superintendent Parrs put her beyond my powers of manipulation.

Perhaps if I remained a passenger in the investigation she'd request a transfer but, then, was that really what I wanted? Questions had begun itching at me. How do you get close enough to stab an armed policeman? And who murders a man days away from death?

The only thing I was sure of after our surprise trip was that I couldn't afford to keep coasting, for fear Naomi would keep catching our suspects, and me, off guard.

When I looked at my phone I had another missed call from a withheld number.

Someone was trying to get hold of me.

11

It was late in the day but Frank Moore never broke eye contact while we were speaking, and I had to crane my neck to look up at him. I found it interesting that, where Kevin Blake, a man I'd assumed would be from the old world, had dealt so comfortably with a female officer, Moore, a much younger man, seemed to struggle. Whenever Naomi spoke, he'd listen carefully and then direct his answers to me. Perhaps it was less about her being a woman and more about his military past, my supposed seniority. He struck me as the kind of man who might ask to speak to the manager.

If only he knew.

After dumping Constable Black in the CCTV suite for a few hours I'd tried to leave the station without her. When I reached the car she'd been sitting there waiting for me. I'd pretended I was expecting that, and got in without comment. We drove out to Frank Moore's home in our now customary silence, with just the glitch and crackle of the scanner for a soundtrack. He lived in a symmetrical new-build redbrick in Heaton Mersey, and he paused as we stepped inside.

'We usually take our shoes off . . .'

He led us in, past a set of family photographs that matched the order of the house. I might have taken them for stock images, bought with the frames and never removed, if I hadn't seen Frank's pained symmetrical smile beaming out of every one. They showed him, his new partner and their three children in various configurations, so stage-managed they felt like mortgage adverts.

When Frank led us into the similarly ordered front room I didn't know whether to sit down or not. The two sofas were covered with opaque, protective vinyl wrap. When I looked to Naomi she was having the same dilemma. We remained standing, awkwardly, beside the decorative fireplace. There was a large bookcase built into the wall with a handful of titles. They were all motivational in nature, and it occurred to me that I'd never read a self-help book in my life. Maybe that was my problem.

Mostly, the bookcases were filled with more framed pictures of the kids. Singles, group and full family shots. After what had happened to his first three children, it seemed only fair.

'Well, Mr Moore,' said Naomi. 'We'd like to ask you a few questions about Martin Wick.'

'Fire away,' he said, looking at me as if I'd spoken. 'Although I never knew the man.'

'It seems like no one really did,' I said. 'The biggest event of his life was 11 Briars Green, with very little of note before or after.'

Moore loomed. 'It was a pretty big event for me, too.'

'Of course,' said Naomi, taking over. 'Did you ever meet or speak to Martin Wick?'

Moore shook his head. 'I saw him at the trial, but he didn't give much away.'

If it had been a staring contest between Martin Wick and Frank Moore, I was surprised they weren't still standing there.

'But you never had any doubts that they arrested the right man?' said Naomi.

He frowned. 'Why would I?'

'He could never provide a full account of that night.'

'Why would he?' He looked at me again, as if I'd understand him more easily. 'More rope to hang himself with . . .'

'Fair point,' said Naomi, trying to keep Moore's attention. 'How did you feel when you heard he was dead?'

He bowed slightly, touching the white streak in his hair with an index finger. I thought he might like to stick it in her eye. He smiled again instead.

'I didn't think much about it.'

'You weren't glad, then?' Moore frowned at this but Naomi continued. 'Most people we've met would have happily handed him his hat . . .'

'Not sure I'd enjoy your line of work,' he said, addressing his answer towards her for the first time. 'As you saw earlier, my line's helping people who are drowning in grief. I can't drag them out alone but I can offer a hand. One thought I always had about Martin Wick was that he was probably adrift in all that grief himself. If he'd reached out to me, we might have helped each other.'

'He didn't, though?' I asked.

'No, I'm afraid not.'

'Forgive me for saying so, but your counselling model seems geared towards a different class of person.'

'I can't apologize for my paid seminars. They're my living, but that's by-the-by. What appeals to me about them is that they fund our work with at-risk groups.'

'How do you define at-risk?'

'People who need our help and can't afford it. Might be a bereaved mother, someone with substance abuse problems, or a man off the street. I want to prevent the next Martin Wick from reaching his breaking point. I've even spoken to a few police officers, in my time.'

'Did Kevin Blake ever come to you in that capacity?'

He shook his head. 'Kev's more like you are.'

'How's that?' I said.

'Keeps everything inside. Sorry, I can always tell. I found it interesting that he left the force immediately after Martin Wick's conviction, though . . .'

'How so?'

'Proof of its magnitude, I suppose. If it were needed. He didn't just destroy my family, he destroyed everyone who came into contact with him as well. I think Blake coped admirably.'

'Would you say the two of you are friends?'

'Nothing like that, he's a hard nut to crack. Our paths cross socially every so often. Charity events and things . . .'

'Were you briefed about Martin Wick's life-expectancy?' said Naomi.

'I was. Your family liaison officer, very sweet girl, told us there were hopes that he might reveal the location of Lizzie's final resting place.' His voice cracked unexpectedly at the subject of his daughter, and his hands went involuntarily to his chest, as if to indicate where she really was.

'How did you feel about that?'

'I think I said they were wasting their time.' He must have seen Naomi glance at me because he expanded. 'You've got to understand that Lizzie was declared dead along with the rest of them. That helped in a way. I could . . .' He held his enormous hands out as though they were gripping a large object and forcing it down to the ground. '. . . I could put it all in the same place. Turn the page. You have to move on when a tragedy like that happens. That means forgiving and forgetting.'

'You forgave Martin Wick?' said Naomi.

An impatient shake of the head. 'I forgave myself.'

'May I ask what for?'

'Survivor's guilt. There's a reason we settle in families. Mothers are there to raise the kids, provide the conscience to a home. Fathers are there to provide food, warmth and protection. I failed.'

I didn't agree, but it was a complex statement to respond to, because in his case it was actually true. There was a chance that his wife and kids would still be alive if he'd been there.

'I believe that you and Margaret were separated at the time?' said Naomi.

'You believe that, do you?'

108

'We're just trying to get the sequence of events straight,' she said easily.

'We'd separated, but I don't think either of us thought it was permanent. We were both cooling off.'

'Cooling off from what?'

'One day,' said Frank, 'when you're a bit older, when you settle down, you might understand. A marriage is like the ocean. Endless, bottomless, mysterious. But also tidal, versatile, unpredictable. We were going through some stormy weather.'

He ended the sentence abruptly, and I realized, amazingly, that was his answer.

Naomi pushed. 'What kind of stormy weather?'

'If you want it warts and all, I'd fallen in with a bad crowd,' he said, evading the question in a different way. 'I wasn't the perfect father or husband, but I was able to take some learnings from it.'

'Learnings, such as?' said Naomi, and I realized she was going to keep asking until she got a straight answer.

'I've been able to teach my kids a very valuable lesson,' he said, nodding at the frames inside the bookcase. 'Treasure every day. Live each one like it's your last.' I thought that sounded like a hard lesson to impart to toddlers, but I tried not to let it show.

'I hate to push,' said Naomi, 'but what made you imperfect the first time around?'

'I was fighting things,' he said, a sliver of menace in his voice.

'Things like?'

'Maggie. The kids. Myself.' He listed them as though they were all entirely separate entities. 'Now I have a motto I try and live by. Go with the flow.'

'I'll try to remember that one,' said Naomi.

He angled his chin upward, like he was straining to hit a high note. 'Do you think there's anything else?' he asked. 'Only, they'll be home soon, and I prefer all this not to touch them.'

'Of course,' she said. 'It would be helpful to know where you were on Saturday night and Sunday morning.'

'I'm the luckiest man alive.' He beamed. I thought about his slain children. It seemed like a strange definition of the sentiment. 'I was here, in bed, beside my wife.'

'Well, thank you,' said Naomi. 'And thanks again for your time.'

'I'll see you out,' he said, escorting us to the front door. Putting my shoes back on in the hallway, I looked at the family pictures again. I was struck by the resemblance between Frank's new partner and the murdered Margaret Moore.

'We were meant to be,' he said, following my eyes to the photo of his second wife. 'Things have a way of working out.' I must have frowned again because he'd begun improving on the statement when we heard voices out on the driveway, a key in the door. It opened and three children stepped inside. At first I thought they were surprised to see us, shy at the sight of strangers talking to their dad, then I realized this was how they always entered.

Silently, holding their shoes.

They stood there like ducks in a row, waiting for their mother to come in and lead them. When she stepped forward it felt like meeting Margaret Moore. She looked identical, right down to the French plait.

Naomi smiled at the kids. 'Well, this must be . . .'

'Elizabeth,' said the girl's mother, nodding at her tallest child. 'And this is Arthur and Mary.'

'Becky, my wonderful wife,' said Frank. We said hello, then she led the kids through into the living room.

'Mrs Moore,' said Naomi, following them. I watched Frank's frozen smile turn in their direction as we heard her confirming his alibi. 'Thanks,' said Naomi, reappearing when she was finished. She said goodnight and walked out towards the car, huffing her parka up round her head.

It was dark out and I felt the chill of the evening.

'They're a godsend,' said Frank as I stepped outside.

I wanted to return to the subject of his family, of things working themselves out. The look of concern had never quite left his face after saying it, and he seemed to realize he'd made a misstep some-where. I lingered in the doorway, taking him for the kind of man who liked the last word. 'Detective, your colleague asked me how I felt about Martin Wick's death and I'm not sure my answer was completely truthful.'

'Oh?'

'It can be helpful to repeat those mantras to yourself. To let things go. But when I see my family now, when I think about everything that man took. Well. If it were up to me, we'd dig him up and set fire to the bastard again.' I didn't say anything and he smiled. 'But that's just my personal opinion.'

'Of course,' I nodded. 'Good evening, Mr Moore.'

I went down the drive thinking we might as well have spoken to one of his framed photographs. His incendiary closing statement seemed to be an intentional distraction from something else. When I got into the car, Naomi and I sat in silence for a moment with the engine running. 'The kids,' she said. I nodded and looked back at the house, where Frank Moore's silhouette was framed in the win-dow, watching us.

Arthur, Elizabeth and Mary. They were each named after one of his murdered children.

III
Remurdered

1

I woke early, changed into shorts, T-shirt and trainers, and jogged along Thomas Street towards the Irwell, crossing it on to Black Friars Road, heading south-east in the vague direction of Spinningfields. The revelation about Frank Moore's children had been disturbing, and I'd thought he had some kind of problem with Naomi, some kind of problem with women full stop.

Not a good look for a man with a murdered wife.

I left the Irwell, speeding up, braking around the Science and Industry Museum and looping back to the Northern Quarter, cutting the final kilometre and a half at a sprint, leaving most of my problems, temporarily, for dead. I couldn't shift the feeling that there was something enormous moving beneath the Moore case, though. Tectonic plates shifting.

When I reached my building and got the key in the door I heard a car pulling up behind me, turned to see Chief Inspector James in the driver's seat. I'd only met him once, when he'd taken my statement about the events that had occurred at St Mary's. He'd worn a bland suit and, in his soft-spoken flatness and gentle, sweeping hand-motions, he'd reminded me of a TV weatherman. He cut the engine and climbed out, leaning on the car roof and speaking across it.

'I'd heard you were a speed addict but this is ridiculous . . .'

'Can I help you?'

'You help me?' He smiled. 'Unlikely, friend. I'm just passing through . . .'

'The Samaritans are the next street over,' I said. 'Have a good one.'

'While I'm here, there was one thing I wanted to talk to you about . . .'

'If it's the case then don't bother. As far as I'm concerned, it's all yours.'

'You volunteered, from what I heard . . .'

'Do you think anyone volunteers to work for Parrs?'

'So Parrs is the one who's hard for Wick. Well, that makes sense . . .'

I waited.

'. . . What I hear, he's not long for this world. Chase is about to step up, and they've never seen eye to eye. This Wick thing's the final straw. He wanted to run the investigation, put his best man on it but she refused, so he went in, cap in hand, saying you felt some personal responsibility. You were all heartbroken about Sutty and begged him to work it. Anything to keep his foot in the door,' he said, shaking his head, as if some previously obscured corner of humanity had been revealed to him.

'All good to know,' he continued. 'But I'm here on another thing. Where did you go immediately after the firebombing at St Mary's?'

'I was in with Parrs for a while and then I went home. Why?'

'You drove home, I take it?'

'I walked.'

'Only, there was a nasty assault, just off Piccadilly. Early hours of Sunday morning. Bloke got his head kicked in and the assailant was a man matching your description.'

'Like I said, I walked home.'

'Stop anywhere?'

I shook my head.

'So, you didn't slip into old habits after a bad night on the job? Bit of meth to calm the nerves . . .'

'I came straight home and went to bed. If you think I'm using, request a urine sample.'

'Would you provide one?'

'I think I could hit you from here.'

'You don't want a pissing contest today, boy.' He came around the car with a CCTV printout, a picture of me, time-stamped from the early hours of Sunday morning, after the attack.

I was staring directly up at a camera, the look on my face past description.

'So?' I said.

He showed me a second, almost identical printout, time-stamped some six minutes later. I'd barely moved, and I realized I was staring up at the Light Fantastic.

'See, after this assault was reported, we canvassed the local businesses. One guy said he'd seen something strange. He'd been closing up his club when he happened to look out of his office, on to the street. Said he saw an angry young man, staring up at the window. He stayed there for the best part of ten minutes. The description he gave matched that of our assailant, so we pulled the footage. Imagine our surprise . . .'

'It had been a long night, I was deciding whether or not to get a drink.'

'It was closed,' he said. 'All locked up. The uniforms working it recognized you, file-noted it upstairs. The note worked its way through Central Park and ended up on Chase's desk. She asked me to come and have a quiet word, off the record . . .'

'A quiet word about what?'

'Look,' he said, like he was levelling me. 'No one cares about the assault – some street dealer, forget about it. But I have to ask if you know the man who owns this club?'

'No,' I said, hearing the shake in my voice.

'You weren't tryna prove some point by staring up at him, then?'

I shook my head.

'Funny that. From what I hear, he used to be your dealer. Next time you find yourself passing the Light Fantastic, do us all a favour. Walk into the road without looking both ways.'

2

I went up to my flat and slammed the door behind me. The Light Fantastic belonged to a man named Zain Carver. Trace it all the way back, and Carver probably owned a percentage of every drug sold in the city. In that sense, perhaps, he had been my dealer, but somehow his reputation was better than mine. You might see his name in the news occasionally, but only attached to property portfolios and construction companies, stocks, shares, businesses and buildings. If you asked him, he'd tell you that these were all simple investments, by-products of his personal wealth.

Zain's real talent was for buying people.

Prostitutes, politicians, police officers. He was no more or less ruthless with these individuals than he was with any other resource. When his stocks slumped, he dumped them. When businesses tanked, their holding corporations were declared bankrupt, assets liquefied. When buildings were no longer of any use, they developed sudden electrical faults, went up in flames overnight and paid out on their insurance.

So, when a person who Carver had invested in slumped, he dumped them, too. When they tanked, they found themselves mysteriously bankrupt, liquefied.

When they were no longer of any use, they went up in flames.

It was inevitable that sooner or later, this fate would befall the Light Fantastic, because it belonged to Zain Carver. I looked at the printout that James had left me, feeling vaguely sick. Because in a sense, I'd belonged to Zain Carver once, as well. I cast my mind back, thinking of all the people I'd known who he'd bought over the years. Could I really be the last one left?

Superintendent Parrs had been wrong when he said I'd sold my soul to him. It had already been mortgaged up to the hilt.

3

I took a long hot shower and sat down to a strong coffee, trying to look like a man at ease. It didn't come naturally. After James's visit, the news that I'd been seen outside the Light Fantastic, there were three overpowering impulses fighting inside me.

The first felt like self-preservation, a biological imperative to let the case go cold, along with the suggestion that I'd been the intended target of the hit, to run away from it all. The second impulse came from my conscience, something I hadn't heard from in a long time, and I resented its sudden intrusion. It suggested there were lives at stake, that I needed to take this seriously. The third impulse came from my own curiosity. I couldn't help but wonder if Martin Wick was telling the truth when he died. What if he'd had nothing to do with the Moore family murders? What if their real killer was still out there?

When I thought about Carver, I felt my heartrate picking up, and I looked at the ceiling, grateful for the go-bag I'd hidden there. The cash, the plastic envelope and all it represented. Some hope of a new life. Some possible release from the threats and intimidation that had dogged this one.

But everything went very still as I saw that the light fitting above me was loose.

The last time I'd touched it, the previous morning, I'd put it carefully back into position before answering the door to Naomi.

I went out into the hallway, trying to ignore the ringing in my ears, retrieved the stepladder and stood it in the centre of the room. When I climbed up and reached out a hand I saw that it was shaking. I moved the fitting and reached inside the void but there was nothing there. Climbing all the way up I craned my neck, forcing the top half of my head inside the space. It was too dark to see, and I ripped my phone from my pocket, shining the torch all around.

The bag was gone.

I tried to breathe but felt my chest tightening, folding in on itself. The stepladder was rattling and I realized that the shake in my hands had spread into my arms and legs. Concentrating, I climbed down, sat on the floor and watched the room spinning about me. A galaxy of sunspots unfolded in front of my eyes and I realized I was having a panic attack, losing all control.

Ugly names and faces flashed through my mind.

Anyone who might be capable of doing this, and I lay back, gasping, gripping my chest, trying not to think about them. I lost consciousness for a second but at length the attack subsided and I found myself shivering on the hardwood floor, feeling the cold sweat beneath my clothes.

The bag had contained a large sum of money, literally my life savings, and an expensively produced counterfeit passport, featuring my face and a new name. Someone breaking in and taking the bag told me I was in immediate danger, but with my only means of escape missing, there was no way I could leave.

I didn't know what to do.

4

I'd dragged the ladder back outside and begun searching through every room, cupboard and drawer in the flat. At first I'd been methodical but as the fear started bubbling up again, I found myself moving faster, ripping clothes out of wardrobes and books off shelves. Turning the contents of drawers out on to the floor in something close to a frenzy, trying to outrun another panic attack.

I jumped when the buzzer went.

It was 5.30 a.m. and I wasn't expecting anyone.

I glanced at the intercom but went to the window instead, where I saw Naomi standing in the street, staring up at me. Her expression was unreadable, and, after a moment's hesitation, I threw open the window.

'The Super wants to see you,' she said.

I nodded, leaning into the frame, wondering what they knew. Naomi was the only person who'd been inside my room in the last few days, when she'd arrived unannounced and seen the stepladder against the bookcase. I didn't like that she'd reappeared at this particular moment.

'Where are we going?' I said.

'St Mary's Hospital.'

'Parrs must be getting that heart transplant . . .'

'I think he's still on the waiting list,' she said with a wary smile. 'Are you OK?' I nodded, feeling like there was a car parked on my chest. 'We need to be there in the next twenty minutes.'

I glanced back at the chaos of the room. 'What's going on?'

'I don't know but it sounded urgent.'

We arrived at St Mary's before six and went towards the activity, following a film crew up three flights of stairs. When we reached the top, we turned on to the ward where Martin Wick had been murdered. I'd expected it to remain cordoned off as a crime scene but the corridor was filled with people, fizzing with activity, and I looked closely at Naomi, wondering if I was being set up.

I'd been watching her as she drove.

She had the intensity of someone who'd been awake all night, and it made me trust her even less. I wondered what she'd been doing with her free time. Uncomfortably, I began to see how this situation might look to whoever had discovered that bag. The only police officer unscathed in a daring, bloody assassination found in possession of a false passport and a large sum of money. I'd framed myself.

We turned to see Superintendent Parrs speaking to a young man who had his back to us. His red eyes lit up and he put a hand on the man's shoulder, turning him in our direction.

'Aidan Waits,' he said. 'Meet your replacement.' Two deaths on day one, no leads on day two and reassigned by day three. A new personal best.

The man looked familiar.

He was somewhere between his late twenties and early thirties, and wore a similar dark suit to mine. His shirt was crumpled and his hair was short, neater than I'd managed but still scruffy, and his jawline was sharp, almost gaunt-looking. He had a five o'clock shadow and hollow, liar's eyes with bags beneath them.

'What's going on?' I said.

'We're filming the reconstruction.' The man smiled. 'I think I'm you.'

'My condolences . . .'

I was distracted by a man dressed like Sutty, forcing his way through the corridor. All reason seemed to be spiralling away from me, following some kind of dream logic, and I was afraid I might look down and find myself naked.

'Excuse us,' said Parrs, nodding at me to follow and then guiding me back the way I'd come. Either he knew, and I was about to be arrested, or he didn't and someone else was out to get me.

I couldn't decide which was worse.

We went into the stairwell and up, away from the voices and action below. I turned when I saw a woman in a green tracksuit who had tattoos drawn on her face. Parrs shook his head wearily. When we reached the exit that had led out on to the roof a few days before it wouldn't budge, so we stood hunched over in the doorway beneath a bare light bulb.

'I didn't know this was happening,' I said.

'Join the club.' He stabbed a look over my shoulder to make sure there was no one within earshot. 'The thrill of the Chase,' he said, referring to the Chief Superintendent. 'If she'd asked, I'd have suggested you play yourself. You've got some experience pretending to be a detective, after all. Where are we?'

'There isn't much to report. We spoke to Sloane but he made a song and dance about protecting his sources. He did suggest he might speak to James, though.'

'No doubt. The Chief Inspector should be in adult diapers. Can't get from one side of the room to the other without leaking. Sloane's the key here.'

'He was pretty firm on the subject.'

'If I could lay hands on Detective Inspector Sutcliffe and heal him, I'd do it,' he said. 'But because I can't, you are my vessel. Sloane's firm, so pay him a visit, get your little wooden hammer out and tenderize the bastard. Because if you can't tell me who took that picture by the end of the day, I'll have to start looking closer to home. Would you enjoy that, Aidan? A bit of scrutiny?'

'Is there something you're not telling me, sir?'

He took a breath. 'Cranston goes at the end of the year,' he said. I nodded, thinking on what James had told me about the delicate balance of power between Parrs and Chase. 'Unofficially? Chase has already been anointed as his replacement, and she doesn't want any dirt on her halo. Naturally, she's looking for someone to blame for all this, which has put me, very temporarily, in the hot seat. Don't think I won't get up and offer it to you, though.'

'Me?'

'No one's closer to this than you are, remember that. You'd better be attacking this from all angles, playing fucking crazy golf to prove you're not involved.'

'I'm not involved.'

'Clearly,' he said. 'Kevin Blake got any more press appearances planned today?'

'We didn't know about it until he was on the air. We're doing the best we can.'

'I'm sure one of you is. Remember, son, I can always, always tell when you're lying to me. It's when I can hear the sounds coming out of your mouth. If you let this case go cold I will send your temperature plummeting, believe that.' I didn't say anything. After the morning's events he might have to get in line. 'Come on,' he snapped. 'The rest of it.'

'Still no ID on the tracksuit girl, no prints from the ward or the car, and no—'

'I get the picture,' he said, hurrying me along. 'Nothing. The revenge against Wick motive, where are we with that?'

I shook my head. 'Frank Moore's a bizarre guy. I can't tell if he's really gone New Age or if it's all bottled up. He named his three kids from a new marriage after the ones Wick murdered.' Parrs looked vaguely interested in that but I didn't have anything else. 'He's built his whole life, or the front for it, around moving on. Forgiving and forgetting. He teaches classes in surviving grief.'

'If we get through this I'll sign us all up.'

'I thought there was probably something lurking beneath the surface, but . . .'

'Yeah,' he said, catching my drift. 'His family was murdered,

125

how wouldn't there be?' He dug inside his inner jacket pocket and pulled out a screwed-up newspaper. 'Seen this?'

He pressed it into my hands and I held it up to the light.

Murder Ink, read the headline.

In the story beneath, with Charlie Sloane's byline, it described how firearms had manhandled a young woman with facial tattoos, before realizing she wasn't our suspect. He went on to write that the one man arrested in connection with the killing had been released without charge.

'This is Wick's ex-cellmate?' I said.

Parrs nodded. 'Spice dealer, goes by the name Short Back and Sides. James's team bailed him this morning, so he should be out and about . . .'

'Did they get anything?'

'Gonorrhoea if they got close enough. Scrote's got an alibi but who knows what that's worth. One thing James's team didn't have were the talents of your Constable Black. She was up all night reviewing CCTV footage from St Mary's. She can put Short Back in the vicinity in the last seven days.' That explained Naomi's raw-eyed tension. 'Are the two of you not on speaking terms, Sergeant?'

'I'm still getting up to speed,' I said. 'Is there anything directly connecting this Short Back and Sides to the attack?'

'Not yet, but unless they've started performing chemical castrations here, I can't see why he'd be hanging round.'

'We'll have a word.'

'Make it a series of four-letter ones. And don't bother bringing him in. The fucker's spent half his life in interview rooms. Made mincemeat of James and co. Again, I appreciate that this would have been more suited to Detective Inspector Sutcliffe's talents, but please, do your worst.'

'Is there any word on him yet?'

He flashed me a look. 'You still haven't been to see him?' I started to speak but he shook his head. 'With friends like you, eh? Detective Inspector Sutcliffe's still under. In fact, he's two floors beneath your feet right now. You've got a few days before they bring him round. You could stick your head in on your way out.'

I didn't say anything.

'Read the rest of that while you're here,' he said, nodding down at the newspaper. I scanned ahead and saw that Sloane had returned to his favourite subject, former constable Tessa Klein. He said that in spite of new leads, officers had refused to investigate her disappearance.

'New leads?' I said, looking up.

'That was what I asked him this morning. Something about her booking a holiday before she topped herself.'

'Do you want us to look into it?'

'Absolutely not. Chase is already aggrieved to see Klein's name in the papers again. She asked me to confirm that *you* hadn't leaked this information to Sloane during your conversation yesterday . . .'

'I didn't know anything about it,' I said. 'I still don't.'

'Keep it that way. As far as we're concerned, Klein was a civilian when she died, and she died by her own hand.' His insistence on the subject gave me a bad feeling but I didn't push it. 'Where are we with that third motive?'

'We wanted to focus on Wick to begin with. There's so much to follow up with him that it seems unlikely—'

'It seems unlikely that you'd disobey your orders, Sergeant. I want you to eliminate the possibility that *you* were the intended target of this hit. I'm sick of all these surprises.'

'Where does the intelligence originate from?'

'Finally,' he said. 'Asking the right questions. Again, I suggest you speak to your partner. I hear Constable Black was digging into that last night, too. Accessed the relevant files at eleven forty-nine p.m. It seems that she's more interested in your well-being than you are, Sergeant.' I didn't like that she'd been searching around in my history but it was a shade better than her searching around in my room. 'Now,' he said. 'This Louisa Jankowski business . . .'

I'd left Parrs a message the previous evening recommending her confinement to desk duties. I didn't know what was happening with her, but it felt wrong to allow a plausibly compromised officer to walk the streets with a loaded gun.

'When I raised your concerns with Chief Superintendent Chase there was a long silence, then she asked me to meet her here. She's doing an interview that'll air after the reconstruction. Said she can give us five minutes.' He looked at me and squinted. 'Have you been drinking?'

'Not this morning.'

He nodded and began descending the stairs. 'Well, it might be the time to start.'

5

They shot the interiors for the reconstruction quickly. The main event would be the external shots showing the woman in the green tracksuit fleeing the scene. Nominally, the reason for the reconstruction was to jog the memory of anyone who might recognize her. More than that, though, it seemed like a public relations exercise. After years of headlines highlighting police corruption, it was difficult to foster a feeling of public sympathy for a dead officer, especially one who'd died protecting a convicted child killer.

I watched as the scene replayed in front of me.

There was no sense of foreboding from Martin Wick in the reconstruction, no shifty behaviour on the part of Rennick, and the man playing Sutty portrayed no burgeoning suspicion of unfolding events. The actor playing me seemed slow-witted, constantly missing cues and fluffing his few lines. It was the only part that felt true to events, and there was a strong resemblance between us.

Maybe they'd use him again if I went missing.

The difference between the reconstruction and the reality was so stark that it crystallized the actual events in my mind. Something had been going on that night, under the surface. Wick's sudden change in behaviour, Sutty's worried small talk while he tried to get me out of the room.

Something had been deeply wrong.

'OK,' shouted the director. 'Thanks, guys.'

The crew began packing up equipment and I saw Chief

Superintendent Chase emerge from the crowd wearing a smart business suit. Her hair wasn't tied back as it had been during the press conference but cascaded elegantly over one shoulder. Humanizing the force single-handed was no easy task, but she made it look like one.

She nodded at Parrs and me to follow her.

After trying three or four doors and finding people at work behind them all, we settled for the toilets where Sutty and I had our conference on the night of the attack. We were inside before we realized that someone else was in the cubicle.

Chief Inspector James emerged. 'Excuse me,' he said, trying to edge out of the room.

'No,' said Chase. 'I'd rather you stayed for this.' There was nowhere for him to stand so he went back into the cubicle. He avoided my eyes, as if our conversation that morning hadn't happened.

Chase smiled at me and nodded. 'Detective Sergeant. I've heard an awful lot about you. Now, this Louisa Jankowski situation . . .'

'Ma'am,' said Parrs, taking his cue. 'As I mentioned, Sergeant Waits has raised concerns about the reliability of—'

'Yes, yes,' said Chase. 'I'll tell you why I don't like it. First, I'm yet to hear any credible evidence against Constable Jankowski. Second, Sergeant Halliday from firearms has raised his own concerns. He believes that the wrong move here could isolate her and alienate his team. Third, the conclusion drawn by the press and her colleagues will be that she's complicit in the murder of Constable Rennick. That could prove especially painful as we fight for more armed police officers in our budgets and on our streets.'

She looked between us.

'Now, all of these objections go away in the sight of any information proving that Louisa Jankowski is involved in some conspiracy.' She waited. 'Her record's terrific, test scores above average and, most importantly, she has the faith, friendship and belief of her colleagues.' Chase looked at me. 'I set a lot of stock by that, Sergeant.'

'Ma'am,' I said. 'There was no one else on that corridor when Wick's picture was taken.'

'That you know of.'

'And she denied having even seen it twenty-four hours later.'

'Is that so strange?'

'That picture was everywhere, it'd mean that she'd seen no newspapers, seen no news broadcasts, on a subject that personally involved her.'

'Did you read the newspapers a couple of years ago when you were suspended on drugs charges, Sergeant?'

I hesitated. 'Not closely.'

She turned her attention to James. 'You've spoken to Jankowski. What do you think?'

'I think she seemed distressed at the accusation,' he said. 'I did push her on not having seen the picture. She said it's not her thing. She didn't read the reports saying she was a hero, either.'

Chase's eyes moved back to me. 'What we do know about Jankowski is that her actions and quick thinking last Christmas saved the lives of dozens of people. Come back to me when you're getting that kind of press, Sergeant. Let's not forget there were other officers at the scene who could just as easily have been involved . . .'

Parrs took a breath. 'It seems unlikely that either Rennick or Sutcliffe would be complicit in a plot to maim and murder themselves.'

'From what I hear about Inspector Sutcliffe it's not a stretch. And Rennick was green. Besides,' she said, still looking at me. 'There was one officer who left the scene completely unscathed . . .'

'Is that what I was?' I said.

Chase looked amused at my response but there was a knock at the door before she could chastise me.

'Be right out,' she said. She lowered her voice, and her eyes darted to the toilet cubicle. 'James is concerned about contamination with two teams working this case . . .'

'That's right,' he said. 'It would have been easier if we'd been first to interview Jankowski. Might have saved us all this bother.'

'Is that why you didn't tell us you were interviewing Wick's former cellmate?' I asked, as mildly as I could.

I thought I felt Parrs drifting further from my side.

Chase looked at him. 'James is perfectly qualified to run this investigation without a shadow, Alistair. While I appreciate that this is your mess and you feel some ownership in cleaning it up, if Waits can't bring anything to the table then I'd suggest that he wraps up his role in the next couple of days, resumes his night shift duties. We've got a dead police officer on our hands. This isn't the time for learning on the job.'

'I could probably find a position for Constable Black, though,' said James.

I half-laughed, wondering what kind of position he had in mind.

Chase nodded. 'Now, if you'll excuse me.'

She walked past us and left. Parrs waited for the door to close before leaning round to look inside the cubicle. 'Fuck off,' he said to James.

The Chief Inspector emerged, eyeballing him. 'Things are changing round here, Al.' He glanced at me. 'Take all the time you need, Waits. You're not getting anywhere.'

He walked out and Parrs glared at me, lowering his voice.

'Did you hear that?'

'Sir?'

'She made a mistake there, son. This isn't my mess, it's yours, and the day that care bear tells me that things change is the day I fucking transition. Bring me something I can use, today. Tell me who took that picture or I'll ruin your life.' I started to respond and he talked over me. 'I'll ruin it even more.'

6

'Can I talk to you?' said Naomi. We were driving out to the registered address of Christopher Back, aka Short Back and Sides, Martin Wick's former cellmate.

Naomi had remained intense all morning, and now I'd spoken to Superintendent Parrs I had some idea why. Up all night reviewing CCTV footage so I couldn't ease her out of active casework during the day.

'What do you want to talk about?' I said, not looking at her. There had been a matt-black Mercedes, three cars back, following us all the way from the city centre and I didn't want to lose it.

'Well,' she began.

My phone went off before she could continue, and I answered.

'Aidan Waits?' said the woman at the other end. The same woman who'd been disconnected the previous day. For a moment I wondered if she was in the car behind us, but I could clearly hear office noises in the background.

'Speaking.'

'Hello, Mr Waits. My name's Sandra Allen. I'm a social worker with Brighton and Hove City Council. Is this a convenient time? I've been trying to get hold of you for several days.'

'Now's good,' I said, glancing at Naomi. 'How can I help?'

'Can I confirm that your mother is a Mrs Christine Farrow?' I took the handset away from my ear and almost cancelled the call. There was a flash of white from the side-eye that Naomi gave me, and I turned to the passenger-side door before continuing. 'Mr Waits?'

'Still here,' I said. 'This actually might not be such a good time.'

'It really is important that I speak to you.'

I closed my eyes. 'The honest answer is, I don't know. I don't have any kind of relationship with my mother. It's possible that she is this . . .'

'Christine Farrow.'

'Right. She was Christine Waits when I knew her, but that was more than twenty years ago.' I tried to think what else to say. 'I suppose she married.'

'I see,' said Sandra, drawing the words out. 'Mr Waits, when was the last time you saw your mother?'

I could feel the weight of Naomi's presence beside me. The near-certainty that this conversation would be repeated verbatim to Superintendent Parrs. If I handed him one more screw to turn on me, he could probably have my body mounted on the wall. I thought for a second, straining to articulate the relationship in a more neutral way before giving up.

'We haven't spoken since I was eight years old. Her first name's Christine, but that's about all I can tell you.'

I was telling the truth for a change.

We'd had no real contact in decades and I didn't know if she was dead or alive. I could have stated a preference, though.

When Sandra didn't answer, I asked if there was anything else.

'Mr Waits, I'm sorry to be the one to inform you, but your mother, your birth mother, has a long history of mental illness.'

'I was there for the start of it, so I'm well aware.' I heard the tone in my voice, felt Naomi shifting uncomfortably and tried to take it up a notch. 'But as I say, it's been a while.'

'These episodes, they go back a long way, then?'

'From what I remember. Now, if—'

'May I ask how they manifested at the time?'

I saw a shimmer of sunspots pass through my vision and closed my eyes against them. The last thing I needed was a panic attack in the car. 'She was in an abusive relationship, and she passed it on.'

'To you?' said Sandra, after a slight pause.

'And to my little sister,' I said, opening my eyes. 'Do you usually discuss this over the phone?'

'This is just background. Anything we can do to help her case. Did Christine ever have any diagnosis that you were aware of?'

'No, and I doubt she ever spoke to a professional about it. She self-medicated and we moved around a lot. They were different times.'

'Not so different, unfortunately. But there was less help available.'

'I doubt you'll be able to help her now, either,' I said. 'I assume that's why you're calling?'

'Well, yes. Yesterday we were issued with a warrant to enter your mother's premises, to make a mental health assessment.'

'I can probably save you the bother if you want mine . . .'

'At this stage, given what we already know, the assessment is mostly a formality. At the close of this meeting, Christine will be sectioned under the Mental Health Act . . .'

I buzzed the window down an inch and waited.

'. . . This assessment will probably take place in the next week or so, depending on police availability.' I'd attended numerous such interventions in my time as a uniformed officer. It meant that my mother was considered a danger to herself and to others. I could probably have told them that twenty-three years ago. 'I'm calling because, ideally, a member of her family would be present . . .'

'She has no family that I'm aware of.'

'I do appreciate your feelings on the matter, but this is a sensitive issue. You mentioned a sister.' I could hear her moving papers around, searching for the name. 'Erm . . .'

'I'm sorry, what did you say your name was?' I asked.

'Sandra Allen.'

'And you're with Social Services? Can I ask how you got hold of my number?'

'I'm above board if that's what you're worrying about, Mr Waits. Your name was on file, and when I asked, your mother gave me the number.'

I could see the street streaming by, everything moving too fast.

'How would she have my number?'

'I didn't ask her but you're more than welcome to. I suppose she looked you up.'

I didn't say anything.

'Here,' said Sandra, reading the file. 'Your sister. Birth name Anna Waits, brother Aidan. She'd be twenty-eight years old now?'

'I think she goes by Anne,' I said, not liking the sound of my voice.

'Do you think Anne would be able to spare us some time?'

'Our mother used to use her arms as ashtrays,' I said, dropping all pretence of a polite conversation. 'So, no. I doubt that she would.'

I felt the speed gently increasing.

Naomi trying to get us to our destination quicker.

'Would you be willing to pass on Anne's contact details to me?' she said. 'I'd like to speak to her formally.'

'We were separated when we became wards of the state. I haven't spoken to her myself since I was eight years old.'

'I'm sorry to hear that, and as I said, I'm sorry to bother you . . .' I sensed that she was rallying for a final effort and tried to kill the conversation.

'You're serving a warrant on my mother, where you'll make a mental health assessment with a view toward sectioning her,' I said. 'Well, that's understood. That makes sense to me. If you could remove my details from your records and not contact me about this again, I'd appreciate it.'

I felt Naomi's eyes move on to me.

'Very well,' said Sandra after a pause.

'And thanks for calling.' I hung up, pressing my thumb into the phone until it started to hurt. At length, I looked at Naomi. She kept her eyes on the road but her skin was flushed. 'I'm sorry about that . . .'

'Everything OK?'

'Fine,' I said. 'What was it you wanted to talk about?'

'I think it can probably wait.'

I nodded, then thought to look for the matt-black Mercedes I'd seen following us.

It was gone.

7

Short Back and Sides lived on a sink estate in Harpurhey, an inner-city district with a hard reputation. It had been named the most economically deprived neighbourhood in the country at one time, with sky-rocketing rates of crime and unemployment. As Naomi drove, both our heads turned to a large message written in graffiti beneath a bridge.

SPICE WORLD

Spice was the one part of the local economy that was booming, thanks largely to dealers like Short Back and Sides, who worked tirelessly to get their hooks into young men, many of them homeless or otherwise at risk. It was a synthetic designer drug, packaged in glossy foil-wrap containers that looked like they might contain sweeties. Unfortunately, the product tasted like burned plastic and caused heart palpitations, panic attacks, vomiting and near-apocalyptic confusion.

That was at the light end of the tunnel.

It was also linked to psychosis, kidney failure, heart attacks.

That a little oblivion was worth all the risk said a lot about the way we lived now, and the visible effects of the drug across the city were impossible to ignore. Usually, high fatality rates limit the spread of a drug, but with austerity it seemed like the death toll would never outpace the speed at which the homeless population was growing.

I'd begun reading Short Back's file eagerly, reaching for some distraction from my missing bag, from the phone call about my mother, the car I'd thought was following us, but all I could feel now was a colossal tide of anger rising up inside me, turning my brain black. According to his paperwork, Short Back specialized in a particularly toxic strain of the designer drug called Posh Spice. He'd spent the last fifteen years bouncing from prison to public sector housing, and had a record that read like an exhaustive A–Z of criminal offences. Kevin Blake's information that his last conviction had been quashed was correct, and I felt my eyes losing focus as I read the details.

He'd allowed one of his regulars, a homeless man, to rack up a spice debt worth £100. When the man couldn't find the cash, Short Back and Sides had suggested an alternative payment method, what he called a five-finger discount.

He proposed that if he punched the man once for each pound he owed, then the debt would be forgotten. To really make his point, he'd do it in one of the squats, in front of a few other people who were themselves in drug arrears. Some of the transients left, some gathered round, concerned or fascinated by what they were seeing. Some tried to intervene, but were prevented from getting to Short Back by his handlers. While he remained conscious, his victim had protested to the crowd that it was OK, even as it became clear that Short Back was enjoying himself, not pulling any punches.

Even as it became clear that he was wearing a pair of brass knuckles.

Short Back delivered all one hundred blows to the man's body. He lost consciousness somewhere around the seventies and never woke up again. A pre-existing condition, plus his economic status, meant that his death was tried, with minimum effort, as manslaughter. When the judge asked Short Back if he really thought he'd avoid jail time, he'd answered with what amounted to a shrug. He'd probably sell more Posh Spice inside Strangeways than outside it. Naomi saw me look up from the file and rub my face.

She nodded. 'It's the people that make this job worthwhile.'

8

We buzzed the number for Short Back's flat, which was on the top floor of a brutalist ten-storey council block. The building looked like it had survived one controlled explosion then been evacuated in anticipation of another. Looking up I could see several tattered England flags hanging from windows, like it was a destroyer sailing to war. There was no answer to the buzzer and the door wouldn't budge. We tried a few more flat numbers but no one answered, no one would.

'Now what?' said Naomi.

I'd insisted we take my car that morning, thinking it might make her easier to shake off later in the day, and I had a flash of inspiration. Returning to the boot I found the lock-pick set hidden beneath my spare tyre. Then I went to the door, inserted the torsion wrench and selected a clipped piece of copper.

Naomi raised an eyebrow.

'You heard the call about my mother?'

She nodded, a half-formed expression on her face.

'We were home-schooled.'

The lock clicked and I pushed open the door.

'Your mother sounds like quite a woman . . .'

'She was a psychopath,' I said, surprising myself. 'Sounds like she still is.'

We stepped into a dank, stale-smelling lobby covered in graffiti. The call button for the lift had been ripped out of the wall, and there was torn crime scene tape hanging from the doors. We went up the narrow staircase instead.

'Do you ever think about reaching out to your sister?' said Naomi, and I looked at her without quite meaning to. 'I couldn't help but overhear . . .'

'No, not really.'

'I'm sure she'd love to hear from you.'

'Or she'd feel the same way I do, getting that call about my mother.'

Naomi hesitated. 'How do you feel?'

I looked about me, the narrow staircase, the long drop and low ceiling. 'Trapped,' I said, before moving quickly on. 'Blake said your dad's a cop?'

'Was,' she said, closing down the conversation, and I felt vaguely short-changed. It occurred to me that I knew as little about Constable Black as I had about Sutty.

When we reached the top floor I turned to Naomi, expecting her to be breathing hard but she hadn't even broken stride. We passed an overturned shopping trolley with someone sleeping inside it and came to Short Back's flat. There was a filthy poster of Victoria Beckham pasted to the door, and when I banged on it a dog started barking.

'Police,' I shouted. 'Open up or we'll break it.' Naomi frowned at me but sometimes you need to sound crazier than the people you're talking to.

After the morning I'd had, I was starting to feel it.

'What do you want?' said a gruff voice from inside.

'To know how Vicky wrote all her hits, what do you think?' I booted the door a few times to make the point.

'He's already talked to you lot.'

'He's talked to a traffic warden with ideas above his station, and we're not going anywhere until he's talked to us. If he feels like leaving, he'll have to climb out the toilet window. Hell of a drop, though . . .'

The door opened on a thick, heavy-duty chain, revealing a large skinhead with HATE tattooed across the knuckles of his visible hand.

'So you can spell,' I said.

'Like talking, don't ya?'

'I don't have any words written on me so I have to communicate somehow. Can we come in?' The man gave me a gold-tooth smile and slammed the door in my face. He took off the chain, opened it again and led us into a sparse living room.

He had HATE tattooed across the other hand as well.

There were two sofas, haggard with cigarette burns, arranged to face each other, with a mirrored coffee table in between. The curtains were drawn but they were so thin that switching the light on was unnecessary.

We could see enough.

It had the feel of a low-rent reception area, and I guessed this was where they sold product. There was an overflowing ashtray that smelt of burnt plastic, the rings left by a million cans, cups and glasses on the table. The pit-bull barking in the next room was insurance in case one of their customers got ideas, or started negotiating on price with a kitchen knife. I went to the coffee table, looked at my reflection for a moment, then put my boot through the centre, smashing it to pieces.

'The fuck?' said the skinhead.

I reached into the debris for the longest shard, holding it out like a knife. 'Call me paranoid,' I said, sitting down on the sofa facing him.

He looked at Naomi. 'This guy come with a leash or something?' She didn't say anything but sat down beside me. 'Well.' He clapped his hands together. 'My name's Axel, can I take anyone's coat?'

'Would you mind telling Short Back and Sides he's got visitors?' I said.

'Sides is out cold. Will be for a few hours yet . . .'

'I'm sure you can warm him up,' I said. Axel's hands were still pressing together from when he'd clapped, and I saw that each one was kneading the other. '. . . If you have any trouble we could always try tickling his toes with this,' I said, holding the glass shard up to the light.

'I'll see what I can do.'

When he went through the door, the dog started screaming again, straining against the chain. I glanced at Naomi and saw a sheen of perspiration on her skin. It wasn't from the stairs, and she looked away from me quickly.

We'd been waiting for a few minutes when the door opened and a weedy man walked in wearing an open dressing gown and a pair of off-white Y-fronts. He had the scrunched-up facial features you'd associate with foetal alcohol syndrome. A small head with sharp eyes, a narrow nose and thin lips. His face was the colour of a day-old bruise, but even this paled against Short Back's main defining feature.

There was a dent in the centre of his head.

One side was darker than the other, comprising a scar tissue patchwork of emergency skin grafts. Someone had caved his skull in. After reading his file, it seemed like a shame they hadn't taken another crack at it. He had several tattoos, the most prominent being a large number written across his neck in gothic font. *105*.

He dropped on to the sofa, facing us with a chemically assisted thousand-yard stare. I tried not to look at his head, and instead glanced at the hand he had inside his pants, visibly cupping his balls.

'You know they won't fall off if you let go of them,' I said.

'What do you want?'

'And if you're counting them, we can probably save you some time there, as well . . .' When he smiled I saw that he was wearing a grille made of gold. He looked between Naomi and me then withdrew the hand from his underwear, holding it out for one of us to shake.

Neither of us moved.

His mouth went to a tight smile and he pushed the hand back beneath his waistband.

'Don't worry about this,' he said, talking out the side of his mouth, looking at Naomi. 'Helps me think, like.'

She smiled. 'In that case, you might want to use both hands. This is Detective Sergeant Waits and I'm Detective Constable Black. We're—'

'I loved that coffee table, Constable Black,' he interrupted. 'Was a lot like your gash. I could see my face in it . . .'

I examined my shard of glass. 'Thanks for meeting us today, Christopher.'

'Keep my name out of your mouth.'

'Then keep your mouth shut for a minute. We're here to talk about Martin Wick and nothing else.'

'I've just got home from all that – ask your mates at Central Park. I haven't seen or heard from him since I got home from Strangeways. The end.'

'Did you know he was sick?' asked Naomi.

'Better than most . . .'

'What does that mean?' she said. He didn't answer. 'He was your cellmate for six months, you must have known him well.'

'Look, I tried to do him inside. He survived. It happens. I don't hold some big grudge about it. Unless you've been away, you probably wouldn't understand.'

'You were making your bones,' I said.

He cracked his neck. 'Out here, I hang my nuts all the way over my shoulder.' He gave them a shake for illustration. 'Everyone knows it. Inside, you've gotta make a name quick.'

'Simple as that?'

'Simple as that.'

'You said you knew better than most that Martin Wick was sick,' I said. 'Why?'

'Did I . . . ?'

He shrugged and put his free hand to the dent in his skull.

He could almost fit his entire fist inside.

'. . . Don't remember.'

'Then squeeze your nuts as hard as you can and think for a second. The way we see it, you're the sick one. You killed a man over a hundred quid.'

'Court said that didn't count, he was ill.'

'Most people are after they get punched a hundred times.'

I felt Naomi looking at me.

At the glass shard I was pointing towards him.

I lowered it and tried to get back on track. 'I think Wick was a good guy on the inside, quiet, kept to himself. That's what you couldn't stand.'

'Good guy?' he sneered. 'All right, Columbo. A good guy with pictures of kids in his pillow.'

'What kids?'

'Are you fucking dim? Them ones he killed. Mainly that girl he had a boner for.'

'Lizzie Moore?'

'The blonde one.'

I nodded. 'So why didn't you tell the screws about these pictures?'

'That's not how it goes inside, is it? Anyway, what would they do? Tie his wanking hand behind his back?'

'Seems like it got to you . . .'

'*Kids* . . .' He shook his head. '. . . That's how I got this.' He motioned to the dent in his skull. 'Tryna stop my stepdad going in on my little sister.'

I looked at the floor, seeing sunspots creep into my peripheral vision.

'So you decided to punish him yourself,' said Naomi.

'Man has to have some standards about who he shares a room with.' Short Back took his hand out of his pants and smelt it. 'I've been through all this with the others. I was over it the second I got out, like. Outta sight, outta mind.'

145

'So how come you were hanging round St Mary's Hospital twice in the last week,' said Naomi. 'You haven't been through that . . .' He didn't say anything for a moment then slowly slid his hand back beneath his waistband, moving it in a circular motion like another man might massage his temples.

'Had to go have my head looked at.'

'Sounds like a good idea,' she said. 'Only thing is, you were never checked in as a patient.' He showed us the grille across his teeth. 'So why would you be hanging around the same hospital where Martin Wick, this guy you'd forgotten all about, was laid up dying?'

'Visiting a friend . . .'

'Sure,' I said. 'Axel was getting his frown removed and you took him some grapes.' He didn't say anything. 'Our colleagues bounced you earlier because they didn't have the full picture, but we do and you're in it. If we conclude that you were involved in the murder of Martin Wick, it won't be hard to put it on you. With your track record, your previous attack on him, as well as the CCTV putting you in the area, we'd need our heads looking at if we let you walk.'

'I've got an alibi for Saturday night. I was here with Axe. If you can't put me there then you can't prove shit. That's the law.'

'Never heard of it,' I said. 'Why were you at St Mary's?'

'I was visiting a friend,' he repeated.

'Describe her for me.'

His expression changed and at length he nodded. 'Some hood-rat slag,' he said. 'Tattoos on her face.'

I reached inside my pocket for the screengrab we'd taken of the woman in the green tracksuit, unfolded it and handed it to him.

He nodded. 'Makes her so important?'

'She's the number one suspect in Martin Wick's murder. You're number two. If we find her, it might make your life a lot easier.' He didn't say anything but I could see from the churning motion of his hand that he was thinking. 'What's her name?' I said.

He looked at the ceiling. 'Said I should call her Esther . . .'

'Esther what?'

'Esther Fuck Knows.'

'How did you meet?'

'Fuck. Off.'

'105,' I said, looking at the tattoo on his neck. 'Was that the highest number you could count to or does it mean something?'

'It's the age I'm gonna live to, chief.'

I thought for a moment. 'Frank Sinatra?'

' "Young at Heart",' he said, impressed. ' "If you should survive to a hundred and five . . ." '

'The problem is, you'll be counting off those years inside Strangeways unless you tell us how you met Esther. This isn't like anything you've been involved with before, Short Back. It's a cop-killing we're talking about. The kind of shit that always sticks to someone, and if we can't lay hands on her . . .'

'She turned up here last week, said I could make some quick cash.'

'Cash how?'

'Said she was a reporter.' He laughed. 'Not like any I've seen but it takes all sorts. That was how she found out where I lived. She wanted a picture of Wick, like, dying for her paper. People really wanted to see it, she said. Only, there's no pictures since he went inside, so no one knew how he looked these days. She needed someone who'd recognize him.' That made a twisted kind of sense, I thought. Martin Wick's appearance had altered so much in the last twelve years that the picture would have been worthless without independent verification. Who better to verify it than his recently freed ex-cellmate? Short Back shrugged. 'So I went. She showed me the picture, I gave her the nod. She paid me, the end.'

'How much did she pay?'

'A grand,' he said.

'Did she say where she got it?'

'You're the fucking copper. Talk to her paper.'

'Do you have any way of getting in touch with her?' asked Naomi.

'Nope.'

'I find that hard to believe,' she said.

'I've got something right here you'd find very hard to believe, Constable Black . . .'

Her eyes went to his crotch and she smiled. 'It looks like a braille bump, Chris.'

'Why don't you shut your eyes and give it a rub, then? Like I said, she came here, then told me a time and a place for the hospital. Wouldn't give me her number or nothing. First time she tried to take the shot she couldn't get to him, but she paid half so I'd go back again.' We waited. 'Straight up. I tried to get her number. Thought she might be up for some Richard.'

Naomi looked between us. 'Richard?'

'Gear,' I said. 'What was her reaction to that?'

'Looked at me like I was shit on her shoe.'

'Sounds believable.'

'Bit rich from a girl who drinks soap . . .'

I nodded. 'Before he died, Martin Wick told me he wasn't responsible for killing the Moores. You were in a cell with him for the best part of a year. Did he ever say anything like that to you?'

'That he was an innocent man?' Short Back looked between us, going from a grin to uncontrollable laughter. 'If you believe that, then my arsehole's got a Michelin star.'

9

There was laughter coming from inside Charlie Sloane's hotel suite, and a room service cart of empty dishes sitting on the floor outside it. We hadn't known where to reach him but guessed that, like most of the press who'd travelled up from the capital to cover Wick's death, he'd be at the Holiday Inn on Oxford Road. The front desk had confirmed this to Naomi, and told us we'd find his room on the third floor.

Naomi hadn't mentioned me putting the boot into Short Back's coffee table, or any of my other abrasive behaviour, but I thought she was standing a little further from me than usual.

I tried to knock on this door with more restraint.

'There's no one here,' said Sloane, with a bark of drunken laughter.

'It's the police, Charlie. They'll come and unlock it for me if I ask.'

We heard voices and then footsteps coming towards the door. Sloane opened it a crack and I pushed it the rest of the way. 'I've got company,' he said.

I looked over his shoulder into total disarray.

Towels, bedsheets and clothes strewn all across the floor, with bottles and fast-food wrappers intertwined. The curtain was drawn and the only light came from a twenty-four-hour news channel on mute. I could see the outline of a woman getting hurriedly dressed on the other side of the bed. She was pulling her clothes on, speaking furiously in what sounded like Romanian.

Sloane looked at me with wine eyes. 'If you don't sin, then Jesus died for nothing . . .'

As the woman emerged from the room, still speaking, I saw that she was several months pregnant. She kept talking to him but he just looked at us and ignored her.

'Where's your wallet, Charlie?' He rolled his eyes and nodded at the bedside table. I went in, removed the two fifties inside and handed them to her. She smiled, said something more to Sloane and tucked the notes inside her bag, then she walked out, adjusting her skirt.

I opened the curtains, then the windows, as wide as they'd go, and watched Sloane squinting, helplessly, into the light. I knew a hangover when I saw one, and it looked like he was juggling three or four of them at once. He walked round the bed, moving with the grace of a wheelie bin, then crashed down on top of it with an arm across his face.

'Business and pleasure,' said Naomi from the doorway.

'I was doing her a favour . . .'

'Really? What was she, five, six months pregnant?'

'Think of it as a going out of business sale.'

'I'd rather not.

'Sounds like your constable's been triggered,' he said, winking at me. 'These bleeding hearts, eh, Waits?'

Naomi took a step towards him. 'Talk about me like I'm not here again and I'll put you through that fucking window, Charlie. How's that for a bleeding heart?'

Sloane looked at her, his face flaming red.

'I didn't think they still made shit that went this deep,' I said. 'But here you are snorkelling in it. Or was that the breaststroke we walked in on?'

'You two are like a bad joke,' he grumbled. 'What's black and white and full of shit?'

'Your newspaper?' said Naomi.

'We get it right more often than you two,' he said. 'And I've done my homework on you, Aidan Waits.' He looked at Naomi. 'Your partner's a dodecahedron, sweetheart. Fucker's got twelve faces according to my friends on the force. Went from cop to criminal and back again.'

'And I might relapse any moment, so let's try and make this quick. Not only were you holding back who sold you that picture, it just happened to be our number one suspect.'

'Oh, Christ, I never met the girl who sold me the picture. How should I know she's your number one suspect? To be honest, I didn't think you'd get that far.'

'How did you find her?'

'Well, a lot like your arse and your face, Sergeant, you've got that back to front. She found me. She'd read a few of my articles on Wick over the years. Asked if I'd be interested in a picture of him croaking it? I said thank you very much, what'll it cost me? She said ten grand and we haggled down to five.'

When he finished speaking he was out of breath, and his face was as red as raw meat. I thought I believed him, though. It explained how the girl had been able to give Short Back his thousand-pound payday.

'And then?'

He held out his arms. 'And then she sent me the picture.'

'You paid cash?'

'Delivered to a supermarket drop-box,' he said.

'How did you know it was genuine? There weren't any recent pictures of him until this one came along . . .'

'Said she could find someone to verify it.'

'And who'd know what Martin Wick looked like these days?'

'Shitloads of prison guards? Didn't matter much to me, long as they were legit . . .'

'She didn't use a prison guard, though, did she?'

'She had the name of some ex-cellmate.' He shrugged. 'Said if I could dig up his address then she'd do the rest . . .'

'She certainly held up that end of the bargain. You do realize that, if she's a contract killer, then you used the resources of your newspaper to identify Martin Wick for her?' For the first time since we'd met, Charlie Sloane looked at a loss for words. 'And that's before we even talk about you giving his location away to a man who'd tried to murder him in the last six months.'

'I didn't give him the location, she did.'

'A thin line to be walking on with your frame, Charlie . . .'

He looked at Naomi. 'You heard that, sweetheart, he fat-shamed me.'

'That'll be when I drag you through the lobby in nothing but your pants and a pair of handcuffs.' I let him stew on that before adding, 'Probably not a good exit in a hotel full of reporters. We've just been to see Wick's ex-cellmate, by the way. Quite a guy . . .'

'Yeah, yeah,' he drawled. 'Did the riverdance on some homeless bloke's ribcage, he'd take my neck and make it snappy. What you're forgetting is, I didn't put them in touch, I just found out where he was living. How could I know all this'd happen? The girl was well spoken. Did she fuck set fire to a hospital ward.'

'Well spoken?' said Naomi. 'You told us you didn't meet.'

'They have these things called telephones,' said Sloane.

'Her number, now.'

10

Naomi called in the number that Charlie Sloane had given us while I sat in the hotel lobby, watching people checking in and out. We'd left Sloane with the promise that his name would feature prominently in our report to Superintendent Parrs, something he understood to be infinitely worse than a simple arrest. Now, with any luck we'd be able to trace the phone and find the woman who'd photographed Wick – Esther, if Short Back and Sides was to be believed.

My anger seemed to have increased the pace of the investigation, leading it further from any potential connection with me. There was still the matter of my stolen bag, though. That couldn't get any closer to home. I felt my phone vibrate with a text.

Peter Collins?

I read and re-read it. Then I cleared the screen, opened it and read it again.

Peter Collins was the name on my counterfeit passport.

When Naomi got off her call and came to find me, I was still staring at the text, and fumbled my phone away.

'They'll call back with the trace but it might take an hour or so,' she said. 'As for the owner, they're gonna start calling service providers today. You look pale.' I nodded, not really listening. 'Look, Aidan. I know it's not a great time, but maybe we could have that talk if you've got a minute?'

'Sorry,' I said, getting up. 'I've just remembered I have to be somewhere.'

'What about the trace?'

'I'll be back as soon as I can. If it comes through before then, give me a call.' Then I was through the door and walking down the road, away from the hotel, looking over my shoulder to make sure I wasn't being followed. I was looking at my phone, my finger hovering over the call button, but I resisted. I didn't want to make things worse by leaving unnecessary records that linked me to whoever was on the other end of this number.

I found one of the city's few surviving payphones, forced far too much change into the slot and dialled. It rang for a minute, finally cutting out.

I tried to think of more options. Tracing it through official channels would only lead back to me, as would replying to the text.

I'd left the phone box and started to walk when it rang. I went back inside and ripped the receiver off the cradle.

'Payphone?' said the woman at the other end. 'Maybe you're not as stupid as you look.'

I recognized her voice. 'What do you want?'

11

We met in the Gas Lamp, another of the city's subterranean bars. It had been a children's mission, back in the 1800s, when Deansgate was still a slum, serving free meals to those who'd otherwise go hungry, acting as a homeless shelter for neglected boys.

I'd never liked the place, having grown up in care myself.

They still had the original tiles on the floor and I thought they needed another couple of hundred years for the despair to really wash off.

I'd suggested the Gas Lamp because it was discreet and close by, and I got there in time to burn the back of my throat with a double Jameson's. I saw her in the mirror behind the bar but let her come up and tap me on the shoulder. As far as I was concerned, she was in charge, and when I turned to a smiling Constable Louisa Jankowski, I saw that she felt the same way.

'Hi,' she said, leaning in for a hug.

Anyone watching would have thought we were on a date. She was dressed casually, black jeans and a leather jacket, but it was impossible not to see the thrill in her face. Eyes widened, as if to take it all in, not far removed from the look she'd had at the firing range. I'd wondered at the time if she'd manage to find the best vantage point in our conversation, but she'd gone a little further than that.

'Can I get you anything?' I said.

'I don't drink, but a soda water would be nice.'

I ordered the highest percentage IPA I could see and a soda

water, then followed her to a table. The Gas Lamp was a warren of alcoves and side rooms, and it was simple enough to find a secluded corner table. There was a candle on it and not much space, so we were pressed close together. As Louisa smiled and wriggled out of her jacket, I got the sense that she was enjoying herself.

'Cheers,' she said, holding up her glass. I looked at her, extinguished the candle between forefinger and thumb, then took a long drink from my pint without touching it to hers. When I put it down again she smiled, showing me her perfect teeth. 'Never been here before, I think—'

'What's going on, Louisa?'

'There's no reason this can't be friendly.' Her eyes met mine. 'We don't have to be enemies.'

'I didn't think that we were.'

'You didn't rein in your partner when we spoke, though. I thought she was very rude to me.'

'Really?'

'This might sound bitchy . . .'

'You broke into my flat. Please don't worry about staying on my good side.'

'She seems like one of those women who feel they need to rip other women down. I didn't see her giving any of the guys a hard time.'

'None of them were on duty when a picture was taken of a protected prisoner. She was only asking questions for Rennick, your friend . . .'

'And I told her the truth, I had nothing to do with Rennie's death, or Martin Wick's.'

'This is a funny fucking way of proving your innocence.'

She looked at me for a moment then put her hand on mine like we were lovers. I'd arrived expecting threats, intimidation, blackmail, but she acted as though it was our third date.

'I didn't say I'm innocent. I said I had nothing to do with Rennie's death. I needed some insurance, that's all.'

'Insurance against what?'

'Overzealous, self-loathing female officers, for one thing.'

'I'm self-loathing but overzealous and female's pushing it.'

'Very funny. What I mean is, you can put the bitch on a lead.' I pulled my hand away. 'Hit a nerve, have I? How are the two of you getting on?'

'I don't know what you're talking about, Louisa.'

'Yeah, right. I think you want a collar round her neck as much as I do.'

'And why's that?'

She laughed with her whole body, with the whites of her eyes. 'Why would they assign their resident golden girl to a shadow investigation with their resident bad boy? To put him on the straight and narrow, or to nail his coffin shut?'

'You're way off . . .'

Louisa moistened her lips and leaned in. 'I'm friendly with a guy in records. He says Constable Black was rooting round in your files last night.'

'I asked her to catch up on some paperwork—'

'That must be why she was trawling through your reports, your arrest records, your known associates . . .'

I hesitated. 'That still doesn't explain what we're doing here.'

'You're filthy, Aidan Waits. I'd heard the stories – drugs, girls, underworld connections. I thought if I followed you home I might find something I could use. Meeting the wrong people, maybe, or screwing your constable. Never in my wildest dreams did I think—'

'OK,' I said.

'It's not OK.' She leaned in and whispered. 'In fact, I think it's a fake passport. A good one. Where do you even get hold of something like that?'

'Friends in low places.'

'I should be the one questioning you.'

'You haven't, though. Which tells me you must know something.'

She smiled and leaned back. 'Listen, Louisa, there are dangerous people involved here.'

'And I think you're one of them,' she said, taking my hand again, digging her fingernails into my skin.

I pulled it back. 'People who might want me dead.'

'I wouldn't want that to happen.'

'So, what do you want? Why are you doing this?'

'Maybe I know what it's like to have secrets.'

'If this is your idea of sympathy, then—'

'Please. I've just had a crash course in people using mine against me.'

'Using them against you like this? Like blackmail?'

'Oh, grow up,' she said. 'You're not the first person to get climbed over because people know your business. Do you know how many chief inspectors I wish I could unswallow?'

I didn't say anything and she went on, voice hardening.

'There's no question I'm the best marksman on the force. No question. And do you know what? I still couldn't get drafted until I'd sucked and I'd sucked and I'd sucked. Until I'd sucked all the fucking air out of myself.' I looked away and she went on. 'What I'm saying is, I know our secrets don't make us bad people. It's just that, occasionally, we have to do bad things to keep them.'

'So, come on,' I said. 'What's your secret? I know it's not screwing some married cops.'

She took my glass and drained it, her head weaving a little afterwards.

'I'm not supposed to drink, for one thing.'

It felt like the tip of the iceberg. 'What else aren't you supposed to do?'

'Men, women, colleagues especially. It gets messy. Drink,' she said, nodding at my empty glass. 'That gets messy, too. We'd probably have a great time if we got to know each other.'

'None of this sounds like a reason to break into my flat.'

'So dare me to tell you,' she said. Her pupils were dilated and she was breathing harder.

'This is ridiculous.'

She widened her eyes.

'OK, I dare you to tell me.'

'I met a girl at St Mary's a couple of weeks ago. This green track-suit one, your person of interest.'

'Esther,' I said.

She looked impressed. 'You're doing better than I thought. Esther wanted access to Martin Wick while she took a picture. She'd be in and out, she said. Wouldn't even come up the staircase. All I had to do was keep my back turned for five minutes . . .'

'For how much?'

'Two grand.'

'You risked throwing your life away for two grand?'

'Not bad money for five minutes' work.'

'I don't buy it.'

She shrugged. 'I play poker when I can't sleep. For some reason I've hardly been sleeping at all, lately. I had a cash flow problem.'

'Two grand wouldn't help if things were that bad . . .'

'It got me started, though, started and then some. After finding your stash, I'm finally winning again.' I closed my eyes. 'I mean it. I've doubled your money. Like I said, I see us as friends.'

'So what went wrong?' I said, dragging her back to the reason we were here. 'You're not telling me this out of the goodness of your heart.'

'Nothing went wrong,' she said. 'The girl gave me the cash and took her picture. It was that simple.'

'Unless she planned a murder while your back was turned.'

'She'd have done it there and then if that's what she was about.'

'There must be something wrong or I wouldn't be hearing all this. A couple of dead men aside, it sounds like you got away scot-free.'

'I had nothing to do with any dead men,' she said seriously. 'I wasn't even there when it happened. Nothing even connects me to this girl except the phone she called me from.'

And there it was.

I sat back and looked at her. If we found Esther in possession of this phone, and if it had Louisa Jankowski's details on it, she was sunk.

'I was thinking I could give you the number, you could trace it . . .'

'We've got the number already,' I said. 'And the trace is processing as we speak.'

'Ah.'

'Why didn't you trace it yourself?'

'How would I explain having her number? And anyway, I'd just be placing the phone in police custody.'

'That's all you'll be doing if you lead me to it.'

'But we're friends now, aren't we, Aidan? You say you're tracing it already?' She thought about it. 'That's even better. I won't need to make an anonymous tip. All I ask is that my number isn't on that phone when it's logged in as evidence, that there's nothing saying she called me. That's it. Then you can have your bag back, your passport, your cash, no questions asked.'

'I can delete a number from a phone,' I said. 'But sooner or later they'll pull the call records. I take it you'll be in there.'

'You're working the case. Follow it up, report my number as a burner, a dead end.'

'And what if we find Esther with the phone? What if she wants to talk? You can't wipe a person's memory quite as easily.'

'Well, that's the hard part.' She looked down at the table. 'I suppose it'll depend on how much you don't want to go to prison.'

I shook my head. 'Burying a phone's one thing . . .'

'But you've got to think, though, haven't you? If they find my number on there, or if they find her and she tells them what happened, they'll find your stash in my possession when they come to arrest me. Your fake passport. I could probably even use it to negotiate my sentence down.'

'You probably could.'

'It really is a miracle, when you think about it, that you were

160

there at the scene of a double murder and walked away without a scratch . . .'

'I've always been lucky that way,' I said.

'. . . So if I were you, I'd be working very hard to keep me out of this.'

I thought about it, and finally nodded.

'The phone won't be enough,' I said. 'Not killing her, either. You'll be piling one lie on top of another until they all fall down on you.'

'Until they all fall down on us, you mean? Why are you being difficult? You don't seriously believe some junkie killed Rennick or subdued Sutcliffe. You said you had doubts . . .'

'And I've still got most of them left.'

She smiled. 'I'm doing this for Rennie, as well as for myself. This is good information. You're following the wrong leads. All I did was turn my back for five minutes while this girl took a picture. If you solve it properly, find the real killer, then no one even needs to think about Esther. Or me.'

I nodded, distractedly.

'By the way?' she said. 'Who's Anne?' A shimmer of sunspots passed before my eyes and I gripped the table. 'I didn't read the letters, not either of them. They looked personal . . .'

I pushed my chair back and stared at her, trying to control myself.

The letter my sister had sent me and my aborted reply. I'd left them both with the bag when Naomi knocked on my door.

'I'm fair game, Louisa, absolutely, but do me a favour, one human being to another. Leave her all the way out of it, please.'

Louisa thought for a moment and then nodded, looking almost moved by my display of emotion. She reached into her bag and produced my sister's letter, handing it to me.

'A gesture of good faith,' she said, getting up. 'Call me, Aidan. You've got my number.' She kissed me on the neck and spoke into my ear. 'I've certainly got yours.'

12

I'd been gone for less than an hour when I returned to the Holiday Inn, but it felt like a lifetime. Naomi hadn't been in touch, and I assumed that the trace still hadn't come through. With luck, I thought, perhaps the phone had been damaged, switched off or destroyed.

I couldn't even begin to work out what I'd do if we found it.

As Louisa said, it would all depend on how much I wanted to avoid jail time. On the walk over I'd found myself thinking about Tessa Klein. Leaving a suicide note and no body behind, being declared dead. I was starting to see it as a viable option for myself.

Naomi was sitting in the lobby.

'I'll call you back,' she said, ending a phone call.

'Sorry about that. Any joy on the trace?'

'Nothing yet. Look, Aidan—'

'You said you wanted to talk, so let's talk.'

'You're sure you've got time?'

I held eye contact for a second too long and then nodded, leading us through to the hotel bar. It was quiet, just one or two couples sharing bottles or afternoon cocktails. I approached the barmaid and looked at my partner. I hadn't liked the way that Louisa had talked about her and, after my recent behaviour, I wondered if she might accept a position on James's team after all.

'Whatever you're having,' she said.

'Two pints of Guinness, please.' While she took a seat I ordered another double Jameson's and threw it down my throat.

We sat at a corner table looking out on to the street. I caught Naomi's eye and saw that same watchfulness from earlier. Even in the pantheon of a double murder investigation, this felt wrong. I couldn't tell if it was Superintendent Parrs's uncharacteristic distress, the phone call about my mother or the case.

The Louisa Jankowski situation was something else entirely, and I tried to force it as far down in my mind as it would go. As Naomi worked up to what she wanted to say, I began to acknowledge, uncomfortably, that I might be the problem here. When my eyes came back to the table, I saw that I'd drained about a third of my stout without realizing.

Naomi was still watching me. 'I've never drunk on duty before . . .'

'Makes it all worthwhile,' I said, trying a smile. She didn't reciprocate. 'Don't feel like you have to.'

'Oh, please,' she said, raising her glass, touching it to mine and taking a drink. She swallowed and looked at me. 'That stuff about your mum, earlier . . .'

'Let's not.'

'So, what Sloane was saying about you having twelve faces . . .'

'He's misinformed,' I said. 'It's just the two of them, I swear.' When she didn't laugh I went on. 'I'm sorry about today. Sloane, Short Back and Sides . . .'

She shrugged into her parka. 'Two more men who've overdosed on their tiny-dick medicine. It's not unusual.'

The way she looked at me implied I might be a member of the same club.

'So what did you want to talk about?' I said.

'Do you recognize the name Stuart Hawley?'

'Sounds familiar . . .'

'You and Sutty arrested him six months ago.'

I thought about it. 'He broke into the Whisky Shop on Exchange Street. They were shut, it was the middle of the night.'

'Then what?'

'We arrested him, took him back to the Park.'

'Did he resist?'

'The opposite. When we arrived he was just sitting there with a bottle. Even introduced himself and asked who he had the pleasure of speaking to . . .'

'And you told him?'

'Course,' I said. 'He came quietly.'

'Any heavy stuff?'

'No.'

'Not even from Inspector Sutcliffe?'

'No.'

She produced her phone and placed it on the table between us, glancing down at the screen and scrolling to a picture. It was Stuart Hawley, the man I remembered from the arrest.

He'd been beaten black and blue.

Both eyes were swollen shut and his lip was split in two places.

'No,' I said, looking up at Naomi. It didn't sound quite so firm any more. 'Think whatever you like but that's not me.'

'I don't know, I thought you might put another dent in Short Back's head earlier.'

'Would you blame me?' I tried to say it lightly but she nodded.

'I would, actually, yeah.'

'Look, it hasn't been a great week . . .'

'And that's what I'm wondering,' she said, looking at her phone. 'Was this a bad week?'

'There's plenty of dirt on me but nothing like that.'

'Well . . .' she said, touching the screen again.

I watched as she scrolled through more pictures. Faces I remembered, or half-recognized, from disturbances, interview rooms and crime scenes across the last year. All of them altered by bruises and scrapes at the least, real head wounds and broken bones at the worst.

'None of them have complained about you by name. They all say they were jumped shortly before or after an arrest, or that they recognized their attacker as a police officer. They're just putting the dots out there and waiting for someone to join them up, Aidan. It sounds like Parrs has, now me, and there'll be more.'

I thought, darkly, about Chief Inspector James's visit that morning. An assault near the Light Fantastic, as I'd happened to be passing.

The assailant had looked like me.

Naomi tried to draw me back. 'If this is some kind of plot against you, then it's advanced stuff.'

'Criminals lie about excessive force all the time,' I said.

'Yeah? What about sexual assaults? Because the first says she was groped. An officer matching your description suggested she could walk away from an arrest if he got a taste . . .'

'What's her name?'

'Seriously?' She looked at me. 'I'm not telling you that, don't even ask.'

'What do you think I'd do about it?'

I saw her eyes go unconsciously to the phone. 'That's not important,' she said. 'What's important is you've got dozens of people suggesting excessive force. The same again suggesting sexual misconduct. All people you've interacted with in the last year. Sooner or later, someone will see this pattern. This is subtle work. Whoever's motivating these people to come forward wants you crucified.'

'We can agree on that, at least.'

She looked at me. 'You're handing them the hammer and nails, I don't get it. Let's say for a second that there's no substance to these complaints.'

'There is no substance to these complaints,' I said.

I saw heads turning in our direction.

Naomi lowered her voice. 'Someone still pulled them all together.

That means finding people willing to put themselves in these situations in the first place, risking criminal records. Then causing these kinds of injuries, coaching them through complaints and actually making them follow through. On this scale. I've never seen anything like it, have you?'

I had to shake my head.

'This is someone with a lot of time and a lot of money, someone with connections.' She paused and took a breath. 'This is someone with a lot of hate, Aidan.'

I took a drink.

'And you know who it is, don't you?' The mass of everything she'd told me was too dense to lie through, and I nodded. 'This friend of yours that the Super was on about,' she said. 'Tell me about him, you owe me that much.'

I spoke slowly. 'What do you know about Zain Carver?'

I was looking at the wall, over her shoulder, but I saw her head lower a little.

'You've probably heard that I had a substance abuse problem,' I said. 'That I was caught stealing drugs from evidence. You've probably heard more besides.'

'I don't *do* gossip—'

'It's true, Naomi. All of it.'

She closed her eyes for a second. 'And now you're in hock to him?'

'Yeah, something like that.'

'But I don't get it. He can't hold this kind of grudge against every cop he's crossed paths with.'

'He doesn't,' I said. Then I finished my drink and stood. 'We should probably get going.'

Naomi stayed where she was, staring straight ahead at the chair I'd vacated. 'I'm trying to help you here, I'm trying to understand.'

'And I'm asking you not to, all right?'

'What's your problem with me?' she asked. 'Because I know it's not my work.' Her phone started to vibrate against the table and I picked it up, grateful for the distraction.

'Detective Sergeant Waits,' I said. 'Yes. Yes. Thank you.' I put the handset back down on the table, harder than I'd meant to. 'We've got a location on Esther.'

Naomi nodded, collected her phone, got up and left.

13

The phone had been traced to the Cornerhouse, a former arts centre and independent cinema that had shut down three or four years ago, standing empty ever since. It was roughly five minutes away from where we'd found the burned-out car the previous day, and Naomi had the good grace not to remind me that she'd suggested we search the area.

It was dark now, the road a mess of intersecting lights. Taxis, buses and bikes battling it out with storefront neons.

The building was on the corner of Whitworth and Oxford Street. Even during its time as a cultural hub, it had always had a thrilling, derelict air about it. Nothing looks quite like abandonment, though. Sandwiched between modern apartment complexes, and standing opposite the Palace Theatre, it looked like a dead tooth in an otherwise gleaming smile. For some time after it shut down, the cinema's marquee had carried a thank you message to former patrons, but the letters had either fallen away or been stolen, replaced by spray-painted logos and political slogans.

I'd been vaguely aware of the graffiti's changing tone in the last few months, but I saw now that it was militant in language and made reference to MAN, the Manchester Activist Network, a group of anarchist squatters who'd been making headlines after seizing several empty properties in the area. The city has the highest rate of vacant business premises in the country, with almost a third of them standing empty. Alongside the exploding homeless population, it had led to several of these so-called super squats in and around the centre. They were raided every few months, when bailiffs would descend en masse in the night, with riot police waiting in the wings, throwing people back out on to the street and confiscating what possessions they had. The whole process cost the city more than it would to lease some of the buildings and turn them into official shelters, but that would have meant acknowledging the problem.

We went to the door and tried to look through the glass. I thought I could see shapes moving in the gloom, but it was too dark to be certain. I made a fist of my hand and banged the base of it into the frame.

The shapes inside stopped moving.

We waited a moment and then a bearded face appeared out of the blackness.

'What do you want?' he said, sounding afraid.

'Police—' But before I could go on, he backed away from the window. 'We're trying to trace a missing person,' I shouted, pressing both hands into the glass. I thought I could still see the shape of him, paused, a few feet away.

'You need an eviction notice,' he shouted back, getting louder with each word.

'We're not here to evict anyone, we just want to talk.'

There was no response and I looked at Naomi.

She looked away.

I was about to start formulating some other plan when a bus drove by. Its headlights swept the building, illuminating the lobby for a second. When it did, we saw the bearded man, at the back of the room, not more than five feet away, talking to a skinny yellow-haired woman.

'Please,' I called through the door. 'Someone's life might be in danger . . .'

I was referring to Esther's but I might as easily have been talking about my own. Another moment passed and then there was a flash of pale skin, bleach-yellow hair, and the woman we'd seen appeared at the door. She stared at me through the dirty glass, then at Naomi, standing behind me. The look in her eyes said fight or flight but I was hoping for a third option. She glanced about the street for anyone else and I stood aside so she could see that we were alone.

'Whose life's in danger?' she said, with a hard Irish accent.

'A young woman, and if it makes any difference we think she's sleeping rough.'

She looked at me again and seemed to make up her mind. I heard a jingle of keys. The click of a padlock being opened and then a chain being drawn out from the door handles. She opened up and stood in front of us, rigid, wiry, continually twitching, picking at the skin around her fingernails.

It looked more like nerve damage than the shivers.

'Jazz,' she said, introducing herself. She had extremely red, flushed cheeks and wore a large, thick hoody over formerly pink leggings. Naomi and I stepped inside, giving our own names as she re-chained the door behind us. 'Follow me,' she said, lighting a small torch and leading the way in like an usher.

We went through the lobby and into one of the old screening rooms, where it seemed they'd set up camp. The cinema seats were still in place, all pointing towards a large black void where the screen would once have been. There were portable lights set up in here, and it made the space seem ageless. Although we were right beside a busy road, the room was hermetically sealed, and felt like a forgotten fallout shelter, all set up to watch the end of the world. The beard we'd seen at the door was talking to a group of five or six vagrant men. Their eyes moved on to us distrustfully, and they fell silent when we drew near.

'So,' said Jazz, still twitching, looking anywhere but at us.

'We're looking for a girl,' I said. 'Or anything you can tell us about her.'

'What you see's what you get,' said the bearded man.

Jazz put a hand on his shoulder. 'Why do you think she's here?'

'We've traced her phone to this address,' I said. They looked between themselves. 'Look, as far as I'm concerned we're in your house. You've got every right to tell us to stick it, but this girl's in trouble . . .'

'What kind of trouble?' asked Jazz.

'The worst. She was at the scene of a violent crime a few days ago, and there are some dangerous people looking for her.'

I sensed a shift in the tone of the room.

'Dangerous people like who?'

'I can't tell you that, but—'

'How do we know you're not dangerous?' asked the bearded man.

'Because the easiest way in for us would have been with a fire-arms unit. We could have broken that door down and had you all turfed out or in custody in five minutes flat.' When one of them took a step towards me I realized I wasn't speaking in hypothet-icals. It was a scenario they'd probably all experienced. 'I'm not saying this as a threat, I'm saying there's a difference.'

'What's this girl like?' asked Jazz.

'She's about your build, anywhere from twenty to her mid-thirties. Most distinctively,' I said, reaching inside my pocket for the printout, 'she has these facial tattoos.' I held it out to the group and one of them took it. 'It's not a clear picture, but those are pent-angles around her eyes, like stars.'

As the group looked at the photograph, one of the men took a step back. He walked the long way around the cinema seats, keep-ing his eyes on me and then exited the room.

After a second, two more of them followed.

'I take it that rings a bell?'

'Big fucking Ben,' said the bearded man, himself edging away from us.

Jazz handed back the picture and nodded. 'She was here, all right.'

'Was?'

'She's gone now. She was round earlier, after her stuff, but I wasn't here, so—'

'What stuff?' said Naomi.

'A bag,' said Jazz. 'We've got a lock-up on the top floor and I'm the only one with a key. I wasn't here to let her in.'

'Her stuff's still here then?' Jazz nodded. 'And do you know her name?'

Jazz looked to the bearded man. 'Esther's what she told us,' she said. 'None of us knew her, though. She'd only stayed here a couple of nights.'

'Can you take us to her stuff?' said Naomi.

'Have I a choice?'

'Not if you want to help her . . .'

She thought for a second then nodded, walking past us towards the exit.

We started to follow when the bearded man called after us.

'Don't both need to go, do ya?'

'I'll go,' I said, walking on before Naomi could argue.

Jazz led me through to a narrow staircase and she clicked on her torch again.

The last time I'd been inside this building was when it was still open, one Christmas, four or five years ago. I'd walked in off the street a little drunk and gone to a matinee showing of *It's a Wonderful Life*. When that finished, I'd had a drink at the bar and then worked my way up through three floors of art galleries, going from frame to frame. The art had been so contemporary that the paint was probably still wet, but it was a nice memory.

I'd walked out on to the street and called the suicide prevention hotline.

After about twenty minutes or so, it sounded like I'd talked the man at the other end into it. It all felt so far away from me now that it might as well have happened to someone else. My mind went to the phone call I'd received earlier about this stranger, Christine Farrow, being sectioned under the Mental Health Act. Somehow, it made me think about the way Naomi had been looking at me all day, trying to anticipate my alternating states of anger and paranoia.

Perhaps I was my mother's son, after all.

When we reached a locked door, Jazz took a key and opened it. Her hands shook so badly that I thought she was either coming down or trying to go cold turkey. Either way, she'd been to hell and back with it. I could tell because I'd made the same journey myself a few times. She squatted, searching inside the cupboard, and dug out a dirty-white backpack.

'This is it,' she said, holding it out to me.

Accepting it, I looked inside. I recognized the green tracksuit that Esther had been wearing when I saw her on the hospital ward and, digging further, found the phone that we'd traced. A spark of relief started glowing inside me. I didn't know what to do next but it gave me some semblance of control. 'Thank you,' I said. Then my own phone started to vibrate, making us both jump. I answered it to Naomi.

'You'd better get back down here,' she whispered. 'Now.'

14

When we reached the ground floor, Naomi was waiting in the stairwell, blocking the doorway. 'They've closed off the road,' she said. 'And they must have picked up on the trace because there are four or five TAUs out front.'

'Fuck,' I said, trying to think.

Jazz looked between us. 'What are TAUs?'

'Tactical Aid Units,' I said. She went immediately for the door but I got hold of her wrist. 'This isn't the time to panic.' I looked at Naomi. 'Where are the others?'

'The screening room.'

'Jazz, if we tell them what's going on, they might react badly. Someone could get hurt.' I let go of her wrist and she rubbed it, angrily. 'I'm sorry, but give me a chance to go outside and talk.'

She nodded but she was still shaking hard, and her cheeks had flushed to a painful, purple red.

I was doing the calculations.

Louisa Jankowski had left the Gas Lamp soon after I'd mentioned our pending trace on Esther's phone. If she'd reported for her shift afterwards, then she might be outside with an assault rifle. Perhaps I could get the bag to her directly, defuse the situation, save us both.

I started for the door but Naomi held out her hand.

'It's Esther's?' she asked. 'The phone, too?'

I swallowed. 'It's in there.'

'If you hand it over to them and there's information leading back to this girl, she could get hurt. You said so yourself.'

We were each holding on to a strap of the bag now.

I tried to factor that into my thought process, that handing it to Jankowski and saving myself might mean damning someone else. In the end I saw there was no choice, and let go.

Naomi slipped it on to her shoulder and turned to Jazz. 'Is there a back door?

She nodded. 'A fire exit goes out to the station . . .'

'And I'll need the key to the front door,' I said. Jazz was really shaking now, dropping the key on the floor before she could hand it over. 'It's OK,' I said, picking it up. 'If anything goes wrong, if either of you see a gun, get your hands in the air and do whatever they say.' They nodded. 'Give me one minute and then go.'

I walked into the lobby, counting down from sixty.

My heart was going like a war drum and I could hear a police helicopter overhead. Its spotlight was trained on to the building, meaning they could see me but I couldn't see them. They'd brought out the big guns, and they'd be pointing them right at me when I left. I shielded my eyes and went to the door, snapping open the padlock and unwinding the chain.

When I stepped outside the noise of the helicopter was overwhelming.

I started forward, the spotlight trembled about me and I heard the shrill feedback from a megaphone. *Armed police, down on the ground!'*

I already had my hands in the air but dropped to my knees and shouted back that I was a police officer. Squinting into the light I could see four or five riot vans, blocking off the junction in all directions, as well as the high-vis jackets of uniformed officers surrounding me. They weren't the ones I was worried about, though.

Firearms would blend into the darkness.

The helicopter descended a little and I could feel the blades, slicing the air, the light burning my eyes. I thought I could see Louisa

Jankowski's sergeant, Halliday, on point, pointing a G36 assault rifle right at me. Looking about I saw several other members of the team flanking him. I knew Jankowski was here as well. I was actually grateful when Chief Inspector James took a bewildered step out of the glare towards me.

'Waits?' he said.

'Am I glad to see you . . .'

'What the fuck are you doing here, Sergeant?'

'Sir, I was following a lead relating to the woman in the green tracksuit.'

'Unassisted?'

'She's not in there,' I said, avoiding the question.

He took another step towards me and shouted. 'I asked if you were alone?'

'Inspector.' I turned to see Jankowski, now in full tactical gear, leading Naomi back towards us. 'I found her leaving through the fire exit,' she said.

Jankowski was so transformed from the woman I'd spoken to a couple of hours before that it was hard to believe. Her gun wasn't pointing directly at my partner but the threat was implied.

James looked at me and shouted over the noise of the helicopter. 'I don't believe this. Is that the bag our suspect was seen carrying at the scene of the car fire?'

'We believe so, sir.'

'Constable Black,' he said. 'Surrender that bag to Jankowski, immediately.'

Naomi hesitated, caught my eye.

As she saw it, we were losing our one lead, and putting Esther's life in danger. I knew it was worse than that, but there were even uglier ways this could go down. All I could see was that gun pointing vaguely towards her. I nodded and she handed over the bag. Jankowski ripped it out of her hands and began backing away.

'Constable Jankowski,' said James. 'Can you confirm that the phone's in there?'

Jankowski unzipped it and looked inside. 'Confirmed, sir.'

'I want it logged into evidence, immediately.'

He was still staring at me and missed the relief passing across Jankowski's face. She walked towards one of the TAU vans, her pace increasing as she went. If she was about to destroy or tamper with evidence then I knew I should say something, but that would be signing my own death warrant.

'Get up,' said James. I got to my feet and he took a step closer, so I could hear him clearly over the air being battered about us. 'Is there anything we should know before we go in?'

'I'm not sure that's—'

'Is there anything we should know, Sergeant?'

'Sir. Five or six unarmed vagrants inside. They don't know the girl and she's not in there.' James nodded at Halliday, who motioned to two members of his team to follow him.

'Not firearms,' I shouted over the noise. They looked at me and for a moment there was only the glare and the engine, the air chopping down on us. We were all standing in the spotlight. 'These people have complied every step of the way, no one needs to get hurt.'

James tensed visibly then turned to Halliday. 'We'll send uniform in first, see if we can do this quietly.'

'Sir,' said Halliday, staring at me.

'As for the two of you, I'll be making a full report about this to Chief Superintendent Chase. I suggest you get your stories straight and get out of my sight.'

Naomi and I both walked beyond the perimeter, out to where a crowd of people was gathering. I'd been keeping an eye on the van that Jankowski had disappeared into. As it started up and pulled out I saw another vehicle behind it. A matt-black Mercedes, the same kind that I'd seen following us earlier. I looked for the licence plate but it started up, drove out too quickly.

As Naomi and I turned the corner, further from the main road, I became aware of our heavy breathing. The distant buzz of the helicopter like a dissipating headache.

Before I could speak, she shook her head and took her phone from her pocket. Except it wasn't her phone, and I stopped dead.

'Swapped it for mine before they grabbed me,' she said. 'They've just got some pictures of your man-handled arrests . . .' She hesitated for a second before handing it over. '. . . It's locked, but you should probably see the home screen.'

I swiped up.

The background picture on Esther's phone was of the murdered Moore family.

I looked up at Naomi and saw that she was thinking the same thing. It wasn't the screensaver of some mercenary hack, however well she might have disguised herself. It was the screensaver of someone who was personally connected to the case, personally involved.

'Who is this girl?' said Naomi.

IV
Disintegration

1

'I'll need to see some identification,' said the guard. He was stationed outside Sutty's hospital room at St Mary's, and looked
visibly surprised when I told him we were partners. He looked
closely at my ID, then at me. Finally, he looked over my shoulder
at Naomi, who he seemed to trust at a glance. I walked through
and closed the door behind us.

'What was that all about?'

'He's been stationed here four days,' said Naomi, without looking at me.

'So?'

'So, I guess he thought Sutty's partner might have visited him by
now.'

I nodded and walked towards the bed. There was a curtain
drawn around it, and I looked through the gap for a second. Sutty
was unrecognizable in white bandages, still in the medically
induced coma which prevented him from cardiac arresting due to
the pain. I sat down, wondering what he'd do if the situation were
reversed. He might not have brought me flowers by now, but he
probably would have found my attacker.

I could feel Naomi's eyes on me, a burgeoning new tension
between us. It had occurred to me in the night that in her close
observation, in her trawl through my arrest records and personnel
files, she'd never been trying to bury me at all.

She'd been hoping to clear my name.

'Y'know,' she said. 'When we interviewed Blake over at the BBC, he was talking about Sutty . . .'

I looked up. 'When was this?'

'When you went for the car. They'd run into each other somewhere recently, some old-timer's leaving drinks. He said Sutty mentioned you.'

'Yeah?'

'He said you were brilliant.'

I looked at the curtains surrounding the bed. 'I don't think so.'

'You don't think he said it or you don't think you're brilliant?'

The door opened before I could answer and Superintendent Parrs strode in. It was 8 a.m., and we were meeting here at his suggestion.

'Sorry about this,' he said, 'but I'm not sure either of you should show your face at the Park until I've smoothed things over with Chase. After all, it's not every day we scramble a police chopper for one of our own, is it, Sergeant? I thought Sutty's bedside would be the last place anyone'd look for you. You've given me a lot to think about. I suppose I did tell you to get involved . . .'

I glanced at Naomi. 'We were at the Cornerhouse on my sayso, sir.'

'Very noble, son, but there are other swords I want you falling on. As far as I'm concerned, you were following a promising lead and you got there first. James and co are just sore losers.'

'How did they trace the phone there?' said Naomi.

'They didn't,' Parrs answered. 'They received an anonymous tip about this tattooed woman. Maybe one of those homeless guys read the newspaper he was sleeping under, saw that she was wanted.'

Either that, I thought, or Louisa Jankowski had followed us to the Cornerhouse and then called in an anonymous tip of her own. She'd had nothing to lose once I'd told her that we were already tracing Esther's phone, and her plan to grab it would have worked perfectly if Naomi hadn't swapped the handset for her own.

Standing in the street with Naomi the previous evening, she'd insisted we call Parrs and put him in the picture. When I had, he'd asked me to keep hold of the handset until he could meet us in the morning. I'd tried to guess the access code, the date that the Moores had been murdered, but it hadn't worked, and I hadn't dared try again in case I locked it.

If Jankowski's number was saved on there, then it was very likely she'd be arrested, very likely I'd be next. The cash and the counterfeit passport would convincingly incriminate me in Wick's murder. After a lifetime of bending the rules and breaking the law, it felt like a lethal dose of irony to go down for something I hadn't done. At length, I realized that both Parrs and Naomi were watching me. I handed the phone, now in a protective plastic baggie, to the Superintendent.

'Still locked?' he said.

I nodded. As long as it was, and as long as the service provider dragged their heels over the call records, I still had some time. Parrs pressed the home button, letting out a breath when he saw the picture of the Moore family being used as a screensaver.

'It feels like this tattooed woman has a personal stake in the case,' said Naomi.

'Prints?'

'This morning,' I said. 'It must have been wiped down because the only matches were myself and Constable Black.'

'Constable Black, the handset you gave to Louisa Jankowski should have found its way into evidence by now . . .'

'I traced it this morning, sir. The signal went dead immediately after I handed it over. It was at 45 per cent battery so either it was switched off or damaged. The last ping location was the Cornerhouse.'

'You've got a spare you can use in the meantime?' he said. She nodded. 'If your phone's been misplaced or swapped on its way into evidence that would seem to answer the question of Constable Jankowski's involvement . . .'

I didn't say anything.

Luckily, I could already see the Superintendent's mind moving ahead to the next step. Chief Superintendent Chase had declined our recommendation to suspend Jankowski. Used properly, that information might undermine her grip on the force, and especially on the hot-button issue of armed police in the city. It might go so far as jeopardizing Chase's promotion, even her position. Of course, the only important thing to Parrs was that it might improve his.

He gave us both his shark's smile. 'A good result all round.'

He said it like we'd closed the case.

'Can I ask what you'll do with the phone, sir?' said Naomi.

'I've got a tame techie over at the Park who I can trust. He says the latest models are borderline impossible to crack, even the security services are struggling to keep up, but he'll do what he can.'

'Sir,' she said. 'I mean, what would we do with any extracted information?' Parrs didn't answer and she went on. 'I'm concerned about the well-being of this girl if firearms get the jump on us again.'

Parrs looked amused, and was about to answer when there was a knock at the door. 'Come in,' he said.

Karen Stromer, a forensic pathologist, entered the room. She wore a slim black suit over her scarecrow figure and paused in the doorway when she saw us. Not because she was surprised, necessarily, but to make her feelings on this clandestine meeting clear. She stepped inside and drew the door shut behind her. Stromer was a professional in a town which didn't value them, and that made her an outsider. Temperamentally, I thought we were probably quite similar. Professionally, we couldn't be more different. She had short, dark hair, small, deep-set eyes and a mouth so lipless and thin that it only became visible when she opened it.

'Glad you could join us,' said the Superintendent.

'I'm sure there's a good reason why we can't have this conversation at Central Park.'

'I'm afraid you're looking at him,' said Parrs, nodding in my direction.

She acknowledged me with a minimal nod and no eye contact.

'Good morning, Aidan. I'd thought, perhaps, this kind of thing was behind you . . .'

'Like a knife in his back,' said Parrs before I could answer. 'I received three separate complaints about Detective Sergeant Waits yesterday alone.' He looked at me. 'Sloane, Short Back, DCI James. Always knew you had it in you . . .'

'I always rather hoped you didn't,' said Stromer. Her eyes went to the curtain drawn around the bed and she changed the subject. 'How is Detective Inspector Sutcliffe?'

'The elephant in the room?' said Parrs. 'He's making his usual contribution.'

I didn't think Stromer would let that one pass without comment, but she decided to make it quick.

'I suppose in that case I'd better make mine,' she said, opening her leather briefcase and removing some papers from it. 'You all know how Martin Wick died. Usually in instances of fire one hopes for the deceased to succumb to smoke inhalation, but I'm afraid that wasn't the case here.'

'Waits was with him at the time,' said Parrs.

'Yes, of course. What's more interesting is that, upon examination, we discovered a note pressed into the palm of his hand.' She passed around photocopies. I thought about Wick beating his fist against my chest when he died.

He'd been trying to tell me something.

The paper had been charred in the fire, and the writing was difficult to make out.

'I believe he was given to writing such messages?'

'They saved his voice,' I said. 'The problem is, his handwriting's so small . . .'

'So I see. We had the note blown up but it wasn't much help. It says *strangays*, if that means anything to you.'

'Strangeways,' I said, squinting at the sheet.

I felt Parrs's red eyes lock on to me. 'He was talking to Detective Inspector Sutcliffe at the time of his death . . .'

'And whatever he was telling him seemed to put Sutty on edge,' I said.

'Have James's team impounded Wick's correspondence?'

I looked to Naomi and she answered.

'I don't believe so, sir.'

'Then get over there, now.' I was already going for the door, grateful to be getting away without activating his sixth sense for dishonesty. I reached out and took hold of the handle. 'And Aidan.'

'Sir?'

'In all of yesterday's excitement, there was something you still didn't do for me . . .' I didn't turn around. I'd been one second away from walking out. 'I have asked you repeatedly to look into the likelihood that *you* were the intended target of this hit. I believe Constable Black's been digging into what I suspect is a campaign against you?'

'Sir.'

'I've spelt it out three times already, so perhaps you could put it into words for me?'

'Zain Carver,' I said.

'The very man. Talk to him, today. If I have to ask again it'll raise serious concerns about your involvement here.'

'You won't have to ask again.'

'Sure, sure. Stay on top of him, Constable Black. Where Aidan's concerned, failure is most certainly an option.'

I ignored him, opened the door and stepped through it, seeing sunspots. The only thing I felt certain of was that I'd never willingly speak to Zain Carver again. Besides, if the phone records came back and led to the arrest of Louisa Jankowski, I'd be in handcuffs by the end of the day anyway.

2

Her Majesty's Prison was an infamous shithole. To me the name sounded fanciful, like the queen summered there or something. It had been hastily rebranded from Strangeways in the early nineties, when a twenty-five-day riot and rooftop protest resulted in millions of pounds of damage and the deaths of two men, one officer and one inmate. In the wake of these protests, and the spotlight it had thrown on to living conditions, authorities had been forced into drastic renovation work on the dilapidated Victorian compound.

The rebrand hadn't worked, though, everyone still called it Strangeways.

Hatton, the governor, met us on the other side of security. He nodded when we introduced ourselves then said his own name and marched off down the corridor, trailing the smell of stale sweat in his wake. It was the kind of terse welcome I often got when the Superintendent called ahead on my behalf.

'Can't say we were sad to see him go.'

'We haven't met anyone yet who's sad to see him go,' I said, catching up. 'But that's not the point.'

He didn't answer.

'We know that Martin Wick wasn't very popular here,' said Naomi.

'Say that again. We were surprised he got out with his life.'

'If you could call it that . . .'

'Exactly. If he'd croaked ten years ago it would've saved everyone a world of grief.'

'What kind of grief are we talking about?' asked Naomi. We were still touring the corridors and I was afraid we'd spend the whole conversation looking at the fat folds on the back of his neck. His shirt absolutely garrotted him and I wondered if he'd done up the top button especially for us.

'Oh,' he said, waving a hand. 'Just numbers. You send them to us faster than we can . . .' He stopped, put the key in a door and opened it. 'Faster than we can . . .'

'Find them hanging in their cells?' I said. The quickest way to rattle a cop or a prison guard is by not giving them the respect that they think they're owed.

It felt like time to start rattling people.

Hatton stepped into his office and looked back at me. 'You really are one of the Superintendent's finest, aren't you? What can I do for you today, Sergeant?'

'We're here for Wick's correspondence.'

'But while we've got you,' said Naomi, stepping past me into the office, 'we'd be grateful for some background on his time here.'

'I can give you a few minutes.'

Hatton had the proportions of a king-sized bed and wore a permanent scowl. His office smelt so rancid with body odour that it was impossible he didn't know. I wondered if he used it as a means of self-protection. Insulated inside this room, I couldn't imagine many people dropping in for a chat. He told us exactly where we could stand or sit, then wedged himself behind his desk and watched us comply. He was clearly used to being obeyed, putting me in mind of the despot leader of a small, rogue nation.

'Thanks,' said Naomi. 'It's been difficult to get a full picture of him . . .'

'You want a picture of Martin Wick?' said Hatton. He looked about the room for inspiration, then down at his desk, at an empty sheet of paper. He tapped it. 'There you go.'

Naomi smiled. 'If he wasn't responsible for the deaths of four people, we'd probably agree with you. As it is, he's actually quite a rarity. A convicted murderer who was himself murdered.' Hatton shifted in his seat. I thought I could see him mentally cancelling his next appointment. It was the same performative, weary look I'd seen several men in this case giving to Naomi. I wondered if I was one of them.

'Look, when I say he was a blank canvas, it's out of frustration. While the bastard was here, he was completely unresponsive to any and all efforts made with him in mind. At the same time, he inspired such hostility in the lads—'

'Why was that?' I said, picking up on the question that Kevin Blake had been unable to answer.

'Honestly? We never got to the bottom of it. But seven attempted murders in twelve years is good going by anyone's standards.'

'I didn't know you had standards here,' I said, and he made a hand gesture in reply. 'I thought it was strange that Charlie Sloane had the lowdown on how many attempts there'd been on Wick's life . . .'

'Did he?' said Hatton, eyes drifting to the empty wall behind us. Interesting that he recognized the name of a hack reporter without pause, I thought. If he'd been on the ball, his first question would have been: *Who?*

I waited until his eyes came back on to me.

'He did,' I said. 'Raised it as a question at the press conference with Chief Superintendent Chase. I was wondering who told him.'

'If that's why you're here—'

'It's not.'

'Because I can't be responsible for every bit of gossip that gets through those walls. Look, if you want my two cents, Wick's silence was his real problem. He was judgemental, like everyone here was beneath him. To be judged by a child killer can stick in the craw.'

I nodded. 'I suppose Wick was famous as well . . .'

'Which can go either way. Celebrities, guys coming off big cases, they can do well. The lads have to pass the time somehow, if you've got a story to tell you'll go far. But being above it all and, what's the word . . .'

'Withholding?' said Naomi.

'That's how you get yourself a perforated eardrum, I'm afraid. He had no gift for conversation, put it that way. Frankly, I thought he'd have been more comfortable in a straitjacket.'

'So, he had no friends inside that you know of?'

'Seemed to get along with his last cellmate, but he's another story . . .'

'In what sense?'

'A troubled soul, shall we say.'

'Do you think this troubled soul would be willing to speak to us?' asked Naomi. 'I'm sure Superintendent Parrs would appreciate it . . .' Hatton's jaw clenched and unclenched, like he'd put his two cents in his mouth and started chewing them.

'Course,' he said. 'I'm afraid it might take some time to arrange, though. E Wing's on lockdown. With a few days' notice . . .'

'Any particular reason they're locked down?' she said.

'Very much the norm. We don't have the personnel to get them out as much as we'd like.'

'How many hours do they get outside their cell a day?'

'In current conditions, just the one,' he said, holding eye contact with her.

We all knew that the twenty-three-hour lockdown was one of the main points of protest in the original riots. It was hard to believe that the city was back there.

'We don't need any special arrangements,' I said, trying to speed things up. 'We'll talk to him in his cell.'

'I wouldn't advise that, actually.'

'Is it the same cell where Wick was held?' asked Naomi.

'For the last five years . . .'

'Then we'd like to see it.'

'I think you, in particular, might not enjoy yourself, Constable.'

She smiled. 'I'm not here to enjoy myself, Governor, believe me.'

'OK,' he said like she was being unreasonable. There was a gloating tone in his voice, and I thought he'd probably be quite happy if the worst happened while we were in there. 'Give me a moment.' He unwedged himself from behind his desk, got up and left the room.

Naomi widened her eyes. 'Something stinks in this place . . .' It was her first time here and I had a feeling she wouldn't forget it. I stood to see if I could open the window, which looked out over the courtyard. She joined me and we watched a group of men filing out into the light.

'Their one hour a day . . .' said Naomi. Neither of us spoke as we watched. They walked, heads low, around the courtyard in circles. 'Funny,' she said. 'All of them going clockwise.'

I nodded. 'Probably trying to make the time go faster.'

3

Category A's have a sense of hopelessness that's hard to articulate. Most offenders are high risk, serving life sentences, with little likelihood of release before death or old age. Strangeways had recently beaten out stiff competition for the highest suicide rate of any prison in the country. When the walls are sixteen feet thick, it's the only realistic means of escape. We were escorted to the segregation unit, while the prison officer filled us in.

'Most of these guys can't hack it in the main pop for one reason or another. You've got your fruitcakes, you've got your juveniles being tried as adults and you've got your self-harmers.' He turned a key in a beaten steel door, leading us on to the wing. 'And obviously, you've got your chomos.'

'Chomos?' said Naomi.

'Child molesters,' he said, closing the door behind us.

It crashed shut and he turned the key again.

'They're on the same wing as juveniles being tried as adults?'

'I know,' he said, misreading her tone. 'Poetic justice, eh?'

He led us into E Wing. Four floors of barred cells with steel-grid walkways. It sounded like a soup kitchen falling down a flight of stairs. As we passed the cells I heard conversations go dead. Inmates shifting forward to watch us, eyes trailing Naomi. No one shouted or did anything to disturb us, and I got the feeling they were memorizing her.

'What's our man in all this?' I asked.

'Man?' he laughed. 'You'll see . . .'

'We're excited enough without the element of surprise,' I said.

'Well, I suppose Adam's what you'd call a switch. Sometimes he's a he, sometimes a she. Today he's somewhere in between.'

'Is that why he's segregated?'

'That and substance problems.'

'What's his poison?'

'Spice,' said the guard. 'Same as all the others. Makes the time pass quicker so it's popular stuff in here.'

I'd heard of family men coming here sober, leaving with unbreakable bad habits. Life failed them first, followed by the system. Buried inside Strangeways, they acquired the skills to fail themselves.

When we reached Adam's cell, the guard asked the other man inside if he'd give us a minute. He agreed with a docile shrug, waiting while Adam was cuffed to a restraint. This was done gently, on account of the overlapping new and old self-harming scars covering both the prisoner's arms. He was slim and wore his hair in short pigtails with light make-up.

It didn't quite cover his black eye.

He had a single tear tattooed beneath it, which I took to mean that he'd murdered someone. No one spoke until the prison guard had taken the other cellmate, jingling down the gangway. I started to introduce myself but Adam got in there first.

'Know this place was built in 1868?'

I shook my head and let my eyes cast over the peeling paint. The dim lights and the dents in the walls. 'I thought it looked older,' I said.

He laughed easily. One short burst but right from the nose.

'Was built two years after Dostoevsky published *Crime and Punishment*.' He pronounced the author's name phonetically, and I thought he'd probably never heard it said out loud. 'What does that tell you?'

'That the architect didn't read it very closely,' I said.

He snorted again and I asked if we could sit down.

He nodded and I perched on the edge of the bed, meaning Naomi would be closer to him. I could see that her presence made him uncomfortable. When he looked away, trying to think of another question in the same line, I took him for a person who enjoyed conversation but didn't get much practice.

'You've read *Crime and Punishment*, then?' I said, helping him out.

'Fucking living it,' he snorted. 'Have you?'

'I've started it a few times . . .'

'That's the problem. Need a life sentence to finish the fucking thing.'

'You liked it, though?' said Naomi.

'I haven't got a life sentence,' he said, sounding confused. He was sitting opposite us but scrunched away slightly. 'I did like it, though. It's amazing. Doesn't end like you'd think, either. You should read it.' He nodded at Naomi and me both. 'You lot should all read it.' He glanced up and saw that I was formulating a question. 'How old are you?' he said quickly.

'I'm thirty-one.'

'Same.' His head sank a little.

'Adam,' said Naomi. 'We're here to talk about your former cell-mate, Martin Wick . . .'

'Was good, that, for a minute. A proper talk.'

'No one else in this case has been capable of talking books,' I said. 'Believe me.'

'Plenty of reading time, it's all I've got. Do you know who killed Martin?'

'That's what we're trying to find out.'

'Don't know why you've come here, then. No one here knows anything, I mean literally.'

'The two of you spent a lot of time together. You could be in a unique position to help us.'

'Martin . . .' He gently rubbed the scars at his wrists. 'He wasn't like a real person.'

'A few people have said similar things. What do you mean by it?'

He thought, seriously, before he spoke. 'Have you ever seen that old horror film, *They Live*?'

'John Carpenter,' I said.

'No, I can't remember who starred in it, but he finds these sunglasses and when he puts them on, he can see that some people aren't really people, they're these creatures walking round in disguise. He was like one of them.'

'Like a monster?' said Naomi.

He frowned. 'More like the other way round, like one thing dressed up as another. Everyone saw a monster but underneath it all he seemed simple to me. Sometimes I wondered if he was special needs or something. Did you ever see his handwriting?'

'Once or twice.'

'He was embarrassed about his spelling, I think that's why it was so small. He could hardly even read before he came in here.'

'Did the two of you do much talking?' asked Naomi.

'I just said.'

I could see that her presence was antagonizing him, and I cut in. 'Towards the end of his life, he actually recanted his confession. Did he ever talk about that?'

Adam shook his head.

'We heard from another former cellmate of his that he used to hide pictures here, including some of his victims.'

Adam looked at the floor.

'How did you feel when you heard he'd been murdered?' said Naomi.

'How do you think? Firebombs on top of cancer. Like having to die twice . . .'

'Why do you think someone would have wanted to do that?'

'Because we're fucking scum. Obviously.'

'Adam,' I said. After a few seconds his eyes came back to me, and some of the heat seemed to go out of them. 'Can you think of anyone who might have wanted to kill him?'

'Besides half of Strangeways?'

'He wasn't popular?' said Naomi.

'I know you think we're animals,' he said in a low voice. 'But we don't wrap our arms round child killers.'

I gave him a second. 'There are plenty of child killers who make it inside, though . . .'

'Some get treated like royalty,' he said.

'Well, it is Her Majesty's Prison.' He smiled again but I could see he was straining to control his temper. 'I was wondering if you had any thoughts on what set him so much apart? How come they hated him?'

'Child killers,' said Adam. 'Yeah. Rapists. Yeah. You can make a go of it with the right attitude. But Martin looked down at everyone, y'know?' He was rubbing his scars compulsively now, and I saw that one of the wounds had opened, smearing blood across his wrist. 'Was just how he looked at us.'

'How did he look at you?' He was staring at the floor now, and several seconds went by. 'Adam,' I said gently.

'Like that fucking bitch is looking at me now. Like I'm a fucking germ. And if she doesn't stop in three fucking seconds I'll have her fucking eyes out for it.'

Naomi looked at me, uncertainly.

'Constable Black, perhaps you could give us a moment?'

'Sure,' she said. 'Thanks for talking to us, Adam.' She stood up and left the cell in one motion, and I smelt a sudden rush of her perfume. We listened to her footsteps leading away then the sound of the guard opening the gate. Adam was shaking.

'I'm sorry,' he said, picking at his nail varnish, rubbing his face. 'She's too pretty, I'm sorry.'

Sitting there in the segregated wing of Strangeways, wearing pigtails and covered in self-harming scars, I thought I'd never seen someone so alone. When I shifted closer he winced like I might hit him. I held open my hands to show that I wouldn't, and he looked up, half-smiled and nodded. He wiped his face with his prison-issue shirt, smearing some of his make-up.

'Can I ask what the tear's for?' I said, referring to the tattoo on his face.

'It's for when you kill someone . . .'

'You don't strike me as a killer, Adam.'

'It's for me, for when I kill myself.' I didn't say anything. 'Look, if I showed you something, something you asked about, do you think you could help me?'

'What kind of help do you need?'

'Lend me some money?' he said. 'I owe . . .'

'I could lend you some money or I could talk to the guards . . .'

'Never mind,' he said quickly, shaking his head.

I dug out my wallet. 'How much do you need?'

'Fifty,' he said, through his fingers.

I found two twenties. 'That's the best I can do right now.' I held them out. 'But I want to know one thing first . . .'

'What?' he said, looking from the cash to me.

'Who's running the spice inside?'

'Come on . . .'

'There was a guy here until recently,' I said. 'Short Back and Sides, does that name—' But he'd already started laughing.

'Sides? Think I'd be shitting it over fifty quid to Sides? All he'd do's kill me.' I waited, watching the courage rise up inside him. 'It's worse than that,' he said, voice dropping to a whisper.

I became conscious of the pulse beating in my ears. 'Is it Zain Carver?'

'*Voice down*,' he hissed. 'Jesus fucking Christ.'

I nodded and handed over the cash. 'Are the guards in on it?'

'Everyone's in on it. Screws get the stuff in, the dealers sell it on . . .'

'If the guards are just muling, then why are they giving you trouble?'

'Doesn't matter,' he said, rummaging round inside a pillow. 'You asked about this . . .' He took out a crumpled envelope and I accepted it. It was addressed to Martin Wick in clear, expressive handwriting. Inside were numerous paper clippings but they were all photographs of the smiling, twelve-year-old Lizzie Moore.

I felt my head sink lower, repulsed by Wick's obsession with the girl.

'Right,' I said finally.

'They're skimming him,' whispered Adam.

I looked up from the envelope. 'The guards are skimming Carver?'

He nodded, then looked at the fist that my notes had disappeared inside. 'I think I'd like to be on my own now.'

I got up and put a hand on his shoulder.

Leaving the cell, I looked back, then down the walkway at the guard who'd led us in. He'd been too far away to hear our conversation and I was grateful. If they really were double-crossing Carver, they'd kill to keep it a secret.

4

'Think you're really slick, don't you?' said Naomi.

We were leaving Strangeways, passing slowly through security. Hatton had one of the guards waiting for us with a box full of Wick's correspondence. It wasn't much and, given what Adam had said about his literacy, I wasn't expecting revelations. I signed the release form and took it.

'Slick? What do you mean?'

'You made sure I was sitting closest to him, you let me say everything he didn't want to hear.'

'I'm really not that good—'

'It wasn't good, it was stupid and manipulative.'

'I'm sorry you feel that way.'

She paused for a second as a guard passed. 'It's not my pride that's damaged, it's that man in there. Did you see the state of his arms?'

'Of course I did.'

'No sympathy, though?'

'Is that what you think?'

'I work with what I'm given,' she said. 'You can't go around treating everyone you meet like Short Back and Sides. Sutty must've really rubbed off on you.'

I laughed. 'Please rephrase that statement.'

The final door opened and she walked ahead of me, through to the car park. I followed, wondering if she was right. I'd started working with Sutty with a sense of dawning horror, despising his cynicism and cruelty. It occurred to me that Naomi might think of me the same way. When I caught up with her I put the box on the back seat and got in on the passenger side.

'What did he say after I'd gone?' she asked.

I looked back at the walls of the prison. Thought about the envelope that Adam had given to me. The self-harm scars covering his arms and the debt he owed. The involvement of the guards and, worst of all, the man he was so afraid of. The man I was afraid of, too.

Naomi didn't need Zain Carver in her life, no one did.

'He didn't say anything,' I said. 'Just wanted to apologize for snapping.'

'Why don't I believe you?'

'You're a born cynic, Naomi.'

5

We were back at the Park, working our way through more than a decade's worth of Martin Wick's correspondence, most of it in the form of legal letters, when the phone rang. 'Waits,' I said, glancing up at Naomi. She put her letter down and, without looking at me, picked up the extension to listen in.

'This is Linklater, we spoke earlier . . .' The techie who Superintendent Parrs had pressed into action on Esther's phone had taken the job grudgingly, telling us it was unlikely he'd be able to pull anything from it, and resenting that he had to keep the work from his colleagues. A part of me had hoped that was the last I'd ever hear from him. '. . . I think you should probably come down here. Can you drop by now?'

I knew it was unlikely that he'd broken into the phone, so the service provider must have come through with the call records. *Fuck*, I thought. *Fuck. Fuck. Fuck.*

'Well . . .' I said, testing the water. Naomi's eyes flicked up at me. 'Of course, we'll be right with you.' I hung up, collected my jacket and left the room without speaking to her. Maybe she wouldn't follow and I'd have some chance of containing this.

I went directly to the lift and pressed the button without looking back.

When I got inside she was right behind me.

Linklater was waiting for us by his office door, eager to get this over with.

'It's good news and bad news, I'm afraid,' he said, ushering us in. 'What you've got here's an X, the latest model. We can break androids and Samsungs like there's no tomorrow, but Apple see it as a challenge. Each new generation outpaces the tech. In a month or two, I'll probably be able to get into this no problem, but . . .' He shrugged.

'So what's the next step?' said Naomi.

'Usually, I'd suggest making a warrant application to Apple.'

'Are they helpful?'

'Rarely, and you'd be handing the phone over for a few months. As I say, by then we'd probably be able to get inside ourselves. The question is, why would a homeless woman be using the latest iPhone?'

'And the answer?'

'It was stolen,' he said, smiling between us. 'I couldn't get into the phone itself, and we're still waiting on the data from the service provider, but I found a print.'

'It's already been printed,' I said.

'Not on the SIM card. I lifted a partial.'

I read the Post-it note he handed me and closed my eyes.

'Kevin Blake?' said Naomi, leaning over me. 'Kevin *fucking* Blake?'

'So there's nothing else you can tell us about the handset?' I confirmed, feeling the paper beginning to tear in my hand.

He shook his head. 'But now you've got the name of the owner, you can talk to him. Get inside using his biometrics.'

I nodded, but somehow I had to stop that from happening.

'Parrs made it clear that this stays between us?' I said.

'Ex-cop involved in a murder plot? I don't even want to know about it.'

I nodded, got up and left the room. If we took the phone to Blake and he unlocked it, we'd find Louisa Jankowski's number inside. I'd have no control over the following sequence of events.

Her arrest, swiftly followed by mine.

I didn't look at Naomi when we got into the lift.

'We need to do this quietly,' she said.

I was watching the floors go by, trying to breathe normally. My vision was blurred, gone static with sunspots.

'You're jumping the gun,' I said at length. 'We need to put Parrs in the picture, think it through. We've strayed pretty far from official channels already, arresting a former police officer might push us over the edge.'

'Not arresting, just speaking to. We need to get into that phone and—'

'There'll be a time for that,' I said, checking my watch as we exited the lift.

I walked on, light-headed, straight into the toilets, where I locked myself in a cubicle and ripped open the top button of my shirt. My ears popped, ringing painfully, and I dug my fingernails into my knees, trying not to panic. I let out one anguished scream into my forearm, trying to muffle the sound. At length the ringing in my ears subsided, and I could hear myself gasping for breath.

I could only think of one thing to do, and I returned to the office before I could talk myself out of it, collecting my jacket and telling Naomi there was somewhere I needed to be.

'As ever,' she said.

I went on, trying to ignore her tone. 'I'll speak to Parrs but I wouldn't expect anything more on this today.' She frowned. 'We've done good work here. We've got some promising leads, we just need to attack them in the right way.' I was speaking too quickly, acting too strange. 'I'll see you tomorrow.'

I left the room before she could formulate a response. As the lift descended I felt a rush, and held out my hand to see it shaking. The phone belonging to Kevin Blake was a jaw-dropping development, a connection between the former detective responsible for Martin Wick's conviction and the young woman who we suspected of his murder.

That connection could be anything.

Perhaps she'd stolen it, targeted him because of his involvement with the case. Perhaps he'd given it to her. The fact that she was able to access the device implied the latter to me. Either way, Naomi was right. The next logical step would have been speaking to him and finding out, but I was operating outside of all logic now.

I exited the building and crossed the car park.

'Aidan,' I heard. I turned to see that Naomi had followed me outside. 'Tell me what the fuck's going on here.'

'I don't know what you're talking about, Constable.'

She hesitated at my invocation of rank. 'Am I missing something? We should be following up on the Blake angle right now. This could be the thread that leads us to Esther, to Wick's killer.'

'I agree, and we will follow it up. Tomorrow morning.'

I turned towards the car.

'That's not good enough,' she said. 'If this were anyone else we'd be bringing him in right now. If I didn't know better I'd think you were intentionally stalling.'

'But you do know better,' I said, turning to face her.

'Do I? You've been dragging your heels from day one, resisting every new lead, throwing underarm to every person we interview . . .' I shook my head but she went on. 'You've even disobeyed the Superintendent's orders to look into this threat against you, even after I went into the files and brought the complaints to your attention. What is it, are they genuine?'

'Do I look like I go round beating people up?'

She hesitated for a second and I shook my head.

'I think someone's trying to compromise you,' she said, recovering. 'Sometimes I think—'

'Sometimes you think what?'

'Sometimes I think they already have.'

'What are you trying to do here, Naomi?'

'I'm trying to take your word as something I can trust. You're making it impossible.'

'I'm not making it anything,' I said. 'This is just a personality clash.'

'Then maybe I should join the official investigation.' She saw the surprise in my face. 'James offered me a place this morning.'

'Yeah,' I said, looking about me. 'Maybe you should. We have different ways of doing things.'

'Fuck you, don't put this on me. I follow leads and you pretend they don't exist.'

'That's one way of looking at it.'

'Well, name another,' she said. 'I'm all ears.'

'All ears, I couldn't put it better myself.'

'What's that supposed to mean?'

'That there's only so much that I can say while you're around.'

'I'm your fucking partner, dickhead.'

'And we both know why.'

'Enlighten me,' she said through her teeth.

'To pass anything I say and do on to Parrs. Deny it.'

'Bullshit, I don't have to.'

'No,' I said, turning to the car. 'You don't.'

'Do you know why I did volunteer for this job, Aidan? Really?'

I heard the shake in her voice and looked around.

'Because I fucking *liked* you.' From the look on her face it was plain that she was telling the truth. 'Because I fucking wanted to work with you.' I opened my mouth to speak but the words wouldn't come. She read my expression and shook her head. 'And that literally hadn't crossed your mind as a possibility, had it? You're not *well*,' she said with some feeling. 'I don't know if it's this case, Zain Carver, this stuff with your family—'

'That's right, you don't know.'

'But you're not thinking clearly. You need help.'

'We'll talk about it in the morning,' I said, turning back to the car, feeling my chest closing, eyes misting over. When I started up and pulled out she was still standing there, stunned, looking at nothing. I made it as far as the first corner before I pulled over, killed the engine and started to beat the steering wheel with both fists, trying to fight off another attack.

6

I went home and poured gin into a glass until it threatened to flow over the brim. Then I sat down and drank as it grew dark outside, staving off my second or third panic attack of the day.

As soon as Kevin Blake unlocked the phone, it would lead the police to Jankowski, and she would most certainly lead them to me. The cash and the passport would look like payment for murdering Martin Wick, and with my reputation, a history of violence, drug abuse and breaking the rules, a life sentence would swiftly follow. Police officers didn't last long inside Strangeways, and there was a pen and a pad of paper beside me on the floor. I was out of ideas and, with shaking hands, I'd begun writing a suicide note.

I'd found myself thinking more and more about Tessa Klein.

Her car abandoned by the river with the doors wide open. I was wondering if I could do likewise, leave a letter suggesting I'd killed myself and then disappear. I'd written one word, *Dear*, before my plan collapsed in on itself and I'd had to laugh. I couldn't think of anyone to address it to. Besides, without the passport, how far could I get, anyway?

When my phone started to vibrate, I welcomed the distraction.

'Waits,' I said, picking up.

'Yes, hello, Mr Waits, we spoke yesterday . . .'

The social worker who'd called about my mother. I took a very long drink.

'Sandra, I thought I asked you not to contact me again . . .'

'I am aware of that,' she said, some urgency in her voice. 'The situation's changed.'

'How so?'

'As I said, we received a warrant to enter your mother's premises—'

'I'm sorry, could you refer to this woman as Christine, please? Or Mrs Whatever?'

'OK, yes of course. We were hoping to make an assessment with regards—'

'And I'm a police officer, Sandra, I'm familiar with the process.'

'I see. Well, I decided not to serve the warrant until I'd made contact with your sister, erm . . .'

'Anne,' I said. 'And I thought we'd agreed that you wouldn't do that?'

'With respect, Mr Waits, that isn't your decision to make. Particularly given that you yourself admit to being estranged from your sister.'

'Separated,' I said levelly.

'I really am trying to do the right thing here.'

'I'm sorry,' I said. 'I don't want you to think I'm being confrontational about this, and I know it's not an easy job, believe me. We're just talking about someone who was bad news for us all the way round. I'd rather my sister was left to get on with her own life.'

'In any event, I decided to delay proceedings until I'd at least spoken with her, but I'm afraid your mother, Mrs Farrow, was hospitalized last night.'

'What happened?'

'She tried to take her own life.'

My eyes went to the notepad beside me on the floor. 'Right,' I said, climbing to my feet, trying to get away from it.

'I thought you might want to know.'

'Of course. Thank you.'

'Now, more than ever, it would be invaluable to have a member of Christine's family present when we make our intervention. I don't know if last night's events in any way alter your feelings?'

'You're still making the intervention?'

'It might seem insensitive, but the problem here is that we can't guarantee her safety. With proper care—'

'It sounds like if you just forget about it she'll solve all your problems, Sandra. And mine. I say leave her to it.'

She didn't speak for a second.

'I'm sorry, Mr Waits. You asked me not to contact you and I did. The mistake was mine and I won't make it again. Good evening.'

'Hang on—'

She disconnected the call before I could say anything else. It seemed like a fair reaction. I stood there, the phone dead in my ear, staring at the notepad. It had always been tempting to think of my mother as a malevolent force, a simplistic idea of everything wrong with the world, but I knew she'd only ever been beaten down by life, trapped in mundane ways.

Emotionally, economically, mentally.

By the difficulties of being a single mother suffering with undiagnosed schizophrenia. By the manipulative and violent man who'd moved, unpredictably, in and out of our young lives. And she had been young when I was born. An image came into my mind of her holding me in a hospital bed, alone, as she almost certainly would have been, and I wished that I could have been there as an adult, somehow. Someone should have been with her, I thought, someone should have held her hand.

I kicked the notepad across the room and tried to confront the reality of my situation. Within twenty-four hours I'd be behind bars, and my only hope of escape was in the possession of an unstable firearms officer who expected me to clear her name.

Draining my glass, a kind of lightness came over me.

I'd been reluctant to follow the Superintendent's orders, to look into the threat against me. Even when Naomi provided evidence of how deep Carver's grudge went, the work he'd done to tarnish my name, I'd known that speaking to him again would only shorten my lifespan. That seemed like a moot point now. So I slammed my glass down and went for the door.

Perhaps I could use my last few hours to help someone else.

7

The Light Fantastic felt like a gateway into another world. It was a modestly sized club which had appeared seemingly overnight a couple of years before, becoming a fixture for people who could afford not to look at their bill.

I'd been avoiding the place since I found out who owned it and I was confused when the man at the door greeted me like a regular, ushering me inside without paying the cover charge.

The room was big enough for a few hundred people, but it was only around half full. Low-key electronic music played from unseen speakers overhead, but the real soundtrack came from the tables. Some of them were booths, built into the walls, and some were discreet circulars made for two. From all of them came the buzz of easy conversation, the sound of confidence and accord, and most of all, laughter. Whatever was happening in the outside world, times were good for the patrons of the Light Fantastic. They'd inherited good times when they were born and they'd pass them on to their gilded children again when they died.

I was heading for the bar when a hostess glided towards me. She wore a black cocktail dress and had a smile that looked like the answer to all of life's problems.

'Good evening, Mr Waits,' she said, surprising me. 'This way, please.'

I hesitated a second and then followed her further inside, dissolving into the surreal, neon gloom, passing beaming, smartly dressed members of staff. Their smiles, the whites of their eyes, caught ultraviolet lights which seemed positioned for the purpose, making them glow with synthetic, electric youth.

I was seated at a moodily lit table for two.

'Will anyone be joining you?' asked the hostess.

'I don't think . . .' I trailed off as Naomi emerged from the darkness and sat at the table opposite me. 'It's just the two of us.'

The waitress smiled and vanished in the same movement.

'Always wondered what you did with your evenings,' said Naomi.

'How did you find me here?'

'I'm a detective,' she said, looking about her. 'I followed you. Nicer than the last place we drank in.'

'Don't be so sure.'

The hostess reappeared with a tray, carrying two frosted tumblers filled with Hennessy on ice.

Naomi looked at her. 'Where does the Light Fantastic come from?'

'It's Milton,' said the hostess, pleased to be asked. '*Come and trip it as you go, on the light fantastic toe.*'

'Do they make you memorize that?'

The girl smiled. 'I'm studying for my masters in English. Now, Mr Waits, if there's anything else I can do for you, please press here . . .' She indicated a small button built into the table. It looked like a silent alarm, except it had a smile and a drink on the other end instead of the police. She took a step back, made a slight bow and sank into the darkness.

Naomi examined her drink. 'Well, here's to your health.'

'It feels like a lost cause,' I said, touching my glass to hers anyway. Our eyes met, differently than before, and I broke away first, taking a mouthful of Hennessy, feeling it go glowing right through me. Our relationship was complicated enough without looking at her for too long. 'If you want to come up with me then you should have a drink.'

'Why?' she said, searching my eyes again.

'The man upstairs probably won't see us until you do. The drinks are on him, and he likes to own a little bit of everybody . . .'

211

She took a drink. 'How much of you does he own?'

'You really think that, don't you?'

She shrugged. 'You're drinking in his club, the staff all know your name . . .'

'I've never been here before tonight. I've never met that girl or the man on the door. As for him owning me? Parrs says he's got my soul, you've got my balls, the force has my brain, I don't know what that leaves . . .'

'Your heart?' she said, suppressing a smile.

We both had to laugh. 'For some reason I can't give it away.'

She looked down into her drink and her face straightened. 'You could always just tell me what it is between you . . .'

'You don't want to know,' I said, as I saw someone drawing towards us.

'We appreciate your patience,' said the hostess. 'Mr Carver can see you now.'

I downed the rest of my drink and held out the glass. 'We'll need two more of these.'

8

We followed the young woman back of house, up a steel spiral staircase. By the time we reached the top my glass was empty again. Just as the hostess reached a closed door and raised a hand to knock, it slammed open, and another young woman in an identical black dress walked by, covering her face. Naomi gave me a concerned look but I thought we'd probably done her a favour by interrupting them.

Zain Carver was a magician when it came to ruining women's lives. He surrounded himself with these beautiful young assistants and then delighted in sawing them up, making them disappear. Sometimes a new girl on his arm might end up on the game, or in hospital, or back with her parents feeling five years older, a permanent faraway look in her eyes.

Sometimes you just never saw them again.

I felt the temperature dropping as we stepped into his office. It was roomy, dark and minimally lit from unobtrusive light sources. The hostess motioned us to two seats and then nodded at the hibernating psychopath sitting behind the desk. When I'd first met him he'd dressed in cutting-edge streetwear, on the high end of what his young customers could afford, camouflaging himself against them. Now, he wore a tailored designer suit, the suggestion that he was moving through a different strata of people.

He smiled, letting his eyes trail after his hostess, even once she'd stepped through the door and closed it, like he could sense her on the other side, listening.

'Good evening, Aidan.' He let his eyes drift over to me. 'Or should I call you Detective Sergeant Waits now? I hope you don't mind me presuming on your choice of drink. I thought we should toast your promotion, for old times' sake . . .'

'Let's not dwell on the past.'

'You should give it a go. From what I hear, you might not have much of a future. You seem to be dry, there,' he said, nodding at my glass.

I'll have anything as long as you drink from the same bottle first.'

Carver got up, poured us both enormous measures of Hennessy and then held the bottle up to Naomi. She watched, unmoved, as he filled her glass.

'No ice, I'm afraid . . .'

He stared at her for several seconds until I interrupted. 'You could always chip off a bit of your heart for us if we get desperate.'

He smiled. 'won't you introduce us, Aidan?'

'Zain Carver, this is Detective Constable Black.'

'Naomi,' he said, perching on the corner of the desk, bottle in hand. 'Is it OK if I call you that?' She nodded. 'How's your dad getting on, Naomi?'

She looked from Carver to me.

'He's fine . . .'

'He's back at home, then?'

Her mouth moved but she couldn't quite speak.

'You're quite an upgrade on his last partner.' His eyes moved to me. 'I hear he's sleeping on the job a lot, these days?'

'That's what we came here to talk to you about,' I said, steering the conversation away from Naomi. Carver raised his eyebrows, got up and sat back behind his desk.

'I really hope you didn't. I'm square now, Aidan.'

'And what does that mean? Sharp on all four corners?'

'Sounds like you're the sharp one tonight. It means I've been so busy with the club I haven't kept up with the news. Why would you want to talk to me about all that?'

'You've heard of Martin Wick?'

'This guy who butchered his family . . .'

'Someone else's family. He was lying in St Mary's, days away from death. Then someone broke in and sped up the process.'

He nodded. 'If you ever find his killer you should give him the keys to the city.'

'Him?' said Naomi.

'I apologize,' said Carver, looking at her. 'Everyday sexism. Whatever their pronouns, I don't know them.'

'Wick's killer also took out a cop,' she said.

'You're fond of cops, then, these days?' She didn't say anything. 'I thought, what with all those years you didn't talk to your dad, you must have some kind of problem with them.'

She smiled and spoke to the floor. 'Am I supposed to be impressed by this, Zain? You should hear some of the shit they say about you.'

'Nah, you shouldn't be impressed by me looking you up. We all do extensive research on our new friends, don't we? I could have saved you some time pulling Aidan's records, though. The good stuff's all between the lines . . .'

Carver kept various police officers on his payroll.

Some through blackmail and intimidation, others through untraceable cash payments made on the first of every month. It was his business to know what was going on, who'd been promoted and why, and it had kept his record clear for more than ten years of organized crime. He occasionally liked to let it slip as a flex, though. A reminder that this city was his, and we were just living here.

'We were talking about Martin Wick,' I said.

'So I changed the subject to one I actually know about. Why would I be interested in him?'

'Because I was supposed to be on the ward at the time of his execution. Someone with your access to police intelligence would have known that.'

'*Police intelligence,*' he said satirically.

'You know I've been promoted, you know Constable Black's family history . . .'

'Lucky guesses . . .'

'And there's a price on my head.' No one spoke for a moment and I continued. 'You put it there. One theory is that I was the intended target of the hit. Wick, Rennick and Sutty were all collateral damage.'

He let the playfulness fall away from his voice. 'You know I had nothing to do with this.'

'How do we know that?' said Naomi.

Carver nodded at me and I answered for him.

'He wouldn't have fucked it up,' I said. 'I assume you've got an alibi for Saturday night?'

'I could get an alibi for this fucking conversation if I wanted one. I could put you through that window with her as an eyewitness and get the mayor to swear blind I was at his house.'

I waited.

'I was at home,' he said, twisting the wedding band on his finger.

'Congratulations.'

'Everyone has to settle down one day.'

'We'll need to confirm that alibi with your wife,' said Naomi. 'Can we have her contact details?'

'Over your dead body.' He smiled. 'I can prove it without involving her, though. There's round-the-clock police surveillance outside my house, you could check in with them.' Naomi looked at me, uncertain of what to say. 'I'll make it easy,' said Carver, taking up a pen, making a note and handing it to her. 'That's the licence plate of the unmarked car they had out there that night. Your colleagues can vouch for me, I'm sure. Anything else I can do for you?'

'Thanks,' she said, accepting the note. 'You being at home doesn't put you in the clear, though. A man of your means might farm out the job, button man, getaway driver . . .'

Now Zain laughed for real. One of the few occasions I'd ever seen him do so.

'Let me explain something about a man of my means. First, it wouldn't have been this hospital clusterfuck that could get innocent people killed. Not my style. Not my style at all. Second, a getaway driver? Do it right and you can walk off whistling with your hands in your pockets. Third, and most importantly, the timing would have been perfect.'

'Perfect how?' she said.

'Why would anyone kill Aidan while he's still a cop? Why bring the world down on your head when he's so soon for the chopping block anyway?' He stared at Naomi. 'I think a man of my means would bide his time. Add a few grand to the vig every so often, just to keep some blood in the water, some sharks circling. Just to make sure Aidan's name and address is in all their little black books. A man of my means would make things clear. Not a penny paid if he dies on duty. Then a man of my means would just wait while the complaints stack up against the spiralling fucking sad-sack, wouldn't he?'

'Complaints?' said Naomi.

'Another lucky guess, but you must have noticed he can be a bit heavy-handed? Ask yourself why he's been promoted all of a sudden? For failing to prevent a bloodbath? They've got more dirt on him than Earth Day. They just need a decent-sized head to roll when all this goes tits-up. After that?' he said, with a smile. 'He's fair game. After that, whatever happens, happens. After that I could do him in broad daylight, walk off whistling with my hands in my pockets.'

'Why do you want him dead?' she asked, surprising both Carver and me.

Zain smiled. 'You wouldn't believe it if I told you. What was her name again, Aidan?'

'That's enough,' I said, standing up.

'It's almost like she dropped off the face of the earth, isn't it? How long's it been, now? Two, three years?'

'You want me to believe all this is over some woman?' Naomi's voice shook but she looked between us. 'Come on, we're not worth it.'

'It's worth over a hundred grand to me,' said Carver.

Naomi shook her head. 'That'd be the highest-paid hit on record . . .'

'That's because the only ones on record are the ones who get caught. There's no ceiling, believe me. Plus, we'd be talking about Aidan as an ex-cop,' he said, weighing me up. 'And there'd be the special instructions to consider . . .'

'Such as?' said Naomi, trying to sound like she was still in control.

I started to interrupt.

'*Make it painful*,' said Carver.

We all sat in silence, letting it sink in.

'Is he good to you, Constable Black?'

'We're partners,' she said.

'Look how that worked out for the last one. They drop like flies around you, though, don't they, Aid? Must be getting hard to keep track. You should get a little tear tattooed on your face for each one . . .'

I nodded. 'If I recall correctly, some of those tears would belong to you.'

'The difference is I'm not crying about them. Don't go buying this sad man routine, Nae. Once the switch flips, he can turn in a second.'

'Speaking of tears, we were talking to Wick's ex-cellmate earlier.'

'Oh yeah?' said Carver. 'Where's he?'

'Strangeways.'

'Never had the pleasure, myself. I can't get arrested in this town.'

'Don't bet on it. He was telling me about the spice racket inside . . .' Carver didn't say anything but his smile seemed to freeze, and I felt Naomi looking at me. 'I couldn't believe what I was hearing,' I said. 'A man like you, involved in prison distribution for a homeless drug. I knew you'd fallen from grace but crime must pay like a fucking paper round these days.'

'Your point?' he said, the smile twisting from his face.

'I think you know the guy's getting a hard time from the guards.'

'Sounds like he should keep his mouth shut, then.'

'About them skimming your cash?' I said, finally getting round to the real reason I'd come here. Naomi's appearance had forced me to pay lip service to Parrs's ludicrous suggestion that Carver was involved with Wick's murder, but I believed the man sitting opposite me. If he wanted me dead, I wouldn't be here.

'Skimming,' he said, becoming thoughtful. 'Is that so?'

'It is,' I said. 'If he whispered it in the right ear, maybe the guy's time might pass a bit easier?'

Carver looked genuinely concerned. One of the reasons he manipulated people so easily was an effortless access to great stores of empathy. He just used it in a different way.

'Having it rough, is he?'

'Very.'

He nodded. 'If there's any truth in it, I'm sure someone would be grateful to know.' He smiled. 'I knew you must be here for a good reason.'

'The drinks helped,' I said, standing up, eager to leave before anything else was said or done. Naomi went ahead but I wasn't fast enough, and I turned when Carver called after me.

'I was sorry to hear about that former detective constable who went missing,' he said. 'What was her name again?'

It took me a moment to answer. 'Tessa Klein?'

'That was it.'

The way he smiled made my blood run cold. 'They sent her undercover to get to you, didn't they?'

'She committed suicide, from what I heard,' he said, the smile vanishing from his face. 'Is it normal for the body not to turn up?'

I shook my head.

'Well, I s'pose it's always the last place you look, eh? Don't come here again, Aid. You might end up beside her. I've seen guys flirting with disaster before, but you walk it home hoping for a kiss.'

I nodded and began backing out of the room. 'Everyone has a type.'

9

'One for the road?' I said, as we reached the bottom of the spiral staircase. Naomi walked straight through the bar and out on to the street in answer, and I followed. 'Wait,' I called after her, as she walked ahead.

'What the fuck was that?' she said, wrapping her arms round herself.

'A day in the life.'

'Jesus Christ, Aidan.' She shook her head and we walked on in silence for a minute, crossing Piccadilly towards the Northern Quarter. 'Swear to me you're not in his pocket.'

'I'd rather die than be in his pocket,' I said.

'So what is it between you two?'

'It's everything.'

'Go on.'

'He let his guard down around me, once.' As we walked on I felt a dull, numbing pain in my right knee. 'I think I must have let mine down, too.'

'This woman?' She stopped walking and looked at me. 'Look, I get it. There's a storied past, but if we're gonna keep working together I need to know what's at the root and how deep it goes.'

I nodded, down at the ground, saw people passing us on the pavement.

'We were both in love with her,' I said finally.

'Fuck.' Neither of us spoke for a moment. 'What happened to her?'

I tried to steady my voice. 'When Zain's finished with someone they tend to go missing. I guess he was finished with her.'

'Fuck . . .'

'She wasn't the first, she won't be the last.'

Naomi shook her head. 'How . . . how does he get away with it?'

'Young women, runaways, some sex-trafficked, some with drug offences or mental health problems. No one cares.'

'You do,' she said.

We started walking again. 'And what makes you think that?'

'I heard he had you beaten black and blue . . .'

'As well some other colours I didn't think my skin could manage.'

She smiled. 'Then the way I see it, you must have done something right.' We walked on in silence for a minute, and I could see she was still thinking. 'You said young women with mental health problems . . .'

'After you left his office, he mentioned Tessa Klein.'

'We need to tell Parrs, we need to—'

'No,' I said. 'We tell no one.'

'He implied he's involved in a police officer's murder.'

'And Parrs probably sent her there. He's the one who sent me.'

'So, what? We're just stuck between them?'

'Like having a devil on each shoulder.'

'Tell me you've got something to drink . . .'

When I got my key in the door and looked back, we were inches apart, and I felt glad that she was with me. Glad, in a sudden rush, to be alive. She gave me a small smile and I hesitated, trying to ignore how much I wanted her, trying, consciously, to enjoy the feeling anyway. We climbed the stairs in silence but there were voices on the landing, and I saw Robbie, my new neighbour, talking to a young woman.

'Here he is,' he said.

Louisa Jankowski turned to me with a smile. Her lipstick was fire-engine red, matching the dress she was wearing. Her smile didn't change when she saw Naomi standing beside me.

'Hey you,' she said, touching my arm. 'Did I get the wrong night?' Before I could turn to Naomi I heard her footsteps going down the stairs, the door opening and then banging shut behind her.

10

I opened my flat and walked in without speaking to either Robbie or Louisa. I went to the window, still in the dark, and stood facing it until I heard the door close behind me. Louisa switched on the light and I turned. She was standing with her back to the wall, one foot against it, wearing a high voltage red cocktail dress and heels. There was a small black purse on her shoulder but I could see that she hadn't brought back my bag.

'Was I interrupting something?'

I just looked at her.

'You tried to fuck me,' she said.

'I really didn't.'

'Not in quite the same way you were trying to fuck your constable . . .' She pushed herself off the wall and walked into the centre of the room. '. . . But you swapped the phone.' I didn't think she needed any more animosity towards Naomi so I nodded. 'That wasn't a good idea,' she said, coming closer.

'I was afraid of what you might do if it led you to Esther, but I'm still trying to keep you out of it, I'm really trying.'

'How?' she said, angling her head to one side. 'I know it's already gone to tech support at the Park.'

'But the call data hasn't come back yet. They can't get inside it.'

'What if Esther turns up?'

I was afraid that she wanted to find the girl, to make sure that couldn't happen. 'The phone was actually stolen from someone else,' I said.

'From who?'

'I can't tell you that.'

'Why not?'

'Because I don't want them to get hurt, either.'

She smiled, taking two more steps so she was right in front of me. 'Sometimes it's better to see eye to eye, don't you think? Do you know how easily I could ruin you?'

'I know, the passport.'

'Oh, more than that. It's no wonder you didn't want me reading that letter to your sister, it's like a signed confession. When was the last time you did amphetamines, by the way?'

'You said we'd leave her out of this.'

'She's not the one you should be worrying about . . .'

'Ruin me and you're on your own.'

'Tell me who the phone belongs to and I'll give your things back. Cash, passport, letter. You can leave tonight if that's what you want.'

I closed my eyes, rubbed my face, tried not to look like I was thinking about it. Finally, I shook my head.

'You think I'd hurt them?' she said.

'I just wouldn't want to underestimate you again, Louisa. You don't happen to drive a black Mercedes, by any chance?'

'On my salary? I'm afraid not. Do I take that to mean that there's someone else keeping tabs on you?' She laughed. 'Remember who got here first, yeah? Why don't we have a drink, put our heads together and—'

'There's nothing to drink here.'

'Try that line on someone who hasn't searched your flat.' Her skirt brushed against my leg. 'I'm sure it wasn't the line that you were about to try on young Constable Black . . .'

'What happened to you?' I said.

225

'I killed a man.' The words seemed to disturb her. 'From what you wrote to your sister, I thought you might know the feeling . . .'

For a few seconds I couldn't speak.

'From what I hear,' I said, responding selectively, 'you saved a dozen more.'

'Exactly.' Her eyes shone with a film of tears. 'It's all a game. Taking one life might win you a dozen . . .'

'Have you talked to a professional about this?'

'You have to take chances,' she said, as if I hadn't spoken. 'The bigger the better.'

'One day you might lose everything.'

'But not today.' She wiped her eyes. 'I gambled on you and now you're mine . . .'

'As far as I see it, we're even.'

'Oh?'

'You've got something that could kill me, I've got something that could kill you. Neither one of us wants the other dead, so let's just call it a night, OK?'

She swallowed, putting a clumsy hand to my neck. 'Keen to get your head down?' she said. Her skin was freezing cold and it occurred to me that she must have been waiting outside for some time before Robbie let her in. I began to get a sense of how lonely she was. 'We don't have to be enemies . . .'

'No,' I said, removing her hand.

'Have it your way.' She turned for the door, spurned, forgetting me already. 'But don't ever try and fuck me again.' She didn't look back when she left, and I heard heels going down the stairs to the street entrance.

'Same to you,' I said, once I was sure she'd gone.

I found my phone and scrolled to Naomi's number, wondering what I'd say now. I needn't have worried, though. I got three rings before she sent me to voicemail. When I called back again her phone was switched off.

V
Into the Fire

1

It was still early so I waited until I saw lights on inside the house. I gave them another half hour then walked up the path and knocked. A large man of mixed race came to the door wearing a towel, regarding me with some confusion.

'Morning,' I said. 'I'm looking for Naomi.'

'Aidan Waits . . .'

'My reputation precedes me.'

'You could say that.'

He looked me up and down, then called over his shoulder.

I thought he might invite me in or at least go back inside and carry on getting dressed, but he left me on the doorstep, watching me like I was a vampire. When Naomi appeared, still pulling on her jacket, she froze at the sight of me, then came forward, touching the man's arm to signal that he could leave.

'How do you know where I live?'

'I'm a detective, too,' I said. 'Sometimes.'

'And?'

'And I wanted to apologize for—'

'Time for school!'

I looked over Naomi's shoulder and saw an elderly black man staring at us. Then the young man who'd opened the door for me put an arm round him, telling him that Naomi's friend was taking her to school today.

When I looked at Naomi she waved me quiet, stepped through the door and closed it behind her. The morning birds were still singing in the trees, and we were both washed grey by a sunless, overcast sky.

'Your reticence around this case,' she said. 'The leads not followed, the mood swings. Disappearing on the job, acting weird when I turned up at your flat, it all makes sense. You're screwing Louisa Jankowski.'

It was one of several conclusions she could have come to, and when I lowered my head to think of a response she took it as a nod in the affirmative.

'Oh, Aidan . . .' I saw that I'd travelled in her estimation again, only this time I was sure of the direction. 'That's why you didn't want to question her,' said Naomi. 'Christ, that's why you hardly said a word when we did. How long's it been going on?'

'Not long.'

'Not good enough. How long?'

'I guess we met while working protective custody for Martin Wick.'

'She only joined that detail two weeks before the attack,' said Naomi. 'I looked at your shift overlaps. You met her for the first time twelve days ago.'

'I suppose I work fast.'

'On everything except murder cases. Why didn't you tell me?'

'How could I?'

'How couldn't you? I must have looked like an idiot when we interviewed her.'

'No one could make you look like an idiot,' I said.

'Well, I fucking feel like one. Are you still together?' I shook my head. 'Because of the case? Or because you were taking me home last night?'

'Is that what I was doing?'

'It might be what you think you were doing. You work fast, remember.'

'Louisa and me were a one-time thing,' I said. It seemed like the most harmless explanation. 'We just got our wires crossed.'

'You mean you screwed her once and didn't call?' I nodded. 'Then the next time you saw her was for questioning? No wonder she didn't want to talk to us.'

'I guess I have a problem.'

'And I guess so do I, because I can't think of one reason why I shouldn't take this to Parrs right now.'

'I can give you two,' I said. 'First, it's over between me and her. The way I see it, it never began.'

'Illuminating, Aidan. What's the second?'

'I've asked Kevin Blake to come in for an interview this morning.' She looked surprised. 'You were right, we should have spoken to him yesterday.'

'So why didn't we?'

'I was afraid for Adam's safety. I needed to talk to Carver, sort out the situation at Strangeways.'

'That's the only reason we went to the Light Fantastic, isn't it?'

'Zain's not responsible for Martin Wick's murder. I wish he was.'

She looked at me for a long moment. I saw that whatever brief connection we'd had the previous evening was now completely severed, and that she liked me a whole lot less.

'Blake,' she said.

I nodded. 'I want to know what his connection is with Esther, and I want to know what's on that phone. I want to work this case right.'

'I'm not sure we should be working together,' she said quietly.

'Did James really ask you to join the team?' She nodded. 'I can't do it without you,' I said.

'From what I've seen so far, you just can't do it. You're putting me in a really shit position, here.'

The way she looked at me felt like the distance between what I was and what I should be.

'Your dad,' I said, changing the subject.

231

'Dementia.'

'I didn't know.'

'Everyone has their problems, Aidan.'

She wrapped her arms round herself, staring at me, still trying to make up her mind.

2

'Thanks for coming in,' I said as Kevin Blake took a seat opposite.

Naomi and I were sitting in an interview room in Central Park station. She'd agreed to give us the day, more out of obligation to the case than to me. Now I needed to anticipate the movements of the ground falling out from under me, drive things forward without incriminating either Jankowski or myself.

'Anything I can do to help, Sergeant,' said the former detective inspector with a smile. Naomi handed him a CCTV still of Esther from St Mary's Hospital.

'We were wondering if this woman's familiar to you, at all?'

'Course.' He looked up at us. 'This is the girl Chase asked to come forward during the press conference, your person of interest. Hard face to forget.'

Naomi nodded. 'We were wondering if she was familiar to you before the conference, Mr Blake?'

'Call me Kev,' he said, looking at the image again before handing it back. He shook his head at the tattoos around her eyes. 'Afraid not. In my day, the crooks just had a steely look on their faces.'

'In that case,' she said, taking the phone we'd found at the Cornerhouse from an envelope. 'Could you confirm whether this item belongs to you?' Blake's eyelids lowered further than I thought necessary as he looked down at the phone, guarding his expression.

'May I?' he said, not looking up at us. Naomi agreed and he

examined the handset through the plastic evidence bag it was sealed inside. 'Looks like one of mine.'

'Can you explain how it came to be in possession of this young woman?' asked Naomi, nodding at the print-out of Esther.

'Not exactly,' said Blake, sitting up again, regaining some confidence. 'I had a break-in a couple of weeks back, though. This was taken.'

'Did you report this break-in?' I asked.

'Afraid it slipped my mind.'

'That seems like an unusual response from a former police officer, Kev . . .'

'Police officers are known to do unusual things, Sergeant.' It sounded like a personal attack and I thought there was a hint of annoyance in his invocation of rank.

I decided to take it away from him. 'Call me Aidan.'

'Well, Aidan, to answer your question. No, I don't think it's unusual. I meant to call it in but we had no damage, no mess, nothing of any value taken—'

'Aside from the latest model iPhone,' I said.

'We weren't really using it.' He reached inside his pocket and withdrew an identical handset. 'Fiona, my wife, and I both got upgrades at the same time. Frankly, she's still finding her way round the old one. The spare handset went into a drawer in my office.'

'There's a contract against it, though,' I pointed out.

'Yeah,' he said slowly.

'And it's locked as well. How would some random thief be able to get in?'

'I'd made a note of the pin, it was in the drawer with it.'

'And nothing else was taken during this break-in?'

'We left a window open overnight, no great mystery. Someone stepped in and grabbed a handful of stuff from around the desk. They must've been disturbed because there was a computer and TV sitting there untouched. Kids probably.'

'Either that or they knew exactly what they were after. What was this other stuff from around the desk?'

'Some papers, nothing important.'

'And when exactly was this break-in?'

He blew out his cheeks. 'I couldn't put a date on it off the top of my head.'

'You should try, the police are usually interested in those kinds of details.'

'Let's cut the attitude, all right, son?'

'Tell us what the papers were, Mr Blake.' He looked at the table, rubbing his forefingers and thumbs together like he was checking the quality of some invisible fabric. 'Were they related to Martin Wick?' I said. He glanced up for a second and I leaned forward to slide the phone back in his direction. 'I'll take that as a yes.'

'Nothing sensitive, just background information.'

'Crib notes on a mass murderer? Sounds sensitive to me.'

I leaned across the table and pressed the home button, lighting up the screen.

The background image of the Moore family.

None of us said anything for a moment.

'Feels like an unusual screensaver for your wife to pick . . .'

'When she said she didn't need it, I decided to use this phone for my writing. That's why there was a contract against it.'

Good answer, I thought, but he'd needed a minute.

'It'd take me forever to write a book on that . . .'

'I'm glad this is so funny, Sergeant. I'd decided to use it for the *research* on the new edition of my previous book.'

'Do you usually use a distinct phone for each project?'

'Yeah, on a project like this. You want to keep this stuff quarantined from your real life.'

'I should give that a try. And you didn't think it was worth mentioning to us when the subject of your book was murdered soon after the phone's theft?'

'I hadn't started the new edition yet. Obviously if there'd been anything sensitive I'd have shouted it from the rooftops.'

'Rather than from nowhere at all,' I said. 'So you set the screensaver?'

He nodded. 'I find a picture like that focuses the mind, reminds you what you're doing it for.'

'There weren't any new developments in the case between Martin Wick's incarceration and his murder,' said Naomi. 'So what would the new edition of your book focus on?'

'Wick's incarceration,' said Blake. 'I knew there'd be renewed interest in the case when he passed away, and with the cancer I knew he couldn't have long. One angle would have been his time at Strangeways.'

'We visited his old cell yesterday,' I said.

'Vile place . . .'

'I don't disagree. Well, perhaps you wouldn't mind unlocking this for us?'

I tried to sound casual but stood abruptly, my chair scraping against the floor, then walked round the desk to look over Blake's shoulder. I avoided Naomi's eye, hoping I just seemed protective of the evidence.

Blake swiped the screen up, through the plastic.

The screen unlocked and I leaned over him to retrieve the phone. First I looked at the messages, seeing none beyond automated updates from the service provider. Then I accessed the address book. There were five entries. I scrolled, too quickly, to the one marked *Louisa*, and Naomi stood.

'May I?' she said.

Time stopped, but I knew I was right at the edge of what I could get away with. Handing it over, I backed out of the address book so she wouldn't see what I'd been looking at. I walked round the table as she moved through the same process I had, freezing when she came to the firearms officer's name.

The smoking gun.

When she showed it to me I tried to look surprised. We both sat down, and I was grateful to hear that Blake's breathing had grown heavy, covering my own. He looked even paler than usual, producing a plastic tube of pills, swallowing two of them dry out of his hand.

'Perhaps you could take us through the people you've got saved here?' said Naomi. Blake nodded and I felt time speeding up again, moving in fits and starts. 'Who's Susan?'

'I mentioned that Wick was briefly married for a year when he was a younger man . . .'

'You even said you'd find the ex-wife's phone number for us.'

'Well, as you've demonstrated, Constable, that information was stolen from me. I never spoke to her for the original book but thought some background might be interesting.'

'Frank Moore,' said Naomi, still reading from the phone.

I couldn't think of a way to stop her.

'Seems self-evident. The bereaved. Some might say he's the last surviving victim of all this.'

Naomi nodded. '*Surviving* sounds like a very Frank Moore word.'

'I didn't realize he had the copyright . . .'

'Let's not give him any ideas.' She smiled. 'It was you who suggested Frank's survival seminars to us. Did you ever get along to one yourself?'

'I suggested it as an illustration of a person pulling themselves together, if I recall correctly.'

'And that wasn't something you needed to do after the original case?'

'I'm not sure I understand the question, Constable Black.'

'I'm just curious to know if you ever attended any of his sessions . . .'

'Not for me, not my kind of thing.'

'If you weren't shaken by the investigation, then why did you leave the force immediately after Martin Wick's conviction?' she asked. 'I mean, it was the case of a lifetime and you brought it home. You could have written your own ticket . . .'

'I did write my own ticket.'

'You wrote one book, ten years ago. I mean, you could be sitting in Chief Constable Cranston's chair now.'

'Again. Not for me, not my kind of thing.'

'You wouldn't say that this case destroyed you, then? Those were Frank Moore's words.'

He thumped down a fist. 'You can see me sitting here, can't you?'

'On the wrong side of the desk,' said Naomi.

'Destroy me?' He folded and unfolded his arms. 'You'll find, Constable, that I'd already handed in my notice when the Wick case arrived. I saw it through out of a sense of duty, because it was the right thing to do. It had no impact whatsoever on my leaving.' He leaned forward, pointing his finger at her. 'And if you're trying to imply some strange relationship between myself and Frank Moore then you're miles off. I've got a lot of time for Frank. As I've said, we cross paths at various charity functions—'

'Such as?'

He bristled at the interruption. 'Compassionate Friends, a charity for the family members of murdered children. The Good Grief Foundation, The Howard League—'

'That's prison reform, isn't it?' I said, hoping to hold us on this line of questioning. He nodded and I looked down at the phone. 'Is your commitment to that cause why you've got Christopher Back, aka Short Back and Sides, saved in here?'

'That would, once again, be because of his link to Martin Wick. The prospect didn't exactly fill me with joy, but he'd spent a substantial amount of time with the man.'

'Had you managed to speak to him before your phone was stolen?'

He shook his head. 'Gives me time to get hold of a hazmat suit in extra-large . . .'

'You might want to leave it on for the next guy in here,' said Naomi. 'Charlie Sloane.'

'Sloane's got a big gob and probably the world's largest collection of venereal disease, but he's a bloody good writer, and principled with it.'

'We found him helping out a young mother just yesterday,' I said.

'All I know is, he covered the Martin Wick case with sensitivity and tact twelve years ago.'

'Fair enough, but I thought this phone was for research?'

'It is.'

'Then why would you need to talk to Charlie Sloane about pieces he wrote twelve years ago?'

Blake shrugged. 'He might have information he didn't print at the time.'

'Shouldn't he have been getting all his information from you, Kev?'

'You know how the press are. Listen, are we about done here?' He gestured, vaguely, at the heart medication on the table. 'Only I've got an appointment . . .'

I nodded, ignoring the look that Naomi gave me.

I didn't want to see his reaction to Jankowski. Him not recognizing her name would confirm that Esther had saved it there, that the two of them were linked and that Jankowski was seriously involved in the case.

'We'll need to hold on to the phone,' I said, trying to get him out of the room. 'If you could jot down the passcode for us?' I slid a pen and piece of paper towards him, and Blake wrote four digits. 'Thanks,' I said, taking it back, standing, going for the door.

'Sorry, Kevin,' said Naomi. 'There's actually one number left . . .'

She turned the phone towards him and he blanched.

It was more convincing than much of what we'd seen so far.

'I don't know it.'

'What about the name?' she insisted.

He shook his head. 'I didn't save that in there. I don't know any Louisa.'

239

3

I was walking Blake out of the building, thinking about following him and not coming back. If I didn't leave now, I'd be forced to accompany Naomi while she questioned Louisa Jankowski. Faced with incriminating evidence, I had no doubt she'd show my partner the bag and send me to hell. When Blake and I reached reception without a word, I drifted slowly back to the situation at hand, asking him for his home address.

'Why?' he said, a sudden flash of authority from his former life.

'We need to send a squad car round for a statement on that break-in.'

'Is that necessary?'

'Absolutely,' I said, lying to us both.

I was grasping at straws, for some means of dragging the case away from myself. He produced a business card from inside his pocket. It looked like it had been in there a while and, by the time I was done reading his address, Blake had cleared security, stormed out of the building without looking back. That left me with the problem at hand, and I stood for too long in the lobby, feeling eyes on me, fellow officers wondering what I was doing.

A third desperate option came to mind.

I could call Louisa. Warn her away from work, out of the house, away from wherever she was.

I went to the payphone and searched calmly through my pockets for change. Then I found the number she'd texted me from and began dialling. I was halfway through when I heard someone say:

'Sergeant?'

I turned into the wall and kept dialling.

'Sergeant Waits.'

'Yes,' I said, looking towards the voice. It was a young constable.

'Superintendent Parrs asked me to check that you're not leaving . . .'

'Excuse me?'

'He'd like you to join him and Constable Black in interview room nine.'

I hung up the phone, seeing the sweat my palm had left on the receiver, then walked back through reception towards the interview rooms. Opening number nine I found Parrs leaning against the far wall staring at nothing, while Naomi sat at the table, rigid and drained.

'Superintendent.'

His red eyes fell to me. 'We thought you'd done a runner . . .'

'Just organizing a squad car to visit Blake's home.'

'You think he's connected to this junkie from the ward?'

'We don't know,' I said, wondering if I was walking into a trap. 'But I think we can row back a bit on the theory that the junkie's personally involved. The information she has on the case, maybe even her access to people like Short Back and Sides, seems to come from documents stolen from Blake's home, as well as the phone we traced to the Cornerhouse. Even the screensaver was chosen by him. She might just be some opportunist after all.'

'Not sure I'd agree, Sergeant.' His eyes lowered to the phone sitting in front of Naomi. 'I think you should probably see this . . .'

Naomi glanced up at me as I came around the table. Then she accessed the camera roll and opened the single video item. There was a flash of Esther, the girl in the green tracksuit, as she fumbled the camera. I recognized the toilets from St Mary's Hospital. The door came, shakily, into focus before opening a crack. Naomi turned

241

the volume all the way up and we could hear the murmur of voices, somewhere on the corridor, before the phone was edged out, with the camera facing in their direction.

It was the wing that Martin Wick had died on.

The camera was at a bad angle, but showed what looked like the bottom half of a man standing at the nurses station. It looked like he was talking to Rennick. Then the two of them shook hands, and the man reached suddenly across the counter. It was impossible to see exactly what happened without the top halves of their bodies in view, but this had to be the moment that someone stabbed him. Realizing the magnitude of that, and the danger she was in, Esther pulled the camera back into the toilet and the screen went black for a few seconds.

The sound of her clothes rubbing against the mic.

Her close breathing.

Then glass breaking, followed by a shout, a roar of flame. The camera was edged back out the door, catching the legs of the man leaving the ward through the fire exit. Once he was through the door, the girl started to follow and the fire alarm went off, covering everything else.

The video cut out.

Four or five seconds longer and it would have caught me passing her in the stairwell, on my way up.

Esther had been chasing the killer down.

'Congratulations,' said Parrs. 'You've just cleared your only suspect. And as far as your theory that she's not personally involved in all this . . .' He waited for Naomi to open the individual photographs. I recognized the first as that which had appeared on the front page of the *Mail*.

Cereal Killer!

Scrolling through the rest, I saw what Parrs meant.

The camera got closer and closer to Wick, moving from the doorway to his bedside. Until he was smiling at the person holding the phone. The final shot showed Esther, the woman with the tattooed face, in bed with him, one arm wrapped around his neck and the other stretched out to take the picture. It was the first time I'd seen a clear image of her face, and I became suddenly, disturbingly certain that I'd seen her before.

Worse than that, she and Martin Wick were kissing.

4

Parrs was in conference with Chief Superintendent Chase, updating her on the possible complicity of Louisa Jankowski in Martin Wick's murder, requesting her suspension for the second time.

Now I was certain that Chase would agree.

In the meantime, we had orders to track her down, and I was wondering what the fuck I'd do if we found her.

Jankowski wasn't due to report for duty until later in the day. I hadn't had time to call ahead and warn her so I'd driven us, slowly, out to her home address. Naomi had been surprised that I didn't know where she lived, and it came as an unwelcome reminder of how easily my cover story would come apart under scrutiny, how soon that was likely to happen.

'I should probably go up alone,' said Naomi. I could see that she didn't want me within fifty feet of her but I shook my head. 'Fine, but don't say I didn't try.'

We climbed out of the car, walking up the path together.

Naomi went to the building's entrance and pressed the number we'd pulled from central filing. There was only a moment's pause before the door was buzzed open, and I made sure I was ahead of my partner on the way up the stairs. I was afraid of what we might find. When we reached Jankowski's flat, the door was ajar and a young woman appeared, looking between us, confused.

'We're looking for Louisa Jankowski,' said Naomi. 'We believe she lives at this address?'

'I'm her flatmate,' said the woman. 'Is everything OK? You do know she's an officer as well?'

'We're hoping she can help us with our enquiries. It seemed like you were expecting someone?'

'I'm working from home today, waiting for a delivery.'

'Is Louisa here?'

'She didn't come home last night . . .'

Naomi glanced at me. The last time she'd seen the firearms officer, she'd been standing outside my door.

'Were you expecting her home?' I asked.

'She said she might be late, she might be staying with a friend . . .'

'Did she mention the name of this friend?' asked Naomi.

The woman shook her head. 'Some guy, I think. All very mysterious. She is OK?'

'We've got no reason to think otherwise,' said Naomi, handing the woman her card. 'I'm sure she's with this friend, but if you see or hear from her, would you let us know?'

'Of course.'

We walked back down the staircase, which seemed to grow narrower with every step, then through the door and to the car. I was undoing the top button of my shirt, trying to breathe. We sat in the car and Naomi stared straight ahead.

'What happened after I left last night, Aidan?'

'Nothing happened.'

'Louisa didn't make it home . . .'

'I clarified our relationship and she left my flat five minutes later.'

'And she left happily?'

'Said I didn't know what I was missing.'

'You don't think she might've been upset? A danger to herself?'

She was humouring me now, and I shook my head.

The scanner glitched into life and I picked up. 'Waits receiving.'

Dispatch connected me with the uniformed officers we'd sent to Blake's home. They'd arrived to the scene of a disturbance.

5

Blake lived in a large, semi-detached house in Burnage, a few miles out of the city centre. Someone had smashed in the ground-floor windows and written *KILLER* across the building in green spray-paint.

'Vandalism,' said one of the uniforms, approaching us on the drive.

'I didn't think it was a confession. Where's Blake?'

He led us inside, through the hall and into a spacious living room, where the former detective inspector was nursing a short glass of amber liquid. The same man who couldn't drink coffee.

'What have I done to deserve you,' he said, eyes washing past me.

'That's what we'd like to know.' I turned to the constables. 'Could you give us a minute?' They backed out of the room, drawing the door closed behind them. 'The first time we met, you told us to follow our instincts. Call me crazy, but when someone involved in a murder has *killer* painted across his front door, I go and talk to him.'

'These things happen sometimes when you're in the public eye.'

'It looks like you spat in it, Kev. Was anything taken?' He shook his head. 'And you've got no idea who it was?'

'None.'

'Or why they might target you?' He shook his head again. 'You have to agree it's an inflammatory message . . .'

'And I can't tell you anything about it.'

'Your wife wasn't home at the time of the attack, Mr Blake?' asked Naomi.

'No, thank God. She's staying with Lucy, our daughter, at the moment. She's got a new baby.' He nodded at some pictures on the mantelpiece.

'I see,' she said, looking at them closely before turning back to him. I'd had the same fleeting thought on the way in, but Blake's daughter definitely wasn't Esther. 'While we're here, do you think you could show us where the original break-in took place?'

His expression was that of a man who'd run out of options. I knew the feeling, and I wasn't eager for Naomi to see the same look crossing my face in a few hours' time.

The study was a small room at the rear of the house, and I was surprised when I went to the window and saw a steep descent to the back garden.

'Looks like quite a climb,' I said. 'You implied that someone passing probably stuck their hand through an open window . . .'

'Maybe you heard what you wanted to.'

'Sergeant Waits can be a little selective,' said Naomi. 'But I must admit, that's how I heard it, too.'

I inspected the window frame. 'And this fitting's brand new. They broke in, didn't they, Kev?'

Blake avoided our eyes. 'There might have been some incidental damage when they climbed through, but what do you expect?'

'The truth?'

'I've given you a lifetime supply of the stuff, Sergeant, as much as I've got. I've got nothing new to say and I've already given you a lot of time today—'

'Are we keeping you from something?'

He'd grown more and more pale since we'd first met, more and more pale since we'd entered his home, and he sat down with a hand to his chest.

'As it happens,' he said, 'I've got a meeting for . . .' He trailed off.

'A meeting for what?'

'For the new edition of my book,' he said breathlessly.

'Who with?' He avoided my eyes and I waited for him to look at me again. 'Who with, Kev?'

6

'Well, Charlie, we meet again,' I said, approaching the journalist in the outdoor seating section of Sinclair's Oyster Bar on Shambles Square. It was one of the oldest pubs in the city, having twice been taken down and moved, brick by brick, to new locations. Seeing Sloane hunched over the table, his fist wrapped round a pint of ale, you could almost believe he'd been with the place since the start, moving as part of the restoration process.

'Fuck me,' he said, struggling to his feet. 'What do you want?'

'Sit down or we'll arrest you for obstruction.'

'Of what?'

'The course of justice, your arteries – you name it.' He considered this for a moment then landed back on his chair with a thump. 'You're looking better than the last time we saw you, but maybe that's the effect of being fully dressed . . .'

He rolled his eyes.

'We found the phone that was used to take Martin Wick's picture,' said Naomi.

'You haven't been completely wasting your time, then?'

'Not completely,' she said. 'The picture you put on the front page was actually part of a set.'

He tried to mask his surprise but couldn't hide his interest. 'In that case, I think the others might rightfully belong to me.'

'I'm not sure you'll want them,' I said, reaching inside my jacket pocket for my own phone. I held it out and began scrolling through the pictures of Esther lying with Martin Wick. 'Seems like you might have paid five grand to a mass murderer and his girlfriend . . .'

Sloane's mouth slackened.

'What makes it worse is that she's still on the loose,' Naomi continued. 'Running round with your money. That's less like obstructing the course of justice and more like . . .'

'Aiding and abetting,' I said.

'Well,' grunted Sloane. 'There are real detectives in this town, and I happen to be meeting one any minute, so—'

'I'm afraid Kevin Blake's a bit busy at the moment,' said Naomi.

Sloane looked from her to me.

'It's true,' I said. 'Someone smashed in all his windows and wrote *killer* across his house in spray-paint. You should send a photographer round before he gets the white spirit out. We're wondering who might have done it and why?' He didn't say anything. 'Seems like all your friends end up with question marks hanging over them, Charlie.'

'Seems like . . .'

'What was it you were meeting Blake about today?' He didn't say anything and I looked at the four full pint glasses on the table. 'Seems like you had a lot to talk about. Come on, Charlie. He's completely compromised. The phone that Wick's girlfriend used to send you the picture was stolen from his home.'

'And for some reason, he never reported it missing,' said Naomi. 'Almost as if he and this girl are connected, somehow.'

I nodded. 'And what with you paying her five grand, you're quite the threesome. When you factor in that she gave your money to a convicted spice dealer, it starts turning into an orgy.'

'You should get a room,' Naomi suggested.

He gave a long, open-mouthed sigh. It smelt like something inside him was dying. 'There's nothing there,' he said. 'I don't even know Blake, aside from the odd chat with him twelve years ago. He got in touch with me recently.'

'What about?'

'Said he was getting to work on a new edition of his awful book, to be published when Wick croaked it. He was after dirt on Frank Moore.'

'Why would he come to you about dirt on Frank Moore?'

'Rumours,' he said. 'Stories I put to him back around the original case. A private eye for the paper dug it all up and I wanted to run them past him. These days, your Frank's an articulate man, but back then he had trouble expressing himself.' He smiled. 'Did a lot of talking with his fists, if you know what I mean.'

'Where did these rumours come from?'

'Ever ask yourself why the neighbours in a semi-detached house at the end of a cul-de-sac heard nothing while a mother and three kids were butchered next-door?'

He took a drink, wiping his mouth with the back of his hand.

'They heard something, all right. Only, they were so used to the sound of shouting and fighting by then that they just went to bed on it. Never let the sun go down on an argument, kids.'

'Did you speak to these neighbours directly?' I asked.

He nodded, holding eye contact, then reached inside his bag and produced print-outs of signed, dated statements. Naomi and I looked over the sheets while Sloane finished one pint and started on a second.

The neighbours had seen Margaret Moore with a black eye.

They'd heard regular fights coming through the walls. Broken plates, and windows. Slammed doors, fists and skulls. They'd seen the kids wincing away from their dad when he moved too quickly.

Frank Moore, *family man.*

'How come none of this ran at the time?' I said, looking up.

'If they hadn't caught someone so quickly, it might have. As it is, Sergeant, the press are no different than the police. We deal in heroes and villains. When your lot picked up Wick, we had our villain, didn't we?'

'One of them,' I said, collecting the statements and getting up to leave. 'Listen, I know this isn't usual police procedure but, please God, leave town.'

'Music to my ears,' said Sloane, draining his second glass.

7

We arrived unannounced at Frank Moore's home. Its perfect sym-
metry seemed sinister to me, but perhaps that was the result of
reading the statements made by his ex-neighbours. He was a big
man, and I could only imagine how imposing that made him to a
child. We knocked on the door and waited a minute. Rebecca,
Frank's second wife, answered, and I was struck once again by her
physical similarity to his first, Margaret.

'Mrs Moore,' said Naomi. 'We were wondering if Frank was
home?'

She stepped out and drew the door closed behind her.

'He's working,' she said quietly. 'Not here.'

'Is this a bad time?'

'Why do you ask?'

'No reason. Is Frank doing one of his seminars?'

She glanced back at the house again. 'Today it's at-risk groups. Is
there something I can help with?'

'Frank's alibi for Saturday night,' said Naomi.

'Oh.' Rebecca looked relieved. 'He was here all right, we had
people over.'

'They can vouch for him until midnight?'

'Until gone midnight. Frank was still carrying them out to cabs
at one a.m.'

'And there was never a time when he was out of everyone's sight,
say for an hour, even less?'

'You don't know Frank, do you? He wasn't out of sight for five min-utes. He was hosting, looking after people, doing what he does best.'

'Sounds like quite a night.'

'We're not party animals but a few times a year Frank likes to invite some of the more well-to-do survivors round for dinner. After what a lot of these people have been through, it's a credit to him that we have such a fun night. Believe me, all eyes were on him, going in-depth on his favourite topic.'

'Which is?' I said, half-expecting to hear Martin Wick's name.

'Saving the world.'

I smiled. 'I hope he gets round to it, one of these days. Would you mind letting us know how we might contact these guests? It'll just make sure we don't have to think of Frank in this light again.'

'OK, do you want to come in?'

She asked in a way that told us not to accept.

'Absolutely,' I said, walking past her.

We went down the hallway lined with painfully staged family photos, through into the lounge. Their eldest daughter, Lizzie, was on the sofa. I was surprised to see that its plastic cover had been removed and Rebecca caught my look.

'We're not so keen on laminating the furniture, are we, Liz?' The girl didn't look up or answer and Rebecca rubbed her head. 'And we're very blue to be at home sick today . . .'

Naomi smiled. 'I used to secretly love sick days.'

'It's a waste of time,' said the girl.

'You like school, then?'

'It's just important not to fall behind.'

It sounded like a quote from someone else and Rebecca tried to soften it. 'Our kids hate being cooped up, they take after Frank that way. All go, all the time.'

'Wish I knew their secret,' said Naomi.

'My brother and sisters got killed,' said Lizzie, unexpectedly. Naomi and I glanced at each other, not knowing what to say. 'So we don't like to waste our lives.'

Her mother rubbed the girl's head again. 'Why don't you go brush your teeth?'

Lizzie got up and left the room quietly, and Rebecca went on trying to paper over what she'd said. 'She's getting to that age where it's not cool to be home or hang out with your parents. You know what mothers are like,' she said, looking at me.

I nodded and looked away, at the family photographs scattered around the room. The kids were all pictured straight-on, upright, smiling rigidly. The pictures seemed less like keepsakes and more like reminders of how they were supposed to look and act at all times.

If Frank had his way, he'd probably laminate them.

'You thought you could get us the contact details of your party guests,' I said.

'Of course.' Rebecca found an address book and allowed Naomi to copy down the details of four people.

'Can I ask why Saturday's invitation was for his wealthiest survivors?' I said.

'Economics. We're a registered charity. You can't be squeamish about putting your hand out. One thing Frank's always seen is the way grief unites the classes. It's a good way of getting one group to help the other.'

'We do have a slightly more delicate question,' said Naomi.

'Come on, I can take it.' I saw that was true. She'd taken in a broken man, been a big part of his rebirth, starting a new family in the shadow of his last one. It had taken strength and belief, and she still had plenty of it left.

Naomi continued. 'I've been looking through the old case file, and I was surprised to see that you were Frank's alibi twelve years ago as well . . .'

The smile stiffened but didn't leave her face entirely.

'Well, that's slightly different, but yes. He spent that night with me.'

'The two of you were close at the time?'

253

'We'd been seeing each other, off and on . . .'

'For how long?'

Rebecca gave a shrug that was more like a twist of the shoulders. 'Weeks, maybe months.'

'So while his family were murdered, Frank was with you.'

'He was still a big drinker back then. He'd had a bad night and passed out, blind drunk, in a chair. I was scared he'd choke on his tongue or his sick, so I sat with him all night. He never even stirred.'

It counted him out of the killings, and it wasn't what I'd wanted to hear.

I asked a forthright question in response. 'Was there any overlap between the two relationships, Rebecca?'

'Overlap?'

'Were you having an affair?'

'Frank and Margaret were dead and buried when—' She heard what she'd said and held up a hand. 'They were over when we started up.'

'He told us they were still in love,' I said. 'That the plan was always to get back together after their separation.'

'Did he?' she said, staring at me. It wasn't the kind of question you answer but I nodded anyway and she pursed her lips.

'Well, either way, they were over by the end of that night, weren't they?'

'Dead and buried,' I said. 'And he never moved?'

'Not a muscle.'

'He has plenty of muscles, doesn't he?'

'Excuse me?'

'We've heard that he was a hands-on kind of parent, back in the day . . .'

'Aidan,' said Naomi.

Rebecca stood up, looked about and then fixed me with a stare. 'You didn't come here to ask questions. You came here to take your anger out on me. I think you're a very hurt man, Detective Waits.

I think it's given you a great talent for hurting others. It's a shame Frank isn't here, I'm sure he could explain it better.'

'I'm sure he could,' I said.

Naomi broke in. 'We know there wasn't always total harmony in the Moore household. That makes sense – they split up, after all. We're just wondering if it went beyond arguments and into something physical.'

'The problems in that house came from Margaret,' said Rebecca, some colour coming into her cheeks. The only time she sounded legitimately angry was at this invocation of Frank's first wife. 'You want affairs? Believe me, it wasn't Frank who had trouble keeping it at home.'

For a moment it looked like she might go on but instead she brushed down her dress and announced that she was late to collect the other two children from school.

'Don't you find it disturbing that they're named after three dead kids?' I said, going so far past the line that I couldn't even see it.

Rebecca seemed pleased, though. Like I'd shown my true colours.

'You'd need to have no love in your life at all to think that.'

I felt Naomi's hand on my arm and when I looked at her she was blushing. 'We've probably taken up enough of your time,' she said. 'You thought Frank would be with one of his at-risk groups, may we ask where?'

'Her Majesty's Prison.'

'Her Majesty's Prison?' I repeated. 'Frank works at Strangeways?'

8

None of us had spoken for more than a minute when I went to the window and forced it open. Hatton, the prison governor, was wedged behind his desk giving off an odour that might confuse a corpse-sniffing dog. The yard outside was empty and a light breeze came, mercifully, through the window.

'Do you usually let people walk in off the street to work with your inmates?'

'Off the street?' said Hatton. 'I think that's a bit dramatic, friend. Mr Moore's a prominent counsellor, cleared to work with vulnerable people, popular with the lads. Perfectly qualified to be here.'

'How long's it been going on?'

'Since before my time, even . . .'

'And how long have you been here, Governor?'

'Five years.'

He said it like a sentence that had been handed down from the high court. If my suspicions about Frank Moore were correct, then he might find himself looking at the real thing.

'And nothing struck you as odd or unusual about a man volunteering to work in the prison where the convicted killer of his family was doing time?'

I turned from the window and he shook his head. 'Obviously the two of them never interacted, I can guarantee that, but I've got a duty of care to every one of these lads. Moore's a net benefit to them.'

'What about your duty of care to Martin Wick?'

'Got out of here alive, didn't he? Some might say that's more than he deserved. And as I recall, his violent death came while he was under your protection, not mine.'

'Not for lack of trying from your lads, though.'

'That's completely unrelated to Frank Moore's presence here.'

'How can you be so sure? Did you accompany him during his sessions?'

'Course not.'

'Did you discuss it?'

'Not as I recall.'

'So, what? You just had a good feeling?' I waited for an answer but he remained silent, eyes drifting to the window like he was wondering what he might have for lunch. I shook my head. 'I've heard of people looking the other way before, but they don't usually get whiplash.'

'You think of all the clever things to say, don't you, Sergeant?'

'Wick killed the man's children,' I said, as the door opened.

Hatton, Naomi and I all turned to see Frank Moore step inside the office. He had to duck under the doorframe, flashing the streak of white that cut through his black hair. As ever, he wore his uniform of a fitted shirt, blue slacks and loafers.

There was a look of near-amusement in his eyes.

It was a bad moment for him to walk in, and I tried to recover. 'What are you doing here, Frank?'

Gamely, he turned, closing the door behind him. 'On Wednesdays, I—'

'No, what are you doing here?'

'If you'll let me finish. On Wednesdays I work with at-risk groups.'

'I'd think they're especially at risk when the family members of their victims are on staff.'

'What are you implying?'

'We'll get to that. I know the horse has bolted somewhat, but it goes without saying that you can't come back here.'

Hatton rose from his seat. 'You might wanna get your weight up before you come in here and start throwing it around, Sergeant.'

'Governor, this probably isn't the cause you want to take a stand on. Your next five years here could be in slightly more cramped confines. Can you give us a minute?'

He sucked his teeth, then began labouring out from behind his desk. Between the four of us we'd reached a point of unanimous mutual loathing, and I thought one less body might make things easier. He patted Moore on the shoulder, hedging his bets, before walking out.

'Take a seat,' I said, motioning Frank to one of the low chairs opposite Hatton's desk. Moore ran a lingering hand through his hair, as if he drew strength from that lightning bolt shock of white in its centre. Then he smiled again, lowering himself calmly, like it was the best seat in the house, the perfect spot to watch the combined histrionics of Naomi and me.

I went to the other side of the desk, leaning back against the wall so we were eye to eye. Naomi was closer, standing to his right beside the window. He'd have to crane his neck to look at her when she spoke, but if our last conversation was anything to go by, I thought he probably wouldn't bother.

'You seem upset with me,' he said. 'I hadn't realized I was supposed to inform you of my every movement . . .'

'Mentioning that you've been within fifty feet of the man convicted of your family's murder, every week for at least the last five years, might have been helpful.'

'Helpful how? It's no secret.'

'What were your reasons for coming here?'

'I work with at-risk groups who—'

'Your real reasons, Frank. When we first went out to your house you told me that if it was up to you, they'd dig Wick up and set fire to the bastard again.'

'That doesn't sound like something I'd say,' he returned. It was a statement of fact which also implied I was lying, without directly lying himself. I was impressed.

'Good to know what level of reality we're operating on,' I said.

'Say what you like about me, I've heard all of it and worse, but I take my work seriously and I won't let you talk it down.'

'And what is your work?'

'I'm a survival expert. A counsellor for vulnerable people with no one else to talk to.'

'Well, I think you're a salesman.'

'I see this all the time, Sergeant. You're a mess, your personal life's a no-go zone, you're disintegrating. You see me, my integrity, my family, my home, what I've survived to get it, and naturally you feel jealous.' I kept my expression blank. 'You might as well be wearing your antidepressants as a necklace.'

'Nice,' I said. 'Did Margaret ever get depressed?'

Moore closed his eyes and his fists at roughly the same time.

'And what do you think puts you on a first-name basis with her?'

'You re-married, Frank. It might be confusing to refer to her as Mrs Moore.'

When he opened his eyes again they were looking dead at me.

'Is there anything wrong with re-marrying, Detective?'

'Not at all, especially when your relationship with the second wife predates the death of the first.' He rose slowly from his seat, staring at me, and he was so tall that it took a couple of seconds for him to reach full height. 'But hey,' I said. 'At least you managed to forgive yourself.'

There was a twitch in his face which transformed into a smile.

He resumed his seat. 'I'm sorry, go on . . .'

I just looked at him and allowed Naomi to talk into the side of his head. I couldn't think of anything that would annoy him more.

'Replacing your wife's one thing,' she said. 'We wanted to talk to you about the kids . . .'

'What about them?'

'Their names.'

'This is offensive.'

'How so?' she said.

'It's a tribute, the highest one it's in my power to give. Is that honestly why you've come storming in here? The names of my kids? They're on their birth certificates. Again, no secret.'

'So let's talk about secrets. What would the walls from 11 Briars Green say if they could talk?'

'You said something about our level of reality . . .'

'OK, let's go further. What would the neighbours behind those walls say? What would they say about your first marriage?'

'I think I've been honest about our problems.'

'You said you were fighting things,' I said, producing the witness statements that Charlie Sloane had given to us. 'I didn't realize you were speaking literally.' I dropped the papers on to the desk between us. Moore leaned forward and began looking through them, his head sinking lower as he did. 'Keep them if you like, we've made copies.'

He moved back in his chair like he couldn't bear to be near them, then looked about the room as if he'd just woken up here.

'We need to know what started all this, Frank. And how it ended.'

'We all know how it fucking ended,' he said tonelessly.

'In a sense. Were the fights about your relationship with Rebecca?' He looked up at me. 'We recently discovered that she was your alibi for the murders . . .'

'Well, yes, but—'

'Did Margaret discover your affair and throw you out?'

He moved his chair back, further from me. 'Could you put those things away?'

I didn't move and he cast the papers violently off the desk, breathing hard.

When he spoke he was looking at nothing.

'I think they call it the seven-year itch, don't they? Well, Maggie and me must have been late bloomers. We'd been married about twelve years when I started to itch. Then it turned into a rash. When I went to get it checked out, I found that my wife had given

260

me chlamydia, Sergeant.' He smirked, looking suddenly unhinged. It was the same look I'd seen on the faces of several men in the seconds before they hit me. He nodded at the sheets of paper, now strewn across the floor. 'Perhaps I could have handled it better.'

'Your neighbours were so used to the sounds of violence coming through the walls that they didn't even report it when someone turned up with a knife. I'd say you couldn't have handled it much worse.'

He blinked rapidly. 'Why all this stuff about Briars Green? Tell me what you're thinking.'

'Martin Wick's last words were to recant his confession. Since then, we've come across a few irregularities in the case.'

'I didn't kill her,' he said passionately. 'For God's sake, not my kids. And you know for a fact I couldn't have killed Martin Wick, I was with people. If I'd known he was dying at the same time I'd have broken out a bottle of the good stuff. But given I was at home, with witnesses, what does it matter?' He leaned forward and kicked at the statements on the floor. 'What does any of this fucking shit matter?'

9

'He's got a point,' said Naomi, once Frank Moore had left the office. We were both standing beside the open window again, letting the breeze clean out our lungs after twenty minutes of Governor Hatton's fumes. I could see that she was still angry about how I'd spoken to Rebecca, how I'd spoken to Frank.

'In what sense?' I said.

'I don't see where raking over all this old ground gets us. Those statements were worth looking into, absolutely, but he's accounted for them.'

'Accounted for knocking his wife and kids around?'

'I'm not saying I like him, I'm saying he's explained it – her infidelity. I'm saying I believed him. Didn't you?' I glanced at her and nodded, grudgingly. He'd still been incensed about his wife giving him a sexually transmitted infection. 'But most importantly,' said Naomi. 'Whether we believe him or not, we know he couldn't have killed Martin Wick. He was with people.'

'According to his wife. All we know for sure is that Mr Forgive and Forget isn't above acts of violence when things aren't going his way.'

'Sound like anyone else we know?'

'Oh, get fucked, Naomi.'

'With you around, I've probably got a good chance,' she shot back.

I paced to the other side of the room.

'Think what you like, but don't put me in the Frank Moore bucket.'

'I haven't put you anywhere, but you don't get to act like a dick and then object to the label.'

'I'm sorry I'm not what you thought I'd be, OK? I'm sorry that this case is a smouldering fucking car fire.'

'Don't talk to me like I'm some fucking schoolgirl with a crush. All I ever expected you to be was a decent person.'

'Well, you set the bar too high.'

'Clearly. The only reason you're so interested in Frank Moore, a man whose entire family was murdered, is because he leads away from the one person who we're certain *was* involved, your fuck buddy Louisa Jankowski.'

It took me a second to recover.

'I'm interested in Frank Moore because he's a liar and a scumbag. But, hey, maybe it takes one to know one?'

'Don't put words in my mouth.'

'You just said I was trying to fuck you.'

'Well, isn't that why you took me back to your flat?'

Her voice broke and I realized for the first time how hurt she was.

'If I recall correctly,' I said, lowering my voice, 'we went there at your suggestion.'

'For a drink.'

'And what makes you think there was anything else on my mind?'

'You.' She swallowed. 'The way you looked at me when you opened the door.'

'How did I look at you?'

'Not like a colleague and not like a friend.'

We were both silent for a moment.

'I'm sorry, then,' I said. 'Of course I'm sorry.'

'No, I'm sorry. Because I still walked up those stairs with you . . .'

I rubbed my face and turned to the wall. 'I'll talk to James. See about transferring you to the official investigation.'

She nodded.

'Let's call it a day. I have some things to do while we're here, anyway.'

'Seeing Adam?' she guessed. I turned and nodded. 'You want to see if Carver kept up his end of the bargain, to keep him safe.'

'If you make a deal with the devil you should at least get your money's worth.'

She smiled. 'In that case, you could have quite a windfall coming your way.'

'I just can't stop winning.'

We looked at each other for one second too long, then she came closer, touched my arm and left.

10

I waited for Hatton to return and asked him to arrange an escort on to the floor. When the guard arrived, I was expecting him to take me back to E Wing but he shook his head.

'Lad was moved yesterday.'

That sounded promising, and I followed.

As we walked I thought about my fight with Naomi. She'd taken the job because she'd hoped I was a decent man, but it had taken less than a week to relieve her of the notion. My supposed relationship with Louisa Jankowski had been her breaking point and I reflected, bitterly, that the truth would only make it worse.

A grubby blackmail plot, fucking the case to save my own skin.

Adam's new cell was a third larger than his previous one, and when we came to the barred door he was reading beneath a lamp. He wore thick-rimmed glasses now and smiled when he saw me.

'Five minutes,' said the guard, walking back up the gangway. Adam turned in his chair and held out his hands as if to say, *What do you think of the place?*

'Looks like you've gone up in the world,' I said.

'More like sideways but it feels a bit further from the edge. Thank you.'

'Don't thank me,' I said, making sure he understood. He nodded then got up from his chair and went to the corner of his cell, where there was a decent stack of books.

'I was hoping I'd see you again,' he said, returning with a large, battered paperback. 'Thought you might want this.' It was a copy of *Crime and Punishment*. I thought it might not fit through the bars but it just needed a push, and I accepted with a smile.

'You're sure?'

'I've had enough of it to last me a lifetime.'

'How much longer have you got?'

'Six years,' he said. 'Still good days and bad days, so if you're ever in the neighbourhood . . .' He took his glasses off and I saw that his black eye was already fading. It felt good to have done something right for a change, and I thanked him for the book, turning to leave. I was almost at the exit when it struck me.

'Adam,' I said, returning to his cell. He'd gone back to his chair and a book. 'Your tattoo's gone. The teardrop . . .'

'I've decided I don't need it any more.' He looked confused by my speechlessness. 'It was only a temporary,' he said.

As I worked my way through security I examined the close-up images we'd pulled from Blake's phone. Esther, in bed with Martin Wick. I knew where I'd seen her before.

11

Val's was a notorious private homeless shelter in Ardwick. I'd first heard it mentioned as a dark joke shared between vagrants when I began working the night shift. The gist was that a casket would be more comfortable to sleep in.

Less likely to get you buried.

It was a dreaded name to charity and council officials, and a despised one to emergency services. A dilapidated warren of sixty-plus rooms, a place you were lucky to leave on your feet. I knew that there had been hundreds of emergency calls logged from Val's in the last twelve months alone. These covered cases of alcohol poisoning, overdoses, spice fits, stabbings and even a violent death or two, but with a transient, distrusting populace, what really went on inside was a mystery.

I'd never been particularly curious, but speaking to Adam had given me an idea of where Esther might be, and I'd called into Central Park to find out where the Cornerhouse squatters had been placed following the raid.

By the time I arrived it was dark.

The hotel was a four-storey row of terraced houses, occupying the entire block. Scaffolding covered a quarter of the building, but it looked as though it had been there for some time. Less about restoring the place and more about keeping it upright. The plastic sheeting had come away, with frayed, filthy strands moving in the wind, no sign of ongoing work. Some windows were boarded up with balsa wood and the facade was coming away from the brick-work in places.

Four entrances, three of them sealed shut with steel sheeting. One way in and one way out.

I went up the steps to the door.

The first thing that struck me was the smell. Like someone had deep-fried bleach and then lit a cigarette to cover it. I could see the marks where No Smoking signs had been ripped from the walls or painted over.

That was one way of doing it.

The carpet was almost entirely bald, greying with decades of grit, and I couldn't tell what colour it had started out as.

'Help you?' said the man behind the front desk.

He had heavy jowls, a red, booze-filled face, and his belly was resting on the counter. He was sitting behind a plastic screen so covered in grime that he looked out of focus.

'DS Waits,' I said. 'I'm looking for a group of people who came here from the Cornerhouse squat.'

'You'll have a warrant, then . . .'

'I don't need one if I'm in pursuit of someone who's committed a crime.'

'And who would that be?'

'I'm afraid I don't have names to hand but there was a woman with them.'

'Narrows things down a bit . . .' He heaved open the guestbook and flicked through. 'We've only got one woman,' he said. 'Room 31. From what I saw you'll wanna knock real hard, there, Detective.'

He buzzed me through into a dark corridor-cum-communal space, where five or six men were sitting round smoking, all of them playing cards, drinking from bottles of fortified wine. The walls were nicotine yellow and I could see a hole in the ceiling where the smoke alarm had been ripped down. The conversation stopped when they saw me but I didn't recognize any of them from the Cornerhouse.

I passed through, into a tight-fitting hallway with a staircase at the end.

Climbing up, I passed men face-down on the floor, doors propped open with fire extinguishers. From inside the rooms I heard tinny music from mobile phones and the tail-ends of conversations.

The doors were about as secure as toilet cubicles. Their original locks had been broken and replaced with others over time, then broken and replaced again, and every one of them was different. I found room 31 and knocked.

When I got no answer I banged on the ajar door to 32.

'Yeah?' said a man.

'I'm looking for the woman in 31 . . .'

'You'll have to do more than knock, my friend. She was legless when she went in and that was a while ago.'

I went back to the door and tried again but there was still no answer. Although it looked weak, it wouldn't budge when I pushed, so I retraced my steps along the corridor, down the stairs and back to the plastic screen.

'I'll need the key for 31,' I said.

'What's this woman wanted for?'

'Her own protection.'

I realized that a group of men from the communal space had followed me through, only now I saw that they'd been joined by the bearded man from the Cornerhouse.

'He's the one,' he shouted. 'Had us all evicted two days ago and now he's back for more.'

The man behind the screen glanced over my shoulder. 'No one's being evicted,' he said levelly. His eyes returned to me. 'I can't give you the key without a warrant.'

I was about to make an issue of it when a beer can bounced off the back of my head, and I turned to see the men crowding me, getting closer. One shoved me and I walked out, stalking back down the street. As I went I heard the sound of glass breaking. It wasn't out of place in this neighbourhood and I didn't think much of it, turning the corner and returning to the car, sitting inside rubbing my head while I requested back-up. With two squad cars on the way I decided to park closer.

I didn't want anyone going in or out.

When I turned the corner, I saw immediately that something was wrong.

Men were filing out on to the street, some helping less able residents to walk. I stopped the car, got out and started walking, then running towards them. There were broken windows on the ground, first and second floors, each with smoke pluming out, and it struck me that there was no alarm going off. I pushed through the people on the street until I found the man from the front desk.

'Fire brigade?' I said. He took his phone slowly from his pocket and made the call. While he did, I searched through the others. 'Has anyone seen the woman from 31?'

There was a sound like an open-throated groan, then something like a sharp intake of breath, followed by a roar. I turned to see a thick cloud of smoke billowing through the front door. Then I went from man to man, shaking shoulders, asking if any of them had seen the woman from 31.

'Suck my arse,' said one.

I took him by the arm, dragging him towards the scaffold. 'Give me a leg up.' He looked at me like I was mad. 'I'm a police officer, just fucking do it.'

He linked his hands and I stepped into them, pulling myself up on to the first level of scaffolding. A ladder from there went all the way to the top. As I climbed, the smoke intensified, and by the time I reached the third floor I could taste it.

Rolling, living, thick.

The fire inside sounded like sizzling bacon, and the people below were shouting at me to come down. I found a loose iron bar and broke open a third-floor window, then I took a breath and climbed in. There was no fire inside this room, and I edged through into the smouldering corridor, to 31, where the door was still closed.

I slammed my shoulder into it, still trying to hold my breath.

'Go away,' a woman slurred from inside.

I stepped back and kicked the door open but a heavy piece of furniture had been pulled in front of it.

She obviously hadn't trusted the locks.

The smoke was starting to burn my eyes and I could feel the tears streaming from them. I went as far up the corridor as I dared, found a fire extinguisher then returned to 31, smashing the top half of the cheap, balsawood door, revealing a chest of drawers pushed up against it. I climbed over, into a narrow little coffin of a room, feeling the splinters grazing my hands and head.

Lying on the camp bed was the woman who'd let us into the Cornerhouse.

Her cheeks were still bright red, but now I saw it wasn't from drink or exposure, it was from scrubbing away the fake tattoos that had been around her eyes. She was high, laughing and limp, and as I lifted her up I saw pills scattered across the floor. I hoisted her on to my shoulder, rolled her across the chest of drawers then carried her down the corridor, now fuzzy with smoke. It billowed up the staircase and I retraced my steps to the room I'd entered through, covering my mouth with my forearm.

I found the window and rolled her out of it.

She landed heavily on to the scaffolding and I climbed out after her. The heat was incredible now, and I could feel my clothes sticking to me, my eyes stinging with sweat.

With the woman on my shoulder I started down the ladder.

When we reached the lowest level I saw that two constables had arrived and were pushing people away from the building. Some men saw us, breaking ranks, running over to help. They reached up for the woman, and I rolled her into their arms before jumping down myself. I leaned into the first man I saw and went with him, as far away from the fire as he'd take me.

When I looked back at the building I could see shapes in the windows, and it took a moment to realize that there were still men

271

trapped inside, trying to get out. One broke through the glass and, overwhelmed by the flames, threw himself from the fourth floor.

I closed my eyes and heard a bone-crunching thud.

When I opened them again the other shapes had disappeared, the building was fully aflame.

12

I was breathing into a respirator with a blanket wrapped round me. My temperature had plummeted, I'd been unable to stop shivering and my teeth were chattering so hard I thought I might need to see a dentist. I tried to stand, fell immediately back down, then saw a familiar face breaking through the crowd. It was a minute before I could say her name.

'Naomi.'

'I leave you alone for five minutes . . .' She squeezed my arm and looked over her shoulder, at the fire brigade still bringing the flames under control. 'They might save the building but I think you're a goner.'

'What are you doing here?'

'I was in the neighbourhood . . .' I waited. '. . . I didn't like how we left it so I went to check on Moore's alibi from Saturday night, his party guests.'

'And?'

'It's iron-clad, Aidan. I've talked to three of the people who were there. A couple were drunk but swore blind he was with them all night. The designated driver was a priest. Said he'd put his hand on the Bible if necessary. Frank Moore was nowhere near St Mary's when Martin Wick was killed.'

I waved her quiet and she stopped.

'Sergeant Waits,' said one of the uniforms, approaching us tentatively. 'You said you wanted to be informed of any developments . . .'

I nodded.

'Most of the windows on the ground floor were boarded up. The ones that weren't, well, the first they knew of all this was when something smashed through the glass. We've got one guy, on his way in, thought he saw someone running in the opposite direction, a young woman. He wouldn't have thought much of it but she was staying low behind parked cars, crouching while she went. He just saw a flash of blonde hair.'

'Thank you,' said Naomi.

'Jankowski,' I said, once the constable had left us.

'I wanted to wait until you felt better,' said Naomi. 'Chase agreed to her suspension but Louisa called in sick, never reported for her shift. She'd signed out two firearms yesterday and never returned them. She hasn't been home and she hasn't been back to the station.'

I looked at the flames, finally coming under control, then to the ambulance that Esther was safely inside. It pulled away, leaving a space in the road, and I found myself staring into it. Someone had to have followed me here, someone who was desperate to stop Esther from talking. Someone with no reservations about raising the stakes. When I looked out into the darkness I wondered if Jankowski was looking back.

274

VI
Teeth Dreams

1

I came to with a scream lodged in my throat, eyes streaming, hands round my neck, struggling to breathe. It felt like the hangover of a lifetime, and I already had a few of those to compare it with. The room was dark, and I felt lost for a second, until it all came crashing back to me. A butchered family, their murdered murderer, the impossible, fist-sized knots of my own compromises. And now an unstable firearms officer at loose with live ammunition and a grudge.

When I staggered to the window and looked out I saw that I'd slept through most of a wet day, and the rain was blasting off neon-drenched streets. Despite two showers the previous night, I still smelt of burning, and when I caught the scent on myself again I pulled off my T-shirt, threw it across the room.

I knew Esther had been taken to St Mary's, still out cold from the combined effects of a suspected overdose and smoke inhalation. Naomi had organized two armed guards, vetting them for possible links with Louisa Jankowski. I hadn't told anyone else about my fears that she'd followed me to Val's trying to silence Esther for good.

I took as deep a breath as my lungs would allow and turned on the news, feeling my stomach drop. One man had been pronounced dead at the scene of the fire and three more were missing. I pulled the plug out of the wall, poured one third of a bottle of Scotch into a pint glass and sat with my back to the front door.

When the buzzer went a few minutes later I took a very large drink, climbed to my feet and went to the intercom.

'*UPS.*'

'Just a minute,' I croaked, before pulling on some clothes.

I wasn't expecting a delivery, and if I was about to die on my doorstep then it wouldn't be in boxer shorts. The man had a speed-freak intensity but I signed for the small package, carrying it back up to my flat and kicking the door closed. It was about the size of a hardback, sealed in plastic wrap and secured with overlapping layers of brown tape. I was looking it over, digging through a kitchen drawer for some scissors, when I heard my phone ringing in the bedroom. I dropped the package and the scissors on to the bed and picked up.

'Naomi,' I said.

'You sound like you've been gargling barbed wire. Sleep well?' I grunted in response. 'Well, the good news is that Esther's awake and responsive, after a fashion . . .'

'A fashion?' I said, cutting at the package, still soggy from the rain.

'She can talk but apparently she won't. She's refusing to say anything, even to the doctors and nurses.'

'If her throat feels like mine, I don't blame her.' I picked, thoughtfully, at the tape. 'What happened to the survivors from last night's fire?'

'The other guys from the Cornerhouse? I had the same idea. They've been removed to a charity hostel run by the Lime Tree, I'm about to speak to them now.'

'If they can tell us about Esther's relationship with Martin Wick it might be a life-saver.'

'I'll be sure to ask. You get some rest, OK?' She waited for some response from me but I'd finally got the package open and realized I was staring at a large, pink purse. 'Aidan?'

'I'll call you back,' I said, hanging up.

Pulling the purse free from the packaging and turning it over in my hands I saw that it was made by Chanel. The size, colour and cut all looked familiar but I couldn't remember where I'd seen it before. I opened the clasp and looked inside. There were no photographs, no cards or coins. Opening it wider I saw that there were dozens of small, circular objects lining the bottom. I went to the window and threw open the curtains, letting the streetlight in. Then I dropped the purse, its contents scattering across the hardwood floor.

A full set of human teeth, ripped out at the bloody root.

2

It was early evening, outside normal working hours, and the station was an echoing maze of quiet, fluorescent-lit corridors. I pushed through into the Superintendent's office without knocking and found him in conference with three senior officers. I was soaked from the rain and their conversation ended abruptly when they turned in their seats to look at me.

'Perhaps you could give us a moment?' said Parrs, eyes locking on to mine. The men assumed he was talking to me until he clarified. 'Gentlemen, perhaps you could give us a moment?' Two of the officers evaporated from the room while the third left with the maximum amount of fuss possible. Once he'd finally walked through the door, he turned.

'Alistair, if we could—'

I slammed it on him and looked at Parrs, throwing the package across the room. He swiped it out of the air, spritzing himself with rainwater and squinting down at the UPS label. He took a breath to say something then stopped, deciding he'd see what was inside before telling me exactly how much trouble I was in.

He frowned as he unwrapped the pink purse.

Looked up.

Déjà vu.

'You might remember it from this,' I said, pulling a screwed-up newspaper from my jacket pocket. I crossed the room, pressed it into his desk and then returned to the door, my back to it. He looked down at the photograph of former Constable Tessa Klein on a night out, carrying the purse.

'Where'd you get this?' he said, voice low.

'Special delivery. Although UPS had no record of it. Take a look inside.'

He unfastened the clasp and opened the purse, glancing down for a second before closing his eyes. He put the purse down on the desk and pushed his chair back a few inches.

When his eyes opened again they were on me. 'Where did you get this, Sergeant?'

'It came to my flat this evening. Still looking like a suicide?'

'I can see that you're upset—'

'Upset?' I said, hearing my shredded throat break. I took a step closer, making sure he could still hear me. 'You as good as killed this girl.'

'And how did I do that?'

'You sent her undercover with Carver, knowing what would happen.'

He got up from his seat, came round the desk and perched on the edge, head low like a predator contemplating attack. 'What tipped you off?'

'She's missing for one thing. You know that's how he likes them.'

'And for another . . .'

'He raised it when we spoke. Said wasn't it strange that her body had never turned up? Funny stuff, when he probably knows how many pieces they cut her into.'

'Klein resigned her position—'

'Because Carver saw through her like he sees through everyone, played her like he plays everyone, got her to leave the safety of her job and killed her right under everyone's noses. She should never have been there in the first place, she—'

My voice gave out and I went into a prolonged coughing fit.

Parrs poured a glass of water from his desk and held it out to me.

I just looked at him until he put it down.

'Was that the plan all along?' I said. 'Get me to go and rattle his cage so you'd know for sure?'

He nodded, wearily. 'Sounds like it.'

'Sounds?'

'I had nothing to do with this,' he said, looking at the purse on his desk. 'And as for Zain Carver, we both know he had nothing to do with the attack at St Mary's. All that flash isn't his style.'

'So why insist I go and speak to him?'

I could see that he was still putting it together in his head. 'Chief Superintendent Chase only agreed to your shadow investigation on the condition that you had some facetime with Carver. I was curious as to why, but I couldn't know for sure until you paid him a visit . . .'

He gave me his shark's smile.

'. . . With your usual finesse, Sergeant, you hammered everything else in sight before finally hitting the nail on the head.'

I looked down at the damp patch I was leaving in the carpet, realizing what I'd just handed him. A bullet with Chief Superintendent Chase's name on it.

I shook my head and went for the door.

'Stay right there,' he hissed. 'If you walk into this room forgetting my fucking rank again, I'll have it branded into your eyeballs.' He nodded back at the purse on the desk. 'Do you know what we have here, Sergeant? Aside from the exact measurements of the Chief Superintendent's coffin?'

'What?'

'An object lesson in what happens to you if I decide you're no longer useful. Klein crossed Carver then left the force. Here's what's left of her.' He gave me a moment to appreciate that. 'Sounds like you finally got some work done last night, though.'

I nodded.

'And the fire would also suggest that Wick's killer is still out there . . .' It sounded like a test and I didn't answer. '. . . Because who else would be following you, trying to wipe out the one eyewitness?' When I still didn't respond he went on. 'This tracksuit girl from Val's won't talk to DCI James or his team. You saved her life, such as it is. Maybe she'll talk to you?'

'She swallowed a lot of smoke—'

'Hasn't shut you up, has it? I suggest that you take this outrage and channel it into the case you're supposed to be investigating. Stop wasting my time and start wasting hers.'

'What about them?' I said, nodding at his desk.

'Not a word to anyone until we've taken a bite out of the Chief Superintendent.'

3

I sank back through the building, returning to the incident room on autopilot, disturbed by the lip-smacking zeal with which Parrs hoped to exploit Tessa Klein's death. I wondered how he'd react if a set of my teeth were hand-delivered to him one morning. Maybe he'd brush his own a little more thoroughly that night but I wouldn't bet on it.

Naomi walked in and sat down opposite, making a welcome intrusion into my thoughts.

'What are you doing here?' I said.

'Shouldn't I be asking you that? I just got done talking to the Cornerhouse lot.'

'How was it?'

'You remember the paranoid guy with the beard? Big fan of yours . . .'

'I can imagine.'

'He had no idea Esther had been creeping out to St Mary's, says he doesn't even know her that well. One interesting thing, though. Someone else turned up to the Cornerhouse looking for her, a couple of days before we did.'

'Let me guess . . .'

She nodded. 'They only spoke to him through the door but when I asked for a description it sounded like a certain former detective inspector . . .'

'Blake,' I said. 'That's why he never reported his phone missing. He was using it to trace her.'

'So either this Esther girl has some dirt on him, or there was something incriminating on that phone . . .'

'Incriminating of what, though?'

'This might sound mad,' said Naomi, 'but I'm starting to wonder what Kevin Blake was doing on the night the Moore family were murdered.'

I thought for a second, listening to the rain, then started moving papers about on the desk, searching for our copy of Blake's book.

'Here.' I held open a page and handed it to her. According to a personal aside in the second chapter, Kevin Blake had been in attendance at a regional police conference on the night that the Moore family were murdered. Naomi read this passage and then turned to the glossy pages at the centre, finding a photograph of him in a suit at the event, alongside several other high-ranking officers who were named below.

'Well, at least it's good for something,' she said, closing the book. 'I thought you weren't gonna read it . . .'

'I guess I got interested. You're not missing much, anyway. Just his version of events padded out over three hundred pages.'

Naomi sighed. 'If we eliminate any more suspects you'll have to arrest me for it. Do I get to ask what you're doing at work today?'

'Motivational speech from Parrs.'

'It worked, I see. Should you really be here, Aidan?'

'Is that a philosophical question?'

'Partly. And I'm worried that Louisa still hasn't turned up . . .'

'I know, me too.'

'I'm worried that you've developed a smoker's cough overnight. Mostly, I'm worried that you looked happy to see me when I walked in.'

'The smoke must have damaged my vision, too,' I said, and Naomi smiled. 'I was happy to see you, I always am. If I've let you think otherwise then that's a failing on my part.'

'The smoke's made your voice sound even more sarcastic than usual . . .'

'My name's Aidan Waits,' I said, testing it.

'Sarcastic . . .'

'My partner's Naomi Black.'

'Sarcastic . . .'

'She's the most promising detective I've ever worked with,' I said, catching her eye. She smiled and held it for a second, then looked at the rain through the window behind me. After another moment, I leaned forward. 'That was sarcastic.'

'Watch I don't throw the book at you.'

'Anything but that,' I said. We looked at each other. 'I'll talk to James about your transfer tonight.'

She dropped the book on to the table. 'You don't think Martin Wick killed the Moores, do you?'

'He told me that he didn't, right after someone went to the trouble of setting fire to him.' I thought of Wick's fist, beating against my chest. Black eyes, lit with anger, staring out from charred, blackened skin. 'I believed him.'

She gave this serious consideration. 'We know Frank Moore couldn't have done it. He was passed out with his wife-to-be. We know Blake couldn't have done it. He was surrounded by half the force at this gala event. Esther would have been a kid at the time . . .' Naomi caught my eye. 'So why's she so obsessed with Wick?'

'That's what Parrs wants me to go and ask her.'

'Now?' she said, checking the time. I nodded and she got up. 'Come on, then. You shouldn't drive in your condition. I guess your medal for bravery's in the post?'

I nodded. 'That and a few more things.'

4

We were a long way outside of hospital visiting hours but Naomi laid it on thick and they agreed to give us a few minutes. Esther was so thin that it was hard to believe there was a human body beneath the bedsheets. She'd been drinking an electrolyte-infused cordial for rehydration and the mixture stained her lips red, making her skin seem even paler.

Perhaps that was why I thought she looked younger.

When we'd first met in the hospital toilets I'd put her somewhere in her mid-thirties, but looking at her now I revised that down by a decade.

Even so, there were marks of the lifestyle on her face.

A livid constellation of broken veins about her nose, likewise in her cheeks, and the lines beneath her eyes looked like they'd been cut with a scalpel.

Her arms were resting on top of the bed covers, fists clenched like she might still sit up and box the world. It was only as her weary pink eyes moved on to mine that I saw some of the fight had gone out of her. The doctor had explained that she'd had her stomach pumped for sleeping pills, been treated for smoke inhalation.

'If she'd been carried out of there a couple of minutes later, you'd be visiting her in the morgue,' she said. 'Just don't expect her to be grateful.'

When we walked in, Esther opened her clenched fists and I

saw that her fingernails were bitten to the quick. I couldn't see any green paint from the graffiti at Blake's home, though, and that struck me as odd. She saw me looking and closed her hands again.

'Mind if we sit?' I said. She gave a non-committal shrug. Naomi went one side and I went the other. 'How are you feeling this morning?'

'Your voice . . .' she said, with the same smoked-out baritone as mine. 'You're the one who got me out.' I nodded. 'You shouldn't have bothered.'

'The way I felt this morning, I'd have probably agreed with you.'

'What happened?' she said. Her accent was somewhere between the hard Irish I'd heard at the Cornerhouse and the softer one I'd heard in the toilet at St Mary's.

'You remember being at Val's Hotel?'

She nodded.

'You overdosed on sleeping pills.'

'Not that . . .'

'It was arson,' said Naomi. 'Petrol bombs through the windows. And whatever you might think of your own life, it's looking like three or four men might have lost theirs.'

'Because of me?'

'Because the building was unsafe,' I said. 'The exits were blocked and there were no functioning smoke alarms. Mainly, though, it's because of whoever did it, and only you can help us find them. I'm Detective Sergeant Waits and this is Detective Constable Black . . .'

'We've met,' said Esther.

'That's right, you let us into the Cornerhouse. Gave us the phone.'

'I didn't wanna drag them into my shit. Thanks for getting us evicted, though.'

'After last night, I'd say we're even. You could at least tell me what your name is.'

'Already told you,' she said. 'Jazz.'

'Not Esther?' Naomi suggested. The woman shrugged and Naomi pushed it. 'That name was given to us by a man named Christopher Back, although you might know him as Short Back and Sides . . .'

She grunted. 'In my opinion, his barber should take the blade a bit closer than that.'

'You're not a fan?'

'He makes my shit itch.'

'And yet you got in touch with him . . .'

'Did I?'

'You seem to connect everyone in this case,' said Naomi. 'You met with Martin Wick, you sold his picture to Charlie Sloane, you got Short Back and Sides to verify it, and you stole Kevin Blake's phone to take it. Now, for whatever reason, someone's trying to keep you quiet.'

I picked up Esther's electrolytes and took a sip. 'We know you broke into Kevin Blake's home a couple of weeks ago. He's the man who wrote the book on Martin Wick, the man who put him away. We know you stole files relating to the case from him. Using that information, you contacted Charlie Sloane at the *Mail* and told him you could get a picture of Wick on his deathbed. Why was that?'

'Got five grand out of the fat fuck . . .'

I shook my head. 'I think for some reason you wanted the whole world looking at Martin Wick.'

She didn't say anything but I thought I'd hit a nerve.

'OK,' I continued. 'You disguised yourself with facial tattoos and hung around the hospital, trying to get close to him. You got the picture Sloane wanted but you kept on going back for some reason. Why?'

She still didn't say anything.

'You were here on the night of the murder. You saw an armed

guard get his throat cut and two men go up in flames. You fled the scene and then torched the car you stole, hid out at the Corner-house. We traced Blake's phone there and you were moved along to Val's, where someone burned down the building to try and keep you quiet. Quiet about what, Esther?'

'All this talk of petrol bombs,' she said. 'Fire and burning. Christ, I'd kill for a smoke.'

'We think you bribed an armed police officer named Louisa Jankowski,' said Naomi. I watched Esther closely but she didn't move. 'We think you possibly bribed a constable named Michael Rennick as well.'

Esther's eyes drifted to Naomi when she mentioned Rennick. I thought it looked like she hadn't recognized the name and that surprised me. If he wasn't accepting bribes then how had someone got close enough to shake his hand? To stab him?

'I think you were in some kind of relationship with Martin Wick,' I said. Her eyes cut to me. 'We found your deathbed selfies with him, and we're working through his Strangeways correspond-ence now. We'll find the link, Esther.'

She smiled, showing us greying, broken teeth.

'Martin was my sugar daddy,' she said.

'How did you meet?'

'No comment.'

'Maybe you could tell us what you've got against Kevin Blake, then?' said Naomi.

'No comment.'

'Are you annoyed with him for locking lover-boy up?' I asked.

Esther looked me full in the face. 'Yeah, actually. I am.'

'But there's something else, isn't there? What is it between you and Blake?'

'A brick wall wouldn't be thick enough,' she said.

'He never reported your break-in, you know? We found out about it by chance. He pretended he'd forgotten about it, said the phone didn't mean anything to him. Only problem is, your friends at the Cornerhouse say he turned up there looking for it. Looking for you. That all implies some personal connection. A grudge that goes both ways . . .'

'And speaking of grudges,' said Naomi. 'Louisa Jankowski's scared to death that you'll discuss her complicity in this case, whatever that complicity might be. She's so scared that she went missing with a loaded gun yesterday.'

'Not someone you want to cross,' I said, speaking mostly for myself. 'The way I see it, you must have something nasty on her and Blake to get them so worked up. Tell us what it is and you might be saving your life.'

'I'd be a fucking idiot to save my life,' said Esther. 'Kevin Blake, this Louise whatever, you two,' she looked between Naomi and me. 'What've you all got in common? The law. We're not on the same side, so don't pretend.'

'OK, let's talk about your side. Martin Wick. Did you see the man who murdered him?' She held her mouth tight, then her eyes moved to mine and she shook her head.

'I just stuck the camera out the toilet door. I didn't dare look.' She rubbed her face. 'No one dares look . . .'

'What don't we dare look at?' asked Naomi.

'Ancient history.' Esther was covering her face now, crying. 'You're tryna make a jigsaw with half the picture.'

'So what's the other half? The Moores?'

'The saintly fucking Moores . . .'

'What have they got to do with Martin's murder?'

'Martin didn't kill them,' she said fiercely. 'That's one thing.'

I nodded. 'He told me the same thing.'

'He told you . . . ?'

'His last words before he died. This meant a lot to him, Esther.'

'You's talked to the fridge yet?' she said.

'The fridge?'

'That's what Martin called her, his ex-wife.'

'We know it was a man who killed him, we saw your video.'

291

She shook her head. 'She didn't kill him, but she's who you should be looking at if you want to know who did.'

'You're talking about Mrs Wick?'

A nasty smile came to Esther's face, and she slumped down in the bed, closing her eyes. 'Have a root round in that fridge. If you can find something mouldy, come and talk to me.'

5

Martin Wick's ex-wife worked at YouBet, a licensed bookmaker in Salford, just off the A6. The homeless men sheltering under the awning didn't make it seem lucky, but that hadn't discouraged a slew of last-minute customers queuing to get their final bets in. It was almost ten, and I recognized the energy in the room.

That last roll of the dice. The one that might send the day in either direction.

Naomi had called ahead while I drove, dialling the number we'd found saved in Kevin Blake's phone the previous day. Susan confirmed broadly what Blake had told us. She'd been married to Wick for less than twelve months, over twelve years ago. They'd been separated before the Moore family were murdered and she insisted that they'd had no contact since. She couldn't understand why we'd want to speak to her now, and I heard Naomi struggling to provide a convincing answer. The truth was that we were no different from the men and women queuing to put their cash down on something, anything.

Sure things, locks, long odds or million-to-one shots.

We were desperate.

We waited while the queue died down and the chancers went, one by one, back out into the rain. Susan knew the police when she saw them. Her eyes cut to and from us, until the last customer left the building. Then she opened the booth that she sat secured inside, walked past us and locked the front door. As she did, a man

293

appeared at the glass, banging both hands on it, looking from her to his watch in disbelief.

She just shook her head and re-joined us.

'There's always one,' said Naomi.

'Damn sight more than one,' Susan returned, making no secret of looking us both over. In her job she had to be observant, and I could see how that trait might spill over into real life. She had sharp eyes, sharp fingernails, and smelt faintly of smoke. After my experience with it the previous night, it made me feel sick. She took a cigarette and held it, unlit, between her fingers, indicating that we should keep it short.

'Thanks for seeing us, Susan.'

'Suze,' she said. 'I've had nothing to do with Martin since he did what he did. Since before that, even.' It seemed like her voice, face and personality had all been dried out by smoke, and it made my own throat ache in sympathy.

Naomi did most of the talking.

'News of his death must have stirred things up a bit?'

'He killed three kids,' said Suze, matter-of-factly. 'I'm not holding a torch. If I had been, I'd have set fire to him before anyone else got the chance.'

'There was no love lost between you, then?'

'No love full-stop, darling. If you're here asking where I was—'

'Nothing like that.'

'Cos I was here until late, then with my mother.'

'We know a man killed Martin. He was witnessed at the scene. If it's true that you've had no contact in the last twelve years, then we've got no reason to suspect you.'

'Not a word since he signed the divorce papers.'

'You must have needed a magnifying glass for his signature . . .'

Suze nodded. 'Had to help him do it. Martin didn't really go to school. If you don't think I did it, then why are you here?'

'How did the two of you meet?' said Naomi.

'He worked on a loft conversion at the shop I used to own. I had big dreams I'd live above it.' She laughed to herself. 'As you can see, they all came true. My first real partner, Al, helped set it up. Lovely man, but he died in a car crash.' She said this slowly, as if handling something of great value.

'I'm sorry to hear that,' said Naomi.

'So a year later it was nice to get asked out on a date. I can't say we ever clicked, to be honest, Martin and me. He was the roving type. I was the homebody.'

'But you married?' said Naomi.

'I got pregnant.' Suze saw the question in her face. 'We never had kids in the end. I miscarried, but by then we were almost walking up the aisle anyway. I knew it was the wrong decision while I was making it.'

'I know the feeling,' I said.

'So I talked myself into the big day. I thought marriage might be a comfort after losing Al, losing the baby. I found out I was on a real losing streak, though.'

'But you married again?' I said, glancing at her wedding ring.

She shook her head. 'Most of the old boys who come here are drinking in the last chance saloon. All looking for someone to pull up a stool and waste what's left of their lives. It's easier to wear a ring.' She hesitated. 'I could never have remarried after Martin.'

'You shouldn't feel guilty for what he did,' I said.

'Guilt?' she barked out one, joyless *ha*. 'That's one of your modern reasons. Mine's much more old-fashioned. By the time Martin left me I was damaged goods.'

'I don't understand . . .'

'I couldn't have children,' she said.

'Was this because of the miscarriage?' Naomi asked gently.

Suze fell silent, looking at the unlit cigarette between her fingers.

'Like I said, Martin was the roving type. But sometimes he did bring things home with him. In my case, a dose of chlamydia. I developed PID and then scarring of the fallopian tubes.' Her eyes went to the glass door behind me. 'Like I said, I was on a losing streak.'

I glanced over my shoulder and saw that she was looking at her own reflection, wondering when the streak might come to an end.

6

'Something mouldy,' said Naomi, referring to Esther's description of Wick's ex-wife. We'd gone next door to a dark but welcoming pub, where we shared two pints and a bowl of peanuts.

I nodded. 'Sensitively put but she's shoved us in the right direction. Suze can't have kids because of untreated chlamydia, contracted around twelve years ago . . .'

'At the same time that Frank and Maggie's marriage was falling apart because of a sexually transmitted infection,' said Naomi. 'How does Esther know all this stuff?'

'We know from the photos on the phone that she spoke to Wick at least once before he died, and there's the suggestion of a pre-existing relationship before that . . .'

'And I guess there's whatever she stole from Blake's house, too,' said Naomi, looking at me. 'So come on, say it.'

'Say what?'

'That you think the Moores and the Wicks are connected.'

'The timelines match up. Suppose Martin Wick and Margaret were having an affair. It provides a link no one ever knew about. It could even suggest a motive for the original killing. . .'

'Which is?'

'Wick blames Margaret Moore for infecting him, for ruining his marriage. He kills her and the kids.'

'Or,' said Naomi, 'Frank Moore finds out Margaret's being

unfaithful. He kills her and the kids in a fit of rage, framing the man she was cheating on him with.'

'The problem with Frank is he has an alibi for the night his family were murdered.'

'There are more problems than that,' said Naomi. 'What about Wick's Lizzie obsession? Where would that fit into him having an affair with her mother?'

'Maybe that was all cooked up by the cops at the time?'

Naomi shook her head. 'There were witnesses who saw him skulking around Lizzie's school, hanging round the house, watching her.'

'He could have gone to those places hoping to see the mother.'

'They found Lizzie's clothes in his room, and you're forgetting about Short Back and Sides.'

'What about him?'

'His big problem with Wick was that he fetishized pictures of Lizzie Moore in prison. He said he'd cut them out of the newspaper . . .'

I nodded, reluctantly.

It had been one of the few times that Short Back had spoken convincingly about anything. Adam had even gone so far as showing me the pictures that he'd found in Wick's possessions.

'So what if Lizzie and Martin were having an affair?' I said.

'Lizzie was a kid, Aidan.'

'Stranger things have happened. Look at Wick's thing with Esther. Even from behind bars he had her wrapped round his little finger. The age difference there's pretty eye-watering, too.'

'So you're saying Martin Wick has an affair with Lizzie, and gives her an STI . . .' I nodded. 'But, wait a minute, how would Frank contract chlamydia from his own daughter?'

I didn't say anything and saw the possibility cross Naomi's mind.

'What's wrong with you?' she said.

'The jury's out, but it certainly gives Frank a secret worth killing for.'

'Agreed . . .'

'And however it went down, we've got a possible link between the two families that no one seemed to know about before.'

'But what do we do with it? Margaret's like the elephant in the room with Frank. The STI thing only came out because he was shaken from seeing the witness statements.'

'The elephant in the room,' I said.

I took out my phone and dialled the number I had for Charlie Sloane.

'I'm boarding a train,' he said, picking up. 'And I've got my heart set on the quiet carriage.'

'Glad to hear it, Charlie, but I need a favour.'

'Tell it to the dial tone.'

'Y'know, we could still have you arrested.' He didn't say anything. 'Or you could leak a story for us . . .'

'The printed word's something I happen to live and die for, whatever you might think of me. I'm not interested in being someone's mouthpiece.'

'Don't worry, the printed word isn't fast enough, this needs to go out sooner.'

'Like a tweet?' he said, after a slight pause. 'Come on, then. What's the story, morning glory?'

'The Detective Inspector who survived the attack at St Mary's Hospital has made incredible strides towards recovery. He's been brought around from his induced coma and we'll be speaking to him about the attack tomorrow morning.'

'Huh,' he said. 'What time tomorrow?'

'Very first thing.'

'Consider it done, but this makes us even.'

'Sure,' I said, ringing off.

The barman was calling last orders and Naomi was frowning at me.

'Sutty's not awake . . .'

'I want to know who'll pay him a visit if they think he is. In the meantime, I need you to get over to Strangeways. Get hold of Frank Moore's records. Employment, counselling sessions, attendees, everything.'

'Now?'

'It's a prison, you'd hope someone's awake.'

'What about you?'

I drained my glass. 'You were right, I forgot about Short Back and Sides.'

7

'What?' said Axel, staring at me through the chain on the door. I hadn't brought my lock-pick set with me this time, and had to wait in the rain until a little old lady let me into the building. I was still breathing heavily from ten flights of stairs.

'I can't believe I'm saying this, but I want to talk to Short Back.'

'He's not in,' he said, pushing the door shut. I had my foot in the way and he looked up at me. 'We've got a new coffee table, if you need to get your aggression out there.'

I waited.

'He's hosting at the Carlyle.'

'Hosting what?' I said.

'The karaoke. Does it every Thursday night.'

'That's . . .' Axel raised an eyebrow. '. . . Not what I expected.'

'People can surprise you,' he said. 'Anything else?'

'Don't expect him back any time soon.'

The Carlyle was the condemned-looking pub on the corner, with a burned-out car in front. It looked like some daring, charred sculpture left there by an art school graduate. The bar was almost empty, just a few stragglers hanging on for last orders. The sound system was banging out an instrumental version of 'Young at Heart', and Short Back was on stage, delivering a passable Sinatra.

Vocally, at least.

The stage lights were switched on, detailing the crater in his skull. The difference between the way he looked and the way he sounded, between what he was and what he wanted to be, felt like the excavation of a sad, universal truth, and I decided to let him finish singing.

I went to the bar, keeping my eyes on the stage, and ordered a large Jameson's.

Short Back was so lost in the music, so blinded by the lights, that he didn't see me, and by the time the song soared toward its conclusion, his voice breaking with emotion, I'd already downed the whiskey. I turned into the bar as he stepped off the stage, and he came alongside me to order a drink.

I put out my hand to shake his, cuffing him as soon as I saw his wrist.

'The fuck?' he said, eyes flashing pure mania.

I was probably giving him the same look.

'Let's have a drink,' I said.

'Take this fucking shit off me.'

I dragged his arm towards mine by the cuff. 'I said, let's have a drink.'

'The ladies must love you . . .'

I ordered us two large whiskeys and turned to him.

'You said Martin Wick was obsessed with Lizzie Moore.'

'Yeah,' he said, uncertainly. 'That blonde girl he killed.'

'And you found pictures of her in his cell?'

He nodded, looking wary but still disturbed by it. I recalled what he'd said about the dent in his skull coming courtesy of his stepdad and tried to take it down a notch. I removed the envelope that Adam had given to me from my jacket pocket and held it open, showing him the clippings.

'Were these the ones you saw, Chris?'

He looked at the clippings then away from them, revolted. 'Yeah.'

I waited for his eyes to come back to me and then started to unlock the handcuffs.

'Talk to me,' I said.

VII
Violent Past

1

Naomi and I were sitting in Sutty's hospital room with the lights switched off, listening to the steady beep of the heart monitor. It was the dead of night and we'd each taken a seat either side of the door.

If you were looking in, you wouldn't be able to see us.

Sutty's few visitors had known not to bring flowers, and I'd cracked open one of the bottles of Johnnie Walker that had been left at his bedside. When I took a glug and offered it to Naomi she gave me an instinctive look of reproach, then shrugged, accepted the bottle and took a drink.

'Christ,' she said, handing it back. 'No one liked him enough to buy a mixer.'

'I could probably find you some liquid soap . . .'

'Just tell me what you think's coming through that door.'

'I honestly don't know. It might be the cleaner, it might be a petrol bomb.'

'At least then we could see what we're doing.'

'It might even be nothing at all,' I said.

We both fell silent at the footsteps sounding along the corridor.

I thought I could hear two distinct sets, and I held my breath as they drew to a stop outside. The person or persons paused, perhaps looking through the small glass pane into the darkened room. There was a low murmur as two voices conferred with each other, then the door opened and they stepped inside. One of the figures, a large man, approached Sutty's bed, the curtain drawn around it, and I flicked on the lamp beside me.

Frank Moore stopped with his back to us. He turned, looking from Naomi to me, then to his wife, Rebecca, still standing in the open doorway. He drew himself up to his full six feet and four inches, finding a smile for us.

'I always said you were in the dark, Waits.'

'Frank.' I nodded. 'Rebecca. Why don't you join us?'

Moore turned towards the two empty chairs either side of Sutty's bed and went smoothly to the nearest one. He sat bolt upright with remembered military posture. Rebecca followed, a little less sure of herself, moving first to her husband and then to the free seat on the other side of the bed.

Frank moved the curtain, squinting through the gap for a second.

'He doesn't look awake to me . . .'

'They said that before the coma,' I said, setting the bottle down on the floor. 'What brings you here?'

Frank brushed his hand through the lightning bolt shock of white hair in his head. 'We read that Sutcliffe had been brought round. I was hoping he might take over the case.'

'Frank,' said Rebecca.

'There's no reason to take this man seriously,' he said out the side of his mouth.

'We came to offer support,' said Rebecca, arranging the flowers in her hand. 'Frank won't admit it, but he feels responsible.'

'That's a first,' I said. 'We've got a butchered family, a murdered prisoner, a police officer fallen in the line of duty, another one still fighting for his life. And absolutely no one willing to take responsibility.'

'Martin Wick,' said Frank, levelly. 'He takes responsibility, whether the bastard wanted it or not. As for the rest? That's your job, Waits. The world won't come to you.'

'But what if Martin Wick wasn't responsible?'

Frank's head weaved like a punch-drunk boxer, and he gripped his knees to steady himself. 'He wrote a very detailed confession,' he said. 'Maybe you should read it.'

'That's probably more than he managed.'

'What are you talking about?'

'Martin Wick was functionally illiterate, Frank – we spoke to his ex-wife today. They broke up a few months before your family were murdered. She had to help him sign his own divorce papers. How do you think he did with a twenty-five-page confession?'

'Well, blood doesn't lie . . .'

'Sometimes it does.'

'What's that supposed to mean?'

He said it like he was starting a fight in a bar, and Rebecca went on explaining their presence, as if the intervening argument hadn't happened.

'We came here to visit a man who was hurt guarding Martin Wick,' she said. 'We came here because we have experience with trauma and we can help. You're acting like we climbed in the bloody window.'

'You did sign in, I take it?'

'What do you think?' she shot back, sounding suddenly like her husband.

'Constable Black, could you confirm that for us?'

Naomi got up and left the room while we waited in silence.

Frank was so tall that he loomed even from a seated position, and I thought again how enormous he must have looked to a frightened wife and three scared children.

Naomi returned with the sign-in sheet, handing it to me and resuming her seat. Both Frank and Rebecca had signed in, clearly stating their names, contact details and time of arrival.

They'd even given their reason for the visit.

To offer gratis counselling support to Detective Inspector Sutcliffe and his family.

I looked up. Saw Frank's head cast low, Rebecca clutching her flowers. The heat was rushing to my cheeks, the back of my neck burning red.

'I'm sorry,' I said, dropping the pretence. 'As you can probably tell, Detective Inspector Sutcliffe isn't awake.'

'What was all this?' said Rebecca, a jolt of that same strength I'd seen the last time we'd questioned her husband's good name. 'Because I think the media might be interested to hear about it. Charlie Sloane's had your number right from the start.'

'Rebecca . . .' said Frank, trying to think.

'It's the truth,' she went on, pointing at her husband. 'Here you have a man as much a victim of Martin Wick as the people he killed, and all you can see is—'

'Rebecca,' said Frank, more forcefully this time. She looked at him but his eyes were on me. 'Tell me again, Waits. About this confession . . .'

'It might be nothing,' I said. 'But it's the truth. He couldn't read or write. When he signed it he was at least in shock, maybe worse. He didn't have a friend in the world, and as soon as he could, he tried to retract it.'

The look of concern that had been growing on Frank's face was now threatening to overwhelm it. He looked like a man who'd had something of great value delivered to the wrong address. I was certain, suddenly, that he hadn't killed his family, certain that he'd had nothing to do with it.

He'd never doubted Wick's guilt until now.

'There's another crime here, though, Frank, and I have to ask. Did you have anything to do with Martin Wick's murder?'

He held eye contact with me and shook his head.

I looked at Naomi and she stood.

'Why don't we put those in some water?' she said, gesturing to the flowers they'd brought. Rebecca got up and opened the toilet door. She let out a startled cry as Short Back and Sides emerged, wearing a Sinatra-inspired fedora.

'A'ight, Frank?' he called across the bed.

The look on Moore's face hardened, moving from incomprehension to suppressed rage. He held out an arm to his wife and she joined him on the far side of the bed. Then he stood, giving her the chair while he leaned, massively, into the wall, arms crossed. I could see the muscles beneath his blazer, tensed, testing the sleeves to breaking point.

'I believe you've met Mr Sides,' I said.

'What's going on?' said Rebecca. 'Who is this man?'

Short Back emerged fully into the room and took his hat off, revealing the dent in his skull. Smiling, he showed us the golden grille covering his teeth. Alongside the neck tattoo, the chemically assisted thousand-yard stare, he looked a little like a patient who'd made a break for it.

'Mr Moore was my counsellor in Strangeways,' he said.

'What kind of counselling did he give you?' I asked.

Short Back sucked noisily on his grille. 'All kinds.' He focused on Rebecca, the only person in the room he hadn't met. 'You might not have noticed but I have, like, a slight physical defect I sometimes get self-conscious about. Mr Moore helped me see I was a thing of beauty, whatever the weather.'

'You also killed a man,' I reminded him.

'By accident, yeah. That's why I was there. Mr Moore said I should forgive myself, like.'

'How did the two of you get along?' I asked.

'He was good to me,' said Short Back with what sounded like some real emotion. 'Not many have been.'

Frank nodded. 'Glad to be of service, Chris. You were good to me, too.'

'Yeah,' said Short Back. 'You were especially good to me when you found out I was Martin Wick's cellmate. Even more once you heard what I was in for.'

Frank shrugged without looking at anyone in particular, flexing the muscles in his arms as if to remind us they were still there. 'I don't recall anything like that.'

'Constable Black,' I said.

Naomi collected some papers at her feet. 'I've just come from Strangeways,' she said. 'One thing the governor gets right is his paperwork. We pulled the records of every inmate who'd attended one of your survival sessions while inside. Could you confirm these names for us?'

She stood, handing him the sheet.

Moore had reddened, and I could see him trying to think his way around whatever was coming, but he glanced at the sheet and nodded.

'Looks about right. No Martin Wick on there, as I said.'

'No,' said Naomi, glancing at Short Back. 'Chris is on there, though.'

'So he should be,' Frank answered with a smile. 'Look, I could go down this list and tell you about every man on it, I worked with them all, but—'

'Sorry,' said Naomi. 'I think I've given you the wrong list.' She handed him another sheet. '*This* is the list of men you worked with at Strangeways. That first one is a list of all the men who attacked Martin Wick while he was inside.'

Frank looked at the two almost identical lists and smiled, eyes drifting to the door.

I got up and stood in his way. 'How did you manage it, Frank?'

'I don't know what you're talking about.'

'In that case, maybe Short Back can enlighten us . . .'

'He told us what Martin had done to his family,' he said. 'Told us what Martin had done to his kids. Told us Martin stalked his daughter before killing her, that he was a nonce.'

'What about the pictures?' I asked.

'Oh, yeah. He said Wick kept posting him newspaper clippings from prison. Pictures of his little girl . . .'

'Lizzie Moore?' I said, looking at Frank.

'Yeah, mental. Like a fucking serial killer or something. Mr Moore asked me if I'd, like, search our cell, on the low-down. Said I might find some. So I did, and I did. After that, he had me convinced.'

'I don't understand,' said Rebecca.

310

Frank put a hand on her shoulder but she shrugged him off.

'Frank was using his position at Strangeways,' I said. 'He manipulated men with life sentences into attacking Martin Wick while he was inside. What he's holding there is a smartly chosen list of inmates. He targeted violent criminals. Didn't you, Frank?'

He didn't say anything.

'Men who'd gone down for twenty, thirty years. To them, a few more months for assault was worth it, especially with Wick being so loathed. Some of them he paid, some of them he just manipulated. It'd be easy to defend if Martin Wick really killed his family, but now he's wondering, what if he was an innocent man?'

'Come on,' said Frank, turning rigidly to his wife. 'We're leaving.'

'Don't forget to sign out,' I said, waving the sheet in front of him. He frowned, looking at it in my hand. I made a show of studying his writing. 'Now, where have I seen that before?' I dug out the envelope that Adam had given to me, holding it against the sheet. 'Mrs Moore, can I trouble you for one more thing? Is this your husband's handwriting?'

She tried to get up and fell back into her seat, then stood abruptly, not looking at Frank, coming clumsily towards me. She covered her mouth when she saw the envelope. It was addressed to Martin Wick in her husband's handwriting.

'What's inside?' she asked.

'Come on, Rebecca, let's—'

'*What's inside?*' she repeated. I held open the envelope. Her hand went from her mouth to her chest, like she couldn't breathe. 'You . . .' she said, turning to her husband. '. . . You were sending that animal pictures of your dead daughter? Your little girl?'

Frank tried turning a wince into a smile but it wouldn't go.

He could lie to me quite happily, but he nodded at his wife, sinking into a seat with his head in his hands, looking revolted with himself. I held the door open for Short Back. He swept his hat back on and left the room with a level of discretion I wouldn't have thought him capable of. Even he could sense the shame in the air.

2

The door opened suddenly and we all turned. I'd been expecting to see Short Back, returning for some reason, but it was former Detective Inspector Kevin Blake. Once he saw me, he couldn't leave, and he stepped into the centre of the room, letting the door fall shut.

He was even paler than the last time we'd seen him. Under the harsh hospital lighting, his skin looked a sickly neon-white.

He stared at the curtain surrounding Sutty's bed, but didn't say anything. The room was silent apart from the steady beep of the heart monitor. If it had been hooked up to me it might have been going a bit faster.

'Evening, Kev. Nice of you to drop in.'

He started with the obvious. 'Doesn't look like he's awake . . .'

'Same old Sutty,' I said. 'But you're right, we've all been had. Naomi and I saw the news ourselves and came running. Looks like you had the same thought . . .'

'What's going on?' said Blake, more to the room than to me. His antennae were still finely tuned, and he turned, trying to get a clear read on us.

Frank looked away, standing, offering Rebecca his chair, resuming his looming position against the wall. He folded his arms tightly across his chest, like he was trying to force shut an open wound.

'Frank's been enjoying his time at Strangeways so much he's gonna start sleeping over,' I said.

'You what?'

'You tried to tell us, Kev, but I wasn't listening.'

'What did I try and tell you?'

'You tried to put us on Frank's trail.'

Frank's expression didn't change but I heard the material in his sleeves flex as he gripped his arms a little tighter.

'I wouldn't say that exactly, his name just came up.'

'But we'd never have made it to his survival seminar without your tip. What did you want us to see?'

'A man who'd pulled himself together . . .'

'Or a charlatan dishing out platitudes for cash?'

'Now, hang on,' said Blake, but as he looked around the room he saw that not even the Moores were prepared to defend Frank's work now.

'Every single time we talked,' I said, 'you kept banging on about Frank's charity work, the poor conditions at Strangeways. You even brought up the subject of Short Back and Sides, like you were trying to put us on to the trail . . .'

'You're giving me too much credit here, pal. Put you on to the trail of what?'

'Frank's work at Strangeways,' I said.

'He was working at Strangeways? News to me.'

'We pulled his employment records today,' said Naomi. 'You're a reference.'

Blake shrugged. 'I can hardly help who puts me down as a reference.'

Before we could push him on this, there was a knock at the door and I opened it to Charlie Sloane. He was out of breath, moving his head from side to side, trying to look over my shoulders.

'This a private party or can anyone join?'

'The more the merrier,' I said, standing to one side. 'I thought you were on a train out of town?'

'I was, until you told me your man was up and at it again.' Sloane sidled inside, clapping his hands together. 'Said anything yet?'

I closed the door behind him. 'Don't believe everything you read in the *Mail*, Charlie. I'm afraid he's still under. We've had a steady stream of well-wishers, though. I take it that's why you're here?'

'Sure,' said Sloane, taking my seat, ripping a handful of grapes from the bunch he'd brought with him.

'We were just discussing the revelation that Frank's been visiting Strangeways every week for the last five or six years.'

His eyes took in the room, the drama, and he laughed. 'No wonder poor Martin couldn't eat a meal that hadn't been spat in . . .'

I nodded. 'Apparently that only occurred to you and me, though. Blake says he had no idea that Frank Moore was a violent man . . .'

'Did he not?' said Sloane, chewing more grapes and looking at the former detective inspector. I could hear the burgeoning journalistic interest in his voice.

'That was a surprise to me, too. Since you showed him the witness statements from Frank's neighbours twelve years ago.'

'Witness statements?' said Rebecca. 'Witness statements of what?'

Sloane spoke with a mouthful of mashed grapes. 'Your husband was getting to know his first wife's face like the back of his hand.'

Rebecca looked at the floor with a kind of quiet dignity, I thought.

'I never saw any statements,' said Blake. 'Sloane didn't tell me shit twelve years ago.'

Sloane glared at him. 'You weren't interested twelve years ago.'

'He definitely got interested again this week,' I said. 'That's why he made sure we saw them.'

'Did I?' Blake clapped his hands together. 'Did I, really?'

'You vandalized your own home when I sent a squad car round to take a statement.'

'My arse . . .'

'Then you just happened to mention that you were supposed to be meeting Sloane.'

'I suppose I broke into my house, stole my own phone as well?'

'No, that's you trying to change the subject. We've arrested the person who stole your phone, don't worry about that.' Blake was trapped between two topics he didn't want to discuss, and he reverted to the previous one.

'Why would I sit on stories about Frank's violence for twelve years?'

'Charlie,' I said. 'You told us why the witness statements didn't run at the time . . .'

'We deal in heroes and villains. Blake had already provided the villain.'

'Simple as that,' I said. 'Making Frank out to be the bad guy twelve years ago wouldn't fit the narrative.'

When I glanced over, Frank Moore was staring right through me.

With a man of his height and physicality, you don't read the expression on his face, but his body language. Emotions seemed to pass through him from head to toe, and he was in a state of continual, agitated motion now.

Arms folded, loosened, re-folded, like he was trying to holster his fists.

Blake swiped the air. 'If I'd known about those statements—'

'We're always hearing about what you would have done, Kev.' Everyone looked at me. 'You would have looked at Frank differently if you'd seen the statements. You would have looked for other suspects if Wick hadn't been covered in blood. You would have reported his abuse in prison if you'd known Frank was working there. You'd have reported your phone missing if you hadn't forgotten. We're supposed to believe all these omissions suiting your story are a series of happy accidents.'

'I'm a long fucking way from happy,' he shouted, clutching his chest. 'What are you trying to tell me? That Frank did it?'

I thought he looked afraid of the answer.

Frank rose up to full height and walked slowly across the room. He leaned into the wall, right in front of Kevin Blake, staring right at him.

His every move carried the threat of physical violence now.

'Let's talk about the mobile that was stolen from your house.'

'This again . . .'

'This again and again, until we hear something that sounds like the truth. Why didn't you report it missing?'

'I didn't get around to it.'

I shook my head. Looked at him. 'Either you didn't want the police to find what was on that phone, or you didn't want the police to find the person who'd taken it.'

Blake trembled. 'Why would I be worried about some fucking junkie?'

'Maybe she told you something you didn't want to hear.'

'Like what?'

'Something that threw the last twelve years into a different light, something that had you scrambling to shit into a desk fan and fire it at Frank Moore.'

'Excuse me,' said Rebecca.

'*Like what?*' shouted Blake.

'Excuse me,' said Rebecca, standing.

We were all on our feet now except Charlie Sloane, who was still eating grapes, watching the drama unfold with amused interest. Rebecca was looking at the heart monitor, which had been steadily beeping faster as our conversation had grown more heated.

'I think we need to get someone for him.'

'I wouldn't worry about it,' I said. Everyone in the room looked at me. 'Detective Inspector Sutcliffe's not here. We moved him to another room two hours ago.'

3

I drew back the curtain and the figure in the bed sat up, peeling away bandages. Once exposed, Esther looked about the room, even more flushed than usual, sweating and sharp-eyed. She started moving the bedsheets we'd used to fill out her figure, ripping off layers of clothes and finally pulling off the pads connected to the heart monitor.

It flatlined into one long, unbroken beep.

'Did you break into this man's house?' I asked.

She stared at Kevin Blake and nodded.

'Who is this woman?' said Rebecca.

Charlie Sloane chuckled. 'She's an intimate of Martin Wick's, I've seen the pictures to prove it . . .'

'Then what's she doing here?'

'The two of them corresponded while Wick was in prison,' I said. 'They even managed to meet a few times while he was under armed guard. You might say she's our window into his soul . . .'

'Well,' said Rebecca, folding her arms. 'Some of us would rather not look.'

'Esther, can you tell us when you first met Kevin Blake?'

'At his house,' she said, watching Blake twist under Frank's glare. 'A few weeks ago.'

'You told him about the campaign of violence against Martin Wick. You must have told him who was behind it, too, because afterwards he went out looking for dirt on Frank Moore.'

'He wouldn't help me, though.'

'How did you want him to help you?'

'I've had enough of this,' said Blake, craning his neck to look up at Moore. He looked weak, sick, wrong, weaving on his feet. 'I can only apologize for this display, Frank. And you.' He stabbed a wild finger in my direction. 'You should be ashamed of yourself.'

'There's the door, Kev.'

He started forward but Frank shoved him back into a chair.

Esther was gripping the bedsheets, trying to keep from shaking. 'Once I knew he wasn't interested in the truth,' she said, 'I thought, fuck him – I went in a back window one night and took everything on Wick I could find.'

'As well as a phone . . .'

'Was sitting there, passcode attached. Why not?'

'And how did you use that information?'

'He had files on where Wick was, what personnel were assigned, all that. He was clearly still friends with the cops, even if he wasn't one any more. One of the other things I got was *his* number,' she said, nodding at Sloane. 'Conned a few grand out of the fat fuck who wrote all those stories about Martin.'

A flash of anger crossed Sloane's face. 'You wouldn't have if I'd known who you were, missy.'

I nodded. 'She'd probably have got a bit more for that.'

'What's that mean?'

I waved him quiet. 'Why did you take the picture, Esther?'

'You were right, I wanted the whole world looking at Martin. We wanted to make dickheads out of them all.'

'Mission accomplished,' said Naomi, smiling, encouraging. 'What did you do with the cash?'

'Some to pay off Short Back, some to pay off that woman cop.'

'Louisa Jankowski?'

'Yeah, some foreign name. I paid her to let me know when Martin was alone, to give me a few minutes with him.'

'Sorry,' said Sloane, waving everyone quiet. 'You said I'd have paid more to talk to her if I knew who she was. Shit or get off the pot.'

Esther looked about the room. 'Men,' she said. 'You've got sex on the brain. Me and Martin, intimate? He was my dad, dickhead.'

Frank turned from Blake, squinting. 'Martin Wick didn't have kids,' he said.

One by one, they all turned to look at me.

'You knew Martin was sleeping with Margaret when you got together, Frank. You must have known there was a chance that Lizzie wasn't yours.'

4

Frank Moore walked to the wall and punched it as hard as he could. The whole room seemed to shake and he turned unsteadily, slamming the heart monitor to the floor. It had been droning in one, unbroken beep ever since Esther had removed the sensors, but he kicked it now, stomping repeatedly until it was just wreckage.

He stood there, in the centre of the room, fists clenched.

'When we confronted Frank with the witness statements suggesting he was an abuser, he told us the truth for a change. That he and Margaret fought because she gave him chlamydia. So it was interesting when Wick's ex-wife told us that Martin had infected her with the same thing, at around the same time. What Frank didn't mention was that Margaret had been unfaithful before.'

Frank was looking closer at the bed, squinting at the young woman inside it.

'Rebecca,' I said. 'You told us the problems in their marriage went back long before you were on the scene. Care to elaborate?'

She glanced from her husband to the woman in the bed. 'Frank never thought Lizzie was his . . .'

'The dates didn't match up,' Frank said distractedly, still standing in the debris of the heart monitor. 'I would have been in active deployment when Maggie got pregnant.'

'OK,' said Sloane, staring at Esther. 'She's Wick's progeny. Does that mean he didn't kill the Moores, or that he did? Where was she? Where's she been all this time?'

'I ran away,' said Esther. 'I'd found out Frank wasn't my real dad, that Martin was. Then I thought he'd killed them all. I didn't have anyone.'

Kevin Blake was undoing the top buttons of his shirt.

'When did you find out Frank wasn't your real dad?' said Sloane.

'All the bullying and threats and bullshit,' she said, looking at Frank. 'All the violence. You do realize she was glad to tell me?'

'You're wrong about one thing,' he said. Some power had left his body, and his voice had weakened with it. 'I was your real dad and I still am, whatever you might think. Whatever the DNA might say. I raised you for twelve years. Loved you for twelve years. I've loved you every day since.'

He took two halting steps towards the bed.

Esther, Lizzie Moore, looked at him like he was poison.

'Don't you get it? DNA doesn't mean shit. You stopped being my dad the day you raised a hand to her. You don't get to decide, Frank. I do. I say that little girl you raised's still alive, my brother and sister are still alive, my mum. You're the only one who fucking died, because we decided it.'

I went to the bed, trying to stand between them. 'Why don't you tell us what happened that night?'

'I can tell you Martin didn't do it,' she said. 'He was with me. It was the first time we'd ever met. To be honest, I didn't even like him. He'd tried to dress up, brush back his hair and stuff, but he couldn't help looking like a loser next to Frank. He took me to a Little Chef. We had an awkward fry-up and he took us home.'

She looked about the room.

'Problem was, his van broke down on the way. We were late. It was dark, and as much as we knocked, no one answered. Martin didn't know what to do, so I stayed with him at his hotel. He snuck me in so there wouldn't be any questions, and we went back in the morning.'

'What happened then?'

'We got there really early,' she said. 'He knocked but there was

321

still no answer. We could see inside a bit now cos it was light, and when he looked through a window he almost fell over. He told me to wait and went round the back. I heard glass break and started to get scared. I wasn't tall enough to see what he'd seen through the window, so I just waited. It felt like I waited forever.'

She swallowed, wiped her eyes.

'Then I went round the back and followed him through the kitchen window. He'd cut himself climbing through but I followed him anyway. I walked into the hall and . . .'

We all looked between each other.

'. . . And I could see blood everywhere. And there was this pile of dirty clothes at the bottom of the stairs. Somehow there was a face attached to them, and somehow it was my mum's. I just stood there with my back to the front door, looking at her. I couldn't remember how to get out. I couldn't even remember how to breathe. Then Martin came down the stairs. He was covered in blood, *covered* in it, and I realized I couldn't hear Arthur or Mary. He said something. Something like, "They're all dead," and I started to scream. He tried to hug me and I hit him. Now I know he was as scared as I was, but then I just thought he'd broken in and killed them. I called him a psycho, got the door open and ran.'

'Where did you go?' asked Naomi.

Esther shook her head like she couldn't remember.

'School, I think. I slept in the games shed that first night, I'd never been so tired in my life. When I woke up and walked into town, Martin was in all the papers. The Sleepwalker, they called him. He'd been arrested. They said he was guilty, and as far as I knew I'd been standing on the driveway while he did it. Some of the papers even said I was dead.'

She put her hand to her breastbone, pressing hard.

'I wondered if I was. It was one of the great disappointments of my life to realize I was still breathing.'

'Lizzie . . .' said Frank.

'After all that blood and death and fear, do you know what the

worst part was? Do you know what really fucking scared me?'
Frank shook his head. 'That they'd send me to live with you.'

All the air seemed to go out of him.

'Whoever took a knife and cut them up, well, at least he made it
quick. Real cruelty's killing someone slowly, over years, with words
and insults and threats and lies. I'll never hate my mother's killer
like I fucking hate you, Frank. You're the reason I ran away that day.
You're the reason I've run away every day since.' Her voice broke. 'I
lived rough. I fell in with a girl who was doing a charity scam with
her ma. They looked after me. They were travellers and it wasn't
long after we ended up in Ireland. I fucked for drugs and money,
Frank, I want you to know that. At first, Esther was my whore
name, but after a while it just felt like who I was all the time.'

'What made you come back?' asked Naomi.

'The papers said Martin was dying and that brought it all up again.
Then I found a copy of his book in a charity shop,' she said, nodding
at Blake. He was leaning into the wall now, like it was the only thing
keeping him upright. 'It was hard to read, and it was the first time I'd
let myself think about what happened. He said the forensics proved
they'd all died on Friday night, and that's when I realized I was Martin's alibi. He'd been with me that entire time.'

'Raising questions about how he wrote, read and signed a twenty-
five-page confession,' I said, turning to Kevin Blake. 'Especially as
an illiterate man.'

'I'd rather not discuss it,' he said, one hand on his chest.

'Dad said they kept him awake for three or four days. Kept telling him what he'd done, over and over again, until he had it down
pat. Then they pressed record and transcribed it. They said he could
sleep if he signed all twenty-five pages. He was already in shock
when they got their hands on him . . .'

'Who,' said Blake, leaning into the wall. There were tears in his
eyes. 'I mean, if it wasn't him, then who . . . ?'

'That was never our question to answer,' I said. 'It was yours.
You might have meant well. Putting a killer behind bars and

making sure he stayed there. But you fitted up the wrong man, Kev. All it took was planting the murder weapon in his hotel room and coaching him through his confession. Your book was the cherry on top.'

Blake looked from face to face, doubling up as he did so.

'Then Esther turned up twelve years later, a cast-iron alibi for Martin Wick. Proof that you'd built everything, your case, your book, your life, on lies. I kept wondering how anyone could get close enough to shake hands with Rennick and then stab him. I was thinking affairs, bribes . . .'

'He recognized me,' said Blake. 'Said, "You're the man who caught Martin Wick. *Let me shake your hand . . .*" '

'Then you stabbed him in the neck.'

Blake swallowed three times in a row, gulping air.

'I hate what happened to him,' he said. '*Hate it*. But I haven't got long. When you get to the shit end of the stick, you start wondering what you stack up to. I didn't want to die discredited, a fucking joke. And Sutty?' He shook his head. 'Whatever. He was no cop and neither are you. It's no surprise you're his fucking protégé.'

'I didn't set anyone on fire, Kev.'

'I told you the first time we met,' he said, clawing at his chest. 'For someone, that fire was the only possible course of action. Well, that someone just happened to be me. I had no choice. I was in and out in five minutes.' He gulped again and then slid down the wall, landing in a heap on the floor.

5

Naomi, Esther and I were on the roof of St Mary's Hospital, staring down at the sodium-lit car park. Frank Moore had been arrested and Kevin Blake was in intensive care, having suffered a massive heart attack. Rebecca Moore, bone-white from the evening's revelations, had been taken home in a squad car, and Charlie Sloane had torn off to write his exclusive.

Once the excitement was over, Esther pleaded for us to take her outside, to get some air. I agreed, leading us up the stairwell where we'd first brushed past each other, this time with Naomi in tow. It had been a long night, but we were all wide awake with the exhilaration of answers, and we were passing the bottle of Johnnie Walker between us as dawn broke.

There was still one question, hanging over everything.

'Who killed them?' said Esther, giving voice to it, the story of her life.

We were all leaning against the wall, looking over the edge.

'I don't know,' I said. 'Blake only became involved with Wick's arrest, we're sure of that. Both he and Frank have alibis, and I'm convinced Frank's certainty about Martin's guilt was genuine. He thought having him attacked inside Strangeways for all those years was justified because he'd killed his family.' I glanced at Esther. 'For a minute I thought about you . . .'

'I was a kid. Hard to believe I ever was one, now.'

As I looked at her, I realized how young she must still be.

Twenty-four or -five at the most. She'd started to shiver, although it wasn't cold, and I wondered how far this might go towards getting her clean.

'What changed your mind?' she said.

'You're Martin's alibi. We can't talk to him now, but you're so certain of his innocence. I believe you.'

'I can't tell if it's the subject or the weather,' she said, 'but I'm fucking freezing.' She was wearing three double-wrapped nightgowns but had declined my long coat on fashion grounds. 'A smoke might get the blood flowing . . .'

I looked at Naomi.

She was wrapped up in her dark green parka and shrugged at me from its depths. It had been the first time I'd been myself, my best self, since we'd met, and I wanted her to like me. I hoped that she did.

'I'll go,' I said, taking the bottle. 'This probably isn't the day for going cold turkey.'

'I'll quit tomorrow,' said Esther.

I nodded and walked the twenty-five feet or so towards the doorway, weaving between an enormous bank of air conditioning units. When I reached the door, I paused to look back. Esther and Naomi seemed deep in conversation, their backs to me.

Just a parka jacket and a triple-wrapped nightgown.

I raised the bottle for a drink and felt an explosion of pain in my jaw.

A moment later it slammed into the ground and I put my hands out to break the fall a second too late. I tried to push myself up but was flattened by another blow to the head. I could taste thick, rich blood, oozing from my mouth, and felt its warmth flooding out and down my chin.

I could see two boots in front of me.

I looked up and saw a flash of Louisa Jankowski for a second before she brought the gun butt down on my head for a third, fourth, fifth blow. When I wrenched myself up off the ground again, I didn't know how much time had passed. My vision was blurred and I could feel one eye swelling shut.

I saw Louisa approaching Naomi from behind. My partner was still leaning against the wall, looking over the edge, and I tried to call out a warning but nothing came. Louisa raised her pistol and I started to move, feeling my way along an air conditioning unit to stay upright. Naomi must have heard me, because she'd begun to turn when the gun went off. The muzzle flash blasted her hood back and she fell, dead, to the ground.

Jankowski turned and saw me.

I backed into the stairwell, turning, belting down the staircase, and the gun went off again.

As soon as I was down the first flight I realized I should have hidden behind the door. I should have let Jankowski pass me and attacked her from behind, but all I could think of was running. I tripped at the top of the next flight and went headfirst, rolling down and landing in a painful heap at the bottom.

The lower half of my jaw felt like it had come loose from my body and I tried to reach up for a bannister, seeing the blood drain out of my mouth. I heard footsteps descending and turned towards them, seeing double, triple, overlapping images.

Louisa turned the corner, drawing her pistol.

'I had no choice,' she said. 'Without Esther, it's just a phone that called mine, it's nothing.' She licked her lips. 'But I really didn't want this.'

She levelled the gun and I heard a deafening bang.

When I opened my eyes I saw blood splattered against the wall and Louisa, sprawled, dead on the floor. I turned to see a large man in a black balaclava on the stairwell beneath me. He cocked his head, almost comically, then tapped his own pistol against his temple, as if warning me to be more careful in future. I got to my knees and started towards him but he turned to leave.

I made it two or three steps more before blacking out.

VIII
Everything Must Go

1

I came awake as an eight-year-old boy in the messy back seat of a family car. We'd moved around a lot in the year before my sister and I were taken into care, often spending nights parked in lay-bys or motorway service stations. Our mother drove all day, never explaining what we were leaving or what we were going to.

She just liked to keep on moving, to keep the world at her back.

It was dark but I could hear the steady breathing of my little sister, asleep on the seat beside me. As my eyes adjusted I could even make out her form, huddled beneath a blanket, her head against a cushion. The windows were misted with condensation and it was disorientating, as if the world had ended while we were asleep. When I smeared my hand across the glass I couldn't see any lights outside and I thought it was strange not to hear passing cars, people or traffic. Sometimes when you sleep next to a motorway it sounds like the sea.

I couldn't remember getting into the car. Confused, I looked to the figure sitting in the front seat. Our mother was sitting with both hands on the wheel, staring straight ahead at the misted windscreen. I could only see the back of her head, her knotted, dark hair, but I knew from her posture that she was awake.

The engine was running.

I tried to open my door but it was locked. Mother didn't turn at the sound of my movement but I heard her applying pressure to the accelerator, causing the engine to rumble louder. My head was sluggish, slow-moving, and I'd never felt more tired. I tried the door again but it still wouldn't open.

Sitting forward, I realized I was strapped into my seat belt.

Pulling the blanket off my sister, I saw that she was, too.

The engine rumbled a little louder and I could taste the fumes in the back of my throat. I unfastened my belt and crawled across the gear stick, into the front, trying to push up the lock on the passenger-side door. My mother reached an arm across and pressed my body back into the seat, her forearm against my neck. When I resisted, she gripped me clumsily by the face, fingernails piercing my cheeks, dragging across them. I pushed up the lock, pulled the handle and kicked open the door, pulling free and falling out on to the garage floor, coughing and holding my face.

I looked back at my mother but she just resumed her position, staring straight ahead, hands on the wheel. I got up, walked round the car and opened the door on my sister's side. She was murmuring, dazed and confused, but she could stand. I held the blanket around her as I opened the garage door and we staggered back towards the house where we were staying, both coughing, breathing the air. When we reached the door, I heard the horn sound three short bursts in quick succession.

Our mother, beating the steering wheel with both hands.

2

'Try not to talk,' said Parrs. He was standing by the window, look-ing out at a steel-grey sky. 'You're in St Mary's – we just can't seem to keep you out. Your jaw's broken in two places, and as for your teeth? Let's just say you should have smiled more when you had a chance. Do you remember what happened?'

I started to answer and felt a shockwave of pain from my jaw.

When I looked at Parrs again I could feel my eyes streaming.

'I said don't talk.' He turned at the sound of my distress. 'You never could follow orders, though, eh? You were causing more damage to your jaw while you were out, so it's been wired shut. Your diet might be even more liquid than usual for a little bit.'

He gave me his shark's smile.

'Don't worry,' he said. 'I told them you're a former drug addict, that painkillers could jeopardize your sobriety . . .'

I was blinking the sweat out of my eyes but when I tried to raise a hand to my brow, it wouldn't move. I looked down, starting to panic.

Both arms were restrained.

I tried to kick out my legs beneath the sheets but they were held fast as well. Straining, I moved all my limbs at once, wincing when I tensed my jaw in the process.

I gave up, panting and sweating, trying not to move my mouth.

'Needless to say, you're under arrest. You do not have to say any-thing, but it may harm your defence if you do not mention when questioned something which you later rely on in court. Anything you do say may be given in evidence. Do you understand?'

I could hear myself panting for breath.

'I'll take that as a yes. In a moment, I'll unfasten your right hand so you can write a detailed confession about what's gone on here. And just to be completely unambiguous, I'd like you to explain why ten grand in cash and a counterfeit passport with your picture in it was found amongst Louisa Jankowski's possessions. She's dead, by the way. So try not to leave anything out. You're going to jail no matter what. In fact, I hear Strangeways have got an opening . . .'

I looked up at him and he nodded.

'Wick's ex-cellmate, your pal Adam. Took the ski-jump yesterday. That's what they call it when a guy hangs himself with his bedsheets. See, there's not enough room to do it from the ceiling, so they wrap it round the bars, tie it to their neck and then lean forward as far as they can. Just a little tip if it all gets too much for you in there.'

I looked from Parrs to the window. If I could have broken a chair against it and walked through, I would have. He saw this and nodded, not unsympathetically.

'You tried, son, at least you can say that. Try to think of the world as hell. Tell yourself the poor fucker got out early for good behaviour.'

He searched inside his jacket pocket for a notepad and pen, dropping them on to the bed. Then he came towards me and unfastened the restraint on my right arm so I could write. I picked up the pen and tried to stab him in the face but he stepped back, watching me swipe at the air.

I could hear my breath catching, and started to rock the bed. Shifted my weight from side to side, trying to turn it over. Parrs just watched, waiting until I'd exhausted myself, then he rested a hand on mine, pulling me into a hug. I looked up at him and he crushed my fingers, using his free hand to grip my jaw, and then someone, somewhere was screaming.

He held on, kneading the broken joints between bony fingers, and I could feel goosebumps and sweat breaking out all over my body. Finally, something broke loose and Parrs stepped back, disgusted, looking down at the bed.

The wet patch spreading across the sheets.

He bent, collecting the notepad and pen that had fallen to the floor, and placed them beside me. There was just the ringing in my ears, the pulse slamming through my veins.

'An hour,' he said, straightening his shirt. 'Otherwise we'll have another little chinwag.' When he left the room, I waited a minute, considering my options. After trying to unfasten the restraint on my left hand, I gave up.

I picked up the pad, seeing that Parrs had already made notes on it himself.

The broad outline of the case, brief summaries of what had happened to the major players. I didn't immediately recall what had occurred on the roof until I came to a line with the words *Constable Naomi Black*.

They were crossed through.

I began with the events of Saturday night and the conclusion I'd arrived at.

That Martin Wick had been sleeping with Maggie Moore all those years ago. That he'd fathered an illegitimate child who Frank Moore had unwittingly raised as his own. I wrote that Frank had discovered the betrayal, the chlamydia, and become a violent, bullying presence in his own home. I still felt certain that he was innocent of their murder. He'd spent the next few years trying to maim the man he believed to be responsible, after all.

I wrote about Kevin Blake framing Martin Wick at the time, compelling him to sign a confession he barely understood, then reinforcing his version of events with planted evidence, a bestselling book. I wrote that Lizzie Moore had been alive all these years, and had provided Wick with an alibi proving a police cover-up. As a consequence, Kevin Blake had come to this very hospital and murdered Wick to prevent him going public.

I knew that was the least of it, and I wrote my own story, too. That I'd secured an expensively produced counterfeit passport. Spent years withdrawing untraceably small amounts of cash from my account. Prepared a go-bag with the intention of abandoning the investigation and escaping the spectre of Zain Carver. I wrote that Louisa Jankowski had taken it from me, that she'd blackmailed me and compromised the case. I wrote right up to the events of the roof. To Naomi's useless, senseless death and the unknown man in the balaclava who'd saved my life.

Every lie told and law broken.

By the time Parrs returned, took the notepad from the bed and sat in the corner to read, the wet patch on the bed had grown cold, and I was starting to shiver. He didn't look at me as he read, but I could see his surprise at my candour.

'I don't understand,' he said. 'If you weren't in on it with Jankowski, why didn't you just give her the phone, that night it was in your possession? Why didn't you destroy it?'

I held out my hand for the pad.

Esther's life, I wrote.

'Just think,' said Parrs. 'You could have been all the way out of it by now. We were wondering how you'd managed to kill Jankowski and dispose of the gun. Did you recognize this balaclava man?'

I shook my head.

'Frank Moore and Kevin Blake were both in police custody,' he mused. 'And I've already checked in on the surveillance detail at Carver's place. He was at home with the wife and kid. Seems like you've got yourself a guardian angel.'

I wasn't so sure.

'It doesn't mean much, but I'm glad to know you weren't directly involved in the conspiracy.'

He met my eyes and gave me a nod.

'Now, I've got some good news and some bad news. The bad news is there's no way I can protect you from all this. It'll be ugly for us. A former detective inspector framing an innocent man,

Frank Moore torturing him in prison, so Chase wants a clean sweep. It's very likely that you'll at least start out in the main population at Strangeways. We can't be seen to be giving preferential treatment. Once oriented, they'll segregate you at the first sign of violence. My advice? Start a fight early on, with the smallest guy you can see.'

I didn't move.

'There is one ray of light, though. The good news is that it looks like I'll be promoted. Chief Superintendent Chase and I came to an agreement on the events surrounding Tessa Klein's death last night. With no new evidence to the contrary, we're both content to call it a suicide, call off the active search for her remains.'

Parrs drifted back to the window, blending in with the grey sky outside. He cast no shadow, and there were moments when I thought he wasn't real, that none of this was happening. Unfortunately, the pain in my jaw proved otherwise.

'The teeth you gave me have been incinerated,' he said. 'You were right, Chase sent Klein undercover to get close to Carver. It seems that she wanted his head on a plate to pave the way for her ascension. It seems she underestimated him. Our working theory is that Carver and Klein had an affair. He convinced her it was the real thing and that she was safe to leave her job. After that, he had her done in.'

He turned, saw the look on my face.

'Don't worry, we're not giving up on him. In fact, that's why Constable Black was assigned to you in the first place. A shadow who could pick up anything and everything about your relationship with Carver before we put her on to his case full time.'

Parrs walked to the door and paused before leaving.

'You got one thing wrong in your notes, there. It was young Esther who Jankowski shot on the roof. Black had just lent the girl her jacket because it was so cold. She got off with a blow to the back of the head. Nasty concussion, but she'll be fine. After all this, I think she's ready to have her crack at Carver, don't you? So, good work, son. In a roundabout way, you did everything we expected of you.'

When he told me that Naomi was alive, I'd never felt anything like it. I set my jaw as firmly as I could and spoke through the wire.

'Turn around.'

Parrs looked amused when he did, seeing the sweat spike out from my skin.

My fists, gripping the bedsheets.

'Send her in against Carver and I'll bury you.'

'If looks could kill, I might take that threat seriously. As it is, you're in no position. You'll be transferred to Strangeways in a couple of days. Let me know how crushed glass tastes as a condiment, eh?'

'How many teeth in the human body?' I spat. I couldn't move my mouth properly and swallowing was painful, saliva bubbled at my lips.

Parrs leaned in closer to hear. 'Excuse me?'

'How many teeth in the human body?'

'Less in yours than most . . .'

'Did you count Klein's before you burned them? Were you paying attention? Because you might be a few short.'

Calmly, Parrs went to the door and opened it. I thought he might be leaving but he just checked there was no one outside. Then he closed it and came towards me, gripping my jaw again.

'I don't believe you,' he hissed into my ear.

When I laughed I sounded insane, and I leaned into his hand, forcing more pressure on to my jaw, looking him dead in the eye, bubbling the blood-spit on my lips until it flecked against him.

He let go and took a step back, frowning, appalled.

He took a handkerchief from his pocket and wiped at his face, then his hands.

'I'll have your car taken apart,' he said. 'I'll rip up your flat—'

'You won't find a thing.'

'So what the fuck do you want?'

'Take this shit off me.'

He rubbed his red eyes with his knuckles, then unfastened the restraint on my left arm, watching me closely.

'I want the bag back.'

'No can do.'

'Then expect Charlie Sloane to get some interesting mail.'

'You're bluffing,' he said.

I just looked at him and he shrugged.

'I'll need to discuss it with Chase,' he said, not looking at me. 'Anything else?'

'Naomi goes nowhere near Carver.'

He tried to gauge the look on my face but my eyes were tearing, bloodshot, and I had red saliva dripping down my chin. My jaw was painfully swollen, broken in two places and wired shut.

It was probably hard to get a read on me.

'I'll see what I can do. I suppose you do know that as a free man you'll be in even more trouble? Carver's been waiting for this, lad. He'll have your guts for garters. Fucking literally.' That hit a nerve and the look must have passed across my face because he went on, seizing the opportunity. 'Why don't we explore some other arrangement here? You've got the teeth. The way I see it, that's leverage. We could have you promoted, say, posted to some quiet backwater, safe and sound . . .'

I thought about Tessa Klein. A young woman manipulated by both sides and murdered without anyone willing to take responsibility. It could so easily have been me, and I wondered, morbidly, what had happened to her. Where her body was and what her final moments had been like. In a few hours, I might find out first hand. I should have cared more, I thought, shaking my head. I should have done something when it could have made a difference.

'Send someone else with the bag. I don't want to see you again.'

'Fine,' said Parrs. 'There won't be a lot of upsides in your future, so have it your way. I'm sure I'll be seeing you again, though, son. Missing persons posters, autopsy reports, cremations . . .'

With that he seemed to just fade out of the room like smoke.

Once he was gone, a thought occurred to me. I pulled the restraints loose from my ankles, climbing out of bed, going unsteadily to the door. There was no police guard or firearms officer posted outside.

I walked to the end of the corridor, ignoring a passing cleaner, and looked round the corner. Parrs was talking to Chase, neither one of them seeming particularly upset. Had I actually been arrested? Or were they just trying to flush out whatever it was I might know before working out how best to handle me? I had evidence proving they'd sent a young woman into an impossible situation, got her killed, then allowed the world to think she'd committed suicide for the sake of their own careers. They must have thought they were buying me cheap. I walked back in the direction of my room and found a nurse.

She made a sympathetic face. 'Painkillers?'

'Give me everything you've got,' I said, through the wire.

3

The painkillers made my jaw more bearable, and I slept in fits and starts, snapping suddenly awake at passing sounds, people who weren't there. My mind kept circling back to Lizzie Moore – Esther, as she'd remade herself. She'd had two very different lives and been stood right at the edge of a brand-new one. She'd come so close to overcoming a lifetime of powerful, negative forces, only to be crushed to death by them at the last second. There was probably a lesson in there for me, but I'd always been a slow learner.

I was watching the day end, the room colouring like a bruise, when there was a knock at the door. A lean, serious young man entered, and part of me wondered if he was working for Carver. Instead, he handed me the bag that Jankowski had taken from my flat and asked me to sign for it. Afterwards, looking through the contents, I had to laugh at his disinterest. How could he know he was saving my life?

I knew I couldn't leave until it was dark out, and I was staring at the window, watching the colour drain out of the sky, wondering where I'd go next, when the door opened. To my surprise, Sutty entered the room. He was wearing a nightgown, stretched see-through across his frame, with bandages around his arms. The ones around his head had been removed and I could see the livid burns on both sides of his face. His hair had been singed right back to his skull and he had no eyebrows.

'You're awake,' I said, through the wire. It was easier to speak now but my voice sounded blunt and uninflected.

'Nah, pal. You've died and gone to heaven. I put in a good word with the big man and we're gonna be roommates for eternity.'

I resisted a smile. 'How you feeling, Sutts?'

'I wish you'd never come to the Temple and dragged me back here, but at least I've still got my looks. How about you? Looks like everything worked out great . . .'

He was being ironic and it hurt when I laughed.

'Well done for landing on Blake,' he said.

'That's what Wick was telling you on Saturday night?'

'Said he'd been framed. That he could produce Lizzie Moore to prove it. When he said she was visiting the hospital that night, I was interested to see what happened.'

'You'd have saved me some trouble if you'd just said so.'

'I showed him that picture of himself in the paper,' he said. 'The one that had been taken on the ward. He told me his daughter had managed to get it because she was bribing cops. I didn't know if you were one of them, I didn't know if I could trust you.'

'She survived all that. For what?'

'The truth,' he said simply.

'I think I've had all the truth I can take. It's like a fucking suitcase full of old notes. It's not worth anything.'

Sutty looked at me. 'I was first on the scene when Wick was arrested, y'know?'

'Yeah, I've seen the tape.'

He nodded. 'Was quite a sight. Guy passed out, foaming at the mouth, covered in blood. I had to get him up and help him out. Was only later, when they worked out who all that blood belonged to that I started to feel sick. Three kids . . .'

He trailed off, producing a small bottle of alcoholic hand wash, cracking it open and smearing the contents on his skin.

'. . . Now, I find myself using this stuff whenever I think about it.' He avoided my eyes and I couldn't tell if he was blushing or if it was a result of the burns, but it was as open as he'd ever been with me. 'That blood was on Wick's hands, too. You got it off. You'll find your own way,' he said with a nod. 'You always have.'

He opened the door and stepped through it.

'Take it easy, Peter,' I called after him, as loud as I could manage.

'Yeah, Aids. I'll catch ya later.'

4

I dressed and left the hospital without speaking to anyone. The painkillers were keeping me upright but nothing could prepare me for my own reflection on the way out. I stopped, double-taking at the bruised, swollen face in the glass.

It was only a short walk from St Mary's to my flat but I flagged down a cab. The first one drove off as I leaned into the passenger-side window. When a second one stopped, I didn't give him the choice, climbing immediately into the back, holding the bag close to my body. I dug around inside it, finding the letter I'd tried to write to my sister. I looked over it one final time and then ripped it up, as small as it would go, littering the pieces out the window.

Some things aren't meant to be.

I got out two streets from my building and paid in cash. Once inside, I took the stepladder down from the landing and carried it into my flat, standing it beneath the loose light fitting. Then I climbed up, restoring the bag to its rightful place. It had occurred to me when I saw my reflection that I couldn't go anywhere until the swelling in my face subsided.

I no longer resembled the man in the passport.

While I was up there I felt around for the envelope in which I'd hidden three of Tessa Klein's teeth. Watching the hours pass in St Mary's, I'd written a full account of what I knew of her story, the complicity of Parrs and Chase. Now, I wrote Charlie Sloane's name on to the envelope, his address at the *Mail*, then stuffed it all inside the bag.

As I closed the ladder and placed it against the wall, there was a gentle knock at the door. I couldn't remember if I'd closed the street entrance behind me, and when I tried to ask who it was my voice came out as an inarticulate drone.

'Sorry?' said the man on the other side.

I opened it to Robbie, my new neighbour.

He took a step back when he saw me, afraid for a second, before squinting and saying, 'Aidan? Jesus, mate, what happened?'

'Car accident,' I mumbled through the wire. 'Looks worse than it is.'

As I spoke I realized that was a lie, it was so much worse than it looked.

'Right . . .' said Robbie, forgetting for a second why he'd come over. 'Right, I just wanted to say sorry about the other night . . .'

I shook my head. The bad nights had been stacking up recently, and I couldn't immediately place what he was referring to.

'The woman I let in, blonde number in the red dress . . .'

Louisa Jankowski.

I nodded and he went on.

'I'd been out two or three times and seen her waiting in the cold. I asked if I could help her and she said she was meeting you, would I mind if she waited inside? I didn't mean to come between you and your lady friend – I mean your partner. Whatever she is.'

'Neither of those things,' I said. 'Don't worry.'

'Right,' he said, wincing again at my face. 'I've learned my lesson, though. A girl buzzed my flat for you earlier when there was no answer at yours.' He searched his pockets and found the note. I could see a phone number but focused on the name. 'Anne?' he said. I accepted the note carefully, holding it with both hands. When I looked up I saw that he was waiting for some kind of response.

'My sister,' I said.

5

My sister hadn't left her address but I knew where she lived. A large, shared house, south of the city, in Fallowfield. I'd driven past a few times, and even stood outside it, once getting as far as the front door before my reflection in the glass, the look on my face, had scared me away.

At least now I was unrecognizable.

I drove carefully because I knew I wasn't thinking straight.

Being pulled over in my condition could be bad, but there hadn't seemed much point in calling ahead and trying to make myself understood over the phone. The painkillers wouldn't show up on a breathalyser, and anyway, from the demented ache in my jaw it seemed like they were already wearing off.

I pulled up to the kerb, cut the engine and climbed out, walking towards the house without hesitation. I'd been careful to keep an eye on the rear-view mirror for the matt-black Mercedes that had been appearing, off and on, over the last few days. I still didn't know who the man in the stairwell had been, my guardian angel, but I knew I didn't want him here.

I knocked on the door and waited.

This would be my last stop before leaving. Afterwards, I'd go to another city, an anonymous hotel where I'd prescribe myself generous doses of Scotch and lie low until the swelling in my jaw subsided. I'd develop a crick in my neck from looking over my shoulder, book the longest flight to the hottest country I could find then pray I cleared security.

I thought about Thailand, Cuba, Mexico. All the places a man might disappear.

The light came on, interrupting my thoughts, then the door opened and she was there. Her hair was darker than I remembered it but her eyes hadn't changed. She had a phone to her ear and there'd been a half smile on her face from the conversation I'd interrupted. It fell away, first in shock at my appearance, then in shock at my identity.

'I'll call you back,' she said to the person on the other end.

I recognized her voice from somewhere, and realized it must remind me of my own. There was a rush of feeling, pressing up through my chest, into my head, past that even, and I felt myself swaying in the doorway.

Anne laughed and touched my arm, as if to check I was real.

'Aidan . . . ?' I nodded. '. . . Will you come in?'

She started to lead the way and then turned back to me, hesitating for a second before crushing me into a hug. Slowly, I lifted my arms and put them around her, and we stood there like that for a full minute.

The front room was comfortably cluttered. Books, records, laptops and blankets, one of which she'd been sitting beneath on the sofa. We both sat and she looked closely at my face.

'Were you in a fight?'

'Believe it or not, I won. My jaw's wired shut.'

'I wish I could say you're looking well . . .'

'I probably should have texted.'

'No, you probably should have come round, probably years ago. I don't even know what to say. Do we have time? I mean, do you?' I nodded, wondering if it was a lie. 'How long's it been?'

'Twenty-two years,' I said, and she nodded gravely. 'Nine months, three weeks, four days, six hours . . .'

She laughed at that.

'Sometimes I thought I'd made you up,' she said, shaking her head. 'Like, remembered it all wrong, you know? Sometimes it seemed like none of it actually happened.'

'It happened,' I said.

'I've got so many questions. Where did you go to when I left The Oaks? I always wondered . . .'

'Some foster homes, here and there.'

'But not with a family?'

'I was too old,' I said, with an honest but, I knew, senseless feeling of shame. I felt myself blushing. 'And I had anger problems. Never really found the right people.'

I hadn't meant to sound so bleak and Anne took it seriously, holding my head, lifting it so we were looking each other in the eyes. 'You've found your people now,' she said.

I nodded and she nodded back, letting go of me.

'What brought you here? I mean, why now?'

'You came around,' I said. By now the painkillers were plainly wearing off, and I was finding it more difficult to speak. 'I wondered if it was important.'

'Well, I had a call from Social Services,' she said. I closed my eyes and she went on, 'I think you had the same one . . .'

I nodded in a way that acknowledged I hadn't handled it well.

'She's not good, Aidan . . .'

'She never was,' I said, opening my eyes.

'No,' said Anne. 'Bad month for me, though. Eliza, my adoptive mother, died last week. I suppose that's why I agreed to go and see Christine. Maybe that's why I finally worked up the courage to go and see you. You're my only real family now.'

Her voice trembled and I had to look away for a second.

'How did you know where to find me?'

'The social worker,' she said. 'Sandra? She said Christine gave her your address. Had the two of you been in touch?'

I frowned, shook my head, wondering why our mother had been

keeping tabs on me. After all this time, I couldn't quite believe it was maternal instinct.

'I thought, well, I wondered if you might come to see her with me?'

I thought of the bag hidden in my ceiling, the imagined hotel room and the minibar I'd set my heart on draining dry. The ticking clock that meant I couldn't possibly agree to this.

Then I looked at my little sister and nodded.

'When do we leave?' I said.

6

I took the spare room, hitting the mattress like I'd been shot in the head. I'd seen it happen twice in the last twenty-four hours, and it was the last thought that crossed my mind before closing my eyes. When I woke up in the morning one of my cuts had opened, sticking my face to the sheets. I stripped the bed and went downstairs to find the washing machine.

Instead, I found my sister asleep at the kitchen table, her head resting on her forearms, laptop closed in front of her. She'd made herself a cup of tea, but it was still on the counter with a bag inside. The mug was cold to the touch and I wondered how long she'd been down here.

I went through to the utility room, loading the sheets into the machine and catching my face in the mirror. The swelling hadn't gone down so much as shifted in its sleep. I found a plastic bottle of paracetamol and a blister pack of ibuprofen, taking four of each before pocketing the rest. When I returned to the kitchen, Anne was awake, looking at the closed laptop.

'I bled on to your sheets,' I said, testing my mouth. It sounded like I was speaking through gritted teeth. When Anne turned I could see that some of the excitement in meeting her long-lost brother had abated.

Now I was just a strange man in her house one morning.

'You don't need to do that.'

I came around the table and sat opposite her so she wouldn't have to twist round.

'I like to destroy the evidence as I go.' She didn't say anything. 'Is something wrong?'

'Do you know how I knew you were a policeman?' she said.

I nodded, realizing what she might have been reading. 'You saw my name and face in the paper. You sent a letter to the station, once.'

'I always wondered if you got it . . .'

'I've still got it,' I said.

'Why didn't you reply to me?'

'I was in trouble,' I said honestly. 'And ashamed.'

Her eyes went to the closed laptop. 'The story was true, then?'

'Some of it,' I said.

'It was stealing drugs from evidence?' I nodded. 'Were you fired?'

'Not then.'

'But now?'

I nodded.

'And what about the drugs?'

'Not any more,' I said, hoping she hadn't heard the rattle of paracetamol as I crossed the room.

'You're still in trouble, aren't you?'

'I never really left,' I said. I hated the sound of my voice. Its abruptness and lack of emotion. 'I haven't always done the right thing . . .' I thought about Lizzie Moore, Tessa Klein, Naomi. '. . . Sometimes I haven't even tried.'

'OK.' She moved her laptop to one side and looked me in the eye. 'So what about now?'

7

We took my car. I drove and she rooted through the discarded CDs in the glove compartment trying to find one that fit the occasion. We listened to *Carrie & Lowell*, then *Hats* by the Blue Nile, Martha Wainright. When Martha started to sing 'Factory', my sister hummed lightly along, not even realizing she was doing it. Then she glanced at me and trailed off.

We were merging on to the M25 when I caught sight of a matt-black Mercedes three cars back, and felt a chill, wondering what I was getting her into.

'All these roads feel so familiar,' she said, breaking into my thoughts long after the final track had played. 'Remember how much we used to drive? I used to think every car on the road was a kind of moving house. I thought they all had families in them like ours, and they all slept in service stations.' We glanced at each other for a second. 'For ages after, I kept waking up in the middle of the night, expecting to be taken out to a car, and in the mornings I always expected to wake up in new places. Do you ever think about it?'

I nodded. 'I stole cars when I was younger.'

She shifted so she was facing me, but I kept my eyes on the road.

'And you think it was because . . .'

'Yeah,' I said. 'I never really went anywhere. I'd just break in and then sleep in the back.' As I spoke I realized I'd never shared this with anyone, and saying it out loud felt like something unlocking inside me. It felt like being cured of a terminal illness.

'Do you remember when we lived in the offices?'

Our mother had found the building one night while driving. A construction crew had destroyed the staircase in the lobby to discourage vagrants from sleeping there. She'd simply fed me through a high window and I'd unlocked a fire exit from the inside.

'You had your own desk,' I said.

Anne laughed. 'You said I was in charge. You made me sick, spinning me on that swivel chair . . .'

'I think you fired me for that.'

'You deserved it.' We drove on in silence, both smiling at the memory. 'What I don't get is, we weren't so bad, were we? Like, why couldn't she . . .'

'No,' I said. 'We weren't so bad.'

After a minute she turned in her seat so she was staring straight ahead again.

'Did you ever feel like you were a mistake?' she said. 'Like we both were?' She glanced at me, saw me trying to answer with anything but the truth, and moved on. 'Do you remember the man? The man who came to live with us sometimes?' I looked at her, feeling my eyes mist over, and nodded. 'I think that's the only thing,' she said, rubbing her arms. She was wearing long sleeves and it made me wonder if she still had the scars. 'That's the only thing I'm really scared of.'

'He's dead,' I said, cutting my eyes back to the road. I could feel her staring at me.

'You're sure?'

'I was there.'

She shifted so she could look away, out of the passenger-side window, and we drove the rest of the way in silence. When I looked for the matt-black Mercedes again, I couldn't see it.

8

We arrived ahead of schedule, after a four-hour drive, pulling into the car park of the Royal Sussex County Hospital. My sister went to get a ticket while I waited in the car, looking up at the gleaming glass monolith in front of me, where our mother was recovering from an attempt on her own life. I lost time for a second and jumped when Anne knocked on the window.

We went inside and spoke to the woman on reception.

'Are you next of kin?'

My sister touched my hand and nodded.

'I'm not finding a Christine Farrow,' said the receptionist. 'Could she be under another name?'

'Christine Waits?' Anne offered.

The receptionist typed then shook her head. 'No . . .'

'We're meeting her social worker here,' I said. 'Sandra Allen.'

'We don't have any kind of arrangement in place for that, I'm afraid. Might be worth getting in touch with her directly?'

We went to the waiting area and Anne dug inside her bag.

Something was beginning to dawn on me, though. A bad feeling about a memory I'd had the day before. When she'd opened the door and spoken to me, I'd thought Anne's voice was familiar because it reminded me of my own. Now I wondered if it had reminded me of the social worker. While she scrolled through her phone I walked slowly out of hearing, keeping my eyes on her. I found the number of the local authority, identified myself as a police officer and asked if I could speak to Sandra Allen, failing that, her line manager.

A few minutes later I hung up and returned to my sister.

'Straight to voicemail,' she said.

'Sandra Allen's not coming,' I told her. 'From what I can tell, she doesn't exist.'

A complicated look passed between us, a lifetime of doubts, in institutions, our family, each other.

'Then who did we both talk to?' said Anne, her face falling as she came to the same conclusion I had. 'Oh, fuck.' I nodded, my mind replaying the bitter conversations I'd had with the woman on the other end of the phone. 'What do we do?'

I looked about and then took her by the arm, guiding us outside for some fresh air. As we passed through the revolving door, Anne stopped, holding up her phone.

Sandra Allen calling.

'Hello,' she said, picking up, holding the phone between us.

There was silence, and then the voice.

'It's so good to see you again,' said the woman at the other end.

I started to look about us, but the car park was on one side and the hospital on the other. I stepped back to look up at the windows but it was impossible, there were hundreds of them.

Anne was trying to hold it together. 'What is this?'

'I wondered if I could do something right for a change,' said the woman. 'I wondered if I could give you back to each other.'

'Where are you?'

'You've got so pretty,' said the woman. 'My Anne . . .'

My sister's voice shook. 'Where are you?'

'Look after each other,' said the woman. 'If I can ask one thing, it's that.'

'Wait,' I said, but the line went dead.

Anne tried to call back but it went straight to an automated voicemail message. 'Fuck,' she whispered.

We both started looking about us, through the windscreens of cars, up at the building, at the people walking in and out, but no one seemed right. I was processing a thousand different feelings at once, but one of them, I knew, was a sense of relief. She'd had my phone number and my address. For days I'd felt as though I was being watched or followed by an unknown set of eyes. Perhaps it had been as innocent as my mother daring herself to get back in touch after all these years.

At the far side of the car park I saw a matt-black Mercedes pull out and cruise towards the exit. I started towards it, first walking, then running, sprinting, until I could almost reach out and touch it. The car turned out of the lot and merged into traffic before I could get the licence plate. When I walked back to my sister, out of breath, my relief had evaporated and she knew.

'You saw that car before,' she said. 'You were watching it in the rear-view . . .'

I nodded, feeling like my real life was catching up with me.

'Why would she have followed us from Manchester when she knew where we were going?'

'She didn't,' I said, turning back to the road. 'That was someone else. There was just a man in the car.'

'Who is he?'

'I don't know. Never seen him before.'

'You look sick, Aidan. You must have some idea.'

Two ambulances were approaching, the sirens growing louder, and I thought about what Zain had told me about having someone killed. *Do it right, and you can walk off whistling with your hands in your pockets.*

I looked about us, then at Anne. 'How would you feel about splitting up, taking the train home?'

She walked back to the car and climbed in, waiting for me with her, going nowhere arms crossed.

9

So we drove all day, sometimes talking and sometimes quiet. When we lapsed into these thoughtful, hour-long silences, there was no telling how they might feel. Sometimes it was companionable, sometimes it was uncomfortable. It was easy, and at the same time difficult. There was some push and pull between us that I thought it might have been good for me to have in my life sooner. I'd had relationships over the years, but when things got serious, went too much one way or the other, I'd ghost, cut and run, disappear. There should be people in your life you can't let go of, I thought, and people who can't let go of you.

Anne's adoptive mother had lived in a converted farmhouse out in the Moorlands, where she'd run a small garden centre and nursery from four greenhouses. She'd been ill for some time and Anne had been helping her to sell the business before she passed away. The house would become a café, restaurant and tea room, while the garden centre and nursery would expand. In the interim, Anne still had the keys, and had been planning to use a few days of this week to box up the remainder of their things.

It seemed like the natural place to go.

When we arrived on Sunday night it was getting late, and we were both exhausted from eight or nine hours in the car, both badly in need of a drink after the day's events.

I thought I'd taken a wrong turn as I pulled into the lane.

It was a steep incline, over a mile long, cutting through woodland.

There was a walled embankment on one side and a sheer drop on the other, with a canal at the bottom. After a treacherous blind turn we reached the top, my headlights illuminating the farmhouse, a grey-brick monster that seemed to fill up our entire field of vision.

Anne said that for the most part it had been just the two of them here, each enjoying their own space. There had also been the labourers who helped her mother in the garden centre, living in a segregated part of the house renovated for the purpose. I got the sense that my sister was proud of the place, that it was important for her to show it to me, as if she was charting a part of herself on a map that I wouldn't otherwise see.

We both showered and then walked down a path through the trees, following the canal for a mile or so by torchlight, to the local pub. We were still talking, still falling silent. Still making life easier and more difficult for each other. The room smelt of ale, hearty food and burning logs from the fireplace. The barman recognized my sister, greeting her warmly.

'Come for one last look around, have we?'

'I'm commuting for your steak and ale pie,' she said.

Nothing had ever sounded better to me but I wouldn't be able to open my mouth wide enough to chew it. I settled for beer, burgundy-red ale, and crisps. When some locals had finished their meal, we managed to get a place by the fire, where we drank quietly. I went up for another round of drinks and caught the barman looking at my jaw, wondering who I was. I tried to smile, paid for two pints and returned to find Anne talking to a young woman and her boyfriend, petting their dog and laughing. I stood back, not wanting to intrude, but when she saw me she waved me over, putting her arm round my shoulder, squeezing until it hurt.

'Here he is,' she said. 'This is my big brother.'

10

We spent most of the next day packing. At around lunchtime I drove us into town, where Anne borrowed a dilapidated old Transit van from the couple she'd spoken to in the pub. It didn't look fit to sit in, let alone drive, and as I followed her back along the lane to her mother's house I wondered how it would handle the incline of the path. I kept my distance, breathing a sigh of relief as she made the final blind turn to the house.

The rest of the day was spent working through the possessions that were left inside. Mainly books, bric-a-brac, the pictures from the walls. As we worked, Anne expanded on what I knew of her childhood and the major players of her young life. Her adoptive mother had been married when she first arrived, but the husband had been a sickly man and died two years later. She'd never really known him, didn't think of him as a father, which meant her chief male influence had been the labourers, working in the nursery. She attributed her being a tomboy to this, but I thought she'd always been that way.

Boisterous and knockabout.

Fascinated by how things fit together or, better yet, how they came apart. Once she'd parked the van, she'd been straight on to the engine, checking oils and fluids, getting her hands dirty in a way I wouldn't dream of unless I was stranded on the roadside. She'd worked away happily for a few minutes before looking up.

She saw me watching her and winked.

Moving into the last room, taking the books down from the cases, I came upon a battered copy of *Crime and Punishment*. I turned it over, flicking through to see notes made in pencil.

'No, no, don't read those,' said Anne, looking over my shoulder. 'Did you like it?'

'Something you'll learn about me,' she laughed. 'I love my Russians. Have you read it?' I shook my head. 'You can have this one. Just let me rub out the notes . . .'

'A friend gave me a copy recently,' I said. I thought of Adam, hanged inside his cell. He'd got away from the prison guards, away from the dealers and Zain Carver, but you can't ever get away from yourself. I wondered if that's what I was trying to do in coming here. Moving to a slightly bigger cell for a few days before the inevitable. 'I'll probably read that. It's sitting on the shelf at home. It's actually where I've put your letter, it's pressed right in the middle.' She smiled and her eyes went to the window, where a streak of pink light cut through the clouds on the horizon. It was starting to get dark. 'Do you fancy a drink tonight?'

'I'd probably rather get this last bit done, but a beer wouldn't go amiss. They'll sell you some if you fancy the walk.'

I agreed to go, looking forward to the walk, the whisky I'd drink at the bar and the bottles clinking in the bag on my way back. Best of all, drinking them with her. I took my coat, followed the path down to the canal and was at the pub within fifteen minutes. The barman served me with less reservation than the day before, happily bagging up some bottles for us, but he still watched me closely.

'She's golden, that girl. We'll miss her round here, and her mum of course.'

I nodded my agreement and he went on.

'You any relation?'

'Just a friend. Just helping her pack.'

He nodded. 'Looks nasty, that jaw . . .'

'It can be,' I said, trying a smile.

He paused as he handed me my change, leaning in confidentially. 'Had a bloke in asking about you last night, after you went . . .'

'What?'

'Big guy. Red in the face but sort of quiet-spoken. Asked if I knew that beat-up bloke who'd been in earlier with Annie.'

'He used her name?' I said. The barman nodded. 'Did he say who he was?'

'Said he was a friend of hers, too.' He looked at me significantly. 'Only, he didn't look like anyone's friend to me.'

I walked out on to the street looking for the matt-black Mercedes, but couldn't see anything or anyone. Then I started back for the house, trying to resist the urge to call ahead. After a couple of minutes I found myself dialling anyway, getting my sister's voicemail.

I hung up and sent a text instead, keeping it light.

On my way. All good?

She didn't respond and when I got back to the house, I went straight into the study where I'd left her. She wasn't there and I called out her name, hearing my voice echo back to me. I started to go room by room, ripping doors open, ignoring the ringing in my ears, until I came to the kitchen, where I found her standing at the sink.

She jumped as I burst into the room, putting her hand to her chest.

'Shit,' she said, trying to read the look on my face. 'Are you all right?' I nodded, feeling the pins and needles tickling through my legs. She looked at my empty hands. 'Where's the beer?'

11

I waited an hour after Anne had gone to bed then got up as quietly as I could. I descended the stairs carefully, trying not to make a sound, and took a bottle of Scotch from one of the packed boxes. Then I went to the front door and stepped out into the night. There were no lights outside, none for miles around, and I let my eyes adjust to the dark over a few minutes.

Once they had, I walked around the house properly, the disused stables and greenhouses, then back to the front door again, seeing and hearing nothing out of the ordinary.

I went to my car, parked beside the van, and climbed in.

The air was so cold that my lungs ached, and I used the Scotch to stay warm, watching the mouth of the driveway until I saw a hue of light in the sky. The false dawn. Then I went back inside the house and slept for a couple of hours. I woke when I heard her moving about, joining her downstairs in the kitchen. She was making coffee and turned to me with both hands wrapped round a mug.

'I thought I heard you leaving last night,' she said.

'Just checking a few things.'

'You were out there a long time. Still sleeping in the back seat?'

'Something like that.'

She angled her head. 'I thought you might be running out on me . . .'

She handed me the mug and I tried to look dependable, like the thought hadn't crossed my mind.

12

Once the van was fully loaded and the house was locked up, we looked at each other.

'I feel like I should probably drive that thing,' I said, nodding at the Transit.

She was amused. 'It'll be like steering a cruise ship going down that bank . . .'

'It could be my next career.'

'I've done it a thousand times but I'm keen to see you try.'

She was half-laughing at me.

'Do you want to follow?'

She nodded and I climbed into the van, adjusting the seat and then the mirrors.

I caught a glimpse of her doing the same thing in my car and had a sudden flash of paranoia. It was my car that this man had followed from the city, my car that he'd be watching if he found us again. I climbed out of the van and went to her before she could start up.

'Change of plan,' I said, opening the driver's-side door. 'You're right, I'm being stupid.' I handed her the keys and she shrugged.

'Wimp.'

She got out, went to the van and started up.

The engine didn't take first time but on the second it roared, and a thick plume of smoke sputtered out of the exhaust. She pulled cautiously toward the mouth of the driveway, cresting the hill that would take us down to the main road. I saw her brake lights come on before she went out of view and I followed. Once I'd crested the hill myself I saw that she was moving fast, even though her brake lights were still on.

I tried my own to no effect as she approached the blind turn.

They'd been cut.

I saw the van waver left towards the walled embankment before veering abruptly to the right, cutting through the trees. It dropped out of view like it had ceased to exist.

There was silence, then the sound of bark breaking, three loud bangs in quick succession. Three and a half tonnes of steel rolling down a hill. There was a gap and then a bone-shaking crash as it hit the bottom.

She'd swerved to avoid a matt-black Mercedes parked across the road.

I pulled up the handbrake and skidded to a stop, five feet from it, breathing hard.

I was ripping off my seat belt when a man emerged from the car, pointing a gun at me. He was big, red-faced and bald. I agreed with the barman, he didn't look like anyone's friend.

I held my hands up where he could see them, watched him close the driver's-side door and start towards me. He stepped between the cars and I went for the handbrake, dropping it and pressing my full weight on to the gas.

I slammed forward, catching him by surprise, crushing him against the Merc.

His upper body was thrown forward so he was lying across my bonnet, looking right at me in astonishment, and the gun dropped from his hand.

I cut the engine and climbed out.

When I did he grasped for his weapon again but I took hold of his hand, digging my fingers into his knuckles, feeling them break apart. Two shots went off into the sky before I ripped the gun free and threw it out of reach.

'Who the fuck are you?' I said, forgetting my jaw.

He watched me dispassionately, the colour draining from his face.

'Come and trip it as you go, on the light fantastic toe . . .'

He reached into a jacket pocket and I hit him in the nose with the heel of my hand, pulling his phone away from him.

He looked down at his legs, crushed between the two cars. 'I need help . . .'

'Tell me something first,' I said, holding up the phone.

'. . . Fuck you.'

'Good luck rolling yourself around on a skateboard,' I said, turning to leave.

'*Wait*,' he panted. 'What do you wanna know?'

'Did you kill Tessa Klein?'

He looked amused, like I couldn't have been more wrong.

'You were the man at St Mary's,' I said, but I could hear the doubt in my voice. 'You killed Jankowski . . .'

At first I thought he was being sick but instead he was wheezing, laughing silently.

A revolting, sick-making sight.

'You really haven't got a clue, have you?'

'A clue about what?'

A mouthful of blood burst from his lips, dripping down his chin. When he smiled at me his teeth were stained red.

'No,' he said. 'I didn't kill Klein. And I've never even been to St Mary's . . .'

His head weaved and his voice was growing faint.

'Then who was it?' I was shaking his shoulder. 'I know it wasn't Carver. Tell me who and I can help you.'

A faraway look came into his eyes and he smiled again, shaking his head. 'You can't help anyone any more, pal. I'd sooner be me than you.' I turned and started towards the trees. '*The phone*,' he screamed.

'Get fucked,' I said, dropping it in the road without turning round.

Reaching the edge I almost fell to my knees, looking at the path of destruction the van had left.

I'd hoped it had collided with a tree or a rock to break its fall, but I couldn't even see where it had landed. The woods were unnervingly quiet and I slid down through the broken foliage, grasping the exposed roots of trees to steady myself.

I reached a ten-foot drop at the bottom and saw the van had rolled into the canal, upside down, at a 30-degree angle. The cab, the entire front end, was completely submerged, while the back, the rear doors and most of the undercarriage was visible above water. I tried to scramble down but slipped, tumbling over, landing hard.

All I could hear was the water lapping, my own jagged breaths.

I ripped off my shoes, pulled off my jacket and threw myself into the water.

It was freezing cold, difficult to see underneath it, and when I surfaced I had to rub the grit out of my eyes. I moved round to the driver's-side door, took a breath and tried to look through the window. Making a visor of my hands I could see Anne, hanging limply, upside down, the water inside the cab rising around her.

I got my hand on the door and pulled repeatedly but the water pressure was too great.

I surfaced again, trying to breathe, moving around to the passenger side. Here, the canal wall meant there wasn't enough space to open the door, even if the water pressure allowed it.

I pulled myself out on to the bank, not knowing what to do, searching through the debris from the van's fall for something hard I could break a window with. I settled on a tough-looking tree stump and went back into the water, half-jumping, half-falling. With the van upside down, the windscreen itself was at the bottom, completely inaccessible. There was just enough room to beat against the glass on the driver's side window, but not enough to arc or get any kind of real swing.

The stump moved, uselessly, in slow motion through the water.

I let it go, pressing myself between the canal wall and the van, kicking both legs into the driver's-side window as hard as I could. I kept on kicking until I had to surface for air, then dived down again, using my hands as a visor against the glass.

I couldn't see a single crack, and my focus shifted, to Anne, inside the cab.

She was conscious now, pressing both hands into the glass. She'd undone her seatbelt and was crouching on the van's ceiling, trying to keep her head above the rising water. I held my finger up to signal that I'd be back in one minute and climbed out, looking at the vehicle. Its angle meant that the back doors were above water, but raised up in the air, out of reach.

If my lungs or my jaw would have allowed it, I would have screamed into the sky.

I dropped back into the canal, gasping now, moving to the front of the van and lifting myself out of the water, on to the exposed undercarriage. From there I crawled up, gripping the exhaust pipe that ran down its centre.

I went carefully, feeling the effect of my weight.

The back end of the van was tilting even deeper down. If the rear doors were submerged, then the water pressure would keep them forced shut, killing my sister. Gripping the end of the van, I flattened myself to the undercarriage, reaching over the edge.

I got my fingers to the handle and pulled.

The doors were locked.

I went limp then, climbing carelessly back down into the water. When I got out on to the bank again I was heavy and flat, panting, looking left and right, up at the sky. The ringing in my ears was so loud I almost didn't hear my phone, going off in my jacket pocket on the floor.

I crawled towards it, dug inside and answered.

'I can't get out,' Anne said.

'No.' I was so out of breath that it hurt to talk. 'I need to go and get help.'

'It's coming up too fast. It's at my head already . . .'

She was out of breath, too, and I could hear her teeth chattering.

'Please don't go,' she said, but there were sunspots creeping in at the corners of my vision, and I threw the phone down on the floor, backed away from it, fighting off another panic attack. I went to my knees, trying to think. No passer-by could get her out. No fire engine could get here in time. I thought about the lock-pick set in the boot of my car but knew I couldn't climb back up the hill, that following the path back to the house would take ten minutes. Even if I threw myself back down, that would be ten minutes too long.

I could see sunspots everywhere now, feel my chest wrenching itself shut, and I hit myself in the head as hard as I could, trying to stay alert. Collapsing beside my discarded jacket, I began searching through it for anything I could use, throwing things on to the ground.

I found my own keys, pulled them off the chain and then bent the circular metal ring so it was almost straight. I could hear Anne, still talking on the phone, but I went back to the water and rolled in, returning to the front of the van, lifting myself on to the undercarriage and climbing to the rear doors.

Reaching over the edge, I touched the metal to the lock. It was too thick, and I just lay there, hanging uselessly from the van.

I looked at my phone, back on the bank.

The cold, combined with the swelling in my jaw, meant that I wouldn't be able to speak anyway. I put a hand to my mouth, just wanting to rip the wire out altogether, to be able to say what I had to, at least. Shaking, I put my fingers into my mouth and felt the metal sewn into my jaw.

It was taut and thin, and I looked down at the lock again.

I wrapped my fingers round the wire, giving it an experimental tug, feeling it strain against my skull. I took a breath, braced myself and pulled as hard as I dared, feeling the metal bite into my fingers.

It felt like I was pulling the teeth out of my head.

I still had the key chain I'd tried to pick the lock with. I put it to my mouth, wrapped it around the wire and pulled, releasing a violent red pain into my head. Pushing through it, pulling harder, I felt a pop, the wire breaking away from my gums. When I pulled again I felt my back teeth shifting, my mouth ripping open, and I dug my free hand into the undercarriage, crying, shouting, screaming out.

Hot wet blood rolled down my chin and I could taste it and smell it and feel it on my fingers.

One, two, three, *pull*. One, two, three, *pull*.

Everything went static white and I beat my fist against the undercarriage to stay conscious. When my vision started to clear again I saw that I was holding the wire in trembling, blood-soaked hands. It was glistening red, and I wiped it on to my clothes, snapping it in two before leaning over the edge again and reaching down to the rear doors.

I put the wire to the lock on the back door and started to pick. It was a pin and tumbler, like every car I'd broken into as a little boy.

It felt like all the luck in the world combined.

I inserted one end of the wire bent upwards, a makeshift torsion wrench, and used the other to brush the brass pins inside it, pushing them upwards. As I worked I felt the van moving beneath me, its back end sliding deeper into the water. I held my breath, trying to stay calm, and kept working until I heard a click. Then, very carefully, I took hold of the handle and pulled.

The door opened.

In the same moment, the van levelled out, throwing me into the canal again, causing water to rush in through the rear doors. The back was packed with boxes, most filled with books, and I started pulling them out with both hands, throwing them over my shoulder, pushing them clear of the doorway, desperately making a path towards the cab. When I pulled the last layer away I saw Anne, holding her mouth up to the two or three inches of air pocket that remained.

There was a metal grille between us, and moving the boxes had allowed the water to flood through, almost submerging us both.

I took a breath.

Pulled against the grille with all my weight.

It didn't move the first time and I pulled again. Looked at my sister. She had both hands on it, too. We counted together, nodding our heads, one pushing, one pulling. We kept on going, counting in threes, our fingers bursting against the steel.

We were both underwater now.

When one corner bolt broke, I moved, concentrating my efforts, tearing it from the fixture and sliding the grille aside. Anne had gone limp, and I reached into the cab and took hold of her, pulling her through the small gap. We clawed through the back of the van and broke the surface, both panting, gasping air, lungs screaming for breath.

We went to the bank arm in arm but I couldn't climb out. My fingers and hands and mouth were bleeding, and I was shaking, crying, shivering, swearing.

Anne pulled herself up first and then helped me after her.

We lay there a few minutes, holding on to each other, and I muttered every swear word that came into my head, again and again, trying to get it all out and get warm, trying to prove we were still alive. There were two deep handprints in Anne's arm from where I'd pulled her through the van.

Minutes passed before we looked at each other properly.

When her eyes came on to mine, I said, 'Give me as long as you can before you call the police.'

She was still shaking, out of breath. 'Where are you going?'

I climbed to my feet and started to gather my things from the grass, putting my keys, loose, into my jacket pocket, collecting my phone, stepping into my shoes. My fingers were shredded from the wire, the grille, and my jaw was hanging loose.

'You're not coming back,' she said, getting up. 'Are you?'

I didn't say anything and her fists clenched by her side. For a moment I thought she might hit me. Instead, she hugged me as hard as she could, pressing her body into mine. I could feel her heart beating through the soaked folds of her jacket.

I looked over her shoulder and spoke into her ear.

'You weren't a mistake,' I said. 'You can't be. Meeting you again was the best thing that ever happened to me in my life.' We broke apart and she turned away, muttering something with her hands in front of her face. When I touched her arm she repeated it, looking at me with raw eyes.

'I said you're talking like your life's over.'

IX
Push the Sky Away

1

I walked back along the canal and took the path up to the house, going inside for painkillers, washing them down with the Scotch and taking the bottle. Walking back down the drive there was nothing that could have surprised me, but I took the blind turn cautiously.

The man was where I'd left him, bled white, plainly dead.

And I'd been afraid of doing time for passport fraud. I collected the phone from the road and unlocked it with the dead man's cold, wet thumb. It was a burner. Nothing saved in the photos, notes or contacts, but I found one message from an unsaved number:

Confirm when in position.

I looked at the man, crushed between two cars, slumped over on to the hood of mine, and tapped out a reply.

In position.

Then I wiped down the phone and put it back in his pocket. I took his keys and began manoeuvring his car out of its sideways position, turning it towards the main road. The man dropped like a sack on to the ground, and when I adjusted the rear-view mirror I caught a glimpse of the horror show I was leaving behind me.

A car covered in blood, the debris of the trees and a person almost cut in half.

I climbed out of the Merc, collected the gun from the ground, then got back in and drove. I was halfway back to the city when my phone rang. My fingers were too ruined with intersecting gashes and cuts to pick up while driving, so I pulled over and answered in a lay-by.

'Aidan, where are you?'

'Naomi,' I slurred, wincing at the way my jaw felt, the sound coming out of it.

I took the pills from the passenger seat and swallowed a handful, washing them down with the Scotch. She heard the bottle.

'You're supposed to be in hospital . . .'

'I felt better,' I said.

'Not if your girlfriend hit you as hard as she did me . . .'

'Jankowski was never my girlfriend.'

'I know, friends with benefits . . .'

'Not friends and no benefits. I lied to you. She was black-mailing me.'

Naomi fell silent but her curiosity won out. 'What did she want?'

'She wanted me to suppress evidence against her. The phone with her number on it.'

'So why didn't you?'

'I thought it might get Esther killed.'

Neither of us spoke for a moment and I spent the time massaging my jaw.

'I can't tell if I hate you more or less for that,' she said finally.

'Well, think on it.'

'You won't tell me where you are?' I didn't say anything. 'Should I be worried?'

'Not about me.'

'Should I pretend I didn't hear that?'

I grunted in agreement.

'Then you do me a favour.'

'If you want a reference . . .'

'I want you to talk to Frank Moore.'

I looked into the mirror. I could probably draw a crowd in a freak show. 'Might be difficult,' I said.

'A phone call, that's all I ask. He wants to talk to you.'

'I'm beyond a survival seminar. What does he want?'

'He won't tell me.'

'Dickhead,' I said.

'Meaning?'

'He has some kind of problem with women. Would never look you in the eye. Always directed answers to me. When he bothered giving them at all. You didn't notice?'

'I don't pay attention to shit like that.'

'You'd better start.'

She laughed. '*Now* you're giving me advice . . .'

'I might not get another chance.'

'It should have been different between us,' she said.

I wanted to say something in return, the same thing, but more. Instead, I heard myself changing the subject: 'I've got time to kill. Put him through. I'm game.'

'You'll tell me what he says?'

'You've got it.'

'And is there anything I can do?'

'Look after yourself,' I said.

'Same to you, hot stuff.'

I ended the call and sat waiting for Frank, tapping out my anxiety and drinking the Scotch for my jaw. Naomi was right when she said that things should have been different between us. So why couldn't I just say it back? Why did everything worth saying have to be crowbarred out of me?

The call came through ten minutes later.

'Waits?' said Frank, as an automated message from the holding facility warned us that this conversation may be recorded.

'How's it going?' I said.

'If you feel like being flippant—'

'Listen, Frank. Since your arrest, I've had my jaw broken, wired shut and then broken again. It literally hurts to tell you this. So if you could cut to the fucking chase.'

'I've been thinking about Briars Green, the night Maggie and the kids died . . .'

'It's about time.'

'I was drunk that night.'

'Blackout drunk?'

'I'm not calling to confess,' he said. 'I woke up in the last place I remember sitting down. In Rebecca's flat, pants round my ankles.'

'Well, thanks for the information—'

'*Listen*,' he growled. 'With everything that came after, I was grateful to her. She was so steadfast in her alibi for me that I believed it myself. I know for a fact I didn't get out of that chair, I couldn't even walk, so I didn't feel bad about her saying we were together all night. I've just been wondering if . . .'

I could hear him breathing into the phone.

'If?'

'I've been wondering if she knew how grateful I'd be. How much I'd need her to cover for me. I'm wondering if she tricked me into being her alibi . . .'

'Jesus Christ, Frank.' He didn't say anything. 'Was she jealous of Maggie?'

'She hated her, and I . . .'

'You told her you wanted to go back to your family.'

'Something like that.'

'You need to call Naomi Black and put all this on the table. Now.'

'I'd rather you and I—'

'I'm not with the police any more, Frank.'

'Just like Blake, eh? I told you, this case kills everything it touches.'

'Unless you want to add your kids' names to that list again, you'll get over your shit and call Naomi. She's the only one who can help you now.'

'I will,' he said. Then he laughed. 'I really believed it all, y'know? I thought I was helping people.'

'It sounds like you believed a lot of things.'

'Yeah . . .' he said, considering the statement. 'I'd still rather be like that than be like you, though. I mean, what do you believe in?' The question surprised me and I tried to think of an answer. Before I could respond, I heard the pips go at the other end. 'I'll see you round,' he said, hanging up, leaving me with the dial tone.

2

I waited until the manager and hostess had exited the Light Fantastic, locked up and left, before I started the Mercedes, my eyes on that solitary lit window on the first floor. I put my foot down and drove right at the main entrance, crashing through the double glass doors and into the empty club, ploughing through tables and chairs, slamming into the bar.

I left the engine running and climbed out of the car.

There was an alarm going off and I could feel glass crunching beneath my shoes.

I found the door leading back of house, followed the corridor to the steel spiral staircase. I climbed up, went to Carver's office and kicked open the door.

He was standing behind the desk, pouring out two large tumblers of Hennessy. He slid one forward slightly before looking up. Perhaps he'd been expecting me, but I could see that he was surprised by the gun, and he frowned slightly as he took in the damage to my hands, arms and face, to my life.

I smiled at him.

He smiled back. 'I'd say you should get that looked at,' he said, 'but I'm not sure anyone could stomach it . . .'

I went to the desk and picked up the tumbler he'd pushed towards me, holding it up for a toast. He lifted his own, touched it to mine and took a drink. I backhanded him with the gun, breaking the glass into his face and he crashed down on to the floor.

When he looked up at me his lips were blood red.

'Sorry,' I said. 'Let me get you another.'

I picked up the bottle and poured the contents over his head, holding the gun on him. He sat there and took it, smiling once I was finished, and I dropped the bottle into his lap.

'Got a cigarette?' he said.

We both laughed and I sat on the corner of his desk, looking down at him. There was a sound at the door and two large men appeared.

Carver shook his head at them. 'Get the alarm, will you?' One of the men backed, uncertainly, out of the room while the other one watched me. Carver gave me his full attention from the floor, sitting up against the wall, waiting for the alarm to cut out.

Once it did, I could hear myself breathing.

'To what do I owe the pleasure?' he said.

'Your man just tried to kill me. He almost killed my sister.'

He wiped cognac out of his eyes. 'That's troubling.'

'That he didn't get it done?'

'That he jumped the gun. You know my policy . . .'

'Maybe he was just better informed than you are.'

'Oh?'

'I'm a free agent now.'

The man at the door took a step towards me and I re-gripped the gun, pointing it at Carver's head, feeling like I could finally do it.

'I hadn't heard,' he said. 'Either way, it's no excuse for what happened.' He sounded like a hotel receptionist telling me that my room had been given away to someone else. 'Let me try and make it up to you.'

'Call off the hit,' I said.

'You know I can't do that, and shooting me won't help. It's out there, it's too late.' A smirk came to his face. 'Maybe you should try and get your job back?'

I thought about the deal between Parrs and Chase. Covering up a young woman's death, and more besides, for the sake of their careers. I shook my head.

'This thing with your sister,' said Carver, climbing to his feet, wringing the cognac out of his designer suit. 'That's regrettable. I can promise you nothing like that happens from here on in. I'm a family man myself, now.'

'So I keep hearing,' I said. 'After this morning there were two places I could go, Zain. Here or Fairview. I've got enough bullets for your wife and kid . . .'

He darkened. 'That a threat?'

'An alternate reality. I came here instead.' The adrenaline was making my hands shake and I took a step back so he couldn't reach me, glancing at the man in the doorway. My vision was just a set of images, as if the office was strobe lit. 'Make it worth my while,' I said.

'Best I can do is make some calls. Say you're still technically a cop until the end of the week, give you a few days at least.' He began pouring himself a new drink, then looked up again, like he was surprised I was still there. 'Take it or leave it.'

3

I left the car embedded in the Light Fantastic, the gun on the floor beside it, and walked back in the direction of my street. I needed to collect the bag, the cash and the passport before leaving. The night seemed more high-watt than usual, eyes, lights, smiles beaming, and I felt the charge all around, making me glow along with it.

Crossing Piccadilly, people moved out of my way.

They looked at my face, the bags under my eyes and the beard of blood I was wearing. My clothes, rotten with canal water and drink, my shredded sleeves, fingers and hands.

I passed men who might have been my friends and women I could have loved, all going wide-eyed with simple humanity. I spun round, walking backwards, looking at them and liking them for it, wondering if they'd remember me.

Somehow, I felt like I was receiving the signal again. Something I thought I'd wandered out of range from was broadcasting to me now, loud and clear. I wasn't a mistake, not panicking or sleep-walking any more, and it felt like a miracle to be alive.

I jogged towards my building, laughing at nothing.

There were no cars outside, no lights on inside, and I ran up the stairs towards a new life, pulling the stepladder down from the wall, dragging it to my room. Once inside, I kicked the door closed behind me, leaving the light off. I stood the ladder in what I thought was the right position and floated to the top, moving the loose fitting, reaching inside.

Then there was a click and the light came on.

'Looking for this?' said a man. I turned to see my new neighbour, Robbie, sitting beside the door, holding a gun on me. The bag was at his feet. 'Why don't you come down from there, eh?'

I heard the ladder fall and suddenly I was sitting on the floor, looking up at him.

'You killed Tessa Klein,' I said uselessly.

He reached into his pocket and removed the envelope that I'd addressed to Charlie Sloane. He handed it to me and then motioned me to the bathroom. I struggled to my feet, holding the envelope against my chest as if it still mattered.

Robbie sniffed. 'In the toilet, I think.'

I opened the envelope and held the three teeth I'd saved in the palm of my hand.

'Wrap them in some tissue,' he said.

I did it automatically and dropped them into the toilet, the letter after them, then he leaned over, pulling the flush, and we watched it all go down the drain. He walked back out into the living room and, at length, I followed.

'You killed Jankowski, too,' I said. Robbie tapped the gun against his head and smiled. 'You couldn't let her kill me because you wouldn't get paid.'

'Had to protect my investment.'

'How long have you been with me?'

'I'd been keeping an eye out for a while, but the price got so high it seemed worth moving in. I'm glad I did, you might have died otherwise . . .'

'We wouldn't want that.'

'Hey, I did right by you,' he said. 'Gave you a few days with your sister, didn't I?'

I nodded. 'You must have had someone watching us . . .'

'Course.' The way he shrugged implied he didn't know what had happened to his friend. 'What's all this about?' he said, motioning to my face.

'You saw the state I was in at St Mary's?' He nodded. 'I left before they'd stitched me up properly. Everything just fell apart.'

'I know, pal. I know. So let's start making sense of it all, eh? I've got something I'd like you to write.'

I held out my shredded fingers. 'I hope it's short . . .'

'Very,' he said, pointing me to my desk. I was feeling dizzy and had to lean on it to stay upright. There was a suicide note typed out beside one of my notebooks.

'I'd rather not, if it's all the same to you. I just spoke to Carver. We've come to an arrangement. He's giving me a few days.'

He smiled. 'I'm afraid that's not what he told me.' He searched inside his pockets, producing a pair of pliers. 'Sorry. Here we go.' He pulled out the envelope that had been behind them, dropping it on to the table.

'What's this?'

'Open it.'

I tore it and found pictures of my sister. Some of them showed her in the city, with friends, or at home. There were even some long-lens shots from her mother's house in the Moorlands.

'Like I said, I've got a guy there.'

'What if I don't believe you?'

He smiled, took out his phone and scrolled to a number. When he handed it to me, I saw that it was a landline. The house in the Moorlands, I assumed.

I hit call and waited until the phone was answered.

'Hello,' said Anne.

'Who's that?' I said, as though I was talking to someone else.

'Aidan, is that you?'

'I see,' I said quietly.

I hung up and handed back the phone. Then I began copying down the suicide note. I still had the one I'd abandoned before, when I couldn't think of anyone to address it to. It just said *Dear* at the top of the page, and I wrote my sister's name after it. My hands were shaking quite badly, now, but I wondered if that made it all worthwhile?

385

'What happened to Tessa Klein?' I said, once I'd finished. 'Professional curiosity . . .'

When I twisted round, Robbie was much closer to me than I remembered, and I wondered how he'd moved so quietly.

'She went and got pregnant on him, broke his heart.'

'I bet. So what did you do with her?'

'I'll show you,' he said. 'If you're that curious. But it's a one-way trip. You've got to really want to know . . .'

I initialled the note and stood. 'I think I do.'

Robbie opened the door and walked out on to the landing, holding the gun on me from inside his coat pocket. I followed him, paused in the doorway and looked back.

When I touched the frame I got a static shock and, in a flash, I saw it all.

The violent, neon ghosts of my past and all the hearts I'd slammed shut on my way out. Exposed foundations and endless regeneration cranes filling the skylines. The people beneath them, crashing into each other like wrecking balls. Half cut, half formed, half finished. The sad, mismatched hospital furniture and the homeless men, weaving through traffic, wearing their sleeping bags like capes. Little boys letting their eyes adjust in the dark, their life savings hidden in their socks. My little sister in the back seat and a muzak version of 'My Heart Will Go On'. Career politicians, failing upwards, always just out of spitting distance, and all the good men with black holes where their eyes should be. Carbon footprints. Panic rooms. Charismatic racists and gifted liars. Salesmen. Businessmen. Salary men. All the good men with black holes where their hearts should be. All the sticks of lipstick smeared into all the collars. Apocalyptic weather reports and the birds, chirping, singing, screaming in the trees. And then I could hear myself breathing, hear myself think. I could see my hand, unrecognizable with cuts and bruises, gripping the door frame. When I let go it felt like the easiest thing in the world. I turned, threw my arms around Robbie and launched us both over the bannister.